RED IN RICHMOND

Red in Richmond

the Color of Love Series

FAY SMITH

Fay Smith

Contents

Chapter 1

Baxter

I heaved the weights up and then down again, the burn in my arms and shoulders a familiar friend. I'd been at it for about twenty minutes, and my shirt was already wet with sweat. Upon being assigned to Richmond, one of the first things I did was find the local gym in the national chain to which I belong. I never neglect my workout routine, no matter where I'm sent or how long I'm there. My body just doesn't feel right if I miss a workout. Blowing out, I heaved the weights again.

My eyes caught the reflection of a girl on the treadmills, slightly ahead of me and to my right. In the bright lighting of the gym, her hair was a brilliant red, not a bottle color, more of the orange-red of natural redheads. It was very intense, and I wondered if it was natural or dyed; I hoped it was real, although I couldn't say why. She just had a sweet girl-next-door look about her with pale skin and a dusting of freckles over her nose and cheeks. She had that "Strawberry Shortcake" sweetness about her that appealed to my sweet tooth.

As I continued to push the weights, I allowed my eyes to travel over her, mainly out of boredom. She was petite; I would have said around five feet two-to-three inches. She was curvy in a way that worked for me, boasting large breasts and full hips that swayed hypnotically as she walked briskly on the treadmill. It was hard to notice more, as she was wearing

"

baggy sweatpants and a grossly oversized t-shirt to work out in. Her hair was pulled carelessly into a messy ponytail that swayed with the cadence of her ass. And while I could see her ample chest moving, she clearly had worn a good sports bra to keep the girls under control. I noticed that she had no makeup on, and I smiled. Although she wasn't pushing herself, she did come to work out and not to put on a show. I could respect that.

Maybe it was just because I hadn't had any female attention in a while, or perhaps it was just because I appreciate a body you can sink into, dig your fingers in without worrying you'll break them, but she was affecting me. She didn't scream 'sexy;' if anything, her appearance screamed, 'don't notice me.' But I could see that underneath all that clothing was a body I'd love to ride. I had to stop watching before I embarrassed myself with a raging boner in the gym.

My arms were starting to give out, and just as I was planning which area I'd work next, another woman strolled down the mat between the machines and headed my way. She didn't hide the fact that she was looking me up and down, impressed with what she saw, before meeting my eyes and smiling devilishly.

Not my type, I decided instantly.

Which was a shame because she was everything most guys want; she was tall and thin, with 'the gap' between her thighs. Her ridiculously loud hot pink leggings, tight t-shirt with a low v-neck, and a full face of makeup told me that she was not here to work out; she was here to get attention. She mounted the treadmill directly in front of me, of course, and as she started it, I saw her in the mirror as she turned to look at the other woman I had just been eyeing. I could see her reflection, and her face was awash with disgust.

Definitely not my type.

She started her workout, jogging with a decided bounce that threatened to unleash her silicone boobs. Unlike the redhead, she put so much effort into her bounce that she lost most of the value in her workout. If she thought I was enjoying her show, she was wrong; I'd take Red over her any day of the week.

As a Behavioral Analyst for the Federal Bureau of Investigation (FBI), I had learned how to read people, and I was usually right. I worked for the Organized Crime Division out of the Boston Office. I had been sent to Richmond, Virginia, to follow a lead on activity involving the Boston-based Giovanni family. I had just arrived that morning, and priority one was getting my workout out of the way.

Just then, I watched from the corner of my eye as Red's attention went to the cellphone she had been using for music.

"Jenna," She beamed, breathing heavily as she took the call. She listened before answering, "No... (huff)... I'm at the gym. (huff) Are you ok?"

Her face fell and her eyes darted nervously, meeting mine for a moment before continuing to scan around her.

"Hold on (huff)... let me get somewhere private." She turned the treadmill off and exited quickly. As she moved past me, I heard her ask, "What's going on, Jenna?"

I was already moving to another machine, so I followed behind with my towel. I wasn't intentionally following her; she just happened to be going in the direction of the machine I had decided to use next, as the ab machine was occupied. In the mirror, the silicone bimbo had an angry frown on her face as I moved away, her eyes following me shamelessly.

Red listened intently as she walked before warily answering, "The one on the corner?... yeaaaah... I remember them." She stopped just outside of the changing rooms, and I went to my machine. I felt a little bad, as I could still hear her conversation, but I wasn't trying to eavesdrop.

Her demeanor changed quickly, her brows drawing down in concern. "Let me guess, that friend thinks if he can get to you, he can get to your boyfriend."

That got my attention. I tried to continue my workout; it wasn't my job to police the world and fix everyone's problems. However, that was precisely the kind of behavior I was trained to deal with. Organized crime used collateral damage all the time to send messages, and no one was safe.

Red breathed out heavily. "Oh, Jenna... I don't know what I can do... if anything, but I'll try. I still have a friend in that family. I can try calling him and seeing if he will meet with you. Can I give him your number?"

I kept my eyes straight ahead as I pulled the weights and set them back again. The term "family" was something I used all the time when talking about the mob... was it just a coincidence? It could be just that: a family member she knew was being petty... but my gut told me there was potentially more going on. After all, it was no coincidence that our intel led me to be stationed in Richmond.

But no one dealing with the mob would be stupid enough to give out their actual phone number...

"Okay, then give me that number," Red said calmly.

A burner phone, I assumed.

She checked something on her phone, nodding, and then told her friend, "Honey, it will be okay. I don't know how, but I promise to do what I can. I have to warn you, though, it may be expensive," she said matter of factly.

The more I heard, the more I was sure I was hearing something I would need to follow up on.

"Okay," Red answered. "Jenna, I want the whole story when this is all over. You may have to come down to Richmond to visit." She was trying to sound cheerful, but a glance told me she was far from it. Her eyes still darted around nervously, and her hands were tightly fisted. Red was scared.

I continued my workout as she turned and returned to the treadmill, but this time she upped the pace to a burning run. As I cranked the weights, I checked in on her every few minutes, and she still ran at breakneck speed. After another twenty minutes and three other machines, I was ready to hit the showers, and I looked over again and saw Red still running hard.

Damn, I didn't think she had it in her.

The silicone bimbo had left mere minutes after I had picked up and moved.

Just in case my gut was right, I pulled out my cell phone, pretending to check something, and snapped several pictures of Red. I could get her contact information from the gym if I needed to. With that, I headed into the locker room to shower and get ready to meet up with my partner.

Twenty minutes later, I walked out of the locker room to see Red still running.

Damn. I love a girl with stamina.

I couldn't contain my smile. As my pants suddenly became uncomfortable, I had to reign in my thoughts again. Shaking my head at myself, I made a bee-line for the front door, making a mental note to visit the gym later and get her info. I had to admit that there was an excited buzz in my gut at the thought of seeing her again.

Red

Fuck my life.

I had been gone for over fifteen years; I had been able to avoid the family. If it hadn't been my best friend Jenna, I would have said there was nothing I could do. But it was Jenna! My best girlfriend from high school, the one who had helped me get through the darkest, shittiest family crisis and was like a sister to me. I couldn't let anything happen to her.

FUCK!

My feet flew beneath me, keeping a brutal pace on the treadmill. I had so much energy to burn and so much anxiety. This was the only way to get it out of my system. This was the only way to keep me safe, by staying in shape and prepared. I blew out a deep breath, fighting to keep the air in my lungs as my legs ached and my lungs heaved.

Jenna had somehow gotten into trouble with my mobster family, the family I had run away from at eighteen. I changed my name from Renatta Giovanni to Natalie Brooks and settled in Virginia. Luckily, they had never found me. Other than Victor, none of them even knew how to get in touch with me, and even Victor only had a number to a burner phone. I wasn't stupid. I knew that if anyone thought he could lead them to me, they would use him. If they ever found out we—

I couldn't finish that thought. I couldn't go there. I shook my head and ran harder, my heart pumping at a frantic and painful rate.

I had to concentrate on helping Jenna. Victor was still in the family, although he was pretty low-level with little pull. We talked once or twice a year to stay in touch, but nothing more. He had been my first real love, and there would always be a place in my heart for him, but we could never be more. I moved away to save us both; that was what I told myself.

I decided that when I got home, I would call him and see if he would be willing to get in touch with Jenna and make a deal. I didn't want to open this can of worms, but I wouldn't risk my best childhood friend, and I knew what my family could do.

And so I ran harder.

Baxter

"Bad news, Murphy." Fiske's voice called out through my rental car speakers.

"Yeah, what's that?" I asked.

"The hotel we were supposed to be booked into had a major water pipe burst last night; they have no water, so we can't stay there. I've already called the home office, and they are finding us other accommodations. Don't get your hopes up; I'm sure it won't be 'Four Seasons' quality."

I chuckled. It was a running joke between my partner and me, as we had been booked in some nasty roach motels over the years. Don't get me wrong; the Bureau was really good to us... it's just that some of the smaller or more rural locations didn't have much by way of hotels. Sometimes you had to take what you could get.

And sometimes you had to put your foot down and sleep in your damn car.

"I'm sending the address to you now," Fiske said suddenly. "Hmm... doesn't look too bad. Maybe not hot and cold running roaches."

I laughed again. "On my way to pick you up now, and we can arrange to keep the rental later once we're checked in."

"See you soon," he replied, and the line went dead.

John Fiske and I had been working together for five years. He was funny, intelligent, and loyal, and I never had to worry about him not having my back. We had been put into pretty shitty situations, and he always came through for me.

We were about the same age and about the same height at a little over six feet, but the similarities ended there. While I had medium brown hair and hazel eyes, Fisk had blond 'surfer god' hair and bright blue eyes for which the women dropped their panties. And while I was clearly bulkier in the muscle department, sporting cut abs and bulging biceps, Fisk was leaner and wirier, although still very ripped in his own right. He always looked like a million dollars in a tailored suit or dinner jacket, while mine were always too tight over my arms and chest, making me feel and look constricted. He looked like a Hollywood celebrity, and I looked like his bodyguard.

In the past, we worked hard and played harder; the worse the assignment, the harder we partied. There was a time when Fiske was a pussy magnet; we couldn't go out anywhere without him collecting a dozen phone numbers, as well as a companion or two for the night. I got plenty of attention, but when he was with me, I was the designated wingman because the girls just couldn't stay away from him. Neither of us had time for a relationship with the hours we kept and the constant travel, but that never stopped us from having a warm body when we wanted it... sometimes two or three, but that was mostly Fiske.

I guess we were maturing, although I hated to think of that. Ever since we hit thirty, it's like the party scene lost some of its appeal. I don't know about Fiske, but I know I haven't called any of my booty calls for a long time...

Has it been over a year already? Fuck. No wonder I'm ogling women at the gym.

As I pulled up to the airport curb, I spotted Fiske immediately. There was a small gaggle of women tittering and giggling around him, one hanging on his arm, as he charmed them with his megawatt smile and his stories. I knew he saw me, even with his sunglasses on, when he started apologizing to the ladies. Kissing one full on the lips as he took her number right in front of the others, he grabbed his bag and headed for the car.

He threw his bag in the backseat and climbed into the passenger's seat next to me, flashing his smile as if it would work on me.

"Did I just save you or interrupt you?" I asked with a smirk as I threw the car into gear.

"Neither. I'll pick up where I left off later." He shrugged, still smiling.

"With the one you were playing tonsil hockey with?" I inquired, lifting an eyebrow.

"Maybe," he said noncommittally, "as long as she doesn't find out I had her friend in the airport already."

I just chuckled and shook my head.

I take it back. Fiske is not maturing at all.

In under twenty minutes, we pulled up to the Marriott, our new home, for a while. We parked and made our way inside to check-in. The hotel was nice, clean, and right downtown for easy access. The Bureau had handled all the details, so we checked in at the desk and got our keys. I was pleasantly surprised to find we had been booked in a two-bedroom suite. The front desk told us there was some convention in town, and most of their singles had already been taken, so we lucked out. There was even a dining room, so we would have space to spread out and work. The only downside would be having to listen to Fiske fucking all night, as recently, that was a given in any new city we went to. I always traveled with earplugs, in case my room was near his.

We settled in, putting our files in the room safe, and Fiske showered and changed into comfortable clothing. I already knew his plans, as he was wearing his 'come fuck me' cologne and way too much of it.

"Going out?" I smirked.

"Yeah... I've got an itch for some strange." (translation: "I'm going to pick up some anonymous woman and get laid.")

"You just had some not a half hour ago!" I laughed. "Don't you have a girlfriend back home?"

"That was just an appetizer." He brushed me off. "And I have more than one in every city we visit. Don't tell me you don't?" He smirked back at me.

"My dance card is full." I lied, turning toward my bedroom so he couldn't read my face.

"Alright then, I'm out. You know how to get in touch with me," he yelled over his shoulder as he headed for the door.

"What are you going to be doing?" He stopped at the door and turned to me.

"I just want to follow a lead while it's still warm. I shouldn't be too long," I answered.

"Great, message me when you're done. You can meet me for drinks." He smiled back.

"Yeah, I'll do that," I lied again and headed into my bedroom, closing the door.

Red

I had showered, changed, and then paced in my tiny apartment with my burner phone in my hand. My gut was screaming at me not to make the call. Victor always called me; I never called him. Truth be told, if it were up to me, we would have lost touch long ago; he always reached out to keep tabs on me to ensure I was safe. It was sweet, but it was dangerous.

My thoughts went back to Jenna, and my stomach tightened again.

Rip the bandaid off; just get it over with.

I pressed the send button, and he answered on the first ring.

"Can't talk now. I'll call you back," he said brusquely before disconnecting.

He was clearly in the middle of something, and I knew better than to push the issue. He was probably surrounded by the rest of the guys. At least his voice no longer made me want to melt or caused butterflies in my stomach. Now his voice brought me a nostalgic comfort, with a twinge of sadness.

Growing up a Giovanni meant I was surrounded by thugs all my life. Of course, I didn't know that when I was little; I just thought we had a tight family. My mother raised me; my dad was always away 'working.' I could tell my mom respected my father, but they didn't have that 'in love' look I saw on couples on TV. It wasn't until I was twelve that I started understanding the family dynamic I lived with. My mom was dad's wife, but apparently, he had several mistresses on the side. He could be moody and violent, and my mother did her best not to say anything if she was unhappy about her situation.

After that, I thought my mother was weak, letting herself be used like that. I worshiped my father, even though he was clearly an asshole. He was arrogant, and everyone treated him like he was a king. I wanted to be that powerful. But being a girl meant I got treated like a princess, fragile and untouchable. I was doted on, spoiled, and protected when I was small.

Puberty changed all of that. Once I had tits, I started getting more attention from the boys. My father made dating impossible. No one outside the 'family' was good enough, and he had them all chased off. The boys feared approaching me at school, and I felt like a leper.

And the guys who worked for the family, well, they all had ulterior motives. Dating the boss's daughter meant they might work their way up the ranks faster. But even then, my father wanted to pick and choose who I should be with. I was a damned piece of livestock.

At fourteen, I had crushed on Victor. He was the son of one of my father's men and had started as an errand boy for our family. He was too sweet for the lifestyle he would eventually become embroiled in. We had to sneak around, always afraid of being caught. I would get punished, but I knew Victor would be lucky to be let off with just a beating. I lost my virginity to him, and I was sure we would run away and get married someday. I was young, naive, and in love.

Someday never happened. As I got older, my father started introducing me to more and more of his people, inviting me to parties and events. He would engineer situations for me to be alone with people he approved of, to "get to know them." It was exhausting and humiliating. I saw it for what it was; he was trying to pair me up with guys he could use to his advantage, sometimes guys his age. It was disgusting.

If Rocky hadn't—

My phone rang in my hand, and I rushed to answer it.

"Sorry about that," Victor blew out, "I was just finishing a job. What's up?" There was so much care in his voice, and I knew he still missed me. I felt horrible having to ask for a favor, knowing that.

"Vic, I'm sorry, but I need to ask a favor." I nibbled my bottom lip uncertainly.

"Ask away," he answered calmly, no indication from his tone as to what he thought about it.

"Well, you remember Jenna? From High School? She's in Boston, and apparently, someone might have a hit out on her to get to her boyfriend. Can you do anything? Maybe call her to get the whole story? I'm so sorry to ask, I just can't let anything happen—" The words tumbled out of my mouth like a waterfall, fear and desperation choking me.

"Hey, don't worry. Send me her contact info, and I'll see what I can do. The guys have changed a lot since you've been gone, and they don't like targeting women and children if it can be avoided. I'm sure I can figure something out," he answered confidently, his tone comforting.

I blew out a breath as tears rolled silently down my cheeks.

"Thank you, Vic. You know this means a lot to me." My voice cracked as I whispered it.

"Red, I'd do anything for you. You know that. I'm going to go, and I'll call you once I know something." The line went dead.

I missed the way he used to call me Nat. When I ran, I had my name legally changed from Renatta to Natalie since most people who knew me called me "Nat" anyway. Then I immediately doubted my decision: it wasn't too far of a stretch to put Nat and Renatta together. Had I been stupid? Should I have changed my name to something else? Becky or Lisa?... In the end, I just tinted my hair more red, away from the mousy strawberry blond it had always been and had everyone call me Red.

Now Victor only called me Red. He would never take the chance that any family overheard him say "Nat." After all, it was he who helped me escape.

Baxter

"Woooow!" The young kid held my credentials in his hand like they were golden, his eyes wide. "I've never had anyone from the FBI in here before!"

I chuckled under my breath. *Yes, you have, kid; you just didn't know it.*

"What can you tell me about this woman?" I held my phone out to him with the pictures I had taken of Red. "She was in here today, at about 7:45 this morning."

"Red! Yeah, I know her. She's in here every day," he volunteered happily. "She comes in early on Tuesdays, Wednesdays, Fridays, and Saturdays... and works out longer on Mondays and Thursdays. Hold on... I can show you her history."

The kid typed away at the computer and then turned the monitor to face me. I read the name at the top of the screen, Natalie Brooks.

"Her name is Natalie?" I verified.

"What? Oh, yeah, but everyone calls her Red. She told me she has Mondays and Thursdays off, so she works out more on those days... here: last Thursday, four hours... the Monday before that... three hours. She's pretty religious about her workouts!" He smiled proudly as if he had something to do with that. I highly doubted it.

"Do you have her address on record? And maybe where she works too?" I asked.

"Uh... Yes, I have her address, but I don't know where she works," he said, seeming genuinely unhappy that he couldn't give me anything more. "Is Red in trouble?" he asked, suddenly stiffening.

"No.. nothing like that. I'm just getting some background information on the people who may have attended an event. Most will come to nothing. I really appreciate your help..." I looked at his name tag, "...Chuck. I'll be sure to let the boys know how helpful you were."

Chuck's face lit up like a Christmas tree.

I grabbed my phone, plugged her address in, and returned to my hotel room. I wanted to get all the details out of my head before my memory could distort them. I hadn't even been briefed yet, and it seemed a case had come to me.

Chapter 2

Red

I put the phone back into the secured box at the top of my closet and took care of all my household chores. The apartment was small, so laundry took up most of my time. I liked my work clothes to be presentable and wrinkle-free. It was already dinner time when I finished all my hanging and ironing.

With nothing left to do, I was still anxious. I hadn't heard back from Victor yet, and I knew I might not for a day or two, so I had to let it go, but the thoughts of Jenna being in danger swirled in my head.

I needed to go out. I needed to get laid. Maybe that could help to take my mind off of the situation. It was a Monday night, but there were always tourists or business travelers in Richmond. I knew a bar in the hotel district that travelers frequented; with any luck, I'd get a few drinks, find some hot body to occupy a few hours, and burn off some more calories.

Like that hot guy I saw in the gym this morning.

I'd only caught his eye briefly, but damn. He was jacked, and my blood warmed at the memory. I shook my head. Guys like that were high-maintenance, and most had small dicks. I could settle for a more average guy with a better dick; that was what I needed anyway.

I pulled out a business-like button-up blouse, a black pencil skirt, and black patent leather stiletto heels. I needed to look the part of the perfect bait to lure in a traveling businessman. My hair was flat-ironed straight, and I had the 'sexetary' look down-pat.

I made my way to the bar. Sure, I could go to the bar in the Marriott, where I worked. Mac was bartending, and he had a thing for me; I'm sure he would set me up nicely. But I had learned from the family, "Don't fuck where you work." Not that my father had to follow that guideline; apparently, he had worked through most of the strippers in his clubs over the years. Still, I wasn't going to ruin the 'sweet girl' image I had worked so hard to build. I'd go elsewhere for my conquests.

Baxter

I scoured the bar from the door. Having finished my notes, I changed into a less formal t-shirt and jeans. The t-shirt fit me just right, showing off all my hard work at the gym. I don't know why I bothered; I wasn't looking to pick anyone up... Habit, I guess? I stood by the door, motionless.

Why was I even here?

The bar was down the street from our hotel. We always stuck to a few hard and fast rules. One was, "Don't shit where you eat, and don't fuck where you work." Vulgar, yes. But if we could, we tried to meet women away from where we were staying, and we took them back to their place or got a neutral room somewhere. They never knew who we were, and we forgot their names if we ever really knew them. But recently, Fiske had made it a bad habit of getting drunk and winding up at his own hotel room with equally drunk beauties.

I should probably have a chat with him about that.

I saw Fiske on the other side of the room at a large circular booth, surrounded by beautiful women. One sat next to him, running her long nails through his hair, while another snuggled up to his other side, her hand stroking his thigh. I sighed deeply, regretting instantly that I had come. I considered just leaving, but then I saw Fiske waving to me.

Too late, he's seen me.

I plastered a smile on as I made my way to where he was holding court with his harem.

"Hey!" He smiled his megawatt smile, standing as I approached. "You made it! Everyone, this is Bill." He introduced me with our usual fake names. At bars, he was Joe, and I was Bill. He then introduced all of the women around the table, not that I'd remember them. He sat back down, and I excused myself to go to the bar and get a drink. Clearly, I was going to need one.

The bar wasn't too busy, and the bartender stepped up to me immediately.

"Scotch on the rocks, please." I indicated the top shelf stuff with my hand, and he nodded in understanding, pulling down an expensive bottle and holding it up for my approval. When I nodded, he pulled out a glass and poured. I took the glass from him and handed him a twenty before he disappeared to the cash register. Another force of habit had me scanning the bar, taking in all the patrons, when a flash of bright copper red caught my eye.

Natalie, "Red," was seated near the end of the bar, sipping a drink by herself. She looked like she had just left a business meeting, except her heels were far too high, and her shirt was unbuttoned, revealing an unprofessional amount of cleavage. My cock jerked at the sight. I watched her from the corner of my eye as the bartender returned with my change. Leaving a few bills, I strolled back to Fiske and the harem, never losing sight of Red.

The girls all slid, allowing me to join them, and Fiske continued his story. The gaggle of ladies all laughed on cue, but I was distracted, watching Red. This went on endlessly until I heard Fiske say, "I need a refill; how about you, Brother?"

(translation: meet me at the bar.) I finished the last of my own drink and smiled up at him. "Yeah, me too. Excuse us."

The girls whined and pouted as Fiske and I pulled away from the group. "I'm ducking out of here soon," Fiske leaned in and informed me. "The brunette and the blonde want a three-way, and I'm sure I could talk them into a four-way if you want in. They're good to go." He flashed his smile again as we walked to the bar.

My eyes crept involuntarily to Red, still sitting by herself. "Nah... I'm good. It will probably be an early night for me. We've got the briefing in the morning," I answered casually. "Make sure you don't bring them back to our place; I'd like to get some sleep tonight."

"Suit yourself," he answered happily. "I intend to spend as much of this night balls-deep in pussy as I can before I go back to work, though." He winked at me conspiratorially.

"Just remember rule number one." (translation: don't forget the condoms.) I said in a stern, lecturing voice, a smile on my face. "You don't need some baby mama ruining your career."

"She'd have to find me first!" He laughed, taking his drink back to the table to say his goodbyes.

Red

The bar was slow. *Well, it was a Monday night; what the hell had I expected?*

Over in the corner, there was a party at a large circular booth; I would have said it was a bridal shower, except there was a gorgeous model-type guy who seemed to have a group of women hanging on the edges of their seats. They were laughing loudly and pouring back the margaritas.

A familiar face caught my attention, and I fought not to spin my head and look. I used the mirror behind the bar and pretended to scroll through my phone as I took him in. With all of the animated women around him, he was hard to see, but there was no mistaking that body, that set jaw, and those eyes; it was the hunk from the gym.

What are the odds?!

I sipped my drink and pulled my eyes away. *He probably has a tiny dick;* I reminded myself. But I had already been sitting on that bar stool for twenty minutes, and no one had approached me. I was far from desperate, but I did need to work off of my anxiety. If I wasn't going to get any action, I might as well go home, change, and go back to the gym. The cocktails weren't helping.

"Is this seat taken?" A deep voice sounded beside me.

I looked up, and up, and right into those gorgeous hazel eyes. The hunk stood beside me, ready to bust out of his t-shirt. His hair was messy and falling over his eyes. I could smell his cologne, and instantly I clenched my thighs together as it sent heat through me.

He smirked and asked, "Do you mind if I join you?" as he sat.

Damn... I hadn't even answered his first question, sitting there like a moon-eyed moron.

"Uh... not at all," I answered after the fact, and I could feel the blush rising to my cheeks. I hated my fair skin tone; blushes always lit me up like a neon sign reading "humiliated."

"Have we met before?" he asked in a silky tone.

I groaned inwardly. I hated lines. And I knew I shouldn't pursue anything with him because he also went to my gym, and I didn't want to have to run into him again and create an awkward situation. And besides... *he probably has a small dick.*

Before I could answer, he cut in quickly, "The gym. I saw you at the gym this morning. That's where I know you from." He smiled, and my panties were instantly moist.

God damn it.

I plastered on my smile. "Yes. You saw me at the gym." I sipped my drink, unsure what to say or how to get rid of him.

My body didn't want to lose him, but my mind kept telling me this was a bad idea.

He sipped his drink for a moment, and there was an awkward silence before he turned his eyes to me again.

"I hate bars. This is so uncomfortable, and I'm starving and would rather get something to eat. Would you like to join me?"

I froze with my drink halfway to my mouth. I turned my eyes to him slowly, trying to figure out what to do.

"Are you asking me on a date?" I laughed with false bravado.

"Most definitely not." He smiled back. "I am asking if you are hungry because I am after my morning workout. And if you are hungry, and I am hungry, then there's no reason we shouldn't eat together. I don't know about you, but I hate eating alone."

"I don't even know your name." It was like my mind suddenly went stupid, and I couldn't think straight in his presence. I was stalling for time, hoping my mind would magically kick into gear.

He smiled genuinely, and it was beautiful. "My friends call me Murphy." He stuck his hand out.

"Red," I answered simply, shaking his bear paw of a hand with my tiny one.

"Shall we?" he asked, putting his empty glass on the bar.

My mind was telling me I should say no, I should leave. But I found the word leaving my traitorous lips before I could stop. "Sure."

Baxter

I placed my hand on the small of her back, she was warm under my touch, and I had to resist the urge to adjust my jeans as I ushered her gently to the door. I didn't know what the hell I was doing. I shouldn't have asked her to dinner. Hell, I shouldn't have approached her at the bar. For all I knew, she was involved in my upcoming case or potentially another one.

I shouldn't let my curiosity interfere with my work. She also used the same gym I would be using, although now that I had her schedule, I could avoid her. But that would mean changing my routine, and I didn't like changes to my routine. This was all a terrible idea.

She looked up at me briefly, and I plastered my smile back in place. It wasn't hard when she looked up with those big brown doe eyes. I towered over her petite frame, but she didn't seem intimidated. Nor did she play coy, hiding behind false giggles; in fact, she had seemed reluctant to leave with me.

While she was all sweetness on the outside, I had seen the intelligence behind her eyes; I was willing to bet there was strength in her, that she was no shrinking violet. And if the stereotype about redheads was to be believed, she was probably as stubborn as hell, with a fiery temper, too.

But none of that mattered when my fingertips grazed the back of her blouse over her skin. My body reacted to her presence. It had been a long time since I had wanted someone as I wanted her; usually, women found me, they made me an offer, and I took them up on it. I couldn't remember a time I had to talk someone into joining me for dinner, but she had this power over me.

It's just dinner. Nothing more. I'll go back to my room alone afterward.

I mentally schooled myself. As I felt her back shift under my hand, I knew I was lying. I wanted nothing more than to bury my cock in her, and I wanted to see her red hair tangled in my fingers and hear the noises she made when she orgasmed.

Why did I get myself into these messes?

"There's a great little Indian place around the corner...," She suggested shyly. Her cheeks were pink, and she looked flustered.

"Lead the way." I wasn't a huge fan of Indian food, but I'd be more likely to keep her talking if she liked it. Indian it was, then.

We were seated at a small table, and I waited until we'd ordered to try to strike up a conversation. I couldn't help but watch her. I did not doubt that she was a sweet person, but I also had no doubt that there was another side of her that she kept utterly hidden. She was a collection of awkward and shy moments, followed by a surge of inner backbone. For example, she fingered her menu nervously like she wasn't comfortable being there, but then she turned to me like this was the most casual event ever and began to talk.

"So, what brings you to Richmond?" She smiled with all false confidence.

"Business, of course," I smirked. "You're not from here; where did you grow up?"

I deflected and countered. Her accent was New England, not Virginian, adding to my suspicions about what I'd overheard.

"I moved a lot," she offered casually, deflecting. I noticed. Game on.

"What do you do for work?" I asked, seeing my double standard after not giving her an inch but asking for more.

"Oh..." She looked down at her blouse, trying to come up with something to say. "I have odd jobs here and there, but I'm an artist. I paint," she answered.

When I scoured her expression, I couldn't find any indicators that she was lying, but she was being evasive. She wasn't telling the whole truth.

"And you, what business are you in?" she asked, a little shrewdness in her voice. She definitely recognized the dance we were moving through verbally.

"I'm a research analyst for the government," I answered, and it was my patent response. "I travel a lot," I added, although I had no idea why I wanted to volunteer anything more.

"So... what do you analyze?" she asked, placing her chin on her hand, elbow on the table, taking me in.

"Lots of things..." I answered vaguely, suddenly feeling like I was the one being analyzed.

"So you're police," she stated factually as if she had just figured it out. "No, you're federal, so CIA, FBI, or NSA." She smiled broadly.

"I can neither confirm nor deny." I laughed.

"Because then you'd have to kill me, right?" She laughed back.

Her laughter was infectious. A part of me wanted to act like a teenager, play the class clown, and make her laugh all night so that I could be there when she did. But another part of me was trying to put me on high alert. Too much about her didn't add up, especially with what I'd heard. I hated to think she was somehow tied up with the Giovanni family, that she would get sucked into their world and made a target, like her friend. I couldn't explain the sudden protective urges I felt about her. I had to get my head back into the game; I had to pull back and be the professional I was.

"So... you must like Richmond if you settled here," I said warmly.

"We're back to the interrogation again?" She smiled wickedly.

"No... no. I just... wanted to get to know you," I said, trying to recover.

Luckily, the food arrived to take the attention off me. We settled our plates, and she looked up, her fork hanging in mid-air.

"Look, I know you don't really care about who I am or where I come from. I didn't come here to learn all of your deep dark secrets. Let's just enjoy dinner." She picked up her water glass with a warm smile as if toasting, and I brought mine up to tap it gently.

It was an olive branch. She thought I had asked her here because I wanted to fuck her, and it appeared my sweet little Strawberry Shortcake was perfectly fine with being my strange for the night: no names, no history, nothing more.

I had never been so tempted. My body was on board, sporting a raging hard-on under the table at the thought. However, it wasn't going to happen. Not if there was even the slightest potential that she was somehow connected to the case that brought me here. I was on a fact-finding mission with a heaping side of masochism.

Red

What the fuck was I doing?! He was a fucking FED! He could ruin everything!

I tried to clear the panic from my mind and keep my face pleasant. I wanted to run from the restaurant, but that would only draw more attention to me. He seemed to buy that I was only interested in him for sex, just like an ordinary, non-mob-related woman would be. I just had to keep up the facade. I smiled at his joke while my heart pounded, and I could hear my blood rushing in my ears.

It wasn't difficult to act like I just wanted his body. Every time I looked at his hands, I could imagine them traveling under my clothing and over my body. I'd nearly combusted when he put his hand on my lower back to walk me here. But what if he wanted to go through with it?! Not that I didn't want him to... or did I? I was so confused. Nothing good was going to come of this. I took another quick drink of my wine.

"So, what do you paint?" he asked casually to make conversation.

I sputtered into my wine glass and put it down before spilling it all over myself.

Fuck... I'd forgotten that I had told him. I should have just made something up!

"All kinds of things..." I started vaguely, wincing at my words as I dabbed the wine on my chin with my napkin. There was no way to converse with each other and not discuss anything about ourselves, but I wasn't willing to give him this secret either. "Mostly... things I see in my head. Like... scenes, I guess." It was the truth, but I knew it was still vague.

"What kinds of scenes?" He asked with interest.

Damn it! Why didn't I just say landscapes?!

"Well... Scenes like... settings for stories. Like backdrops. I've always had a knack," I answered lamely.

"What kind of stories?" he followed up.

Fuck. my vagina had overpowered my mental facilities, and I was sinking fast.

"Um... Crime stories... I mean... crime scenes..." I was stammering and stuttering. I had inadvertently swum into deep water, deeper than I had wanted to take him into the truths about my life.

"Like a police sketch artist? I'd love to see your work sometime," he said with a small smile and reached his hand out to cover mine; it completely enveloped it.

"Sure," was all I could squeak out. I could feel the warmth of his hand over mine as my heart pounded. I changed the subject quickly.

I managed to navigate through dinner and conversation, but it was tough. He looked incredible, smelled heavenly, and seemed very intelligent. He ticked a lot of my boxes, and I liked him more than I wanted to like him. My vagina already had a crush on him, and they hadn't even been introduced.

On the other hand, he could ruin my life in a heartbeat, and I needed to get the fuck away from him before he saw too much and started putting pieces together. He was dangerous. I had worked too hard and long to free myself; I couldn't afford to endanger that now.

The evening was getting late, and Murphy suggested we should leave. My breathing hitched, and I consciously slowed it down. He paid the check and walked me out of the restaurant, his hand on my lower back causing my lady parts to cheer. I smiled but held my breath, waiting to see if he would expect me to accompany him for the night. I tried to mentally prepare my apology for needing to leave. I honestly was disappointed; I would have loved to rock his world if I wasn't me and he wasn't who he was. Once outside, he looked at his watch and then down at me sadly.

"Well, Red, I enjoyed your company very much, but it's getting late, and I have to be at work early tomorrow morning. I'm afraid I'm going to have to say goodnight. Do you need a ride home?" He took both of my hands into his.

I was stunned momentarily. *Did he say he was leaving? He was not assuming we were going to have sex?*

I felt relief instantly, followed by indignation.

Why DIDN'T he want to have sex with me?! What, was I not hot enough?

He must have read the expression clearly written all over my face because he chuckled and leaned into me.

"Red, you are a breath of fresh air, and if I didn't have a work meeting first thing tomorrow, I would definitely be trying to drag you up to my room and worship your body all night. Unfortunately... I can't do that now and refuse to do anything halfway with you. I'm sure I will see you again... if you want to, that is?" His eyes sparkled with hope.

I stood there, looking into those eyes, and my mind went completely blank. Zip. Zero. Nothing. He chuckled quietly, bringing me out of my stupor.

My mind was screaming at me. *Tell him NO! Tell him you're not interested!*

"Yeah, that would be okay, I guess," I said with a small smile. I could feel my cheeks burning.

Suddenly his face was moving toward mine, and before I could gasp, his lips covered mine tenderly. I was frozen... and then I was melting. My mouth met his, and his tongue brushed my lips, requesting permission, and I opened them and met his tongue with mine. It was a gentle dance, our mouths exploring each other, not the hot and hungry kiss I had imagined from him at all.

Not that I had imagined his kiss... well, not much, anyway...

When he pulled his face away, my body involuntarily tried to follow, to replace the warmth on my now chilled lips. He stared at them for a heartbeat before straightening up with a jerk, letting go of my hands as he backed up a step.

"I'll see you around, Red." His smile didn't meet his eyes, as if he had just come to and realized what he was doing.

Did he regret kissing me?

I know I should, but damn it, I didn't.

Chapter 3

Baxter

I slapped my hand over the cell phone to silence the shriek-ing alarm. God, I hated getting up early; why had I decided to get up at... *four thirty?! Fuck, what had I been thinking?* And then I remembered. She'd be there. I wanted to get into the gym early and get most of my workout out of the way before Red got there. I couldn't afford another lapse in judgment like I had the night before. I needed to think with the big head to-day and get to the briefing without potentially obstructing my own case.

It didn't help that it was ridiculously early, and I had blue balls on top of it. *Fuck.me.*

I pulled my gear on fast, grabbed my workout bag and the car keys, and headed for the door. The sky was still dark as I made my way to the gym, and there was very little traffic. In no time at all, I was checked in and hard at work on my legs. I did my sets on one machine and then moved to another. I wel-comed the burn and pain in my hamstrings and glutes. When that workout was done, I moved on to another machine... but not before I noticed the flame of a red ponytail swinging its way in the door.

She was early. Was she trying to avoid me too?

I pretended I didn't see her and kept working. She didn't see me in the back of the room and headed straight for the treadmill; just like the day before, she took off at a run and never slowed. I knew I wouldn't be able to go through my whole routine, knowing she was there. I could already feel myself getting hard. *Fuck.*

I wiped the machine down with frustration and grabbed my bag, heading for the shower. I'd have to come back later for my cardio. She was just too much of a distraction, and I needed a clear head. When I ducked out of the locker room, freshly showered, I saw her still running on her machine, her face red, and her clothing drenched in sweat. *It's a good look on her.* I groaned under my breath and headed for the door fast.

I sat in the conference room with a terrible cup of coffee in my hand. I had gone back to the hotel room and changed into my suit, which was far nicer and more expensive than the clothing allowance the Bureau provided would buy. I didn't care. I valued my appearance; my father had taught me that. My shoes were expensive, Italian, leather, and highly shined. Fiske sat next to me, texting some woman on his cell as we waited for our interim supervisor to fill us in.

"Gentleman, I am Joey Owens; you'll report to me or my assistant Agent Trevor Billings while you are here." The middle-aged man walked into the room, his suit coat unbuttoned. He was balding and wore wire-rimmed glasses that hadn't been fashionable since the seventies.

"I understand you have been following the Giovanni family for quite some time?" he asked us as he took a seat.

"Yes," I answered for us. "Going on ten years for me, five for Fiske here. So what's this new development?"

"So you know Vinnie Giovanni is dying?" he asked. Fiske and I nodded. "And you know that there is a war brewing within his own family? Everyone wants to be the heir apparent."

"Yes, but he named Antonio 'Tony' DiRosi as his successor; he even had Tony change his name to Giovanni to keep the family coherent," Fiske answered.

"He would, considering his own father married into the Lombardo family and then took it over as the Giovanni family once old man Lombardo was taken out," I interjected.

"Right," Owens stated. "Vinnie Giovanni never had any surviving sons, and his only daughter disappeared at eighteen years old. It was rumored that Rudolpho "Rocky" Difiorro, his second-in-command at the time, was given the blessing to marry her when she turned eighteen; instead, she turned up missing, and Rocky was found dead at his home. There was always speculation that Tony took them both out so he would be made second, and if it *was* him, he got his wish."

"We know all of this," Fiske interjected impatiently.

"Yes, but what you *don't* know..." Owens eyed Fiske, "is that intel suggests Tony is here in Richmond."

"That doesn't make any sense," I said sitting forward. "Why wouldn't he be in Boston, waiting for Vinnie to pass, so he could take over the family? There are tons of cousins already making noise about a hostile takeover; they don't like Tony, name change or not. Why would he leave while the family is vulnerable?"

It didn't make any sense to me. Tony wasn't stupid. He'd been working his whole life to take over the family, why leave it when he was at the finish line?

"That's what *you're* here to find out," Owens stated, dropping a file in front of each of us. Fiske groaned, and I mentally seconded it.

Red

I smoothed down my skirt as the bitchy old bat in front of me berated me again for not having all of the information in the world. Her gray hair was coiffed to perfection, and she wore far too much makeup, but it did nothing to soften the sneer on her face.

"I am so sorry, Mrs. Adams. The phone number for the Director of Education is unlisted. I would be more than happy to give you the number for his department—" I tried again in a soothing tone.

"I do not WANT to speak to some lackey in his department," she shrieked.

"Mrs. Adams, why don't you come with me, and I will call down there personally and try to get him on the phone with you? My private office is just this way." Roger, my boss, appeared from behind me and moved around the desk to usher Mrs. Rancid Face away.

She really needed an assistant, and it was not going to be me. She had once sent me on a half-hour errand that nearly got me fired, and thought nothing of it. She seemed to think she was an aristocrat. I mouthed "Thank you!" as he glanced back at me with an eye roll at her behavior. He had dealt with her hysterics before. As he shuffled her off she thanked him for his courtesy and understanding. I snorted in disbelief.

I returned my attention to my computer screen, going over all of the day's reservations. I worked at the concierge desk for the Marriott Hotel and managed car rentals or services, sightseeing or tours, and other activities for travelers, as well as in-house needs.

I heard footsteps approaching and looked up to see the blond model-type from the bar yesterday walking up to me, sans the crowd of adoring women. I plastered my best professional smile in place.

"Good morning. How may I help you?" I gave him my 'eager face'.

"Yes, good morning." He flashed me a huge toothy grin and pulled his sunglasses off while he looked me up and down. "I'm in room 529, Fiske. I need to extend my car rental for another week. God, I hope you can help me with that." He pulled his lower lip between his teeth through his grin as he looked me back up and down again like he was undressing and fucking me with his eyes. I could only see him as a player.

I kept my perma-smile in place. "Let me see what I can do, do you have your rental agreement with you?"

"Yeah, my buddy is parking right now, he'll be here any minute with that. Oh, there he is now!" He turned and waved. As he turned I could see Murphy walking our way.

Fuck.my.life.

He had ignored me at the gym that morning, and now he was staying in the hotel where I worked. I was never going to be able to lose this guy.

Murphy's eyes got wide with surprise before he adjusted his look to something more amused.

"Hello, Red," he said slyly.

Fiske's head whipped between us. "You've met?" he asked Murphy.

Murphy just chuckled under his breath, "Yeah... we've met."

Before they could take this conversation anywhere else I interjected brightly, "Do you have your rental agreement with you?" My perma-smile was damn near breaking my face.

"Why yes, I do." He smiled and handed it over. It was one of the rental agencies we worked with, so I logged into their terminal and made the adjustments quickly. The sooner I did this, the sooner they would be gone. "Did you want to return this on Saturday, or Sunday?" I questioned, never looking up from the terminal.

"Sunday," Murphy said, his eyes boring holes into my forehead as I typed.

I did take the opportunity to notice that his full name was Baxter Murphy, and the other man was John Fiske. So he hadn't lied completely... that was something, wasn't it?

Nope. Not caring.

I printed out the new forms and had them both sign them, agreeing to the new charges. "There you go, all set!" I tore their copies off and handed them to Murphy.

But as my hand touched his I felt the cold chill before the darkness overtook me.

NO! SHIT! Not NOW!

Baxter

Poor Red, she looked completely discombobulated seeing me. I guess I found out where she worked. Was she feeding me a line about painting crime scenes, maybe telling me what she thought I wanted to hear because she thought I just wanted sex from her? I wanted to know every last detail about her.

She held the rental contract out for me, and our hands touched as I took them. Suddenly she stiffened, and her eyes took on a faraway look in them, focused somewhere over my shoulder. I turned to look as I heard her speak.

"Don't go to the docks alone. It's dangerous. They are waiting for you."

I turned back to her, and as I took the papers from her hand she seemed to snap out of it, shaking her head. Her cheeks immediately blushed deeply, a look of embarrassment on her face. She turned to me with horror.

"Uh..." She stammered. "Okay then, if there's nothing else, have a great day! Thank you for choosing the Marriott." Her smile was stricken, and she turned and ran into the office behind her, closing the door quickly.

"What was that all about?" Fiske asked me, looking at the door she had closed hastily behind her.

"Not a clue," I said, feeling concerned.

"Well, I'm hungry, how about you?" Fiske asked suddenly, turning and walking back toward the restaurant in the hotel.

My eyes stayed on the door for another moment, before I turned to follow Fiske, completely confused by what I had just seen.

Red

I was sucking air in through my nose, and blowing it out of my mouth, trying desperately not to hyperventilate. *Fuck!* I hadn't had an episode in a long time, and never in front of guests before. Murphy probably thought I was a head case now.

But is that a bad thing? Maybe he will not want to pursue me now, thinking I'm crazy. Maybe he'll just work on whatever he's here for and forget all about me.

Yes, it would be for the best, but a part of me was sad that it ended that way. He really did seem nice, and I did like him, or at least what I knew about him. A part of me wanted to get to know him a lot better.

But really, where could it have gone? He was a fed, and I was... well, me. We had no future together. As soon as he found out who I was, he would drop me like a hot potato, or worse. I could end up in prison. Chances were he was a player just like his buddy, anyway... and yeah, they probably had small dicks.

I sat down and pulled a sketch pad out of my bag. I carried one at all times for just this reason. I knew the vision I had wouldn't leave me until I got it out, until I drew it or painted it.

I quickly sketched the scene I had seen in my mind. Murphy was on the ground, Fiske had a gun raised at someone out of the scene. They were in a large dark space, with a concrete floor, surrounded by crates and boxes. I felt like I knew Murphy had been shot.

I stared at the barebones sketch. I hoped that it would be enough to stop the vision from haunting me. A wave of sadness flowed over me; I didn't want Murphy to die. And I couldn't tell him what I had seen, he probably already thought

I was a nut. The warning I had given him was already cuckoo sounding. I could only hope he would take my advice.

Fuck I hated this gift.

Tucking my sketch pad back into my bag I opened the door a crack to look out, the coast was clear. Murphy and Fiske must have run for their lives after my little episode. I tried to block the sadness out, and continue working on my rentals for the afternoon, but the sick feeling in my gut wouldn't go away.

Baxter

I ate my burger in silence. Fiske was laying out the review of his threesome last night in great graphic detail. I liked the guy, but I swear, sometimes he was like a teenage horndog. I was only half paying attention, as I kept replaying in my head the weird way Red had acted.

It was like she zoned out, and was then embarrassed. Or had she seen someone over my shoulder, who scared her? Did she know something? Was she involved with the Giovannis and was trying to warn me that they were going to ambush us? If so, she did a crap job. I had no idea what she was talking about, we weren't going to any docks. Clearly, there was more to this, and I had to know what.

"I'll be back," I said to Fiske, dropping my napkin and walking away while he was mid-story. I made my way back out to the concierge desk where Red was back at her computer, typing away. After a moment, I cleared my throat to let her know I was there, and she jumped with a gasp.

Her eyes were wide when she saw it was me, and her cheeks returned to their crimson color.

"Red, what did you mean about the docks?" I asked her directly, all business.

"I... I don't know," she answered softly.

"What do you mean you don't know? You told me it was dangerous, that 'they were waiting.' Who is 'they?'" I pressed.

She looked down, averting her eyes. "I don't know," she said again.

"How can you not know, when you're the one who said it?" I asked, my anger starting to rise. "Did you see someone here? Do you know something about the work I'm here to do?" I could feel she did know something but wasn't going to tell me. Was she afraid?

"Look, I can protect you." I finally bit out.

"I told you, I don't know." She finally looked up. Tears were forming in her eyes, and she looked nervous. But why? Nervous of what?

"Did you know you're being watched?" she said suddenly, her eyes on her computer.

"Is this another cryptic message you're not going to know anything about later?" I asked harshly.

Instead of answering, she pulled her cell phone out of a drawer, and turned the camera on, so that it was showing the screen she was looking at. She held it under the counter so that I could see in her cell phone what she was seeing on her screen.

"That camera shows the parking lot outside the entrance. I use it to see rentals coming and going. If you look in the third row of cars, there is a guy standing behind that SUV. He keeps pulling up binoculars and looking in here. I saw him when you were here earlier, but he wasn't using the binoculars, now he is. I thought you would want to know...." She looked up at me through her lashes, her eyes puffy.

She was right though, there was someone watching me talking to her. I pulled out my cell phone and texted Fiske.

"Can you screenshot that, and text it to me?" I asked her.

She nodded, taking the screenshot, and then I gave her my number. The image came through immediately, and I sent it to Fiske as well.

"Just keep talking and act like everything is normal," I said to her calmly. I didn't need her running off again.

"What should I talk about?" she asked quietly.

"You really don't know why you said the things you said earlier? You're not aware of any plan to ambush us or something?" My voice was calmer now, soothing.

She shook her head. "I'm sorry. I really can't explain it, but I don't." A tear leaked from her eye, and she swiped at it angrily, pulling her head high and blinking away the rest of them.

"OH!" She exclaimed suddenly, and then she turned her monitor so I could see it. Outside, Fiske and two police officers took down the suspicious man in the parking lot as he tried to run. In no time they had him in handcuffs. Fiske would have him brought to the local office for questioning.

"You did really good!" I tried to cheer her up. "Thanks for catching that."

She smiled weekly, and I still felt like shit. It made no sense at all, but I believed her when she said she had no idea why she had warned us. A part of me still wanted to bring her in for questioning, but a larger part knew I wouldn't get anything from her. Either she didn't know anything, or she was too afraid to tell me.

"I have to go deal with this," I said quietly. "Are you going to be okay?" I didn't know what 'normal' was for her, but she seemed really shaken up.

"Yeah, I'll be fine." She sniffed, and this time her smile was a little easier.

"Okay. Well, you have my number now," I told her. "Don't hesitate to call me."

She nodded but said nothing. I stood there for a moment but realized I had work to do, I couldn't stay until she felt better. Silently cursing I headed outside to find out who our mystery stalker was.

Our peeping Tom was a low-level member of the Giovannis, Sal Giovanni: one of Vinnie's younger nephews. He had a record a mile long for drug charges, breaking and entering, and robbery, and he wasn't the sharpest knife in the drawer. They knew our faces in Boston, but I had to wonder how they found out we were here in Richmond so quickly. He wouldn't tell us why he was watching me; in fact, he claimed he wasn't. I could imagine he was here to protect Tony, as he also wouldn't verify that Tony was here.

Three hours of interrogation had gotten us no further information. I left the interrogation room frustrated. Our element of surprise had been taken from us by that dipshit. I walked into the breakroom and poured myself a coffee while I tried to strategize where to go next. Agent Billings, Owen's assistant, found me there.

"We found the car that went with the keys he had on him. You're going to want to take a look at this." He handed me a large manilla envelope.

The envelope was for a commercial moving company, and inside were handwritten notes, obviously in some sort of code. I shook my head in disgust.

"Let's get a team together to check out this company first. Get a crypto team working on this code, see if they can get us any information," I said to the young agent. With a nod, he headed back out of the room.

Forty minutes later we had two cars moving into the industrial park. Fiske and I were coming in from the north, while another team of agents approached from the south. It was after five, but there were still trucks and cars moving through the area. When we reached the parking lot for the business listed on the envelope, deep on the outskirts of the park, it looked deserted. There were no cars, and the asphalt in the parking lot had weeds coming up between cracks. The second team radioed us to say they would take the front entrance; Fiske and I would take the rear.

There didn't appear to be any side doors or cameras on the property. And while it looked abandoned, I knew better than to assume before searching. Fiske and I located the loading bays and a door into the building beside them. Checking in one last time, we made our way to the back door, while the other team was approaching the front. The front door was locked, but the rear door wasn't. We were in luck.

While the second team worked to gain entrance, Fiske and I let ourselves in as quietly as possible. The building was dark inside, with only a few skylights letting in some hazy late-day light. It was completely silent, and we crept along as quietly as we could. We were standing in the loading bay, which was full of boxes, some of which were open, with packing paper strewn around them like they had been unpacked hastily. I walked the perimeter of the room to the left, while Fiske took the right. I walked the end aisle of rows upon rows of metal storage shelving, which extended up twenty feet, just shy of the metal ceiling. I stopped for cover at the end of each and then rushed to the cover of the next. In my ear, I could hear that the second team had just been able to enter the front of the building.

As I made a dash to the last row of shelving I heard the telltale click that always preceded the loud BANG of a gun-shot. I was knocked off of my feet by a powerful blow to my chest, trying to keep my head from hitting the concrete as I went down. Suddenly there were shots everywhere, echoing loudly. Pain radiated out of my ribs, as I tried to move to cover. I couldn't even take a full breath. I managed to crawl behind some boxes when I saw the silhouette of one of the shooters move in front of me. Fiske appeared out of nowhere, his own pistol drawn, and took out the shooter before he could shoot me again.

Within seconds the second team was at our location, and the rest of the shooters lay dead on the concrete floor. I sprawled out on the floor, just trying to breathe when Fiske appeared above me.

"You okay, Man?" He gave me a worried look.

"Yeah..." I growled. "Thank God I wore my vest today." I looked up at him and froze. Behind him, on the wall, was a directory. It labeled the place we were in "THE DOCKS."

I spent the better part of another few hours at the hospital, having x-rays to confirm that two of my ribs were bruised. I could have told them that before they took the x-rays, but it was procedure to get a full medical evaluation whenever there was a physical altercation involving weapons. I was given pain-killers, which I couldn't take until I was back in the hotel room, and sent on my way. Fiske was waiting for me in the hall.

He had seen the same sign that I had. We had shared a look, but neither of us had said anything about Red or the docks. I think we were both just going to ignore it as a coincidence. Or at least Fiske was, I couldn't get it out of my mind. Was it a coincidence, or had she somehow known?

She was the one who pointed Sal out to us, so I found it hard to believe she was working with the Giovannis. Of course, she could have been an unwilling accomplice, which would explain why she pointed him out, and why she had warned us about the docks. But it just seemed really unlikely.

But not impossible. Stop thinking with your cock.

The guys on the docks all turned out to be locals known to the PD for running drugs. I still had no connection between them and Sal, other than the envelope we had found in his vehicle. Dogs had found traces of drugs in his car, but those could have been from Boston. We were back to a dead end.

I just wanted a hot shower and some painkillers, and a good night's sleep.

Chapter 4

Red

I scrambled to my bedroom closet and, using a stool, got my burner phone out of my lockbox. Rushing back into the living room, I flopped on the couch, exhausted. It had been a shit day. The emotional roller coaster and then a freaking episode in front of Murphy, of all people, had left me entirely wiped out. But I couldn't call it a day until I heard from Victor.

I looked at the screen and saw I had a voicemail. I listened immediately.

"Hey, good news. It's being taken care of. You don't need to worry about your friend; she's all set. I'll talk to you later." Victor's voice cut off suddenly as the voicemail ended. I nibbled on my lower lip.

Should I call him back for more information? Or should I trust and let it go?

While I wanted to know every last little thing, the less I knew, the better. Plausible deniability was a thing. If Victor said it was done, it was done, and I had to trust that.

I sighed deeply, feeling like the weight of the world had been lifted off my chest. Jenna was going to be okay. Now I could concentrate on the shitshow that my life was becoming. At that moment, I just wanted to melt into the sofa and never get back up; I needed to relax. I had been pushing myself with my workouts, not sleeping well, and work had been... ugh.

My eyes took in my tiny living room; like my life, it didn't get much natural light, so it was gloomy. The carpet was ancient and worn, and the outdated furniture was all thrift store salvage-vintage. The sight added to my sense of exhaustion and unrest.

A bath suddenly sounded relaxing. I dragged myself off the worn sofa and made my way to the bathroom. My apartment was tiny, and the size of the tub was more appropriate for children. Even at my petite height, I knew that the top half of my body would be out of the water and my knees, but I would give anything just to soak most of myself in hot water and relax.

While the water ran, I put my burner phone away, safe and sound, and got my regular cell to keep beside me in the bathroom. I always had it on hand in case of emergencies. I dumped half a bottle of bubble bath into the steaming water and shed my clothing. Stepping in, I winced at the heat but lowered myself into it anyway, sighing when my back finally settled into the superheated water. I closed my eyes and just breathed.

The buzzing of my cell phone roused me from my stupor. Had I fallen asleep? BUZZZZ. The phone vibrated its annoyance again. Wiping my hand on a towel, I reached out to pull it up to my face.

The caller ID read Baxter Murphy.

Holy fuck! He was calling me! Oh shit!

I jerked upwards in the tub, sloshing water everywhere, and answered the call with trembling fingers.

"He-Hello?"

Way to sound confident, Nat, I berated myself in my head.

"Heeeeey, Reeed!" His deep warm voice pushed out sluggishly as if he was drunk.

"Uh, Murphy?" I asked. It was his voice, but it sure didn't sound like him.

"Call me Baxxxx. All of my closesssfriends do." He drew out suggestively.

"Oooookaaaaay. *Bax*. Are you alright?" Something was definitely not right.

"Yeah! I'm greeeaaat!" he said, his voice pitching up. "I mean... other-th'n being shot today. But don'worry! I got better!" He added cheerfully.

"YOU GOT SHOT?!" I screamed into the phone with horror. I could still see my sketch from earlier behind my eyes: Murphy lying on the ground, Fiske standing over him, preparing to shoot someone...

"Iiiissss okay." He slurred. "Are you *worried* about me?" He sounded giddy with delight.

What the everlovingfuck?

"Murphy—"

"BAX," he insisted.

"*Bax*, of course I'm worried. I would never want you to get shot," I answered him honestly. My gut was twisting.

"You DO like me!" he announced happily in his drunken voice.

"Bax, are you okay? Have you been drinking?" I tried to bring him back to safer ground.

"What? NOOOO. You... you can't drink alc-hol when you take painkillerrrs." He slurred matter of factly.

Finally, feeling the relief of understanding, I smiled. "Good to know, Bax."

"HEY! Hey... I wanna ask youuu som'thin." He slurred, his tone more serious. "Is your hair natch-er-ully that red?"

I tried to suppress my giggle. He was adorable when he was stoned. "Well, Bax, there's only one way to know for sure, now, isn't there?" I teased.

"Damn." He breathed out. "I'll have to compare the carpettt and th'drapessss."

I laughed out loud. He apparently thought he was a real Casanova at the moment.

"I'm glad to hear you are okay, Bax," I said, trying again to bring him back to safer ground, again.

"I ammm." He slurred. "But are YOUUU okayyy?"

"Me? Uh, I guess so," I answered, not knowing what to say.

"Do youuu need me to com'over there? 'Cause I will. I can protect youuu." His deep voice, even with the slurring, was stirring me.

Chivalry is not dead.

"Then I can check th'carpett an'curtainsssss." He continued

I take it back. Chivalry is dead and buried.

"Bax..." I knew I shouldn't be taking advantage of his state of mind, but I really couldn't help but ask, "Why did you ignore me at the gym today?" I held my breath, waiting to see if he'd answer.

"IGNORE YOU?!" He slurred indignantly. "Red, I couldn't take my fuck'g eyes off-f-youu! Do you hafff any idea how embarrssssng it is to try to work out with a ragggnng hardon?! I had to leav'b'fore I bent you over, anburied my cock in youuu! Maybe we could'do thattt sometime? Huh? Afffterr I eat your pussy? Cause, I'd lovvve tudoo thatttt tooo."

My jaw fell with shock. I heard a door slam in the background of the call and a voice calling out; it sounded like Fiske.

"Man, who are you talking to?" I faintly heard Fiske ask.

"I'm talk-ing-to the fffutuuure Mrshhh Murphy." Baxter slurred angrily just before the call went dead.

I threw my head back and laughed hard; I couldn't stop myself. Nothing about this was funny; a fed wanting to fuck me wasn't amusing... But imagining him stoned, with his big puppy dog eyes, begging to eat me out?... Yeah. That was the stuff of dreams.

Baxter

I had sat in my hotel room for the last two days, bored solid, and I was not staying in any longer. My head was foggy, and my mouth felt like the Sahara. I groaned as I tried to roll out of bed, my ribs reminding me that they were still attached and unhappy. I winced and glanced at my phone.

Shit! I had overslept! Probably the damn painkillers.

With a groan, I hauled myself out of bed. My limbs felt like lead. The doctor had said no workouts for a while, and the way I felt, I couldn't even argue. I trudged to the bathroom like I was walking through jello and turned the shower on.

I walked into the regional office an hour later; it had taken me far too long to get dressed and ready. You don't realize how much you move your ribs until they feel like you ironed them with a Mack Truck. Fiske's eyes rose to meet mine with surprise.

"You aren't supposed to be here today," he said flatly.

"Good morning to you, too, Sweetheart," I grumbled.

"There's nothing here—" he started, but I cut him off.

"And there's nothing in the hotel room for me to do either, so I might as well be here," I argued over him.

Agent Billings strolled into the room before Fiske could fire off another shot. He was young, only in his early twenties, but he had a good head on his shoulders and was thorough.

"Hey, I don't know if you guys are interested or not..." He looked down sheepishly, pulling his hand up the back of his neck. "But we have a local person here... a clairvoyant... We use her on cases when we hit a wall..." He faded out as his cheeks flushed.

"A Psychic?" Fiske demanded. "Is this how you solve cases down here?"

"I know, it's unorthodox, but she's amazing. You should try it before you judge," Billings answered more confidently.

Fiske picked up his cell phone and started for the door. "I'm going to review the evidence we got off those guys from the warehouse and off Sal. Call me if your psychic closes the case before I do." I watched as he left the room.

I didn't know a damn thing about psychics other than I assumed most of them were full of shit. If the guys down here actually used her, then she must have a good success rate; so who am I to turn down help? So far, we have nothing, so there's nothing to lose. Not that I'll tell Fiske that.

I turned to Billings. "Make the call; I'll talk to her."

He immediately brightened, then headed back to his desk.

I sat in front of the apartment complex at quarter of seven for my seven o'clock appointment with the psychic. River Heights Apartments was in what I called a more gray area of the city, not a bad part, per se, but not one I'd want a girlfriend of mine to walk home alone in. The building was neglected, and there were signs that the tenants didn't think highly of it either, with junk overflowing off patios and trash on the lawn.

I looked at the screen of my cell phone again. "Osgood Road"... where had I heard that before. It was just out of reach in my memory, but I know I had heard it recently, and I couldn't place where. It was bugging me. It wasn't like me to forget facts, figures, or places. But sitting and staring at my phone wasn't going to refresh my memory, so I got out of the car and headed into the building.

I pressed the buzzer for apartment seven, and without anyone checking, the buzzer sounded to release the lock for the door, not that it mattered because it was propped open. I walked up the stairs and down the hall until I found apartment seven; taking a deep breath, I knocked.

God, I hope she's not some wacky gypsy lady.

The door opened, and I had to stop my jaw from dropping. Red stood in the doorway, equally as shocked to see me.

"Red?" I asked incredulously.

"Bax?" she asked, and I did a double take. How did she know my childhood nickname?

Osgood Road was the address the gym gave me for Red.

"YOU'RE the psychic?!" I asked, still shocked.

"I prefer clairvoyant. Won't you come in?" She turned away so that I could enter the apartment.

"What's the difference?" I asked hesitantly as I took in the dark living room and dated furniture. It was clean but clearly secondhand.

She held her hand out to indicate a chair, and I sat before she explained. "Clairvoyance is a form of psychic intuition. It means 'clear seeing.' I see things... and then they happen. There are many psychic abilities, but I have the ability to see things," she answered quietly. "Can I get you a drink?" she added.

I shook my head, and she sat on the sofa facing me. On the coffee table were a sketchbook and pencils.

"So the crime scenes you paint..." I left it unfinished.

She nodded. "Yes, an unfortunate side effect of my... gift... is that once I have a vision, I have to get it out of my head; otherwise, it haunts me. I'll have dreams, nightmares, and migraines; eventually, my body will shut down. It took me years to figure out how to make it stop." Her eyes were on the sketchbook.

"May I look?" I asked, my curiosity getting the better of me.

She held the sketch pad out to me, and I flipped through the pages. I saw drug deals going down, people being threatened, and sex scenes, but the last page stopped me cold. The last page was a rough sketch of the warehouse, with me lying on the floor and Fiske standing with his gun drawn. She had gotten every detail down to the boxes I was lying behind.

I held the picture up. "Have you ever been inside this building?" I asked. I knew she hadn't; even if she had, the boxes wouldn't have been precisely as they were the day I was there.

"Never," she stated.

"So you just... see things?" I asked, unable to wrap my head around it.

She sighed, clearly uncomfortable. "Bax, I can't tell you how it works. I don't even know how it works. I just know that sometimes I see stuff. If I know someone involved, I can try to warn them, but often I see stuff, and I have no idea who it's for. It's really more of a curse than a gift."

I stared at her for a moment, realizing I would hate to have a gift like this. I couldn't even imagine the amount of pressure this puts on someone. I almost felt bad that I was going to ask for her help, but if it saved lives down the road, wasn't it worth it? She could refuse if she didn't want to do it.

"Red... how does this work? How... What..." I didn't even know the questions to ask.

"Give me your hand," she prompted gently, seeing my awkwardness.

I reached out and took her hand in mine, noticing how tiny it was in comparison. It was warm and soft, and I liked holding her hand.

"I'm going to close my eyes. If you have a recorder, turn it on now, although I will try to sketch when I'm done. If I black out, don't panic, it happens sometimes," she said calmly, as if she had done this a thousand times.

Black out?!

I was suddenly very uncomfortable with this. But before I could say anything to stop it, she closed her eyes and took a deep breath.

"I see a tall building... condos or apartments overlooking the water... high-end. In the foreground, there are shops and cafes on the riverfront. People are milling about, walking, talking, sitting on benches... two men shake hands in front of the newsstand," she stated matter-of-factly before continuing, "The newspaper headline is from Friday, September 23rd. It reads...." She stopped and gasped.

She jerked her hands away from me, her eyes fluttering, before opening wide. I could see tears forming in them. She quickly grabbed her sketch pad and a pencil. Her hand whipped and scratched over the page. I walked to stand behind her and watch her work. As her hand flew over it, I saw her vision come to life on the page. In the background were the high-rise apartments; she had written "Richmond Heights" over them. The perspective was from the street along the waterfront, showing the cafes and businesses, the paths through the green park, and the trees. She roughly sketched people here and there, going about their lives, but spent a lot of time detailing two men shaking hands in front of a newsstand. At the bottom, she wrote, "Newspaper date Friday, 9/23, 'MOB BOSS DEAD'."

Tears streamed down her face as she tore the page off and handed it to me. I didn't know what to say; I felt terrible that this process had taken so much out of her. I instantly had the overwhelming urge to hug and comfort her, to protect her; instead, I stood there lamely, looking at the picture, not knowing what to say. I had to be a professional, but it was testing every last bit of my self-control.

I finally snapped out of my daze. "Hey, Red, are you going to be okay?" I eyed her with concern as she rubbed her temple.

"Yeah, Bax, I'll be fine...," she answered without looking at me.

"How did you know to call me Bax? Did you see it?" I hedged.

Her eyes rose to meet mine in surprise, and then she smiled broadly. My heart stuttered. "No," she said. "You insisted I call you that."

"When?" I started, but my phone rang in my pocket simultaneously. I held up one finger to let her know I needed to get it, and she nodded. Fiske's name was lit up on my caller ID, and I rolled my eyes. His timing was horrible, and I took the call quickly and hissed that he needed to wait a minute.

Putting my hand over the phone, I asked her again, "Are you alright?"

She nodded with a small smile and made a shooing motion with her hands, telling me I could go and take the call. I held up the sketch and mouthed "thank you" as I made my way to the door. She followed behind, and as I picked up the call in the hallway, she gently shut the door behind me.

Red

The door shut with a click, and I locked it. I could hear Bax talking in the hallway, his voice growing fainter as he moved away.

Why the hell could I see stuff about everyone else, but I couldn't see him coming to hire me as a clairvoyant?!

But that was the least of my worries.

If my vision was right, my father was going to die in a week. Good riddance, as far as I was concerned, but would this affect my life somehow? Would any of them come looking for me? Or would I be forgotten right along with him? Victor had told me there were rumors that I was already dead, that Tony had killed me, and then Rocky, to become my father's right-hand man. Maybe I would finally catch a break and just stay dead.

Either way, I had to call Victor and warn him. My father's death was going to cause a massive upheaval in the family dynamic, and he needed to be ready.

I hit send on his contact icon, and he answered on the first ring as usual.

"Hey there!" he answered happily.

"Are you alone?" I asked nervously; I didn't need anyone overhearing this.

"At the moment, yes. What's up?" he answered more seriously.

"My father is going to die on the 23rd." I blurted out, not sure how to couch it.

I heard Victor hiss on the other end of the line. "You're SURE?" he asked.

"Yes," I said sadly.

"Fuck," He grumbled. There was a moment of quiet, and then he said, "Look, I think you should lay low. Tony took off about a week ago; a few of the guys know about it, but no one is telling us anything. I have a bad feeling about it."

"You think he'd come looking for me?" I asked incredulously.

"I don't know," he answered. "I think he believes you are dead, but with all the shit that's about to go down, the timing is terrible, that's all."

"Okay," was all I could say.

"I'll send word if I hear anything. You be safe." The call ended, and I returned the phone to its hiding spot.

I sat on the sofa, holding the phone, trying to process everything. I had so many emotions going through me at once. I hated my father, but he was still my father. I'd never be able to tell him how much I hated him, how much he had fucked my life up. I couldn't even attend his upcoming funeral. Grief and rage bubbled up inside me.

Suddenly I felt the chill, and then there was darkness. I gasped in surprise. I never got two visions on the same day, usually not even two days in a row. I watched as the scene unfolded in my mind in crystal-clear detail before everything went black.

Baxter

Even though it was Saturday, and I didn't have to be in the office my body was used to getting up at a specific time. I showered and dressed more casually than I would for work before heading down to the restaurant for breakfast. Fiske hadn't returned to the room last night; he was probably slinking out of some woman's apartment.

I enjoyed breakfast alone, scrolling through the news, when my phone rang. I strolled back into the lobby to take the call from my father.

"Son!" he exclaimed happily.

"Hey, Dad," I answered with a smile.

My dad was so proud that I was an agent with the FBI. While I was growing up, he had worked his way up the ranks back home with the Boston Police until he became Chief. It was only natural that he would want me to go into law enforcement as he had. I remember clearly how he had tears in his eyes when I graduated from the academy.

"Are you in Richmond yet?" he asked. He had only retired a year before and moved down to Richmond himself.

"Yes, I just got here a few days ago," I answered. He didn't need to know I'd been here almost a week.

"We should get together for dinner! I'd love to catch up!" he chirped.

"Definitely. Let me check my schedule and get back to you."

"I know you're not going to come all the way down here and not find time for your old man," he said in a warning.

And there it was.

I loved my Dad. However, my dad was always the Chief, always running the show... or, in my case, my life. Yes, he was proud of me for joining the FBI, but that was after he had nearly disowned me for refusing to join the police. We got along better when we had several states between us.

"Not if I check my schedule and find a block of time to see you," I reiterated. I was a little too old to be bullied or cowed, respect or no.

"I just miss you, Son," he stated sadly, pulling the heart-strings like he did when bullying didn't work.

"I miss you too, Dad," I said distractedly. My eyes wandered to the concierge desk, where some young man was tapping away at the computer.

I thought Red worked Saturdays.

"Look, Dad, I have to go. I will call you as soon as I can, okay?"

"Of course, Bax. Talk to you soon."

I hung up and headed to the concierge desk.

"Excuse me," I said to Jordan, the name on his name tag, "is Red out today?"

"Yes, Sir, she didn't show up for her shift, so they called me in. Is there something I can help you with?" He smiled.

"No, but thank you," I said as I walked briskly through the lobby to the parking lot.

I had a bad feeling in my gut.

Chapter 5

Red

"She's awake!" a woman's voice beside me said.

I was on the floor in my living room, on my back, looking up at my ceiling. Instantly, Bax's face appeared over mine, his forehead creased with lines of worry. Then he crashed into my body, pulling me close and holding me tight. His breathing was ragged, causing me alarm.

"Wha..." I tried to get the words out.

Baxter pulled back, cupping my face in his hands. "You had me so worried, Red."

"She's stable now." The woman's voice interrupted. "Do you still want us to bring her in, or would you like to?"

I turned to see a paramedic on the floor beside me, her dark braids pulled back. She had clear dark skin and compassionate eyes.

"I'll take it from here," Bax said.

The paramedic gave him a long look but started packing her gear as her partner returned to the room.

I brought my gaze back to Bax, who continued to study me.

"What happened?" he asked quietly as the last paramedic left the room, closing the door.

"How did you get in here?" I asked, realization dawning on me.

Baxter's cheeks flushed pink. "Well... when you didn't answer, and I could hear your phone ringing in here, I picked the lock." He stopped for a moment, looking away, but then continued. "When I found that the bolt was also drawn, I... I broke the door down."

I looked past him to see that the door wasn't entirely shut level and then looked back at Baxter with wonder.

"You didn't show up for work. I was probably the last person to see you last night, and I was worried," he explained. "So what did happen? Did you black out?"

"Not.. not exactly. This has never happened before, Bax; I had a second vision." I felt foolish and fragile, and I wouldn't say I liked it, but I didn't mind how he was holding me and looking at me intently.

"We should get you to a hospital." He started to get up, but I pulled on his arms, keeping him in place. His head swung back to mine.

"No hospitals," I said simply. "I've lived with this a long time. They never find anything; they only make problems for me."

"You can't be sure you weren't hurt," he argued.

"I'm sure, Bax. They won't find anything physically wrong with me, but they will try to get me for a psychiatric evaluation. This isn't my first rodeo. Trust me. This is best."

I could see his internal debate as he looked into my eyes. He was always sexy and alluring, but sitting with his indecision, he was so damned desirable.

"Are you okay?" I asked him, trying to change the subject.

Instead of answering, he pulled me back to his chest again and held me tightly. I wanted to pull away; I wanted to create space between us. I knew that I shouldn't allow him to get close to me. I knew it was dangerous, and still, my arms wrapped around his neck and held him back.

Instantly his cologne was in my nose. My core clenched with desire. His scent made me want him more. I don't know why I did it. I don't think it was a conscious decision; I just started kissing his neck. And once I started, I couldn't stop.

I felt his moan vibrate up his throat as his fingers clutched at my back. His breathing was uneven again. I slipped my fingers along the back of his scalp; his hair was too short to tangle in. My lips found their way to his ear, where I nipped gently before sucking it into my lips and teasing it with the tip of my tongue.

He groaned, and then his mouth began to work feverishly along my neck as well. He kissed, nipped, and sucked on my bare throat. He gently raked his teeth against my sensitive skin, and I gasped as a shudder ran through me. That seemed to spur him into action because his mouth moved over mine, his kiss deep and passionate. His fingers were winding in my hair, pulling my head back, giving him access to my tender throat.

He ran hot kisses down the column of my throat, his fingers following, tracing my jawline, down the sides of my neck, my collar bone, and then... his hands were gently rubbing over my breasts, tentatively. I squeezed my hand over his, letting him know it was alright. And then he was everywhere.

He laid us back on the floor, his mouth devouring mine while his hand moved up under my shirt to massage my breast. He groaned with pleasure, and I could feel the length of his hardness against my thigh.

Definitely NOT a small dick.

He pinched my nipples through my lace bra, and I arched into his hand with another gasp. His hands found their way to my back and quickly undid my bra, sliding it and my shirt over my head. My hands grabbed at his waist to pull his shirt up, but when I got it halfway, he stopped and lurched with a groan. I looked down to see an enormous dark purple bruise along his muscular ribcage, and my breath froze in my lungs. My eyes flew back up to his.

"Maybe we should..." He pulled back and looked away sadly, his breathing still rough, seeming to realize what we were about to do.

I wasn't having any of it.

"Take this to the bedroom," I said. "Yes, you're right, we should."

He looked back at me, indecision warring in his eyes, until I reached down and started to unbuckle his belt. I pressed my breasts against his chest as I kissed him there, my fingers working the zipper of his jeans.

"Bedroom... yes..." he panted and then groaned.

He helped me up, and we scurried into the bedroom together. When we got to the bed, he pulled me in for another soul-searing kiss. I could kiss him all day. There was nothing better than the feel of his mouth on mine, hungry for me like I was for him.

My hands reached down to finish undoing his jeans, and I slid them off his body with his briefs, pulling my mouth away from his and lowering with them. I let my hands skim the outsides of his muscular thighs and calves until his jeans hit the floor.

In my face was the largest cock I'd ever seen, and another shiver of anticipation ran through me like lightning. I was on my knees instantly, needing to feel him in my hands and take him in my mouth. I took him in my hands. He sucked in a breath loudly and then groaned, his head falling back for a moment and then snapping back to watch me and his hands flying to my hair.

I stroked his length as I looked up. His chest was heaving with ragged pants, and his eyes were half-lidded and filled with desire. There was almost a desperate quality to the way he watched my hands stroking his hardness. I cautiously brought my mouth to his now fully erect cock, allowing my tongue to savor his texture, his flavor.

"Red, you're so fucking beautiful," he said between gasps, watching me tease his cock with my hands and mouth.

I ran my tongue up the underside and then swirled around the tip. He groaned again, deeply and loudly. I looked up through my lashes at him.

He understood.

"Please," he groaned.

It was all I needed. I took him deep into my mouth, loving his velvety soft skin and the hard muscle underneath. He tasted sweet, earthy, and slightly salty, and I relished it on my tongue. His groans increased, and his hands tangled in my hair, pulling slightly, sending me into a frenzy.

I wanted to make him come undone in my mouth. I wanted him to lose control. I took him deeper, feeling him at the back of my throat; I sucked harder and gently skimmed my teeth down his length. His hips rocked into my mouth in time with my movements, his hands becoming firmer in my hair.

I reached to cup his balls and gently massage them with one hand. His groan was strangled, and I felt him harden on my tongue. His hips drove his cock further into my throat, as his hands stilled my head while he fucked my mouth.

"Fuck! Red, I... I'm gonna--"

I dug my nails into his ass to keep him from pulling away from me, and I felt his balls pull tight, his breathing loud until he let out a gasping cry. Thrusting hard, I felt him spasm on my tongue, and then he was spilling warmth into my mouth. I licked his salty sweetness, swallowing him down as his rhythm in my mouth slowed.

He pulled me back up and into another searing kiss. I could feel his cock pressed against my body, warm and wet. I wanted him, and I wanted him as I had never wanted a man before. I pulled him gently toward the bed, falling back onto it and pulling him with me. I was careful not to touch his ribs.

He gently laid his body over me, supporting most of his weight on his arms and knees. He brought his mouth down over my breast to suck the nipple into his mouth, and I thought I would come apart from that alone. I arched into his mouth, making mewling noises, my nails raking over his shoulders and scalp.

He turned his attention to the other breast, nipping at the nipple, making me scream, before taking it into his lips and sucking. The sensation made me grind my hips into him, searching for relief. He pulled back, lifting off of me. His hands slid down my body while he surveyed every inch with hungry eyes. Finally, his hands made it to my pants, and he began to undo them with practiced fingers. He slid my pants and panties off my legs and let them fall to the floor.

I was laid bare before him, and he stopped to stare with a look of awe. I knew I wasn't the prettiest girl out there and wasn't in the most remarkable shape, especially compared to his god-like body. Still, the way he looked at me made me feel like I was the most desirable woman on Earth. His look said he was the luckiest man alive, making me wet for him all over again.

He reached down to the floor behind him and picked up his jeans. I popped up onto my elbows and was about to ask what the hell he was doing, thinking he was going to leave. Instead, he fished a condom package out of his wallet. He smirked as he tore the wrapper open and then rolled the condom on, before returning to bring the warmth of his body over mine.

"I've wanted you from the minute I saw you," he said over my mouth before kissing me deeply. His kisses moved down my jaw, nipping at the tender flesh behind my ear.

"When I saw you in that bar, I knew I had to get you out of there. I couldn't let another man touch you. Not when I wanted to be the one to give you pleasure." His warm breath feathered over my ear.

I squirmed against him, desperate to feel him inside of me. My breaths were shallow pants and moans.

"Every time I see you, I can't control myself. I know I shouldn't, but I can't stop. I need to be inside of you. I need to feel you. Fuck, Red, I can't stop wanting you."

I turned my head so that our eyes would meet. "Take me, Bax. Fuck me now." It was more of a plea and less of the command I had wanted it to be, but damn, he had me ready to come, and he hadn't even gotten inside of me yet. I was desperate to feel him.

His hand moved swiftly between us, positioning his head at my opening. He kissed me again as he slowly pushed the head of his cock inside of me. He groaned loudly, pulling his head back slightly, his eyes clamped shut in ecstasy.

"FUCK, Red... you're so damned tight..." His breathing hitched.

He pushed a little more, and I felt the pain. I tried not to, but I yelped. He was so fucking big.

Instantly he stopped moving, his eyes on me.

"Are you okay?" Concern laced his eyes.

"I will be," I said soothingly. "I just need to adjust... It's... it's been a while," I admitted. I could feel my cheeks flaming.

"We can stop if you need to?" He still hadn't moved.

I was dying a thousand deaths of humiliation. I had the most amazing cock, attached to a God, on top of me, and my anatomy was not living up to it.

"No," I insisted and rotated my hips under him to help stretch me out.

This caused him to drop his head into a groan. I reached out and pulled his head to me, kissing him deeply. I could feel his cock throbbing inside of me, wanting to push further, and that prompted the lubrication I had been needing. I gently pushed against him, sliding him in a little further.

"Red! You're so... fucking... tight!" he said with a gasp, followed by a long deep groan as he slowly pushed himself all of the way inside of me.

"Bax," I whispered breathily, "I need you, Bax! Oh my God, you're so fucking big! Fuck me, Bax. Please! Fuck me!"

Instantly he was thrusting into me with abandon, filling me in all the right ways. I let out a moan as my head fell back. My hips bucked up to meet his grueling pace. He slammed into me repeatedly, making grunting and groaning noises with each sharp, deep push. I was so incredibly full, and the sensation was beyond imagination.

I was incoherent, lost in the sensation of the force impaling me on the mattress.

"Yes! Yes! Bax! Harder!" I screamed, and Bax let me have it.

He was an animal, roaring and thrusting. I could hear our groans and the hard slapping sounds of our bodies as they beat together in a harsh rhythm. I felt him get incredibly hard inside me, pushing back against my muscles as they tightened around him.

"I need you to come, Red!" he ordered. "Come for me, Baby!"

And right on command, I felt myself taken to new heights of ecstasy, every muscle in my body winding tighter and tighter like a spring until I snapped with a scream, arching up into him, every muscle shaking with the effort.

He thrust hard, lodged deep inside me, screaming his own release as his fingers clawed into my hips. And then he was pumping into me again, slowing the pace, heaving groaning breaths. An aftershock tore through me, causing me to scream out again, the feeling of his cock against my over-sensitive skin too much.

He finally collapsed on top of me, careful not to crush me with his weight and mindful of his ribs, which I was positive had to be hurting after that performance. We were both slick with sweat and breathing heavily.

"You know..." He heaved, "For a sweet girl... you sure talk dirty." He laughed.

"You don't like it?" I asked through my own ragged breaths.

His eyes lit up. "I fucking LOVED it," he responded.

"You know... "I heaved back. "For a big tough guy... you took it easy on me." I smiled at him.

"You didn't like it?" he teased back.

"You know I did!" I responded instantly. "But I can't wait until you are healed... so I can see what you can REALLY do to me."

I felt his cock spring to life inside of me. Of course, that was when his cell phone rang.

"SHIT!" He cursed angrily, moving carefully off me and down to his cell phone, still in his jeans pocket on the floor. He looked at me, and I nodded.

"What's up, Fiske?" he asked shortly.

I could just make out Fiske's voice on the other end.

"Where are you, man? I got back a few hours ago to find you gone." He sounded a little whiny.

"I'm about to have lunch; I'll catch up with you tonight," Bax said as he smiled over at me.

"You want company?" Fiske asked.

"No. I have company," Bax replied flatly.

"Oh... I'll leave you to it then."

Baxter dropped the phone onto the nightstand and pulled the condom off to dispose of it. He returned to the bed and lay beside me, pulling me into another toe-curling kiss.

Baxter

She was fucking incredible. I don't think she had any idea how erotic she was. She had all of the sweetness of the girl-next-door, all of the things a guy looks for in a good girl to date, but you get her behind closed doors, and she's a wildcat.

The way she went down on me... holy fuck. I think she's ruined me.

I fondled her breast in my hand as I kissed her; I was already getting hard again. My ribs were killing me, and I didn't give a fuck. I'd be inside her all day and all night if she let me. I couldn't get enough of her.

But there was still one thing I still needed to do, and I wasn't leaving her until I did.

I slowly kissed down her jaw and neck, running my tongue along her collarbone. I stopped to spend some quality time with her luscious girls as well. I want to thank her mother for giving her superior DNA and amazing full tits. Once she was squealing and writhing underneath me, I kissed my way down her soft belly. I loved how her full hips felt in my hands; I could dig my fingers in and hold on. She was made for loving, and apparently, she could handle roughness. My cock hardened even more at the thought.

I had started delicately, feeling her out. But she didn't want safe lovemaking, quiet sighs, and gentle pushes; she wasn't fragile. She wanted, had demanded, more. And it was a workout, the kind I could get behind one hundred percent. Balls deep, animal thrusting, taking-no-prisoners-fucking. I must have died and gone to heaven.

My mouth found her warm mound, and she groaned. It was my turn.

"Red, Baby, do you want my mouth on you?"

"Mmmhhhmmmmmmm." She moaned, and I chuckled.

I ran my tongue through her channel, and she gasped, her hips jumping up to meet my mouth. I kissed her with an open mouth, sucking, and she groaned and writhed under my tongue. I brought my mouth up to her clit and flicked at it with my tongue as I pushed two fingers into her velvet wetness.

Her hands were on my head instantly, and she was moaning and crying with pleasure. Fuck, the noises she made almost had me coming; it was like she had a direct line straight to my dick. I latched onto her clit and sucked her hard, making her scream and ride my mouth with her pussy. I groaned as I felt the walls of her core tighten around my fingers, trying to milk them and suck them further into her. I upped my pace, pumping my fingers harder and faster as I lavished her clit with attention.

She was ready; her screams were pitching up, her back arched with a roar, and her pussy clamped down hard on my fingers, sending her wetness down my hand and wrist as she convulsed on me. She was still coming hard moments later, and I just rode her out, enjoying every fucking minute of it. Her pussy was amazing, and I could eat it all day.

I worked her back up to another screaming orgasm before she pushed me away, her clit too sensitive. She was gorgeous post-orgasmic. Her eyes were glossy and sated, her cheeks were all flushed, her hair was messy and spilling around her, her nipples were hard pebbles, and her inner thighs were all glossy with the wetness I had put there. I wish I could get a picture of her like that to keep that memory forever.

She looked up at me with fierce and hungry eyes and curled her finger in a 'come here' motion. I gladly obliged, leaping onto the bed.

She nuzzled her nose just below my ear, wrapped her arms around my shoulders, and whispered, "Please tell me you brought more condoms?"

I nearly blew.

We spent most of the day fucking. The apartment was small, so we christened just about every flat surface we could find and a few vertical ones. After several hours and several good workouts, we were both hungry and sore.

I stroked her hair as she laid her head on my chest. Kissing her forehead, I asked, "You want to get something to eat?"

She looked up at me and smirked. "Are you asking me on a date?" she teased.

"Never," I smirked back. "Because we absolutely should not date. We are doomed from the beginning." I was kidding, but in the back of my mind, I recognized how close to home it hit.

She laughed. "Absolutely!" she agreed. "Hell, we shouldn't even be fucking."

The thought made my heart constrict, but I went along. "Agreed. Let's promise never to do that again..." I paused. "After today," I amended.

"Right." She giggled. "So what's the plan?"

"Dinner," I said. "And then more fucking before midnight, when the day ends."

She squealed with laughter, so I tickled her, sending her into a fit and making her roll into a ball to try to evade me. She was so beautiful when she laughed.

I knew joy at that moment, and I knew I was never going to be able to let it go.

Chapter 6

Red

We sat in the restaurant across the table from each other, the glow of the candle making his skin appear warm. The food had been excellent, and the wine went down easy. Bax was telling me a story, and his voice was rich and deep, laced with humor; the shape of his mouth kept distracting me, making it hard to concentrate on what he was saying. I had to fight back the urge to lean forward and steal a kiss from those luscious lips.

"Red." He laughed.

My eyes flew up to meet his, my cheeks blushing instantly. I had been busted.

"What are you thinking with that look on your face?" he asked me slyly.

"I was wondering how many hours we have left until midnight," I answered. "Wait, we didn't agree on a timezone, right? I mean, it's earlier in California than here," I added, not even kidding.

Christ on a cracker. I was practically unable to walk after our all-day marathon, yet I couldn't wait to jump back into the saddle again. He was right, though; we were doomed from the beginning; for whatever reason, I was just not caring. If I can only have this happiness for a week, I will take it.

He was laughing out loud at my last comment, and he was so beautiful. How did someone as fucked up as I am ever manage to have such a wonderful person choose them... even for a little while?

Duh... because he doesn't know who you are.

I felt shame and guilt flood me, two feelings I rarely felt and had no use for anymore. I had never set out to hurt him, but it was going to be hard not to.

"We can agree to Alaska-" He started to say when a large man stepped up behind him and placed a beefy hand on his shoulder.

"Imagine running into you here," the man said with a broad smile. I noticed he had an uncanny resemblance to Bax, except for his eyes. His eyes were a pale blue, almost gray, and looked cold, whereas Bax's hazel eyes always seemed warm.

Bax looked up with surprise. I caught a flash of annoyance moving across his features before he stood quickly, smiling. I also noticed the smile didn't quite reach his eyes.

"Dad!" Baxter said. He was acting happy, but I saw the tension in his posture; I just didn't know why.

"Interviewing over dinner?" his dad asked casually, his eyes roaming over me.

"No, Dad, this isn't business. This is my ... girlfriend, Red." The pause was slight, more like a hiccough, but I heard it. I sat stunned, not knowing how to react, when I realized they were both staring at me expectantly.

"Oh, hi!" I said awkwardly, "I'm Red. Nice to meet you." My cheeks were flushed.

"I'm Bill Murphy, Baxter's dad. It's lovely to meet you... *Red.*" His eyes penetrated me with an intense gaze that never faltered, and I caught the same pause, this time before my name.

"Would you mind if I join you for just a few minutes?" his father asked as he took a chair, not waiting for an answer. I saw the frustration move through Baxter's features again, this time staying a little longer.

Baxter sat, and the two men made conversation, caught up on mutual acquaintances, etc. I tried not to stare, but Bill looked so familiar to me. Maybe it was because he was Bax's father, and they looked alike. But no, I could have sworn I had seen him before. Something gnawed at my stomach lining.

Bill turned to me suddenly. "So... *Red*... you don't sound like you're from around here. Where do you hail from?" He smirked at me in a very disturbing way, and his eyes were doing that intense staring thing again. It was like a challenge, like he was trying to stare me down.

I noticed even Bax was looking back and forth between us as if there was some tension he couldn't define. I know I couldn't.

"I move a lot," I told him with a smile, trying to hide my discomfort.

"I'll bet you do." He chuckled low.

Baxter shot him an irritated frown before changing the subject quickly, and I studied Bill more intently.

Then it hit me! I knew I had met him! My heart stopped in my chest, and I focused on keeping the shock off of my face. My pulse was racing, and I had to get away. I had to breathe, and I had to get away from HIM.

"Excuse me!" I sputtered in a rush, pushing away from the table. "Just going to the ladies' room!" I walked away far faster than was considered polite, but I was only glad that I hadn't broken into a run in the middle of the restaurant.

I rushed into the bathroom and locked the door behind me quickly. I leaned back against the wall, almost hyperventilating. I had to get myself under control!

The memories all sat queued up in my mind. It all came flooding back as soon as I realized who he was. I tried to push them down, but even I knew that the things you tell yourself not to look at are the first things you look at.

As I forced myself to alternate nose/mouth breathing, my mind replayed the events of the last party where I had seen Bill. It was over fifteen years ago, and he was much younger. He was brash and arrogant, which is why my father gravitated to him. I knew he was a cop but didn't realize he would eventually become the Chief. He was a dirty detective, paid by my father to handle the family's business and keep our boys out of trouble. He made sure the right people looked the other way when my father needed to get "less than legal" things done.

I don't remember what the party was celebrating. It was held in one of my father's many seedy clubs. I was only seventeen, but the alcohol flowed like water. I enjoyed getting out and feeling like an adult for a change, which is laughable now that I know the truth. My father would introduce me to "special friends he thought I might like to get to know."

Bill was one of those "special friends." Bill let me know he was interested in getting to know me, despite the fact that he was older than my father by a few years and married (to Baxter's mother, it now turns out). He had been after me for about a year, trying to stake a claim whenever my father would have me with him at any social event. He would grab my ass whenever I walked by and winked as if it was some mutual joke we both shared. He made my skin crawl. And no matter how many times I told him I wasn't interested, he would laugh at me, like what I wanted was utterly irrelevant. I guess to him, it was.

He tried to grope me at that party; he waited until I was alone in a corner and then backed me against a wall. Luckily, Victor happened along and saw what was happening. He played stupid and did something to pull everyone's attention to himself, and thus Bill and I, so I could escape.

My eighteenth birthday was shortly after that, and I ran.

I was starting to get my breathing back under control, and I hadn't yet started crying explosively. Still, I also couldn't force my feet to take me back to the table, back to where he sat. My worst nightmare was realized: he was a predator of the worst kind, and he knew my real identity!

What if he told my father where I was?

WHAT IF HE TOLD BAX?! FUCK!!!

I shoved off of the wall and rushed for the door. I took deep breaths and slowed my pace as I walked back into the noisy dining room. I cautiously peeked around a corner to see that Bax was alone; Bill had apparently left. I studied him for a moment; he seemed quiet, and I couldn't tell what that meant.

Pasting a slight smile on my face, I slowly walked back to the table, focusing on putting one foot in front of the other. Bax jumped up immediately and pulled my chair out for me again, a small smile on his face, his eyes warm.

Bill hadn't told him. Why?

"Everything okay?" Baxter asked.

"Yeah..." I tried to smile convincingly. "With the episode yesterday, I probably shouldn't have had wine tonight, but it's all good."

"You didn't—" Bax started fearfully.

"No... more like a headache." I lied too easily. "I took something for it; I'll be fine." I felt horrible lying to him, but I couldn't very well tell him the truth, now could I? "Where did your dad go?" I asked, trying to sound casual.

"Ugh." Bax groaned, rolling his eyes. "I am so sorry about him. Sometimes he has no social graces, I swear. After you left, I let him know that I would prefer your company alone. He finally got it through his thick head that three is a crowd.

"He did say that you are lovely, though, and that he looks forward to seeing you again soon." He smiled adoringly at me, completely unaware of the hell I was going through.

The words made me want to vomit, and I fought not to grimace at him.

It wasn't long before we were walking down the sidewalk and back to Bax's car. Our arms were wrapped around each other's waists, although mine was more to help stabilize me than keep him near. I watched out the window as he drove me home, lost in my fears.

"You okay over there?" Bax checked in. He had a slightly worried pinch to his eyebrows that was so cute. My heart did a little flip.

"I'm sorry, Bax. I'm not good company at all. I guess I'm just better in bed than at conversation sometimes," I said with a small chuckle, trying to lighten the mood.

"You don't have to make conversation if you don't want to, Red. I just wanted to know if anything was bothering you. You got awfully quiet after my Dad showed up."

"I... I had a really shitty relationship with my father," I said quietly. "I guess I just let it get in my head tonight. I'm sorry; I didn't want to ruin our perfect day." I smiled up at him shyly.

I didn't know why I was giving him some of my truth. But I wanted to be vulnerable with him. I wanted to trust him, let him in, and let him help me chase the monsters away... even though I knew that wasn't going to be what ended up happening. In the end, he would reject me because I am the monster.

"You don't have to apologize, Red," he said, shooting glances at me. "I don't want you to feel uncomfortable." His hand reached over and took mine.

"Besides." He smiled slyly. "The night is far from over. Maybe I can make you feel better?" With that, he beamed.

He was so kind and sweet. I didn't deserve a good man like him.

Baxter

I stopped on the way home to pick up a slide-lock mechanism for Red's door. There was no way I would be responsible for leaving her alone with an apartment that didn't lock in her neighborhood. I also called her management company to replace the door with a stronger safety door; I put that on my own account. I needed her to be safe. I don't know why I felt responsible for her, but I lied to myself and said it was just because I had been the one to break her door in the first place.

Red had been quiet and withdrawn after dinner; something about my father had upset her. And he had been acting odd as well; I know my Dad, and I know when he's pushing buttons. I don't understand why he felt the urge to needle Red.

I know that after mom left us when I was fourteen, it seemed like he went off the deep end, serial dating, but I chalked that up to losing the love of his life. But as I look back now, as an adult, I see it a little differently; his girlfriends were always too young for him, and there were too many. At the time, I was thinking like a boy, "Way to go, Dad!" But as an adult now, especially after watching him perve on Red at the table... Had he always been this way, and I just never noticed it? He even made me uncomfortable.

I also noticed I got away with calling Red my girlfriend; although to be fair, it probably filtered out of her mind after my father was a dickhead and invited himself to creep on her.

Red and I settled on the couch to watch a movie. She snuggled into my shoulder, on the non-injured side, and I wrapped my arm around her. The film had barely begun before I felt her fingers tugging at the zipper of my jeans, and I was instantly aroused.

A small smile tugged at my lips as I kissed her forehead and whispered, "Is there something I can help you with?"

She looked up at me with a sexy smile and said, "It's still 'today.'"

Sunday morning found us tangled up in Red's sheets. She was sound asleep, her red hair cascading down the pillowcase around her like a halo. Her face was peaceful, like the face of a child or an angel. I just stared at her for a moment, trying to memorize every detail. Reaching the nightstand, I grabbed my cell phone and silently snapped a picture of her. I wanted this memory to hold on to.

I knew this thing with us wasn't going to last. Even if she wasn't somehow attached to the case I was working on, although I still felt like she was somehow, I was going back to Boston when this was all over. I didn't want to let her go, but I couldn't expect her to pick up and move for someone she had literally known for a week. And a week isn't enough to even consider moving for, or moving in with, someone.

I gently slid my way out of bed, careful not to wake her, and headed for the bathroom. While there, I checked my phone: no missed calls and only one text from Fiske, but not critical. I texted him to let him know I'd be out most of the day sightseeing and not to wait up for me. After all the times he had done this to me while chasing pussy, I didn't feel even a little bit bad.

Red

Bax collapsed on my back, a heaving, sweating mess. He had taken me roughly from behind after waking me up with an orgasm courtesy of his divine mouth.

God, I wanted to keep him.

I shook the thought from my head. There wasn't going to be a *happily ever after* for us; he just didn't know it yet. The thought made me sad, and his voice in my ear pulled me away from my melancholy musings.

"What would you like for breakfast?" His breath warmed my ear and neck.

I turned my head, nose to nose with him. "Cock," I said with a smirk.

It took us hours to get out of bed and another half hour of fucking in the shower before we emerged from the bedroom. It would have taken longer, but the water was running cold. I don't think I have ever been this horny with anyone in my life, not even as a teenager. It's like Bax had a magical dick or something.

Bax set a plate with french toast in front of me before getting his own and sitting down. It felt so natural, like what normal couples do... something I had never been a part of. It was like playing house, made all the more special because I knew there was an expiration date.

People like me didn't get 'happily ever afters' to their stories; I can't say I even deserved one. Bax deserved someone as pure and wonderful as he thought I was. My corruption would only eat away at his soul as it had mine.

"So, is your mom down here too?" I asked as I chewed my french toast.

A drop of maple syrup slipped from the corner of my lip, and I darted my tongue out to catch it. I noticed Bax's attention fixed on my mouth, his fork raised halfway to his mouth, and I giggled. He realized I had caught him and straightened in his chair, his demeanor shifting as he answered me.

"No. She ran out on my dad when I was fourteen. I got home from school and found her gone. She left a note saying I was old enough to look after myself, and she wasn't cut out to be the wife of a workaholic detective anymore." He looked at his plate as he stabbed a piece of french toast with his fork. While he said it factually, I noticed the hurt behind his eyes.

"I'm so sorry," I said, deflating. "My mom died when I was young, and I never got to know her. Was your mom nice, at least,... while you had her?" I mentally kicked myself for letting my elephant mouth overload my canary ass. I shouldn't be asking him personal questions. Still, I was curious about the family that had molded him into the man who sat before me.

"Yeah... She was." He sighed. "I thought she was a great mom, and I loved her. That's why her leaving hit us so hard; it's like it came without warning." He looked up to meet my eyes.

"And you never saw her again?" I asked, unable to stop the verbal onslaught of my thought-to-mouth filter breakdown.

"Nope," he said flatly. "Dad looked for years, but Sophia Murphy didn't want to be found, I guess."

I reached over and put my tiny hand over his, willing him to feel my comfort for his broken heart. There was a part of my mind trying desperately to believe that what he told me was truly what happened: a dissatisfied housewife leaving her husband and son.

But knowing that Bill worked with my father, I'd bet money that the truth was far different from the story Bax was told. A part of me wished desperately that I could share something more with him. But what did I have to share? That his dad was crooked? That my dad might have agreed to have his mom killed? It was just so fucked up. And the man in front of me never deserved to be on the receiving end of any of this. Unlike me, he was a good person.

"What about you?" He broke me out of my thoughts. "You said your mom died, so your dad raised you?"

My stomach clenched. "Um, yeah..." I tried to find a way to answer his questions without spilling all of my secrets. "He was a raving asshole and narcissist. My family all stepped in to help raise me, but they are a pretty dysfunctional group," I answered.

"Do you keep in touch with any of them?" he asked.

"No," I said a little too quickly, adding, "They're pretty toxic."

Bax sat looking at me with consideration while he ate, and I stuffed another bite into my mouth to stop me from talking. *Had I said too much? Would he put it together?* I quickly shoved another bite into my mouth before I'd even swallowed the last one.

"Speaking of family...," Bax said. I froze in my chair. "My dad invited us out for dinner one night this week. We could eat at the restaurant at the hotel, and then maybe I could show you my suite." He smirked at me.

"No," I said quickly.

Bax's eyes got wide. "No?"

"I don't want to go out with you at the Marriott. I work there, remember," I said flatly, my stomach filling with acid.

"Yeah, I know; what does that have to do with anything?" he asked.

"Bax, I don't want to be seen there on a date. I don't want my co-workers to see me like that," I told him.

"You don't want them to see you like what? *Like my girlfriend?* You don't want them to see you with me? Is that it?" he asked cooly.

"NO." I hissed. "I don't want them to see me with anyone! I don't want any of them to think of me as dateable material. It isn't all about you, you know," I answered with equal frost.

"So you won't come, even if my father is there too?" he asked with a hard edge to his voice.

I spoke before my mind even caught up with me. "I don't want to see him." I could feel my cheeks flush, but I couldn't back down.

Bax seemed taken aback. "Why not? He really liked you, and you're the first girl I've ever introduced him to that he seemed to like."

My heart was racing as I tried desperately to find a legitimate reason not to meet with his dad. "I... I just don't like him. I'm sorry, Bax. I know he's your father, but there's just something... creepy about him."

Please don't push this. Please don't push this...

"I know he can be a little overbearing, Red, but he's a great guy. Maybe if you give him a chance?" There was heat in his words, and I could tell this was not going to end well.

"No, Bax. I'm sorry. I can't do that." I was trying desperately not to freak out, and I'm sure I came across like a spoiled brat.

"Red, my dad *isn't* your dad. It would make this a lot easier for me if you'd come along; I don't want to give up any time I may get with you." He was getting angrier the longer we talked.

"Why are you pushing me to do this?" I pushed back. "Why is it so important that I spend time with your father? You'd be surprised just how similar my dad and yours are, Bax. I'm not spending a minute with him." I crossed my arms over my chest.

"You don't know shit about my father." Bax fired. "Oh, I see what this is, Red. Is this all just about the sex after all, isn't it? You don't want your co-workers to see us, and you don't want to meet my family? Was this all about just fucking until I left Richmond, no strings attached, so you could move on with your life and fuck the next guy who comes along?" Bax rose from the table with fire in his eyes. "Well, you won't have to worry about that, Red. I'm out. Have a nice life."

He gathered his phone and wallet and headed out the door in a huff, slamming it behind him.

I sat in stunned silence. I couldn't even go after him. This was bound to happen sooner or later; I had just desperately prayed it would be later. I had been living in denial, wishing I could see a future where we could have been together.

But I should consider myself lucky to live the life I already have, even if it is alone. Murderers don't get happy endings.

Chapter 7

Baxter

The drive to the office with Fiske was unbearable. I still couldn't work out at the gym, and wouldn't have anyway, as it was Red's day off. I was bound to run into her, which only pissed me off more. I needed to burn off some anxiety. And to add to my already highly pissed-off mood, Fiske would not shut up about his sex life, I was in no mood to hear it.

"So I said to her, 'Hey Baby, want to ride my magical unicorn horn?', and get this, she says, 'I'd love to... but only if I can bring a friend.'" He even spoke her part in a female voice.

"Fiske...," I said quietly, my head pounding.

"It turns out her friend is another GUY! So I said-"

"FISKE!" I shouted.

He stopped talking and looked at me. "Pussy hangover?" he asked me, audaciously.

"Something like that," I snapped back, pressing my lips into a thin line.

"So who did you get into this weekend? I noticed you were absent for quite a while," he said, smirking.

I put the car into park and got out, heading into the office, not bothering to answer his question.

As far as I was concerned, last weekend never happened. Aside from the picture of her on my phone, which I hadn't been able to force myself to delete yet, it was all just a fantasy.

It was clearly all just fun and games to her, so that's where I'll put her; back on the shelf under "someone I fucked once." In time I would forget all about her.

It was a damned lie, and I knew it.

Fiske hurried to catch up with me but was smart enough to keep his mouth shut.

Inside, the office was in chaos. Owens pulled us into a small room and closed the door.

"Sal's being extradited back to Boston for parole violation," he hissed.

"What?!" I practically howled. "No, we're not done with him yet!" I could see my case slowly dissolving. I had no new information, and zero leads.

"What I want to know..." Fiske muttered, as if to himself, "is why they would send Sal down here, knowing if he got caught he'd do time? They have plenty of foot soldiers, so why him?"

"Maybe they assumed he wouldn't get caught?" Owens said.

"Maybe, but let's face it, he practically begged to be arrested out there with his binoculars. He's just not that smart," I said. "They'd have to know that they couldn't leave him unsupervised, and I didn't see anyone with him."

"I'd feel better about knowing his connection to the drug distribution warehouse we raided too," Fiske said.

"It's out of my hands." Owen shook his head. "Transport is on its way."

The three of us walked out of the room and back to our desks in frustration. Fiske pulled out his laptop and began to review photos. I opened my drawer to get my notebook and again my mind went to the drawing Red had done for me.

I was sprawled out on the floor, hidden behind boxes; Fiske had his gun raised, ready to shoot.

How had she known?

Red

I had cried all night like I had when I was eighteen. I sobbed at the unfairness of the world. I sobbed for the lives I lost. I sobbed with the knowledge that I would never ever have the chance at a normal life. I would never have happiness, not really, not until I was dead too.

I didn't dare go to the gym. I couldn't see him. My heart couldn't take it. I was afraid I would confess to him. I'd tell him it wasn't all about sex. I'd tell him that I had grown to care about him. I couldn't call it love... we'd only known each other a week, but it was way more than friendship and much more than just sex. I'd tell him...

No, I wouldn't. He wouldn't listen. It was over. Stop pining like a teenager and move on. Survive.

Moving through my apartment like a zombie I tried to stay busy, tidying the house, but ran out of things to do just after noon. I stared at my tiny apartment; it suddenly felt empty, instead of just gloomy. I considered going grocery shopping when a loud knocking came from my door. The same door Bax had knocked in only two days before.

My heart jumped in hopes that Bax had come back. I ran to the door and peeked through the peephole, only to stagger backward when I saw Bill Murphy standing in the hall. I slowly crept away from the door, holding my breath, hands clutched over my pounding heart, even though he couldn't see or hear me. Bile rose in my throat.

The knocking became pounding. "Red... *Renny*... open the door. I know you're home!" his voice called in a sing-song tone. I froze. No one had called me Renny since... since my father.

The pounding started again. "Renny, I'm getting kind of tired of this. I suggest you let me in to talk to you. Otherwise... who knows who I might have to talk to..." His threat hit the desired target; although, at that moment I was more worried about him telling Bax than my nearly-dead father.

Fighting every survival instinct I had I started the voice recorder on my cell phone and put it into my back pocket, and then opened the door.

"So it is you, Renny!" Bill smiled smugly. "I like what you've done with your hair." He strolled into my living room like he owned the place, and dropped his jacket over the back of the sofa.

"What do you want, Bill?" I asked him flatly, trying to keep the fear out of my voice.

"What do *I* want?" He smirked. "I would have loved to have you ask me that fifteen years ago, doll." I shuddered with revulsion.

"I guess I just wanted to pay a visit to an old friend..." He looked at me pointedly, his smirk still in place. "You know your father doesn't have long, right?"

I nodded.

"And you know Tony has been looking for you?..." He chuckled darkly. "I take it by the look of surprise on your face, you were not aware of that." He smiled smugly, the bastard.

"Tony has this idea in his head that if he was to marry you, get you knocked up with his babies, it would make the family accept him more easily, less need for bloodshed. Personally, I think it's a shit idea, but you know Tony."

"Why would anyone accept him if he was married to me? I've been gone over fifteen years," I snapped. I had to keep him talking; I had to find a way out of this mess.

"They wouldn't. But again, you can't tell Tony anything. I mean, after all, he's a loose cannon. right? Look what he did to Rocky." He smiled knowingly at me. I stood stock still and said nothing.

"'Cept you and me both know he didn't kill Rocky, don't we?" he said coyly. I remained silent. "See, I was the lead detective on that case, Renny. Those wounds weren't made by a seasoned killer, they were made by someone smaller and weaker, someone who lucked out and hit an artery."

I knew it wasn't "luck" at all. Years of martial art training had taught me exactly what I needed to know to end that fight. It had only taken me two weeks to accomplish it because Rocky had kept me drugged and incapacitated. But I wasn't going to tell *him* that.

"What do you want?" I bit out, already tired of his bullshit. If he was going to kill me, I just wanted him to get it over with already. I didn't want to have to listen to him talking.

"What I want is some goddamn respect, Renny!" He slammed his hand down on the table, and I jumped. "I want what's owed to me! I worked for your father for almost thirty years, and as soon as he's on the decline, his family has no use for me any-more! THIRTY YEARS!" he bellowed.

"So here's what's going to happen, Princess. I'm going to deliver you to Tony, but only if he plays ball with me. You are my invitation to a meeting, understand?" He stared at me.

"And what makes you think Tony's going to listen to a Mick?" I asked flatly. Yes, I was pushing his buttons, playing on the Irish versus Italian rivalry, but I wanted off of this merry-go-round. I'd rather be dead than dragged back up to the family in Boston.

"He will if he wants his drugs to keep running up this route, doll. And he will if he wants you alive." His smile was gone, all of his charm forgotten. This was the dirty cop that had befriended my father so long ago, the one who wanted to have sex with an underage girl, young enough to be his daughter, whether she wanted it or not. He was pure evil.

"But first..." He cleared his throat. "You are going to call my son and break it off with him. I can't believe that I never got a piece of that ass, and here you are, fifteen years later, sucking my son's prick. Un-fucking-believable." He shook his head with disgust.

"He will know nothing about this, or my involvement, do you understand me? You are going to break it off with him, leaving no room for doubt, and you are never going to talk to him again. Because if I find out that you do, I'll make sure to deliver all of the evidence from Rocky's case right into his hands. Call him." He bit the command out coldly.

"But we—"

"CALL HIM." There was no room for argument, not even to tell him we already HAD broken up.

My blood ran cold as I pulled my phone out and clicked his contact.

"Red," he answered flatly, surprising me. I didn't think he'd take the call.

"B-Bax... it's over." I stated, trying to sound forceful. Bill looked at me and rolled his hands as if to say, "keep going."

"We...We're over. I never want to see you again. Don't bother coming after midnight." I hung up before he could insist I say more. I hoped Bax would understand that I was under duress, that something was wrong. But would it matter? If he had to choose between his father and me... he'd already chosen. Bax wouldn't be my knight in shining armor.

"You better not be pulling anything smart, Renny. Your dad ran Boston, but around here I have eyes and ears. I'll know if you go anywhere near my son. You'd better be on your best behavior until I come to get you. Oh... and don't even think about running. You'd never make it to the city limit." He reached out and ran the back of his finger down my cheek, a sick smile on his face, before I pulled away from him. I felt the chill spread. With a chuckle, he then turned and headed back to the door.

"It was good to see you again, Renny! Until we meet again!" He closed the door behind him as he left, his stupid smug smile on his face.

That was all I saw before the darkness overcame me.

Baxter

What the fuck was that?!!! The bitch called me to break up with me after I had already broken up with her? What the fuck is wrong with her? Does she just have to have the last word? How could I not have seen how damaged she is?

Maybe I was thinking with my dick, that's how.

I stared at the phone in my hand. *"Don't bother coming after midnight?"* What did that mean? *She didn't really think I was going back there, did she? She didn't really think I was ever going to touch her again after what she said, did she? Was she really crazy? Was all this psychic shit just a cover for true mental illness?*

Because it hadn't seemed like she was crazy. It had seemed very fucking real.

I remembered the picture she had drawn, the one of me getting shot. It had been incredibly accurate. I pulled out the drawing that she had done for me last, the apartments and the park. I groaned and pulled my hand down over my face. I didn't know what the fuck to think.

Fiske pulled the door open and climbed into the car as I folded the picture and tucked it into my pocket.

"Anything?" I asked him.

"Not a damn thing," he said. "Drive."

Several hours later I sat in my car watching the street ahead of me. I was positioned in roughly the place shown from the perspective of her drawing. In front of me, people walked on the sidewalks, sat on benches, and children played. The river was to my right, and the park was ahead of me, beyond the sidewalks. Above the trees the apartment building rose into the air; it was all just as she had drawn it. I made a mental note to return on Friday, although she never gave me a time.

I went to open an app on my phone, and her picture scrolled by. I stopped it and opened it, just staring. She was so angelic.

Fuck. How had this gone so wrong? Did I miss something?

I had been so angry that she didn't want to be seen with me at work. She said she didn't want her co-workers to think of her as dateable, maybe it *did* have nothing to do with me. Come to think of it, I hadn't ever seen her hanging out in the restaurant over the week I'd been there or the bar. Maybe she really didn't want her co-workers hitting on her, especially considering I was going to pack up and go back to my life in Boston, leaving her behind. Maybe I was being a selfish prick, expecting her to upset her routine here when I had no plans of staying.

My heart squeezed in my chest as I traced her face on my phone like a love-stricken teenager.

But my dad... There was clearly something off between the two of them. He was challenging her, and she was terrified of him. It was like she knew him. I sucked in a breath and felt a chill take hold of me.

Did she know him?

Immediately, my mind went places it should never go. My blood turned to ice in my veins.

Had she picked him up in a bar, like she was trying to do the night I got here? Had she slept with him? Is that why there was so much tension?!

The thought made me sick, but at the same time, I felt like I had to know. I just had to. I dialed my father's number.

Red

Everything hurt. I groaned and rolled my head slowly. I was on the floor again, this time near my kitchen table. My head was throbbing. I reached up to feel a hot bump on the back of my head, where the pain radiated. I dropped my hand back to the floor, and just allowed myself to lay there for another minute.

But the vision came back. It was all I could see. It filled my already painful mind.

I groaned in pain and dragged myself, crawling to the sofa, unable to stand, to the sketchbook on the coffee table. Grabbing a pencil with unsteady hands I began to draw. My fingers didn't want to cooperate, and it took far longer than it usually would. My fingers fought with the pencil, dragging it over the paper, but eventually I got it finished. I heaved out a breath of relief and slumped over the coffee table, completely wiped out.

Why the fuck did he have to touch me?!

I closed the sketchbook with a thwap, and slowly climbed to standing; it took several tries. My balance was off and I was weak; I teetered my way into the bedroom, falling into the wall and leaning the whole way through the room. I was going to need something for the pain. I pulled the bottle of emergency pain pills out of my medicine cabinet with shaking hands, fighting to get the cap off. Nausea threatened to take me under.

For the briefest of moments, I considered just taking the whole bottle and getting it over with... but I glanced back in the direction of my sketchbook. My story wasn't over yet. The thought made me want to cry and I sagged with fatigue.

I swallowed two painkillers, the good stuff I'd gotten from a friend, and called out of work for the rest of the week. I told them I had a concussion, and no one asked any further questions. I guess I would just quit at the end of the week if I couldn't find a way out of this mess. I honestly couldn't worry about that at the moment with the exhaustion creeping into my body slowly. The painkillers started kicking in, making me feel sleepy, so I headed into the bedroom to lie down.

With any luck, I just wouldn't wake up.

Baxter

I had originally gotten up early, with the hopes of making it to the gym. My ribs still weren't fully ready for a full workout, but I had convinced myself a light legs workout would be okay. However, once I got in my car, I found myself driving to Red's apartment building. I parked in a lot half a block away, debating. I hadn't called her. I hadn't reached out at all. And I probably shouldn't.

Something about her call didn't sit right. Why would she call to break up, when we were already broken up? And why did she throw in the comment about after midnight, referencing our "never after today" joke? Was she just unstable, or was there a message there?

And the thought that she and my dad might have been a thing tore me apart. I wanted to confront her. I wanted to scream at her. I wanted answers. I wanted her to deny it all and convince me it was all just a big misunderstanding. I wanted her to hurt like I hurt.

I should probably leave it right where it was, and let it be done. It was already over. There is no future for us, so why bother repairing the damage, just to rip our hearts open again later? Would her heart be ripped open? Did she care at all? Or was I just another nameless dick for a weekend? I could survive it being over, I'd lived through that before, but I couldn't live with not knowing.

I was already out of the car and walking to her building before I made the decision to do it. I got to her building door, to find it propped open. I growled in frustration thinking that nobody takes their safety seriously these days. Taking the stairs two at a time I got to her apartment and stopped short. It wasn't even five am, she might not even be up.

I reached up to knock on her door gently, and it swung open under my hand. My heart stopped. She would never leave the door unlocked. She had been thrilled that I had gotten her the new lock to suffice until the management company could replace her door.

I reached for my service weapon, only to realize I was in my gym clothing, I had no weapon with me. Cautiously I crept inside, shutting the door behind me. I made my way into her bedroom, scanning with my cell phone flashlight. When I saw her sprawled on the bed, and breathed a sigh of relief. However, I continued sweeping through her apartment until I was sure there was no one else there.

I found her cell phone on the floor by the kitchen table, next to a small smattering of something on the floor nearby, and picked it up to bring it into the bedroom. I walked silently to the side of the bed, trying not to shine the light directly in her eyes and scare her; that's when I noticed dried blood on her pillowcase. Reaching my hand back quickly, I felt dried blood in her hair.

The dark spots I had seen on the floor by her table...

She groaned as my hand moved under her head, her eyebrows pulling down wincing with pain, but she didn't wake. I tried calling her name and shaking her gently, but she didn't wake. I shook her more forcefully, calling her louder. I was starting to panic when I noticed the small pill bottle beside her on her nightstand. It was some pretty powerful stuff.

Fuck! If she had a concussion and took that...

I called an ambulance to her apartment for the second time in almost as many days. As I waited for them to arrive I went back out into the living room to look at the stains on the floor, to verify it was her blood. But as I passed the coffee table I noticed her sketchbook was open and had fallen off of the table. I picked it up to put it back, but the picture I saw stopped my heart.

When had she seen this? When had she drawn this? When was it supposed to happen?

I tore the page out of her sketchbook, I don't know why I did it. I suddenly didn't want anyone else to see it. I didn't want it to exist, but I couldn't bring myself to destroy it either. My heart was racing, my world crashing around me.

I could hear the ambulance sirens pulling into the parking lot. I tucked the picture into my bag, and let myself out of the apartment before the paramedics could arrive. I needed to figure out what the hell was going on. I slipped out the door before anyone could see me.

Sitting on my bed in my room, I pulled the drawing out again. In the picture, my father had a gun drawn on Red, and I had a gun drawn on my father. It was a Mexican standoff. The background looked like a warehouse, but it was hard to tell. I had no idea why she would draw this. Even if she had met him before, fucked him before, would she have remembered the details of his face this well? Or was it more likely that she had seen this in a vision? This proved there was some connection between them, or at least... there would be. None of it made any sense.

It took more than twenty-four hours after they had admitted her to the hospital before she finally came to. I had a guard on her door reporting to me. She was now officially a "person of interest" to me, but in a professional way, not the bedroom way. I had no idea if she was involved with the case that brought me to Richmond, but I was going to damned well find out what she had to do with my father and me.

I looked at my watch; I still had two hours until I was due to meet my father in the hotel restaurant for lunch. I was going to demand some answers. But not before I didn't find some of my own.

It was a short drive back to Red's apartment. The agent I had put on the door nodded as I passed him in the hallway. Shutting the door behind me I stopped, letting my eyes wander around the room. I decided to start my search in the bedroom, as traditionally most people hid their secrets close to where they slept.

I searched through her drawers, looking for false bottoms. I checked her desk, and under her bed, without finding anything at all beyond her personal belongings. *There had to be something. I knew there had to be, I just had to find it.* I moved all of the stuff stored in the bottom of her closet, finding nothing but too many shoes; I checked to make sure there were no hidden compartments in the walls. I was starting to feel frustrated as I looked up to the top of her closet.

Bingo!

A locked safe box was hidden under piles of sweaters. I pulled it down, noting it required a small key. I had seen some keys in her nightstand and brought the box to her bed. The first key was too large, and I disregarded it. The second key didn't fit. But the third key fit and turned smoothly. I popped the top open to find a passport, a large stack of cash, and a cell phone.

Turning the phone on I noted that there was only one number in the history, a Boston area number. I would have the number run, but I was willing to bet it led to a burner phone, and it would give me nothing. Still, it tied her to someone near Boston. I had a link, albeit a weak link. Pulling out my cell I dialed the office.

"Agent Myers," a man answered.

"This is Agent Murphy, I need someone to trace some information for me. First I need to find out who owns the phone with the number..." I rattled off the number to Myers. "Next I need a deep background done on Natalie Brooks." I gave him all of the information I had on her, including the number from her passport, and the date of birth, but told him it might not be the correct one. I couldn't assume anything.

I noticed her daily cell phone nearby and pulled my laptop out of my briefcase. I plugged her phone into it and let the program download all of the information from her cell. Then I put her cell phone back where I had found it.

As expected, I didn't find anything noteworthy in the rest of her house. I locked the box with the burner phone in it and replaced it in the closet, hiding it as I had found it. I didn't know why I was hiding the fact that I was searching her place from her, she'd find out eventually; perhaps the burn of perceived betrayal still hurt too much to trust her fully. Maybe our fight had all been a misunderstanding; but the phone call I overheard, the burner phone, and her mysterious connection to my father, of all people, left me pretty sure she was keeping secrets from me.

I looked at my watch again. It was time to see what 'Dear old Dad' had to say about all of this. I packed up my briefcase and headed back to the hotel with renewed purpose.

Chapter 8

Baxter

I walked into the restaurant, searching for my dad. Luckily the place was quiet, with only a few travelers enjoying lunch or a drink at the bar on the far side of the room. He was easy to spot; he sat at a table with two gorgeous young women. The blonde had long hair and red lips; the brunette had dark curls and darker makeup.

I knew they must be over twenty-one because they each had a cocktail, but I would have sworn neither was over eighteen if I had met them on the street. They seemed very flirtatious for noon, mid-week, with cleavage spilling out of their blouses and towering heels on their feet. They all seemed to be enjoying their time together. Suddenly the thought of my dad, well into his sixties, trying to hook up with these women made me sick to my stomach. When had he turned into this?

"Ahh!" My father smiled and waved his arm at me. I was in no mood for his nonsense. I had asked him to meet me so we could talk, and he'd brought 'entertainment' for us. I was livid and not interested in his companions.

"Baxter!" he crowed as I approached, "Come join us! This is Veronica and Sherry!" The women giggled and batted their eyelashes, each crowding on either side of him like groupies, their breasts pressed out on display.

"Dad. A word?!" I demanded hotly, tilting my head away to indicate 'alone.'

"What? But we only just got here…" His eyes met mine with a slight roll of annoyance, and he got up with a huff. "Fine. Fine. Ladies," he turned to them. "I'll be right back! Keep my seat warm!" He smiled and blew them kisses. They whined and pouted, shooting me a dirty look, but didn't move otherwise.

When we stopped a few feet away, my father turned to me, his posture aggressive. "What's climbed up your ass?!" he hissed, never a man to hold back. He showed his annoyance, but the way he was clutching his glass with white knuckles told me he was angrier than even he was letting on.

I crossed my arms over my chest, not allowing myself to get baited into an argument with him. I put myself into my Agent mindset.

"How do you know Red?" I asked him point blank.

To my surprise, he smiled. "Trouble in paradise already, son?" he asked.

"Just answer the question," I answered flatly.

He sighed deeply, looking down and swirling his glass before bringing his gaze back to me. His anger was gone. "Bax, I didn't know how to tell you. You seemed so happy with her, I… I didn't want to say anything to ruin it…"

I kept my face completely neutral, but my heart was pounding. All I could think was that he was about to confirm my worst fears; she had slept with him.

"I knew her from my days on the force," he said. "I worked homicide, but I saw her in the halls many times getting booked… Probably prostitution or drugs, I can't be sure, but she was a regular. I had hoped I could scare her off for you and save you the heartache of finding out. I know she recognized me… Son, you deserve better." He clapped his hand on my shoulder conciliatorily. It should have been a very comforting, fatherly thing to do… but I saw deception in his eyes.

Beyond his police training, my training involved detecting when people were being dishonest or deceitful, and he had too many markers. I kept my face neutral, but my mind was spinning. *Was it all a lie? Was a part of it a lie? Or was it all the truth, but he was using it to deceive in some way? Fuck.* I might recognize a liar, but it didn't mean I knew what the actual truth was.

"She's not worth your time. Come on." My father changed gears, back into happy family mode. "We don't need to dwell on the past when we have these lovely ladies to keep us company, now do we?" He winked at me, clapping his hand on my shoulder as he moved back toward the table.

"You enjoy," I said flatly. "I have to get back to work." Before he could object, I was moving briskly out of the restaurant. The more information I got, the more questions I had. At least now I had a connection to Boston, even if I wasn't sure what it was. If she WAS from Boston AND had a police record, it might tie her to the Giovanni family. At least I could research that. It was a start.

I hadn't slept worth a damn that night; thoughts of my father and Red floated around my brain, taunting me like a puzzle missing some of its pieces. It was now Friday morning, the morning that Red's picture had foreseen. Already the news had broken overnight that Vinnie Giovanni had passed during the night, and the headlines read just as she had written it on her drawing. The old guard was dead, and Tony would take over as the new guard for the Giovanni family.

Fiske and I were staked out by the river, largely hidden from view, although there wasn't much to hide from at five in the morning. The fall weather had turned colder, leaving us bundled up with our binoculars.

"Tell me again why we're here?" Fiske snapped impatiently. "I should still be in bed with a hot woman right now."

"My lead said that a meeting was going to take place today; I want to be here when it does," I answered calmly, sipping my coffee.

"And your lead couldn't do you the courtesy of giving you the time of the meeting?" Fiske grumbled.

I chuckled under my breath. Fiske was used to his creature comforts; sitting out in the cold and waiting was not high on the list of his favorite things. I sighed and settled in for a long day.

And it was a long day.

Periodically, I would send Fiske out for more coffee, food, or stretch his legs, but I couldn't take my eyes off the newsstand. It wasn't until a little after one in the afternoon that we lucked out. Fiske was handing me a sandwich when he suddenly stopped, pointing toward the newsstand.

"HEY. Isn't that Tony?" he whispered urgently.

My head snapped to see a familiar face strolling toward the newsstand, one of his henchmen following discreetly a few feet behind. Relief flooded me. Red's drawing had come through! This might be the break I needed in my case.

"Why the fuck isn't he in Boston?" I whispered. "With Vinnie gone, he'll need to assume control of the family. What's he doing hanging around here?"

Tony went to the newsstand and bought a newspaper; he then made a big show of spreading the pages and reading it leisurely as he stood in the middle of the small square. A few minutes later, another man walked to the newsstand and bought a newspaper. He turned slowly and said a few words to Tony; a conversation ensued.

I pulled out my camera with a telephoto lens and began snapping pictures furiously. The second man had his back to me so that I couldn't get an ID on him. I signaled Fiske to circle wide around the area with another camera and see if he could get a shot from another angle, and Fiske slipped quietly away.

I watched Tony talking to the mystery man; he had a look of annoyance on his face but didn't react at all to anything being said. Finally, after a few minutes of listening, Tony started to do most of the talking, gesturing with his hands casually. The man with him seemed to stiffen, his posture suddenly uncomfortable. With a last flick of his wrist, Tony dismissed the man, turning and walking away. As the second mystery man turned, I snapped shot after shot with the camera until I finally had a full shot of the man's face.

Horror washed over my brain as recognition hit like a wrecking ball to my gut: it was my father.

I watched as my father stormed away angrily from his meeting, clearly unhappy with what had been said. I could only hold the camera in my hands, my palms sweaty. I couldn't believe it. My dad was a COP. Why the fuck would he be meeting with a mob boss? Fiske suddenly appeared at my side.

"Did you get the shot?" he asked excitedly as he shoved his equipment away.

"Yeah," I croaked. I felt numb. My brain struggled to accept what I had seen with my own eyes, my heart shattering. I had worshiped my father, even if he had been hard to deal with. I loved him. I hadn't felt this betrayed since my mother had left.

My mother!

Suddenly my whole life situation had a whole new perspective. HAD my mother left us?! If my dad worked for the mob all this time, there were other, less pleasant, explanations for her abrupt disappearance. My world suddenly felt upside down, and there was nowhere I could go to get out of my own head. I suddenly felt like an orphan, floating alone in the world. I was anchorless.

"Hey, you okay?" Fiske asked beside me, but I couldn't answer.

As I packed the gear away like a zombie, my thoughts floated back to Red. I clenched my eyes closed for just a minute. I would give anything to forget everything right now and feel her wrapped around me, her heartbeat against mine. I just wanted blissful ignorance and the surety of her warm body. I wished I could have that more than anything. She was like a soothing balm to the ache in my chest, a remedy I had to deny myself until I knew her role for sure.

Red

It was already after five in the evening, and my head was reeling. I had seen the news; my father was dead. The national news stations covered the story every fifteen minutes, and I finally had to turn the television off in my hospital room. I couldn't bear to see his picture again. Oddly, only one station had mentioned his daughter, me. The photo they showed was old and hardly looked like me. I could only pray that no one around here had seen it, that Baxter hadn't seen it. I knew I probably wasn't going to be that fortunate.

The doctor told me I was lucky that I hadn't slipped into a coma, taking the painkillers after getting a concussion. They had held me all day for observation, and the nurses had been friendly. Some of me just wanted to go home and hide away in my apartment alone, but another part didn't feel safe going back there. He knew where I lived; it was only a matter of time before he came to get me and drag me back to the life I had fled.

I had no choice; really, I had to run again. Yes, he may find me and stop me, but he would definitely have me if I didn't go. I had to take the chance.

My heart broke again for the thousandth time. When I left at eighteen, I knew I was choosing a life on the run; there would be no roots, no happy family, and no normality. I was lucky I got almost fifteen years of relative safety. This might not even be the last time I had to pull up any shallow roots I had put down, pack up, and move on. This was the pattern for the rest of my life; to live alone, starting over every few years. Close connections were dangerous, and not just to me. Complacency was deadly.

The doctor hadn't returned with my release paperwork yet, but I tentatively got out of bed and awkwardly made my way to the small bathroom. I was still very dizzy, and my head was still pounding, even with the meds they had given me. I got dressed quickly and returned to my sterile room, ready to grab my purse and try to make an escape.

I hadn't taken two shaky steps into the room before I heard the familiar deep voice at the door.

"You're up?" Bax stood with his hands folded in front of him, eyeing me suspiciously.

FUCK!

"I am," I said quietly, in defeat.

If Bill knew he was here... Oh shit! I had to get rid of him!

"What are you doing here?" I asked, trying to appear non-chalant. Panic held my body rigid.

"Miss Brooks, you are a person of interest in a case I am working on regarding the Giovanni's out of Boston; I came to get your statement," he answered professionally. There was worry in his eyes no matter how his words were delivered, and I had to wonder if it was worry *for* me or *of* me.

"I don't know how much help I can be, Agent Murphy." I decided to answer his formality with my own. "I know nothing about the Giovanni's."

"That remains to be seen," he said, surprisingly gently. "I've just spoken to your doctor, and he's cleared you to leave. Why don't I take you home, and we can discuss this privately?" His voice was professional, but my core clenched at the thought, and a wave of dizziness nearly took me off my feet.

In a heartbeat, he was beside me, the warmth of his body supporting me. I wanted to melt into him, but I forced myself to stand up straight. I couldn't let him take me home, and I couldn't be seen with him, now, for very different reasons.

"We can talk here," I said, waving my hand at the small room.

"No, actually, they need the room. I'll take you home," he countered.

"I'll just get a cab."

He blew out a frustrated breath and said, "You can either let me take you home voluntarily, or I can charge you with withholding information and obstruction and have you cuffed and taken to a holding cell: your choice." I knew he was frustrated with me, but even still, he wasn't the cold, heartless man I had faced a few days ago at my table. This was business, but not cruel or personal.

"Sounds like I don't have a choice. Let's go," I said, pulling away from him and taking cautious steps toward the door. It didn't help that my shaky legs could barely hold me up, and he had to practically carry me from the room. So much for my dignity. So much for my one shot at freedom. When I saw a guard posted at the door in the hallway, I realized how fruitless my escape plan had been. I was well and truly fucked.

When we returned to my apartment, I was pleasantly surprised that a new security door had already been installed. I sent up a prayer. I had to hope that Bill didn't know that Bax had brought me here. Maybe he didn't think I was home at all! And if he did, perhaps the new door would keep him out and me safe. *Please!*

I knew it was childish. I knew my Dad's men had a list of ways to remove a door when they needed to get into a room, so Bill would too. There would be no safe place for me.

I slumped on the sofa and scrubbed my tired eyes with the heels of my palms. When I looked up, Bax sat across from me, studying me curiously. I didn't know what to say, so I said nothing. Then I noticed that my sketchpad was open on the table, but the last page had been torn out. Fear rose in my throat.

Did he see it? Did he take it?!

I tried not to look back at it, as if Bax would somehow see what I had seen in my vision. I didn't even know how to begin explaining that drawing. Not without divulging too much and further endangering myself.

Fuck I was so screwed.

I groaned, my head falling back and then jerking sharply as I winced in pain.

"You want to tell me how you got that bump on your head?" Bax asked.

"Not really," I whimpered through the pounding in my skull, my fingers digging into my temples.

"Still hurts a lot?" he asked quietly, concern lacing his voice.

"It does," I confirmed, eyes still clamped shut as if I could tune him out if I just didn't see him.

I heard him sigh and shift on the chair.

"Look, Red... I don't know what the fuck is going on right now. I don't know how you are tangled up in all of this. I really want to believe that it's all just some huge misunderstanding. I want to believe that you were somehow in the wrong place at the wrong time, but I went to that place today, the place you drew. The two men meeting in the square were Tony Giovanni, now the head of the Giovanni crime family..." He paused, and I opened my eyes to look at him. "And my father, the former Chief of Police," he finished, his voice cracking.

"So I need your help here, Red. I'm begging you. Please just tell me what you know. Help me make sense of all of this." He leaned down, resting his elbows on his knees, his eyes full of sorrow, begging me to give him the answers he desperately wanted.

Except I didn't think he really wanted them. I had tried to tell him, and he wasn't ready to see his father as a monster.

I stared at him. I didn't know what I could, or would say. Anything I said could only endanger me further, so I sat tight-lipped.

"I see," he said, with a harsh edge to his voice, as he dropped his head. His head snapped back up, his look direct. "Well let *me* start then. Here's what my dear father told me about you. He told me that he had seen you many times at the station, being booked on prostitution and drug charges and that you were a repeat offender," he spat.

"And, of course, you believed him," I stated, already exhausted.

"What am I supposed to believe, Red?" He threw his hands up. "I know almost nothing about you except that you have mad skills when it comes to sucking cock! Give me something else to work with!" He threw himself back in the chair, his brows drawn into an angry ridge over his eyes and his mouth a thin line.

"So because I gave you good head, I must have been a prostitute, is that it?" I asked him, not even having the energy to be angry.

"Fuck, Red. Help me out here." He swore.

"Uh, I did help you out. And look where it got me," I answered flatly. "I shared my body with you; that's being held against me now. I tried to tell you I didn't want to be around your dad, that he was creepy, and now you want me to what?... Tell you what a great guy he is?... throw myself under the bus and agree to some vile lie he's spinning so you can hold onto your hero worship of him? Even after you saw him meet with a mob boss?

"Yes, I knew him; I've seen him before, a LONG time ago. But here's something for you to consider, Agent Baxter Murphy; the last time he saw me, I was seventeen and two months pregnant, and he was trying to force himself on me at a party." The anger had finally taken hold of me. "So don't ask me for information. I already tried to give it to you, and you were so NOT interested in hearing it that you walked out of my life for good. You two deserve each other. I'm going to bed now. I'm sure you can see yourself out?" I spit.

I clawed my way out of the sofa, staggering as I tried to walk around the coffee table, cursing my damned legs under my breath. I only made it to the outer edge of the coffee table before he was crashing into me, his arms around me, his tongue in my mouth.

I bit his tongue, but he didn't stop. He pulled me closer, tighter, with a desperate passion bordering on rage and hunger. I tried to push him away, but as usual, my damned traitorous body just melted into him, letting all of the pain and frustration rise to the surface to meet his.

He walked me backward into the bedroom, pulling my shirt off as he went, his followed soon after. He lowered me onto the bed with a gentleness that belied his urgent hands, and then we were a tangle of limbs, clawing at clothing and each other. His cock was notched at my mound, and with one hard push, he was inside me, and then we were thrusting.

I couldn't tell if it was rage fucking, or reunion fucking, but we were beating our bodies against one another, our emotions all over the place. All I could do was be; live in that ferocious divine sensation that was his cock pounding into my pussy, stretching me wide, taking me, claiming me. I roared in anger; I wanted to hate him. I wanted to despise him for the way he had made me feel. But I also wanted to love him for all the other ways he had made me feel. My heart was wholly overwhelmed with warring passions. The only thing that was right was him fucking me senseless.

I felt myself growing tighter, winding closer. I could feel his hardness pushing back against me as I squeezed him deeper inside me. And then suddenly, there was only bliss as we leaped over the abyss, both of us locked together for a moment while our bodies spasmed around each other, releasing all of the anguish and pain and feeling nothing but euphoria.

I heaved in lungfuls of air as the tears streamed down my cheeks. Slowly reality bled into my perfect bubble of joy. Bax collapsed on top of me.

"You asshole!" I cried, trying to turn my face away so he wouldn't see my tears.

"Hey! Hey! Don't cry!" He pulled my face back, but I wouldn't open my eyes.

I couldn't look at him. I felt so entirely used; it was as if his father had gotten to fuck me after all. My own weak body had allowed him to take what I had so desperately intended not to share.

"Red, I'm sorry about those things I said to you the other day. I'm sorry that I was so insecure and selfish that I couldn't understand what it might be like for you. I wouldn't ever want you to feel like a target at work, and I should never have pushed you to go out for dinner like I did.

"As for my father, clearly, there's a lot I didn't know about him, and I'm coming to terms with it. But I've already lost the first woman in my life that I loved, and I'm not ready to lose the second woman I've ever cared about. Please stay with me on this. I don't want to lose you, especially not because of a fucker like my father."

"You lost someone?" Jealously gripped my heart with cold hands.

"My mom." He offered me a small apologetic smile.

I paused and then started saying what I needed to say to him. "Bax, I wasn't a prostitute, and I didn't do drugs," I stated.

"I know—"

"But I'm not a good person," I continued. "I have a past, and it haunts me. You can't want me, Bax. I'm bad, and it will ruin your life." The tears flowed down my face as my heart filled with grief. I had to give him up. He was too good for me.

"I'm already ruined," he said, kissing my neck. "Whatever happens, Red, I'm on your team, and you can trust me. We'll deal with it together."

I knew I shouldn't, but I so *desperately* wanted to believe him. I wanted to think he would learn the truth and be okay with it. I wanted to believe that his feelings for me could overcome all of the demons from my past. I was exhausted. So instead of arguing, I kissed him back.

Chapter 9

Baxter

I toweled Red off with care. We had explored each other's bodies until her headache became a pounding cock-block. My cheeks reddened with shame; I shouldn't even be doing this with her in her condition. I shouldn't be frustrated with her, considering she had clearly been attacked. What a selfish fuck I was.

And I still needed information about the attack. As Red dressed, I sat on the edge of the bed, choosing my words carefully.

"Red... I understand that you have no reason to trust me." I started slowly, gauging her reaction. "But I need to ask if there isn't anything you *can* share with me without compromising yourself. Understand that I will do everything in my power to protect you, even from my father."

I wasn't used to begging witnesses for information, but she was more than a witness. She was important to me. I wanted to come out of this case with our relationship, whatever the fuck it was, still intact. I had to try.

Red chewed her bottom lip uneasily, eyeing me warily, before coming to sit next to me on the messy bed. She looked down at her clasped hands, considering before she slowly started to talk.

"Look..." She hesitated. "I can't tell you everything. I just can't. But I can try to help you out if you don't push for more..." She looked up with fearful eyes.

I nodded for her to go on, not wanting to interrupt her flow. She sighed deeply, closed her eyes for a minute, and looked back at her hands.

"I... I had connections in the Giovanni family, but I was never a part of their business. As a girl, I was kept outside of all of that. But that doesn't mean I wasn't around them. That's how I knew your father. He frequented their parties; he had business with them—"

"You're telling me my dad was always a dirty cop?" I asked flatly, not wanting to believe it but knowing it was confirmed after I witnessed his meeting with Tony.

I felt Red stiffen beside me defensively.

"I'm just trying to understand," I quickly added softly. "I'm not saying I don't believe you. After yesterday, I had pretty much come to that myself," I added unwillingly.

She blew out a relieved breath and then went on. "He recognized me at the restaurant. It took me a little longer to recognize him. It was fifteen years ago, after all." She took another deep breath.

"After you stormed out, he came over, banging on my door. He threatened to tell you about my connection to the family if I didn't let him in." She stopped and looked at me, waiting for my response. There was still fear in her eyes, but also the fighting fire I loved about her.

"And I told you the version of the story he spun to me," I confirmed. "Of course, he left out anything tying him to the crime syndicate."

"Yeah, he seemed most concerned that you did not find that out," she said. "He insisted I call you and break it off with you so you'd never find out."

"But we had already broken up, and he didn't know that," Bax thought out loud. "So you called me to keep him from telling me about your connections?"

"That, and he threatened me if I came near you or spoke to you. He...." She looked down again, swallowing loudly. "He had wanted to date me... well, '*date*' is the wrong word... he wanted me when I was seventeen, and I did not return his interest. He seemed pretty pissed that I was seeing his son. I think it hurt his pride."

I sat, completely still, shocked by what she had just told me. My father... my FATHER... had pursued a girl younger than I am for sex while his teenage son was at home, his wife gone. So much for "years of searching" for my mother. I know exactly what he was searching for.

I lifted her chin so that I could look into her eyes. I could see tears wanting to burst free and shame warring with anger washed over her features.

"So... he's here to pursue you?" I asked, trying to put it all together.

"I don't think so... not directly," she sputtered. "He seemed pretty pissed off that the family dismissed him. My dad was fond of him, but some of the other guys never trusted him. He came to Richmond because their drug trade runs through here; he wanted to make himself invaluable to them. He wanted a role to keep that income, so he started setting up a base here to take over the area so that Tony would have to 'play ball' with him, as he put it. I was just a bonus, I think. He said I was his 'invitation to a meeting' with Tony." She stopped abruptly as if she was about to spill something she didn't want to reveal.

I pieced together what she had said and what she had not said. If my father thought Tony would want her, then she did indeed have ties to the family, perhaps more than "not involved." That was the secret she was hiding from me. But how could she be involved? She had said she wasn't a prostitute. If she had been pushing or using with or for them, she could be clean now; I doubt they would still want to punish her fifteen years later. The only other thing they had was muscle; clearly, she wasn't an enforcer. Unless she had stolen from them, turned on them, or murdered one of them, they wouldn't give a damn about her fifteen years after the fact. It still made no sense, but at least she was opening up.

I cleared my throat. "So, as of right now, my father has you on notice not to be near me or contact me, and he threatened to hurt you if you do?" I asked for clarification.

"Yes... and no..." She bit out. "He blackmailed me with things I'd rather not have known about me." She couldn't meet my eye.

This confirmed my suspicions. Something had upset the family, and he was using her role against her.

"Did he say how? Or when?" I probed.

"No... only that I needed to stay clear of you. Oh... and be ready when he comes to collect me. He told me not to try to run." Her shoulders slumped in defeat. Her face spoke of exhaustion, and her hands fell open on her lap as if she had given up.

How long had she been running from her past? She knew my father from when she was seventeen... had she been in hiding since then?!

"Did my father hit you on the head? Is that how you got the concussion?" I bit out through clenched teeth, anger seething at the thought of my own father tormenting Red.

"What?... Oh... no... actually..." Her cheeks blushed crimson. "He touched my cheek, and it brought on a vision. I blacked out right after he left; I must have hit my head on the floor."

"The vision that you drew last?" I asked. She looked at me and nodded silently.

"What did it mean, Red? When will it happen?" I asked quickly, the words flying out of my mouth.

She only shook her head sadly. "You know I don't know, Bax. That's not how it works, and what I know is what you saw on the paper."

And that had been disturbing enough. I had to do something so that it never came to pass. I needed more information, and I needed to get the ball rolling.

It was time to bring 'Dear Old Dad' into the office. I had the photos of him meeting with Tony, and I had Red's statement; it wasn't enough to keep him, but maybe it was enough to scare him into leaving her alone. The problem was, it might backfire, causing him to take out his frustration on her, and I couldn't have that.

No, I needed to get him tailed and see what he was up to until I could get more evidence to put him away. In the meantime...

"Red, just so you know, I have an agent on you at all times. He's there for your protection. I want you to feel safe. I'm not letting that prick get anywhere near you. It would be best if you stayed home as much as possible."

She nodded mutely, and it killed me to see her so defeated. I pulled her into me gently, tipping her head back carefully and kissing her deeply. I could feel my heart swelling with warmth, with an emotion I couldn't name. I only knew that it was because of her. I needed her.

For the first time in my life, I was putting a woman before my career and family. I just hoped this didn't come back to haunt me as she said it would because I would give up everything to keep her.

Red

Bax left to go back to work in that vague way that law enforcement does. I eyed the new safety door to my apartment and breathed a sigh of relief. I knew that just on the other side was the agent we had passed coming in. I wasn't alone, and I wasn't vulnerable. Still, there were things I could do to protect myself.

I made my way back into my bedroom and pulled my lock-box down. Opening it, I pulled the phone out and turned it on to find I had five missed calls from Victor.

Shit! I had forgotten that my father's passing might mean trouble for me. Fuck!

I dialed his number quickly, and he answered on the first ring.

"Thank FUCK!" he all but shouted. "Where have you been?! I've been worried sick!"

"I was in the hospital," I squeaked. "I had a concussion."

Victor became quiet suddenly. "Shit, are you okay?! What happened?!" he asked his voice heavy with worry.

"I'll be fine. Vic, what's going on up there? Do I need to worry?" I bit my bottom lip. My morning with Bax had convinced me I might be able to stay; I might be protected. Had that been premature? My gut twisted with worry. There was a very real likelihood I would still need to run.

"I honestly don't know..." He blew out a breath. "What I know is that Tony got back to Boston, and he has officially taken over as the new boss. There are still some grumblings from your cousins, but no one has the balls to challenge him outright.

"I found out that he has been in Richmond, Virginia. Seems someone has been fucking with his supply route, some new player. If this new player doesn't back off, there's going to be a turf war, and you know what that means."

I could feel the uneasiness in his voice. Victor was never an enforcer and was never prone to violence like some others. He was always strictly a numbers runner or deal broker.

"That new player isn't so new." I breathed out. "Bill Murphy is down here making threats to get back into the action. He's even tried to use me as an in for Tony," I said, knowing I was giving him my location, something I had never done in all the time I had been gone.

"FUCK, Red!" he spit, seething. "Is he the reason you were in the hospital?!" he demanded.

I winced. "Indirectly, yes," I said, knowing I couldn't hide it from him.

"Red, you need to move, NOW!" he yelled.

"I...I can't," I said cautiously. I knew my next words were going to make him explode. "I have federal protection. I can't leave, or they'll BOTH be after me. You know the feds have a lot more resources." I got it out quickly and held the phone back, waiting for the explosion.

I didn't have long to wait.

"WHAT?!" he roared. Even though I was holding the phone at arm's length, his voice bellowed through the room. "RED! Don't tell me you've turned?!"

I knew what he meant: "turned informant."

"NO!" I said vehemently, pulling the phone back to my ear. "We both know why I can't do that. But Bill has already spun his side of the story and threatened to tell what happened. I only told them about Bill's involvement to try to get myself out of this mess," I added hopefully.

"How did they put you two together? How is any of this even possible?" he seethed.

"Well... I'm kind of... dating a fed," I stated, and again Vic bellowed on the other end of the line, almost deafening me when I didn't pull the phone away fast enough. "Oh, it gets better: he's Bill's son," I finished.

I expected Vic to snap, for him to roar. I didn't expect the silence.

"Say something, Vic," I pleaded desperately.

"I don't know what to say, Red," he answered quietly, as if in shock. "How the fuck did you even meet him? How do you know he's not crooked like his father?" His voice cracked. I could hear the fear and utter disbelief. "All this effort to get you to safety, and you're fucking a fed? I can't believe you."

"I have no idea how it all worked out the way it did," I answered truthfully. "I found out after the fact that Bax is here investigating the family, and by that time, his dad was onto me. Now I'm stuck," I said quietly. "But Bax is a straight shooter. At first, he didn't want to believe the truth about his dad, but now he's protecting me until he can get to the bottom of it all. His dad involved me; now, I can't get myself out. And frankly, Vic, I'm tired of running. I'm just... tired." I blew out a long breath.

"But you and I both know that protection will end once he finds out..." Victor trailed off, leaving the rest unsaid.

"Yeah," I said quietly.

We sat in awkward silence for several heartbeats before Victor finally grunted and seemed to push through everything I had just said.

"Look, I'll do what I can on this end, but Red, you know Tony will be gunning for you if he even thinks you're working with them, right? And if your guy, Bax, is it? If your guy drops you, there won't be anything anyone can do to protect you. You have to look out for yourself, first and foremost." His voice cracked again.

I knew this was killing him. At one point in time, we were each other's worlds, back when we were kids. I knew he never really got over me, but I couldn't deal with the fact that I was hurting him now too. Add it to my list of reasons I am a horrible person.

"Let me work on it up here, Red. I'll call you once I have something."

"Thank you, Vic."

The line went dead in my hand. I stared at the phone; the need to cry was overwhelming, but the tears just wouldn't come. How many times can you grieve the same loss? It never changes the outcome.

I put the phone away, safe and sound. I compartmentalized that part of my life into that lockbox with it, as if it was another person who had lived out my fucked up history... as if Natalie Brooks was a whole other person. But my worlds had collided, and there was no separating them any longer. Time was running out quickly, and there was going to be an explosion when my two worlds finally merged and the truth was revealed.

My personal cell phone rang on my coffee table, and I climbed off my stool to answer it, thinking Bax might be checking in on me. A Boston number I didn't know lit the screen. My heart stopped, and I let it go to voicemail. I couldn't make myself answer it. My world was unraveling before my eyes.

Soon, a voicemail notification popped up, and I listened to the message. Bill's voice spoke through my earpiece, and I immediately wanted to vomit.

"Not answering your phone, Renny? Well, that's a shame. It seems that you can't keep your word, can you? Or are you just such a whore that you can't keep your legs together where my son is concerned? Tell me, do you think he'll still want you sucking his dick when he finds out what you did? I know my son; he'll be the one to cuff you and drag you away without a second glance. I'm giving you one last chance, bitch, or this package gets delivered to Loverboy. So you be a good girl, for a change, and do what you're fucking told. I'm texting you an address; meet me there in an hour. Oh, and lose the fed watching you. If you're followed, I can't be held responsible for what will happen to you... or my son."

The message ended abruptly. Panic seized me. I spun in circles frantically, not knowing what I should do. I couldn't breathe. My chest squeezed with fear. *He wouldn't really hurt his own son, would he?!* Thoughts of Bax's mother floated in the back of my mind. He could.

Should I call Bax?

Instantly I shot it down. While he was protecting me now, it was just a matter of time. One way or another, he'd find out what I did. But right now, I could protect him from his father. I was just going to have to face the consequences of my life decisions on my own.

A text came through with an address.

This was it. This was where it was going to end; I could feel it. I sat down on my couch quickly and wrote Bax a letter. I knew I wouldn't get to say goodbye, and he wouldn't want it once he found out anyway, but I wanted to tell him as much of my truth as I could.

I wrote to him about how I felt, how happy he had made me. I told him I wished we had more time to get to know each other better and date like ordinary people. I wrote about the life I dreamed we could have had together and how sorry I was that it would never happen. I also told him to listen to the voice recording I had kept from Bill's visit. I had pulled it out of my cell phone and transferred it onto a small drive I left on the coffee table.

He would have my evidence about his father's role in all of this. It killed me to know I was going to break his heart twice, once with the truth and evidence about his father and the other in knowing he would hear what Bill had threatened to reveal to him. He would never love either of us again.

This was goodbye. I fully expected my visit with Bill to be a one-way trip; honestly, I knew I deserved that. I had postponed the inevitable for long enough.

I went back into my bedroom, into my secret hiding spot, and pulled out my sig. I put it into the waistband of my jeans, at my back, and pulled my loose shirt over it. I took out a small revolver and stuffed it into my boot as well. I wasn't going down without a fight. If Bill Murphy planned on taking my life away, I was damned well going to take his as well.

It wouldn't be the first time I had killed someone.

Baxter

I sat in my car, going over some notes. I had sent Fiske to follow up on a tip we had gotten from a local informant who had an in with the drug pushers in the neighborhood; they had been unhappy with a new guy in town taking over and had been very forthcoming with information.

My phone rang; the office showed on the caller ID.

"Murphy," I answered flatly.

"Murph, I have that info you requested," Myers said. "The number belongs to Victor Gambelli."

My head swam. Victor was a low-level operative for the Giovanni family; I'd come across him several times in my work on the family. He kept his nose clean working for the family, but rarely crossed the law. Was he Red's connection to the family?

"As for Natalie Brooks... you're going to love this," Myers said excitedly. "Natalie Brooks is actually Renatta Giovanni! Looks like she changed her name about fifteen years ago, near Seattle, Washington. Congratulations, you've found the missing mob heiress! Good work!"

Renatta?! HEIRESS?! She wasn't just connected to the mob; Vinnie had been her fucking FATHER!

I stared at my phone in horror. Suddenly, all of the little pieces shuffled into place in my mind. No wonder she hadn't wanted to tell me who she was... Still, she wasn't involved with the family business... at least, I had no reason to believe she was...

So why had she run?

"What do you need me to do next?" Myers asked.

I had forgotten I still had him on the line. "Nothing," I said quickly. "Tell no one about this, Myers. I mean NO ONE. I don't want her slipping away before we get our hands on her." It wasn't the real reason, but I couldn't tell him that.

"You got it," he answered, and the line went dead.

Renatta Giovanni, Vinnie's missing mob princess... and I had been fucking her like a dumb shit. I swiped my hand down my face. What the fuck was I supposed to do now. I had all but confessed I loved her; just that morning, I had been willing to sacrifice everything for her... and she had known. The whole time she had known. She was the daughter of the mob boss I had made it my career to investigate. She had tried to warn me without telling me, but I couldn't have possibly imagined *THAT* was her secret.

Fuck.My.Life.

I started my car and headed back to her apartment.

Fifteen minutes later, I reached her door and immediately noticed that her agent wasn't outside. I swore under my breath as I pulled out a key to her door that I had gotten from the management, a key she didn't know about but that I was grateful for at that moment. I pushed into her apartment quickly.

"RED!" I yelled, my gut sinking. "RED!"

I raced through the small space, only to confirm what I already knew. She was gone. Before I could even pull my phone out, it was ringing. Her agent was calling: the one who was supposed to protect her.

"Tell me she's okay!" I snapped, answering my phone.

There was a brief hesitation on the other end. "Uh... actually, I was calling to tell you that I can't find her. She somehow managed to lose me, and I can't find her now. I've already called in backup and sealed the area... but she's gone." He sounded scared shitless, and right then, he needed to be.

"I don't care how many men it takes; you need to find her ASAP!" I roared.

The line went dead, and I dropped my head, only then noticing the note on the coffee table. I jumped to it, scanning it quickly.

"Bax,

I'm sorry things had to end this way, and I do believe this is the end. I just wanted you to know a few things. First, I care about you deeply. I don't know if you will ever believe that, but I genuinely do. You were the only person I have ever known who would make me reconsider the direction of my life.

Unfortunately, decisions I made when I was younger have dictated my outcome, but I wish...

I wish we could have met under normal circumstances. I wish we could take our time and get to know each other better. I wish I could give you a happily ever after. I wish I could have looked forward to being with you for the rest of my life.

But my time is up.

Please know that I didn't abandon you; in my own twisted way, I am doing this to protect you as much as myself. I have left a voice recording of my interaction with your father on the jump drive. It will give you the evidence you need to understand his role in things, and unfortunately for me, for you to understand my role as well.

I don't expect you to forgive me. I can't even forgive myself.

Just know, for what it's worth, that I do have feelings for you, and I would do anything to spare you from the consequences of my life.

Always yours,

Red"

I pulled out my laptop and plugged in the drive. Clicking on the MP3, I let it play. As I listened to the muffled sound of the recording of my father's voice, my hair stood on end. It was the voice of the man who raised me, my father, threatening Red. I heard the name Rocky, and my attention was caught. Rocky had been killed fifteen years ago. If it was at all possible, my heart sank further.

I listened as my father outlined his investigation of the case, inferring that she was the murderer, that he would tell me... *It couldn't be true! Red wasn't a murderer!*

The final pieces of the puzzle snapped into place in my mind with a sickening click.

The reason she'd run from the family, the reason she was hiding, the reason she didn't want anything to do with my father, the reason she said her past would ruin my life...

I felt the grief trying to rise in my chest, wanting to heave, but I pushed it down. First, I had to ensure she was safe; then, I could deal with the fallout. I pulled out my phone to call Fiske and have him bring a team over to gather evidence from her apartment, but I heard a muffled noise in her bedroom before I could dial.

I raced into the room and headed straight for the closet. In the box, the phone was ringing. With impatient, shaking hands, I got the key and fumbled with the lock until I had the phone in my hands. I answered immediately.

"Red! Thank fuck! Are you still okay?" the man's voice asked urgently.

I had to steel myself against the jealousy that made me want to tear this guy's head off for clearly caring about Red.

"This is agent Baxter Murphy of the FBI; I assume you are Victor?" I said, trying to reign in my anger.

"How the fuck did you get this phone? Where is Red?!" Victor demanded indignantly.

"Right now, Red is missing, presumably at the hands of Bill Murphy," I spit out.

"You mean your FATHER," he spit back with equal venom.

"Unfortunately, yes," I conceded. "And as much as I'd love to have a conversation about my family with you, Victor, my main concern is getting Red back alive. So if you know any-thing, I would suggest you start talking."

"Why should I tell you shit?" he snapped back. "If you guys did your fucking job, she wouldn't be in this mess right now! She trusted you to keep her safe," he yelled.

"Again, I'd be happy to argue with you all day about this… once she is safely found," I gritted out.

I heard him blow out a breath at the end of the line before he finally said something.

"I know that Bill was taking over the drug scene down there. I know he hit a couple of Vinn- Tony's warehouses and is now using them as his home base. I can find and text you the addresses. That's all I have. We haven't heard from Bill in over a year, so all of this is just coming to light. I'll make inquiries," he finished with an edge to his voice.

"Let me give you my cell number—"

"Not a fucking chance, Fed. Look, Red may be thinking with her vag, but I'm not having anyone find a fed's number on my cell phone. Keep this one on you. I'll call when I have something."

The call dropped immediately. Putting it on silent, I pocketed the cell phone and put the open box on the bed. My finger-prints were going to be all over it, so I couldn't very well put it back; I'd rather it looked like I was turning everything over.

The cell phone in my pocket weighed heavily on my soul. It was the first time I had ever withheld evidence. I wondered if this was how my father had started his journey to being a dirty cop.

Chapter 10

Red

I groaned. My head throbbed again. I reached my hands up to cradle my skull while stars danced on the outside of my vision. A wave of nausea hit me, and I had to fight not to throw up. After several moments of deep breaths, my roiling stomach was under control, although it still didn't feel much better.

I took in the space around me. I was in what looked like an industrial storage unit; the floor was concrete, and three walls and a roof were comprised of metal lattice, with one door to provide access. I could see the thick padlock on the outside of the door. The final wall was cinder block construction, with gray paint peeling off in large flakes. The lattice was rusted, adding to the appearance of disuse and neglect. The only other opening to the cage was a small window fitted into the cinder block wall. The glass had long since been knocked out, but there was a rusted metal grate over the opening.

Outside of my metal cage appeared to be a warehouse of some sort, I could see boxes and refuse, but it was fairly dark and gloomy, regardless of the small windows of daylight shining high on the perimeter walls.

I remembered losing the agent they had tailing me at the market; it had been more challenging than I thought it would be. Once he was gone, I got a cab to the address Bill had texted me. I had been foolish to believe he would meet me face to face. Instead, as I entered the dilapidated building, I was hit on the head from behind. He was such a fucking coward. Face-on, I could have taken him down, but there's no defense against the strike you never saw coming. And I had blindly walked into it.

I tried to stand, but another wave of nausea bowled into me like a freight train, causing me to sit still and breathe deeply. I slowly looked around my makeshift cage, taking note of the cardboard boxes covered in dust. Aside from the telltale footprints and the trail left when someone dragged me here, this place had obviously been untouched for a while.

So there was no chance someone would stumble onto me by accident.

Instinctively, my hand flew to my lower back, and I groaned as I felt the empty spot where I had put my sig earlier. I shuffled my foot in my boot, relieved when the small telltale bulge let me know I still had my revolver. Clearly, they hadn't searched me well. It also meant that it was probably just one person, as two people wouldn't have had to drag me, and a second person would have grabbed my ankles, finding the gun.

A noise echoed throughout the large warehouse, a door screeching open. I sat still and waited.

Bill made his way to my prison, his usual smug smile plastered on his arrogant face. I had to fight the urge to shoot him where he stood and only managed it because I knew if I killed him right there, no one would ever find me.

"How are you adapting to your new accommodations, Princess?" he chuckled.

"You might need to have a word with your cleaning crew," I said flatly, running a finger through the dust on the floor.

"Well, I'm sorry it's not up to your daddy's standards, Princess, but you should consider yourself lucky to be alive right now." He sneered.

When I said nothing, he continued. "Imagine my surprise when one of my guys returned from a family vacation in Richmond, Virginia, over a year and a half ago, and I saw a very familiar face in the background of one of his photos." He beamed maliciously at me.

"He stayed at the Marriott," he clarified.

I held my tongue. I was in no shape to spar with him, verbally or otherwise.

"Well, I had to come down and see for myself, now, didn't I? Vinnie's health was already taking a nosedive, and fucking Tony was commander in charge. Tony and I don't see eye to eye.

"It should have been Rocky who took your father's place; Rocky and I had a good working relationship, and I had guarantees for a long career with the family with Rocky in charge. But you had to fuck that up, didn't you?" His heated words seared my already throbbing brain.

"So the way I see it, you fucked up a really good situation for me. It was only a matter of time before Tony had other people in place, and I didn't have the free reign to do what I wanted anymore. You cost me a shit ton of money, girl; you and that wandering pussy of yours.

"Did you know that Vinnie knew you killed Rocky? I made it a point to tell him. He also knew about the baby," he spit.

I couldn't help the shudder that shook my body.

"Didn't think he knew about that either, did you? So sorry for your loss, by the way... I have people watching the clinics, too; we got word when you lost that baby. Rocky was probably too stupid to know it wasn't his, wasn't he?" He smirked condescendingly at me, and I could no longer keep eye contact with him.

None of this was his business.

"And do you know what happened when I told Vinnie that you had killed Rocky and that you had whored yourself out to someone else? I'll tell you what happened: absolutely nothing!" he spat, spittle flying from his lips.

"That bastard was so wrapped up with you that he wouldn't even punish you for taking out his second in command!" he fumed. "I tried to pin it on Tony to prevent him from taking Rocky's place, but I couldn't get it to stick. Tony and I never got along after that.

"I met Tony the day your father died, you know. I asked him for a meeting to put the past behind us and even offered to turn you over, and he flat-out refused me. He didn't give a shit if I killed you."

He continued his monologue like the cliche villain in a movie.

"So here we are." He spread his hands. "It's time for you to atone for your sins, Renatta. You've cost me so much; it's time I finally get my pound of flesh from you."

"If you're going to kill me, shut up and do it already. Listening to you yammer on is worse than torture," I said in a bored tone. I knew I wasn't getting out of this alive; the most I could hope for was to make him mad enough to shoot and kill me quickly.

He chuckled, his smirk spreading.

"Always were a feisty one, weren't you? I often wondered how many of his boys got that pussy before you ran off; did you fight them off like you fought me off, *Renny?* I would have loved to have fucked you while you struggled to escape.

"No... I won't be killing you, Renny, that would be too easy, and it would get me nothing. Instead, I sent your picture to Tony and told him about your situation with Rocky. It's a long shot, but maybe seeing that I'm serious about sending you to him, piece by piece, will make him reconsider doing business with me."

"You really aren't the brightest bulb on the tree," I muttered loud enough to be heard.

"And yet I am the one on the outside of the cage. Interesting, isn't it?" He chuckled smugly.

"Renny, I don't give a fuck what happens to you. I'm just as happy to fuck you and send him pieces of you until he changes his mind, or there's nothing left to send him, but either way, I will get my due from you. I especially look forward to fucking your ass hard and making you scream. Personally, I hope you fight me; I hope you struggle. There is no greater turn-on than conquering a prey." He bit his lower lip between his teeth as he eyed me up and down hungrily.

I tried to keep my look neutral, but I couldn't be sure I was pulling it off. A mixture of rage and pure unadulterated terror was rising in my chest like a tsunami.

"Think on that for a while, Princess, while I get in touch with Tony. I hope for your sake he takes me seriously."

He blew me a kiss before turning on his heel and strolling back to the depths of the warehouse; a few moments later, I heard the screeching of a large metal door and then the clatter as it shut.

I rushed into action. My hands swept over my pockets, but of course, my cell phone was gone too. I pulled boxes closer to me to inspect what was in them, hoping for anything I could use to escape or make an improvised weapon. Unfortunately, the boxes were primarily full of rags or paperwork; only one contained a rusted screwdriver and a wrench.

I counted to one hundred to be sure Bill was truly gone before pulling myself onto shaky legs and going to the window. The sun outside was starting to descend, the better part of the day behind us; soon, it would get cold, and I had nothing with me for warmth or comfort. I examined the grate on the window; it was industrial and strong but also ancient and rusting. It was also meant to be removed from the inside, which worked in my favor.

It seemed like hours passed as I tried to get the bolts out of the grating with the wrench, sometimes using the screwdriver like a chisel, but in the end, they were completely rusted through and weren't budging.

My arms ached with the effort, and my head was still throbbing. I was coated in sweat and dust, and as the temperature dropped slowly, I started to shiver. But there was nothing else I could do, so I turned back to the grate, hitting the screwdriver base one more time, only to have it skip off the metal and hit the concrete block, taking a chunk out of it.

My eyes widened, and I yelped for joy. I could chip away at the blocks themselves if the grate didn't give. It was a shitty plan, but it was the only one I had, so I put my back into it. My arms reverberated with each hit, jolting pain up my shoulder and into my head.

As I worked, I thought of Bax. A sob worked its way through my rib cage, but I stuffed it down, putting my passion into my hands to get me out. He likely knew I was missing and who had me. He had probably read my letter and heard the recording. So now he finally knew the truth about me, even if there was no evidence. I had to face the fact that I was never going to see him again unless my drawing came to pass.

And after that? He's a fed, and he's dedicated his life to fighting crime. And I was a criminal.

If I had the opportunity to run, I had to take it because Bax wasn't on my side any longer. There was no "us." I was alone again, and Vic was right; I had to look out for myself. I didn't know how far I could make it, with both the feds and my family looking for me...

My hands stopped working the window.

If Bill had told my father I killed Rocky, why didn't he come after me? Vic had helped me to escape, using the money I stole from Rocky, which he, in turn, had stolen from my father. At the time, we were both impressed with our ability to get me away completely unscathed, but now I wondered if there was more to it. Had they *let* me go?

But Bill was a liar. Bill had told Bax I was a repeat offender, a prostitute, and a druggie.

But he was the lead detective on the case... and it was almost harder to believe that he would hide that from my father.

And the baby?...

He had probably just told me what he wanted to make me feel worse. And as I slammed the wrench into the screwdriver again, sending shards of red hot pain into my skull, I had to admit that he had done just that.

Baxter

It had been three days of hell. I hadn't heard back from Victor, and when I finally broke down and called him, he yelled that I would just have to wait and hung up on me.

I had turned Red's statement in, as well as the recording she had left, and at that point, I had no choice but to inform my supervisor of who she was. There were shouts of delight throughout the office as if we had solved the most significant case of the century, but I was dying inside. Even though I shouldn't want her, I couldn't help it; the thought that my sicko father had her somewhere was making me crazy. Agents were slapping me on the back and congratulating me for solving the mystery of the missing mob boss's daughter while I was actively trying not to hurl.

When I couldn't take it any longer, I got into my car and drove. I had no destination in mind; I just needed to get away from the office, the pictures of her, and everyone looking at her like she was a thing, not a person.

She was my person.

"Was"... past tense. My chest squeezed around my heart again, my breathing becoming labored. I wasn't ready to let her go... but I had no choice.

The burner phone in my pocket started to vibrate, and I nearly drove off the road, trying to fish it out of my pocket.

"Hello. Victor, what have you got?" I answered in a rush.

"I have some information for you, Agent Murphy, but we need to get a few things straight first, you understand?" he asked cautiously.

"Go ahead," I said, more level-headed. The mob did not help you without getting something in return; I understood this much. I could feel the weight on my soul bearing down a little further.

"We are willing to assist in getting Red back, but we will require certain... assurances... to be put in place on our behalf."

"You want protection from prosecution? Is that what you're asking?" I spit.

"We are expecting that if we extend our necks to help you to get Red back, you aren't going to use that information we gave you and turn it on us," he clarified.

"I can agree to that, so long as you understand that *aside* from this information, our usual investigation of criminal wrongdoings will continue," I stated.

Victor chuckled mirthlessly. "We would expect no less," he stated. "I'm having a courier deliver a package to your hotel as we speak. Within the package, you will find a very interesting history involving our mutual acquaintance Bill. You will have all of the evidence you need to make sure he is no longer a pain in our sides, nor yours.

"Also, Bill has already reached out to Tony, requesting another meeting. He was offering to bring Red with him. You will find the arrangement that Tony has extended to Bill with the meeting time and place. Tony will not be there; you will. While he is willing to set this up on your behalf to try and get Red out alive, he is not willing to risk his own life at this time; I'm sure you understand.

"After the time of this meeting, our business will be concluded. We expect never to hear from you again unless it's on opposite sides of the badge. Understood?" Victor spoke succinctly, his words sharp and clear.

"Understood," I replied, not knowing what else to say. It was more than I had expected, to be honest.

"Oh, and Baxter?" Victor added, "You'd better bring her back alive, or I will hold you personally responsible."

With that, the call went dead.

Grabbing the wheel hard, I jerked it to the side, spinning my car in the opposite direction, and floored it for my hotel.

Red

It had been three days... or had it been four? The sun had already risen, sending small gaps of light into the immense darkness of the warehouse, but I couldn't pull myself up off the cardboard I had spread on the concrete. I was filthy and shivering, and my head was still aching. I imagine getting a second concussion on top of a concussion wasn't good for one's health.

I knew I had to get started on the window before Bill returned. He stopped in once daily to deliver a bag of food and a few bottles of water, which he pushed through a narrow slot in the door. I had resorted to using one of the cardboard boxes as a makeshift toilet and paperwork for toilet paper. Hey, I was alive; I wasn't going to complain now.

Before I could peel myself off the floor, I heard the noise of the door groaning open in the warehouse. Bill was early. Thank God I hadn't already started working on the window, or he would have caught me. He made his way to me quickly, a huge smile on his face; that alone caused my stomach to flip with worry like a fish out of water.

"Get up, Princess!" he sing-songed, "We have a meeting to attend." His smile was vicious and smug as he pulled out a set of keys and unlocked the padlock with a loud CLANG. The door groaned from non-use as he pulled it open.

I pulled myself up as quickly as possible, which wasn't very quick. When I finished last night, I had buried the tools in a box and dumped the concrete bits out the window. I didn't want him to notice my progress on the window sill in case he brought me back here. I staggered toward the open door, my hand on my temple, my vision going double. He reached for me and then dragged me with him through the warehouse without the slightest bit of gentleness.

When we stepped out of the warehouse, the sunlight assaulted my eyes, and I screamed as I fell. It felt like my eyeballs were on fire.

"We don't have time for theatrics, Princess!" Bill hissed as he grabbed my arm roughly, hauling me to my feet and all but dragging me to his car.

Once I was in the seat, and we were moving, I tried desperately to open my eyes and see where we were, to look for landmarks. It was no use; my vision was blurry and hazy, the light blinding me. The pain caused tears to run from my eyes, and I turned my head away from Bill. I didn't want him to think he was making me cry.

The trip was short; only moments later, he was pulling to a stop in front of yet another abandoned building, this one more remote than the last. I knew I should be talking, trying to get him to feed me information, but my brain didn't seem to be working. I had all I could do just to function.

The next thing I knew, his hands were hauling me roughly out of the seat and dragging me toward the door. I felt the chill spreading, and terror radiated through me.

Not now! NOT FUCKING NOW!

The darkness descended on me.

As consciousness drifted back, I studied the scene as if floating above it. It was the last scene I had drawn... but it had *changed.* My body was on the floor face up, a pool of blood slowly expanding around my chest. Bill was crumpled on the floor with a bullet hole in his forehead. And Bax was standing over me and shouting. I watched on with detached fascination. My visions had never changed before. I didn't know what it meant.

The pain told me I was back in my body, and the vision was fading. I could hear shuffling footsteps nearby.

"Don't you die on me before I get what I want, Renny," Bill commanded sharply.

As if I had any control over that.

I rolled to my side and was again hauled to my feet as I heard the noise of a door opening somewhere in the cavernous building. I thanked God that we were inside again; I could almost see clearly, except if I looked in the direction of the scalding light of the skylights.

"You stay put!" Bill hissed in a whisper as he moved forward. I tried to balance myself on my legs, but I felt like a newborn calf. I also noticed that my wrists had been tied. When did that happen?

"What the fuck are YOU doing here?" I heard Bill yell, pulling my attention back to the room just as Bax stepped out of the shadows.

"Why, Dad, were you expecting someone else?" Bax asked with irritation.

Bill moved, lighting fast, raising a pistol to point at me. "Son, you shouldn't be here, but I should have known that you'd come after the whore."

When I looked at Baxter, his gun was also raised, pointing at his father. "If you shoot her, it will be the last thing you ever do."

"Is she worth it?" Bill sneered. "This is Renatta Giovanni, Vinnie Giovanni's missing daughter. She's also a murderer. Are you willing to turn your back on your family for a criminal? The pussy can't be that good, son." He chuckled.

Fear and dread ran down my spine like cold fingers. I had hoped to spare him finding out about my family ties, but I guess once he knew I was a murderer, that paled by comparison. I snuck a look at Bax, but his eyes were glued to his father, and he never once looked my way.

Well, what had I expected?

"I know who she is, Dad, just like I know who you are." His face was cold and hard as he spoke with his father, and he never flinched when his father exposed who I was.

"And just who do you think I am, *Son*?" He punctuated the last word with a growl. "Other than the man who worked his ass off to help you get into the best schools so you could be a fancy federal agent?"

"I know all about your history with the Giovanni's. I have a stack of evidence against you for at least forty cases, so I wouldn't be throwing the 'criminal' label around so loosely. But what I'd like to know is where you buried mom?" His voice was even, his face still cold and hard. If he felt even an ounce of emotion, he betrayed none.

Bill laughed out loud. "That's your biggest concern?" He huffed through his laughter, "Son, she's not dead. I told her I wanted a divorce, and she wouldn't agree, so I told her that her only other option was to disappear and never return, or I'd make her disappear. At least *she* can follow directions."

I stared in shock at them both, guns still drawn, talking as if one of us wasn't going to die here today. I tried to shuffle backward slowly, but after only a few paces, Bill's head whipped back in my direction.

"Going somewhere, Sweetheart?" he teased, bringing the barrel of his pistol back to my chest level.

"Let her go, Dad. She can't help you get anything from Tony," Bax said flatly.

My eyes must have been crazy as I looked at him, but again, he wouldn't even look in my direction. My heart broke a little more.

"Honestly, I didn't think she would, Bax, but here's the thing... This little cunt has ruined my life. She lost me a cushy income with the family, and now she's apparently cost me my only son, so I think it's only fitting that she loses her life in exchange. Maybe you'll get your balls back, learn from this experience, and show your father some goddamn respect after this? Hmmm?" His pistol was on me, but his eyes were on Bax.

I groaned like I was going to be sick and doubled over, dry heaving. I needed to reach my revolver before this got out of hand. Bill shot me a disgusted look and turned his head back to Bax.

"Or... we could both fuck her first? What do you say?" Bill laughed.

I brought my tied hands up with my revolver pointed at Bill. My vision was still squirrelly, but I had no choice.

"Drop it," I said, trying to sound authoritative but just sounding sick.

Bill laughed again as he took me in. "Well, will you look at that? She came prepared! And here I didn't think you had it in you... again. Sorry, Son, there'll be no time for pussy now."

I saw him reach to cock his gun, and I cocked mine. I heard Bax yelling in the background, but I couldn't focus on what he was saying. I saw Bill's finger flex. My finger pulled the trigger just an instant after Bill did, and I felt my shoulder get ripped backward, spinning me on unsteady feet, the room flashing in a blur as I fell toward the concrete floor. There was a blinding pain in my head, and then there was nothing.

Chapter 11

Red

I heard voices murmuring far away, but I could never make out what they were saying. Sometimes I was aware that they were close to me; sometimes, they seemed far away, or like they were underwater.

I felt peaceful but also like I was missing something. I tried to look around me to find what I was missing, but nothing made sense. I felt like the world was foggy. I felt like I didn't have a body, which should be alarming, but it wasn't. My consciousness just seemed to 'float,' to exist. I just was... and it was okay.

...Except that I was missing something.

And then I felt it! That thing I had been missing! I heard a deep male voice nearby, and I *felt* him! His energy was so close to mine, and my heart sang. I could smell his scent and wanted to wrap myself in it, and I directed my attention to where I felt he was.

He felt sad and closed off, and my heart sank. I wanted to scream to him that I was there for him. I wanted to let him know I wanted him... but I couldn't get to him through the fogginess. Finally, I felt his energy pulling away from me, and I panicked. He couldn't leave me! I needed him! I screamed for him, but he only got further away until I couldn't smell or feel him anymore.

And I was back to missing him.

Baxter

I closed the file, sent it in to be archived, and emailed all agents working the cases back home. All of the pieces of the puzzle had come together at last.

By coincidence, my father had found Renatta over a year ago, and as he had been dismissed by the Giovanni's, he decided to retire and take up business in Richmond. He had two motivations: to ruin the shipping lanes for the Giovanni's drugs and to find Renatta and use her as leverage while getting revenge.

His mayhem in Richmond had caused Tony, who was about to inherit the Giovanni family business, to stop down and put things right, which then triggered the Bureau to send Fiske and me to find out what Tony was up to. It was all wrapped up in a nice neat bow that afternoon at the warehouse.

I stared at the file with my heart in my gut as I remembered.

My father and Renatta both fired. My father's shot caught Renatta's shoulder because she jerked when she pulled the trigger, causing her shot to miss by quite a bit. Had she not fired, he would have killed her instantly.

I was shouting at them to stop, unable to take a shot without hurting someone myself, when Fiske's shot caught my father right between the eyes. I was slumped over Red's unresponsive body while my father lay crumpled in a pile, staring lifelessly at the ceiling. I couldn't even spare him a thought; I was overwhelmed with Red. An ambulance was already heading our way as our agents brought in any of Bill's men they had captured around the perimeter and hadn't had to kill, but my entire focus was on my Red. She was losing a lot of blood, and I was losing my mind.

People were yelling instructions, shuffling people out in handcuffs, and just generally contributing to the chaos, but my world was silent as I watched the life flow out of Red's body. I was stricken. I couldn't move. I couldn't lose her.

Finally, Fiske pulled me away forcibly, put me into his car, and drove us back to the office. I was numb. I saw none of it. My mind was seared with the vision of her lying on the concrete floor, bleeding out.

Why hadn't she foreseen it? And if she had, would I have been able to stop it?

I felt the numbness in my mind and body, but I was aware that there was a volcano of hurt just underneath it, ready to explode and consume me. I knew tremors were shaking my body uncontrollably, but I couldn't care.

She couldn't be gone. Even if I had to go back to Boston, I needed to know that she was still out there somewhere, smiling her smile and laughing her laugh. I needed it like the air I breathe. She couldn't be dead; she couldn't be gone. She just couldn't.

That had been a week ago: one of the worst days of my life.

My father was dead; good riddance. It was too merciful a death. The evidence that Victor had sent me was submitted and tied several cases up nicely, as well as exposing a few of his accomplices from the Boston Police Department. This was the kind of bust most agents dream about their entire careers, the kind most will never see. I had it handed to me on a platter, and I could have cared less about any of it. My boss had put me in for a medal.

I didn't want a fucking medal. I wanted Red to be alright.

I slammed the desk drawer shut and stalked from the room. "I'm going for a ride," I called over my shoulder to Fiske as I left.

"Tell her 'Hi' for me," he answered, not bothering to chase me.

A half-hour later, I stood by her bedside. She was still in a coma. She looked ghostly and pale, just a shell of herself with a shock of bright orange-red hair making her look even more frail and sunken. Her skin was almost translucent, and I could see dark circles under her eyes. She was an empty husk compared to the bright flash of life she had been.

The doctors had told me that she had sustained too many blows to the head not to have permanent damage; they had no idea if she would come out of the coma, and she may never be the same afterward if she did. It broke my heart to think of this vibrant woman as anything less.

I let the tears fall. I picked up her soft hand, so small in mine, and just held it. The monitors beeped in the background as a constant reminder that she was still with us... for now.

"Red," I started, my voice breaking. "I am so sorry, Red. I never wanted this for you. You have to know I cared for you, and I wanted some kind of future for us. And now I am so god-damned angry at you for knowing what you did and not telling me. And I am so hurt by you leaving me. But most of all, I am pissed off that we can't be together, that we'll never be together, and I can't even give you a proper goodbye!" I swiped the tears from my face with an angry fist.

"Red, I'm going back to Boston tomorrow. I can't stay here until you're better, but I have people who will let me know you're alright. I need you to come out of this, Baby. I need you to be okay because, Red, I can't be okay if you're not. I need you to be brave and strong just a little bit longer. I need you to come back and make me miss every damned thing about you... I... I need you, Red," I whispered the last part as the tears overtook me.

Three and a half weeks later, I had just returned to my office in Boston from lunch when the call came in. Red was awake! My heart stuttered, and I almost fell to my knees in relief. I followed her progress over the next few days as they ran tests and scans to determine her prognosis, but I already knew that if she fought to come back, she was going to make a full recovery.

I looked at her picture on my phone again for the millionth time. I was doomed. I was never going to be able to get over her. But at least she was alive. I had something to celebrate, even if I never got to see her again.

That night I made my way through the crowded neighborhood to the small bar on the corner. It was a known hangout for some of the Giovanni boys, and I had heard that Victor could be found there. I made my way inside and took a seat at the far end of the bar, ordering a beer as I scanned the room. I caught his eyes a few minutes later, and I nodded subtly before I got up and headed to the men's room. He followed a few minutes afterward.

"WHAT THE FUCK ARE YOU DOING HERE?" he demanded in a heated whisper as he shut the door behind him.

"She's alive. I wanted you to know. She came out of her coma, and there was no sign of any brain damage. They're keeping her for observation and then rehab, but she will recover fully." I couldn't look him in the eye for the same reason he couldn't look at me; tough guys don't cry.

"Thanks, man. Now, get out of here," he ordered, a small smile on his face; and I took the opportunity to get out of enemy territory before I was spotted.

Red

My eyelids were heavy, and I forced one open, just a crack, before it fell back down on its own. It took a few minutes before I could get them both open and keep them open. I was happy with myself, keeping my eyes open until I looked around me.

I didn't recognize the room. How had I gotten there? When I turned my head and saw the equipment and the many tubes running into my arm, I figured it out. I was in a hospital. The question was, why?

I tried to swallow and then grimaced; my mouth and throat would give the Sahara Desert a run for its money. My tongue felt like a piece of dry beef jerky stuck in place. There was nothing to drink, and no one was around. I was pretty well trapped in the bed by all of the cords and tubes, so I chose just to try to take everything in; I mean, what else was I going to do?

At some point, a nurse came in, her nose buried in a chart. She moved swiftly to the bed, hanging the chart at the end, and moved to do something before she noticed I was sitting watching her. Then she screamed and jumped, her hands clutched over her heart.

I tried to apologize, but I only croaked harshly. She rushed to the door, leaned out, shouted for the doctor, and then turned back to me with a huge smile.

"Natalie, you have no idea how happy I am to see you!" She beamed.

I had no concept of time. What followed was an endless version of "hurry up and wait." I was seen by doctors, nurses, specialists, lab technicians, and others whose roles I never understood. There were countless labs, tests, scans... It was endless. There would be hours of note-taking, question answering, and getting vitals, and then there would be hours of nothing and no one.

I was getting frustrated and angry; no one wanted to tell me anything, and no one would say a word about Bax or Bill. They kept all conversation to my "condition" but never wanted to elaborate on exactly what my condition was. They were clearly concerned, based on the amount of observation they kept me under. I never got a full night of sleep because someone always woke me up several times a night for vitals or medications. I was exhausted... and grumpy.

It could have been one week, or several, later when I finally got a visit from the FBI. My heart sank as Agent Pierce introduced himself to me. I knew it was unrealistic to expect Bax to come and see me, but I had hoped. Sadness sat heavy in my chest as I tried to give the agent my full attention.

He was a nice enough guy, probably ten years older than I was, and good-looking; he was all business. Bax must have mentioned our fraternization because while he never said anything outright, his demeanor left no doubt that he was here to do a job and only that. And then, of course, there was his wedding ring. Did they think I had an FBI fetish or something?

He had questioned me extensively about what happened in the warehouse; we spent hours reviewing every detail of what I could remember, although some of it was hazy. At least it didn't feel like an interrogation, even though I knew it was one. He asked questions as if he was simply curious and very, very thorough.

After we had exhausted all his questions, he finally told me what I wanted to know. Bill was dead, shot in the head by another agent, probably Fiske. Bill had shot me, but it wasn't lethal, which isn't to say it hadn't required hours of surgery. And Bax? Agent Murphy had returned to his home office in Boston. He was gone. Just like that, it was all over.

Except it wasn't.

I was then informed that I was being investigated as a suspect in Rudolpho "Rocky" Difiorro's murder. I found out that my room in the hospital was segregated, away from other patients where I could be contained, and I had armed guards posted at my doors to prevent my escape.

I stared at him blankly, having no idea what someone would say to something like that. I sure had a hell of a lot of thoughts on the matter, but I was sure he wouldn't want to hear any of those. Why the hell couldn't I have just died in that warehouse?

The only good thing that came out of his visit was that he left me with a package of my personal items: my sketchbook, cell phone, and burner phone. Agent Pierce left, and I picked up the bag. My eyes went wide when I saw the small spare phone I kept to talk to Victor. They must have searched the apartment. Even though I was alone, I couldn't help but check to make sure no one could see it... not that it made sense; someone had to have put it in the bag... but who?!

DUH!!! They're the FBI! It's not like I hid it all that well! I should have kept it with my guns!

Had they used it? Had they spoken to Victor? Was the family aware of my charges? After all these years, were they going to demand retribution for Rocky's death? I groaned involuntarily and could feel sweat forming on my brow and under my arms.

There was only one way to know... I had to call Victor. I rifled through the bag until I found both phone chargers and plugged them in. Then I waited.

Fuck.My.Life.

Baxter

I looked out over the Boston skylight. Every day felt like every day before that. It felt like I had no reason to get out of bed anymore. The job was the same, and the people were the same, but there was no thrum of excitement for me anymore. There was nothing to look forward to.

My parents were both gone now, and I had no siblings. Holidays were pointless. I didn't want to go out with my friends, knowing I was in a sour mood, and dating was out of the question. After the handful of fire I had tasted in Richmond, women all seemed beige and drab. I still had plenty asking me out, but the thought of dating one of them turned my stomach. Dissatisfaction was like a taste in my mouth I couldn't quite get rid of.

I wanted the spitfire who ran like her life depended on it at the gym. I wanted the smart mouth that called me on my bullshit. I wanted the wanton vixen who made my cock feel like it had never felt before.

But I wasn't going to get that.

Fuck.My.Life.

Agent Pierce had called me as a courtesy to let me know they were holding Natalie "Red" Brooks as a potential suspect in Rocky's murder fifteen years ago. I had heard my dad talk about it in the recording, and I wish I had that envelope full of evidence he referenced, but it was never found. It explained a whole HELL of a lot if she had done it. She was running from the murder she committed, the family's retribution, and prosecution. And then I stumbled in like a country bumpkin.

I turned away from the window, disgusted with myself. I had never been this pussy-whipped, ever. I had been a player: love'm and leave'm. My job was stressful and risky, so ladies were relegated to recreational relationships only. I had always been honest: the women I took to bed knew I was only good for one night.

So how the fuck had I gone so wrong? I had let a woman get to me, and not just any woman: the daughter of the mob boss I had been investigating for a large part of my career. I had foolishly fallen for her charms like a love-sick kid.

She probably knew who I was when she took that phone call at the gym that aroused my suspicion. She obviously knew who SHE really was the first time she fucked me. Did she break it off or tell the truth? NO. She instead used reverse psychology on me, and I ate it up.

"Oh, you don't want me! I have a past! I want to spare you!" What complete and utter bullshit. The more I reflected on our time together, the more angry I became. How had I not seen it sooner? The signs were all there. Christ, this is what I do for a living!

She didn't even tell me when she recognized my father! MY FATHER! At that point, she knew she was a mob princess, I was FBI, and my dad was a former cop... well, a dirty cop, but still... and she was wanted for murder. She knew what this would do to me and my career. Thank God no one knew we slept together! I can't exactly put "dating a murderer" on my FBI resume, now can I?

I can understand not wanting to come out and tell me; I can. What I can't understand is why she went through with seeing me anyway, knowing what she did. Did she have any feelings at all, or was that all part of the package delivered to make it easier for me to swallow? She could act like she was falling for me, let me develop feelings to protect her, and take the hit to my career and reputation to pull strings to protect her.

I downed the last of my scotch as my anger boiled to the surface. I was such a fool. I had nearly thrown away my career for a con artist. She didn't give a damn about me. I'll bet she was laughing the whole time she was fucking the agent investigating her family: using me to get rid of my father for good.

Well, I was done. I had fallen for her before I finally came to my senses and realized just what was going on. I was done with having adolescent feelings for that conniving woman— no more. I placed my glass on the bar top and made my way back to the door, grabbing my jacket. It was time for me to go back out into the world.

Baxter Murphy was nobody's fool.

Red

Days of rehab were long and arduous. I didn't understand why they insisted that I practice walking, picking things up, and speaking... I could already do those things. Yes, I was a little bit weaker after my month-long nap, but I didn't need the hand-holding.

To add to my frustration, I was relegated to my tiny room in the secured ward. The guard wasn't very friendly. I would smile and say "Hi" when I saw him, but he always looked straight ahead, so I had no choice but to stick my tongue out at him or make silly faces. Mature, I know, but this was my life now.

As of the last time I re-entered my room, his attitude had not changed an ounce.

Maybe they'd all been warned about me, "Red, the Agent Eater." I stifled a giggle.

I waited until late in the evening, when things quieted down, to pull out my burner phone and try to call Victor. I was nervous, despite our history. There was a very good chance he wouldn't be talking with me again after how betrayed he had acted when I told him I was dating Bax.

A pang of hurt ripped through my chest. Pushing back the memories, I dialed Vic instead.

"Red?" he answered on the first ring.

I breathed out a sigh of relief. "Yeah, Vic. How are you?" I closed my eyes and relished the normalcy of hearing his voice. It was like a prayer from childhood that you cling to, even if you have left the church behind.

"How am *I*? Red, how are *YOU*? I've been worried sick," he answered uncharacteristically quietly.

"I'm... okay... I guess." I hedged.

"Spill," he said instantly. He knew me too well.

"Well, physically, I guess I'm okay. The doctors all seem shocked that I have no long-term damage other than temporary weakness due to my coma-nap. But..." I chewed my lip hesitantly, "It appears I am now a suspect in Rocky's murder," I finally whispered as if saying it too loud would convict me.

"Well... we kinda knew that was coming, didn't we?" Vic answered slowly but carefully.

I sighed again. "Yes. Yes, we did. I guess... I guess I just hoped..." I felt silly.

"I know, Red. I know. But who knows? Things change all the time, right?" he said with a little too much bravado.

I couldn't even think of something to say.

"Look, Red..." Vic said suddenly, "While I have you on the line... I... Uh... I kinda have a message to relay," he spoke hesitantly, which was not at all usual for Vic.

"A... message? From who?" I asked, trying to mask my shock and then instantly correcting myself mentally for not saying "whom."

"Tony."

That one tiny word instantly made me shrink back onto my hospital bed, sucking in my breath.

"Why would he—" I started.

"I don't know, Red, but I don't think it's anything to be worried about. Can I give him this number? He'd like to call you tomorrow at ten in the evening. Is that okay with you?" He sounded more matter-of-fact, and that alone made me feel better about it.

"Yeah... uh... sure, I guess," I replied, stumbling over my words.

"How is your boyfriend taking it all?" He suddenly switched gears.

My heart constricted in my chest, and I let out a slight gasping wince despite myself. "I haven't seen him since the warehouse," I said quietly, willing the pain not to rise or the tears to fall again.

"What?" he asked, confused. "He hasn't been in touch with you?"

"Just let it go, Vic," I said softly. I couldn't handle talking about it any longer. I couldn't live with the memories, and I couldn't forget them. It was like a weird version of hell.

"Yeah, okay, Nat. So... don't forget, tomorrow at ten, okay?" He jumped back onto the safer topic.

"Yeah, I'll be waiting," I said, still holding back tears. "Hey, Vic, thank you for everything." I don't know what I was even thanking him for; maybe just for being my friend, not judging me, for being there.

"You know I'm always here for you, Nat. Get some sleep; we'll talk soon." He ended the call.

Once I was off the phone, the walls around my heart crumbled, and I fell apart. I was a wet, sniffling, soggy mess of tears. I couldn't honestly say I understood which part of it I was crying over: my past, present, or future. It seemed like they were all concentrated around one event in my life that stuck me there like an anchor, never letting me move past it. I could see everyone else moving on, but I was damned to remain in that one place.

I laid back and let the tears flow until I must have fallen asleep.

Chapter 12

Red

I was on pins and needles the entire next day. I was anxious to get through all of the bullshit therapy and get to ten at night, but of course, that's not how things work.

I had another visit from Agent Pierce, which surprised me. My first thought was that he must know I had talked to Vic; that's why he showed up suddenly, upsetting the relative boredom of my sterile room. A mild flutter of panic started in my stomach at the sight of him, like birds being shocked from the ground into flight. I realized I hadn't even stopped to consider that they might have tapped my phone!

But perhaps I gave the FBI too much credit because Agent Pierce spent the whole afternoon sitting stiffly in a folding chair, re-interrogating me. He asked me many of the same things he had asked me before but worded differently, I was assuming to try to catch me in a lie. He wanted every gruesome detail about my interactions with Bill, and I was thankful he didn't ask about my interactions with Bax. I had enough to worry about already without wondering if there was going to be fallout from our trysts.

I had to bite my tongue with him all afternoon as my anxiety grew with each hour. I wanted to tell him to leave, as if his presence was slowing down time itself. I had bigger fish to fry than worrying whether the FBI thought I was fully honest with them. In the back of my mind, I burned to know why Tony wanted to talk with me. After all, if it wasn't a social call, the whole FBI situation might be moot. While the FBI could convict me and send me to prison, Tony could have me erased.

It was a long and tedious day.

That evening I sat on my bed clutching my cell phone in a death grip. The clock said I still had two minutes, but I had been staring at the phone intently for over an hour. At first I had tried to distract myself, but it only frustrated me further, so instead, I had spent an hour worrying, my guts churning, staring at the phone like it was going to sprout a head and talk to me.

One minute. Oh God, I was not cut out for this.

When the phone finally rang I answered it immediately, my hands cold and shaking.

"H-hello?" My voice sounded small.

"Hello Renny, it's your Uncle Tony," he said warmly. I had forgotten he used to call himself "Uncle."

"Hi Uncle Tony. Vic said you wanted to talk to me?" I asked hesitantly.

Just because he sounded warm doesn't mean he was happy with me. While he had always been one of the kinder of dad's men to me, I knew he had the capacity to be a ruthless killer. You didn't associate with my father because of flower arranging skills.

"Yes, Renny." He stopped and sighed deeply. "I wanted to say a few things to you, to clear the air between us. First, I want you to know that the family harbors no ill will for you. You are welcome to come and visit anytime you want. You're still a part of the family."

I sat in shock, my breath caught in my chest. This was not at all what I had expected to hear from him.

"Also, I wanted you to know a few things about your father."
He paused again. "Renny, I know your father was an asshole to
you, but he did love you."

I must have huffed because he continued.

"Really, Renny. I need you to hear this. He shared a lot with
me, especially after Rocky died. Your father always wanted to
incorporate you into the family business by having you get
close to people so you could feed him information, but make
no mistake, he would have slaughtered anyone who laid a hand
on you. You were always his Princess."

"Well he failed at that spectacularly," I said, before my filter
kicked into gear.

"That he did," Tony answered solemnly. "Your father didn't
find out about what Rocky was doing to you until after Rocky
was already dead, and he was enraged. Anyone who knew
about it, and hadn't told him, found themselves in a similar
boat, Renny. It was a massacre. You have no idea what that
man did for you."

I sat in stunned silence.

"He knew you took off, and he knew Vic helped you. He
ordered us to back down and let you go. He ordered us to check
in and make sure you were safe wherever you went, although
you made that pretty hard for us." He chuckled.

"He wanted for you to be happy, and he knew you weren't
happy here. After what Rocky did, he wanted to set you free,
the family business wasn't for you. And Renny, he was devastated when he found out you lost the baby."

A sob broke out of my throat, and I choked it back.

"He would have loved to have had a grandchild, honestly,
I don't think he would have given a fuck who the father was,
so long as he treated you and the baby good. He told me
how much he missed you all the time, how sorry he was that
he hadn't treated you better. I wish we had this conversation

before he died; he was looking for you at the end. He wanted to apologize."

"I don't know what to say…" My words broke, as I tried to form them. My mind was struggling, trying to consider every-thing he was telling me about the man who had raised me. I didn't know how to feel.

"You don't need to say anything, Renny. Just know that your family loves you. You still have that here, anytime you want. I can't say the same for your fed boyfriend, but you're always welcome." He chuckled warmly again.

"Thank you, Tony. I wish I could come back. I have missed being there," I said wistfully.

"Now… about this bullshit case…," he said, a little more gruffly. "Here's what I recommend: you should confess. Tell them exactly what happened."

"Wh—"

"Because I'm going to send a shit ton of evidence to them proving it was a prostitute that killed him while he had you trapped in his house. There is no way a jury is going to convict you with that much conflicting evidence. Don't take a deal. Go for a full acquittal. I can get you a good lawyer too, if you want."

My jaw fell open. I didn't think Tony could shock me any-more than he already had, but I couldn't believe what I was hearing. The family was going to get me out of this? The family that should be burying me in pieces for killing Rocky was in-stead going to get me off for his murder?! It had to be too good to be true.

"Tony… I don't want to sound ungrateful, because I am so, so grateful… but… why would you do this for me?" I asked quietly, tears streaming down my face.

"Because you're family, Renny. That bastard got what he deserved. If Vinnie had caught wind of it, he never would have gotten off as easy as he did, you can bet on that. We will never leave you out to dry, Renny. You're blood." he said with conviction.

"Now, you have a good night, get some sleep, and when this is all behind you, I would love for you to come up and visit with us. I'll even have Claire make her famous lasagna for you." I could hear the smile in his voice.

"Thank you, Uncle Tony. I love you," I said. And I knew it was true. My heart was warm and happy; it felt full. Maybe my father wasn't such an asshole; maybe I was loved, just in the only way he knew to show it. In one call, just like that, I had family again... something I hadn't had in a very long time.

After I hung up I wondered what would have happened if I had never run? What if I had stayed? Would my father have shown me the love and approval I had craved? Had I wasted my life, worrying about retribution that was never there? My sudden joy at having my family back felt like a hollow reflection of what my life could have been. I had lost my child, I had lost fifteen years, I had lost my father, and now I had lost Bax... If I had ever really had him.

Baxter

Over a month had passed since I returned to Boston. Fiske was back up to his old tricks, and I was finally cutting loose and going out with him again. I couldn't sit in my apartment and mope any longer. It didn't go unnoticed.

"Hey Murph, you up for the shindig tonight?" he asked with a grin on his face. "I could use a wingman."

"You know it," I answered. I wasn't smiling, not yet, but I knew I had to break out of whatever funk Richmond had put me in.

"There's always lots of girls from the 'Naughty List' at this Holiday event." Fiske laughed. "I'm sure you'll find someone to suck your candy cane. Here's your room key."

I smirked for Fiske's benefit, he was always more vulgar than I was. Maybe it was time for me to embrace my inner asshole like Fiske. Fuck and have fun, don't worry about feelings. At that moment, that sounded like just what I needed. I had let my guard down, and look where it had gotten me.

When we walked into the huge ballroom of the hotel, we were not disappointed. It was decked out in over-the-top holiday glamor; a pyramid of champagne glasses, gold and silver sparkling decorations, and with a mountain of presents for the womens' shelters on display. A large orchestra played music, and there were tables of food and drink available near a large dance floor. It was like a gathering of the rich and famous; tuxedos and gowns on display everywhere. The scent of money drew them all in to be seen among the 'in' crowd.

I knew it was a shitty thing to do, going to a charity event to get laid, but it was the perfect setup. There were tons of bored rich housewives looking for a boy-toy for the evening, and even some single gals with their own money who didn't want a man to tell them how to live their lives. They were in for "one and done": no names, no history, no "next times." Fiske lived for these events, and I was his wingman, after all.

I snagged us each a glass of champagne from the tray of a passing waiter as we made our way around the room. A friend of Fiske's caught his attention, shaking his hand while they caught up. I let my eyes wander, looking for my next prey, when I saw a gorgeous creature who instantly had me getting hard.

She was shapely, but firm, no starving model. But what got my attention, everyone's attention, was that she had long, thick, blue hair hanging in loose curls down her back. It was a darker blue, but not quite navy, and it looked stunning on her. Glancing back to see that Fiske was still occupied, I started to make my way toward her. She was intriguing. I was only about five feet away from the blue goddess when a man stepped up to her and handed her a glass of champagne. I slowed my approach, until my eyes caught his.

"Max!" I said with a smile.

"Baxter!" the man replied, extending his hand.

Max had been a friend since college, although we hadn't talked in quite a while. He and I were always serious about working out, and had even done amateur bodybuilding at one point. I could see he'd lost a little of his mass, but like me his suit, while tailored, was a little snug around the biceps and chest.

"What have you been up to, Man?" I asked with a grin. I couldn't help stealing a sneak at the lovely blue angel at his side. Lucky fucker.

"Partner in the firm now." He grinned. "Oh... Let me introduce you to my fiance, Jenna."

I notice he placed his hand at the small of her back possessively, beaming with pride.

"It's lovely to meet you." She smiled.

"Likewise," I said, taking her hand and kissing the knuckles gently.

"Get your own girl, Murphy." Baxter laughed, but I knew he was only half-kidding. We used to be very competitive for the girls when we were younger.

"Well I couldn't be rude to this divine creature just because she has the misfortune of being stuck with you, could I?" I asked, my eyes never leaving hers.

She withdrew her hand, firmly but gently, to nestle into Max's side, her hand on his chest, and I felt a pang of jealousy shoot through me. I chose to ignore it.

"Yeah, well don't be too polite, either." He chuckled. "Hey, we should get together sometime and catch up! Here..." Max pulled out his card and gave it to me, and I tucked it into my pocket. I still had his number; I just hadn't had much time over the last year to socialize. I was solving that problem immediately.

"Absolutely. It was lovely meeting you, Jenna." I nodded to them both, and made my way back to Fiske... something in my memory rubbing me the wrong way.

Jenna... Jenna... where have I heard that name before? I finally gave up, and started recon for tonight's main event.

Red

They had moved me out of the rehab hospital in early November. I was allowed to go back to my apartment, but I was essentially on "house arrest." I couldn't leave town, and I was followed everywhere I went, and I was pretty sure it wasn't for my protection this time.

My apartment brought reality crashing back into me. I owed several months of back rent that had to be taken care of promptly. I had the money; I still had a bulk of the cash I had stolen from Rocky when I ran, and I had invested wisely. I only worked to keep myself from getting bored, so losing that job was never an issue. But the apartment felt cold and empty, even more gloomy than it had been before I left. It occurred to me I should consider getting another place, maybe even buying a house, before I dropped my shoulders, realizing I couldn't really do anything... not yet. I might have a new home, a concrete cell, soon enough.

I was only home a week when Agent Pierce contacted me to say he wanted to bring me in to make a formal statement about Rocky's murder. I had seriously had enough of that dick and his endless questions, and there couldn't be anything I had to say that wasn't already in the many pages of notes he had taken.

But what choice did I have? I couldn't very well say, "No, thanks."

I caught an Uber to the FBI office downtown and was stopped at reception. After the person behind the desk called somewhere, I was given a blue visitor badge, and a guard walked me through the metal detector and then escorted me up the elevator and to the fifth floor. As soon as the doors opened, Agent Pierce was front and center in a very business-like lobby, ready to bring me to a glorified interrogation room, so that I could start all over again.

I rubbed my sweaty palms down my pant legs as I followed him. Honestly, if they were going to lock me up and throw away the key, I was wishing they would just get on with it. The never-ending questions were getting on my nerves. The constant invasion of my privacy, and the repetition were beyond irritating to me.

They had me sit in a chair by a metal table, facing the cliche double-sided glass so some perv could watch the whole thing. I rolled my eyes. Agent Pierce began by turning the recorder on and stating the date...

"This is Agent Bryce Pierce, receiving a statement from Natalie Brooks, also known as Renatta Giovanni, in the matter of the murder of Rudolpho 'Rocky' Difiorro on..." He rattled off the date of the murder, and the address of his house.

"Tell me, Miss Brooks, where were you the day of the murder?" he asked flatly.

"I have already told you, I was at Rocky's house that day." I tried not to sound snarky, but I was exhausted with what felt like his harassing me with the same questions, yet again.

"And when did you arrive there?" he asked.

"About two weeks before," I stated.

"No, when did you arrive at his house that *day*?" he asked, to clarify, as if I was the nitwit.

"I didn't arrive *that day*," I answered, my annoyance starting to show.

"But you just told me you were at Rocky's house that day, Miss Brooks. Please remember that inconsistencies may be considered perjury." The man was seriously freaking annoying.

"Yes, I was at Rocky's house that day. I didn't lie," I replied heatedly.

"Are you saying that you went to Rocky's house two weeks before he was murdered, and you never left... for two weeks?" He eyed me suspiciously.

"That's exactly what I am telling you," I answered, growing impatient.

"And you never left that house in those two weeks, not for any reason at all, not even to step outside?" he asked.

"No," I answered simply.

"Did you go outside at all? Could you have left and forgotten about it?" he tried again.

"No," I said bluntly.

"How can you be sure?" he asked, his own irritation rising.

"Because I was drugged and chained to a bed the whole time so he could rape and beat me. I was only unchained for a few minutes every day to use the bathroom. THAT'S how I can be sure." I glared at him, daring him to challenge me.

"Do you have any witnesses to substantiate this claim?" he asked calmly.

"None that will... Except the employees at the Crosstown Clinic. When I finally got free I had to go there for treatment, I used the name Jenna Gambelli. Rocky didn't know I was pregnant when he took me, and he essentially killed my baby. I had a full workup done there, and they inventoried all of my injuries. They found traces of the date rape drug in my blood, and his semen in my body." I stared straight ahead at the mirror. I would not give him an ounce of my pain. I would not look to see if there was pity in his eyes, because I didn't know which would be worse: seeing pity, or seeing his complete lack of compassion.

"Why hadn't you disclosed this before?" he asked a little more gently.

"You.never.asked." I bit out between clenched teeth.

"Okay..." Pierce moved on. "So tell me what happened the day Rocky was murdered."

I blew out a breath. "They had untied me that morning to use the bathroom, and Rocky had tried to give me my daily drink with the drug in it, but his cell phone rang and he was distracted with the call, so I dumped most of the drink on the bed and covered it with a blanket."

"Go on," he pressed.

"I heard him say to someone on the phone that he was on his way, so I knew he was leaving and I had a chance. I waited until I heard his car pulling away, he had a sportscar with a loud muffler, before I started working to get the restraints off. I had smuggled the head of a disposable razor blade out of the bathroom a few days prior, so I used that to help fray the ropes. I was worried he would be back any minute; I was scared shitless.

"I finally got the ropes free. I threw on some clothing I found in the room, and snuck downstairs as quietly as I could. I headed for the backdoor, through the kitchen, planning to sneak out; but as I rounded the corner I heard someone out-side the door. I grabbed the closest thing to me, a knife out of the block on the kitchen counter. I ran to the side of the door, so that when he opened it, I would be hidden from view.

"I guess he'd been doing some drugs, because he was acting really weird. He started to walk through the kitchen, leaving the door open, and I thought I had a chance. But then he seemed to remember it, and turned around to close it, and he saw me.

"He was furious! I had never seen him that out of control before. He took a swing at me, but he stumbled, so his fist hit the wall instead. I panicked, and I brought the hand with the knife up, cutting him. He went berzerk! I just kept stabbing at him, praying he'd stop, and then all of a sudden he fell over, grabbing his neck. There was blood everywhere. He just... died.. on the floor, in front of me." I looked at my hands and stopped, still seeing his lifeless eyes staring at me with confusion. I wasn't nearly as helpless as I had made myself out to be, but there was no need to point that out to them. I knew exactly the cut that was needed to end Rocky.

His cell phone chirped, and he pulled it out and looked down at it, before pocketing it again and looking up at me.

"We're going to pause for a while, so we can substantiate some facts. Thank you for your cooperation, Miss Brooks. Edgar will escort you back downstairs." He turned on his heel and walked out of the room, the door 'snicking' shut behind him, leaving me with the security guard.

I pulled myself up, mentally exhausted, and followed the guard through the door. As we took a few steps down the hall we passed an open door which led to the adjoining room where I was sure people were watching me give my statement. I turned my head just in time to catch the smallest glimpse of Baxter Murphy. His face was a void, his jaw clenched, and his eyes were cold and ruthless. I felt the air being sucked out of my lungs as my eyes met his for the briefest of moments, a heartbeat. Before I could even react, the guard was shuffling me past the doorway as it swung shut, cutting me off from his face.

The elevator trip to the first floor felt like a descent into hell. *He was there! Bax had been there! He had heard every-thing! What was he thinking? Would this change anything?* But the look on his face... it was like staring into an abyss. It was a cold heartlessness I had seen many times,... on my father's men. It made my blood run cold. I didn't know what that look meant on him, but I knew it wasn't good.

If I had any thoughts that one day Baxter Murphy and I might ever reconnect, they were shattered in that brief moment of eye contact. That one look told me everything I needed to know.

Anything we had was over, and he was my enemy.

Baxter

"When do you fly out?" Pierce asked me.

"Tomorrow afternoon," I answered, still staring at the two-way mirror.

"So what do you think?" the investigator, Agent Melissa Harris, asked.

I looked over at her; she was a small woman, just a little over five feet tall, but she was brilliant at what she did. She would take all of the evidence that the field agents could gather, and weave them into a case for federal prosecution so that when we took criminal scum off of the street, they stayed off.

Pierce stood nearby, watching me.

"Well, it's obvious that she's frustrated and angry with you, Pierce. Also, I noted that her respect for you seems to be slipping, probably due to the aforementioned frustration and anger." I said it flatly, looking at Pierce. There was no love lost between us, but I could say at least he was good at his job, even if he was a raging prick.

"I don't give a fuck if she likes me, Murphy. I need to know if she's telling the truth. That's why you're here," he spat back.

My eyes narrowed in concentration as I mentally reviewed her answers and her body language, before I could answer.

"I didn't see deception markers, so it would appear that she is telling the truth," I said slowly, and Pierce pushed off of the wall to walk out. "HOWEVER...," I continued, "She's a con artist, trained by the mob. I wouldn't take anything she says to be fact without first proving it. She's probably very convincing when she wants to be."

Pierce shot me a look. "Is that everything?" he asked flatly. When I nodded, he continued, "I'll have a copy of the findings sent to you." And with that he moved to the door, and out.

"This is going to be a tough one to prosecute if what she said was true," Agent Harris said calmly, eyeing me. "A good attorney will call it self-defense, and with no weapon, no witnesses..." She let the rest go unsaid.

I pushed up out of my chair and stalked out of the room, my head swimming. What I had just heard had chilled me to the bone. The part of me that had cared for her had broken right down the middle, at the thought that those things had happened to her before she even turned eighteen; not that being older would have made it any easier. It physically pained me to think of any woman having to endure it. But my Red,... just a young girl... and pregnant...

But instantly my mind rushed in to remind me how she had played me already, how she lured me in, and suckered me into feelings for her. This was probably all another extravagant lie, designed to get her out of having to do time for the crime she committed. She was raised by the mob, she had probably been coached in how to play the system, and work off of sympathy. She was trying to make a judge or jury feel bad for her, see her as the victim; just as I had. It was all for show.

What she didn't know was that there was no way in hell I was going to let this stand if it was a lie. I would hunt down all of this fictitious proof she claimed existed, just so I could see the look on her face when I presented the real facts in court.

Natalie Brooks, AKA Renatta Giovanni, was a liar and a murderer, and I saw right through her.

Chapter 13

Baxter

I paced in my room. It had only been a few hours since I saw her face; that look of shock and devastation behind her eyes as she was dragged past the doorway. It had hit me like a wrecking ball to the gut. I kept telling myself that I was over her, that I didn't have any feelings for her but hatred... and the first time it was tested, I failed.

I couldn't keep doing this to myself.

Grabbing my jacket I headed out to do what I always did to clear my head, I got in the car and drove. I wandered aimlessly, barely noticing the city, the beauty of the area. I felt like I had a sucking chest wound that I was trying to ignore like a mosquito bite.

I was angry... furious. With her. With myself. Fuck, with everything. And no matter what else I ever felt, it always came back to the rage. I hit the gas as I pulled out a little faster than was recommended, trying to burn off my emotions with the gasoline.

I shouldn't have been surprised when I looked up to see her apartment building. I cursed under my breath. I was such a fucking moron, running on autopilot. Running right back to her like a good little puppy, begging for a treat. *Well fuck this.* I was here now, so I might as well get it all out. Maybe I could get her out of my system once and for all; confront her. Maybe she would finally just admit that she had been using me the whole time, and make it easier for me to just hate her, without hating myself for it.

I made my way across the lot, and let myself into the building through the door which was always propped open. In moments I was stalking up the stairs with its faded and stained carpets, and standing in front of her door. I had a split second of doubt, before I raised my hand and knocked loudly. I heard her gasp, seconds before the door opened.

Her eyes were wide with surprise, and maybe a little fear. *Good.* She opened her mouth but I cut her off.

"Could I have a word with you Miss Brooks?" My tone was harsh, and I knew my eyes were telling her this wasn't a friendly visit.

"Of course, Agent Murphy," she answered curtly, her expression sour, stepping out of the way so I could walk in.

She walked to the sofa and, pulling her skirt under her, she took a seat not bothering with pleasantries. I sat in the chair opposite her, just as I had the last time. *The last time...* I took a deep breath to clear that thought right the hell out of my mind.

"That was some pretty compelling information you gave today," I said, still staring daggers at her.

"Is there a question there, somewhere?" she asked as she stared at me, having nothing to add.

"You do know that the Bureau will follow up to find the evidence you suggested, and if they don't–"

"What do you want?" she asked, her tone wary and pained.

"What do I want?" I rolled my head up, a sour chuckle escaping my throat. Then my eyes were on her again. "I'll tell you what I want. I want to know why you didn't break it off. Why, if you cared so much, you never told me the truth, or just had the balls to end it. That's what I want," I snapped.

My glare met hers. "I think you should leave," she spit.

"No, I don't think I should. Not before I get what I came for," I hissed back, a smirk on my face.

She matched my smirk, leaning her elbows on her knees. "And just what is *that,* Agent Murphy?"

I gave her a condescending grin. I knew I was going to piss her off, but at that moment I wanted nothing more in the world than to hurt her like she had hurt me; to make her scream and rage. I matched her posture, leaning my elbows on my knees, both of us leaned in, "Well, you have a very talented lying mouth. I think you should come over here and suck my cock one last time, seeing as it's all you're good for."

I expected her to yell at me. I expected her to demand I leave. I was ready for that. So imagine my surprise when she called my bluff and stood up, walking to stand in front of me, and then dropped to her knees between my legs. I tried to keep my face straight, not wanting her to see my shock. She made quick work of my belt and zipper, freeing my cock, which immediately hardened in her hand, despite my effort to withhold it from her.

Fuck!

Her mouth was on me in seconds, taking me in and sucking me down. I groaned despite myself; part of me was thrilled to have her attention on my cock again, and part of me was pissed off that we were, again, going down this road. This wasn't what I had intended when coming to her apartment, and I had to take control back before I was lost to the miraculous feelings of her mouth on me.

I looked down and watched her swollen lips sucking my cock all the way into her throat, her warm pink tongue skimming the underside as she flexed her lips around my girth, sending waves of pleasure through my body. While my cock rejoiced, a little voice in my head reminded me that this was not what I wanted.

"What a good little whore you are. You suck my cock so well," I purred, trying to get a rise out of her.

Instead of making her pull back and screech at me, my words just seemed to spur her on.

FUCK. I tried again.

"You like that, don't you, you little slut? You like having cocks down your throat?" I made my voice arrogant and condescending, but she took no notice, groaning over my cock and almost making me lose control. She was getting off on the dirty talk, and didn't seem upset in the least. Everything I tried was backfiring, and I was starting to fear that I was going to lose this battle against my impending orgasm, based on the way she was taking my cock like a champ. I had to up my game.

"You know what you need? You need someone to put you in your place, you little whore. You need someone to fuck that lying little mouth of yours, and remind you who's in charge. I bet you'd like that, wouldn't you?"

She groaned loudly and nodded her head vigorously around my girth in her mouth. *Shit. Not the response I was expecting. I couldn't back down and let her see that I was bluffing.*

I fisted my hands in her hair roughly, yanking her head still and holding her in place, as I rose out of my chair so that I could thrust my cock into her mouth with force. I groaned as I felt myself hitting the back of her throat, pounding into her, feeling her nose hitting my belly, and my balls bouncing off of her chin. I held her as I fucked her face, hard; her hands clutched at my ass, nails digging in.

Finally! A response! But not the way I had intended. Instead of her trying to assert her dominance, she was instead digging her nails into my ass, pulling me in harder, pushing me for more.

I let her have it, slamming into her mouth, finally enjoying punishing her for everything she had done to me. I could feel my release starting to rise, and I tipped her head back slightly to get even further down her throat. She started to gag and cough, but I didn't slow my pace until she finally bared her teeth, scraping my sensitive skin in warning.

"You fucking bite my dick, and I swear to God I will fuck your mouth so hard I cause brain damage!" I swore, instantly wincing at my choice of words.

Too late, I had said it, and there was no taking it back.

I continued to pound her mouth, pushing my cock deep, as my balls tightened.

"I'm going to come in that sweet little liar mouth of yours, Red. Take it all. Choke on my cock. Fucking take it all," I goaded. I had already crossed the line, and I knew it. I just couldn't seem to stop, I had to see it all the way through. I was horrified at my own actions, but I couldn't seem to back down.

With one last thrust I threw my head back and groaned loudly as my cock spasmed in her mouth. I felt my hot wet release filling her mouth and throat, and held her fast as she sputtered and choked around it, before sliding in a few more times until I was completely empty.

Before I had even recovered she shot up quickly. I felt a blow to my solar plexus, which doubled me over, forcing the air out of my lungs. Next, I felt pain radiating through my jaw, my head snapped to the side with force, before I found myself flipped onto my back, hard. The impact kept me from getting a breath, and I was like a fish out of water. My hands grasped at my chest, as if they could pull air back into me.

And then she was on top of me, her tight pussy impaled on my cock. My body dragged in a ragged breath, finally, as her wetness gripped me and she rode me hard. I pushed at her, trying to get up, and she easily pushed me back down, pulling herself up and then slamming herself back onto me, her muscles milking my cock.

"You think you're so goddamn tough? If it's all about sex for you, FINE. Just quit your whining and fuck my pussy like a MAN!" she roared, impaling herself hard and deep onto my cock.

I was furious! I wanted to tear her to pieces, but my traitorous body only grabbed her hips in a death hold and slammed her onto me harder, my cock getting hard again. I felt her inner muscles ripple around me tight, right before she screamed; her silky warm wetness running over me as she came hard on my cock. My own orgasm was starting to build again as I felt her muscles sucking and stroking me inside of her warmth.

And then she was up again, leaving my cock to feel the cool air against the wet slick she left behind. She headed for the bedroom door quickly, while I scrambled to my feet, trying to figure out what to do next. This had all gone to hell faster than I could have imagined.

"You can see yourself out," she hissed as she stomped into her bedroom, slamming the door behind her.

I stood there both shocked and enraged that she had left me hard as a rock, unfinished. I dragged a hand through my hair as I blew out a breath when I heard a humming noise coming from her bedroom. It was loud, then muffled, then loud...

SHE WOULDN'T DARE... My hand began to stroke my length as I listened.

I ran to her bedroom door and put my ear against it. I heard the humming/muffling speed up its cadence, and a low moan.

THE BITCH!

"OPEN THIS FUCKING DOOR OR I WILL BREAK IT DOWN!" I bellowed, enraged.

"FUCK OFF, AGENT MURPHY!" she screamed from behind the door.

I didn't think. I leaned my shoulder in and charged the cheap door, forcing it open, and tearing off some of the door frame with it.

Red

I shrieked with excitement and jumped. I was sprawled out on the bed, positioned so he could see the large pink vibrator pulsing in my pussy. I knew he would never be able to resist hearing me getting myself off. I hadn't wanted to believe he was the kind of guy who would use sex as a weapon, but he was a moron if he thought I was going to lose at his game. From the minute he told me to suck his dick, I called the shots.

His pants were off in one swift movement, and he flew to the bed and swung, so that his knees were on either side of my shoulders, his face over my swollen pussy in a sixty-nine. His mouth captured my clit as his hand grabbed the vibrator and thrust it back inside me again and again. I gasped, dropping my head back with a groan, before he dropped his cock into my open mouth, fucking my lips again while he worked my clit with his mouth. It only took a few seconds before my body seized around the vibrator and I screamed around his cock, bringing him closer to release.

"You fucking bitch!" he raged, as he slammed the vibrator into me roughly again and again, my wetness leaking out around it. He was wild, out of control, and completely hot.

I could feel his cock stiffening in my mouth, his climax getting ready to wash over him. I reached behind me to the buttplug I had prepared, and I smeared some lube over his puckered hole. This sent him into another loud groan. Just as I felt his balls starting to contract, I pushed the butt plug into him, slowly pressing it deeper and deeper.

"Wha—"

"Still think you're in control?" I screamed, as I pushed the plug into his tight ass. My arms were secured around his hips, holding him in place. He roared in surprise and rage, but immediately the bizarre fullness fueled his climax, and his body locked up. His orgasm surged like a freight train, completely overwhelming him; his cock was lodged down my throat as he screamed his release. He was paralyzed there, his muscles locked and convulsing, his cock draining down my throat while I sucked him dry. He was completely raw and at my mercy. I pulled the butt plug out, and his body went into another round of convulsions.

He was furious. He leapt off of me, turning and bringing his arm under me, and he flipped me onto my stomach, ass in the air.

"You want to play dirty, Bitch?! I'll show you dirty!" He yelled.

I had to fight not to smile. He had me right where I wanted him to have me. I just had to plant the seed.

"You're not fucking my ass!" I demanded hotly, shooting him a dirty look full of challenge. "Only guys I LIKE get to fuck my ass."

He pulled up behind me and thrust into my pussy hard from behind. He pounded me, and I could feel my wetness running down my thigh as his cock relentlessly savaged me. It was glorious!

"What?" He teased menacingly, "You don't want this cock inside your tight ass, Bitch?" He gathered some of my wetness on his finger and then pushed them into my ass roughly. I howled in response. "I bet you're used to plenty of cocks fucking this ass," he hissed.

"You don't get to fuck my ass!" I yelled, but it lacked the heat I had previously. I had to let him think he was getting one over on me. He kept me locked tight to his body as he pumped me hard: his cock in my pussy, and his fingers in my ass. I made no move to pull away.

"Thing is, Red, you're not in charge here," he stated ominously. "Beg me to fuck your ass, Red. Beg me, and I might. Otherwise, I'll just grab my pants and leave."

We both knew it was a lie. There was no way he'd just walk away with my pussy wide and waiting, and his cock hard enough to break bricks.

"Fine. Then go." I said, in between panting thrusts.

Pulling out of me quickly, he pressed the head of his cock against my asshole, and I wiggled against him, cursing.

He laughed at me. "Beg me."

I turned to glare at him. "You either fuck my ass right now, or get the fuck out. I'm done playing with you."

That must have been the right thing to say, because he thrust hard into my ass. I screamed and cursed as he rode my ass before he picked up the discarded vibrator and shoved it into my pussy.

"You fucking asshole!" I hissed over my shoulder, but it wasn't very convincing as my hips rocked back to meet his. He seemed to be in ecstasy with his head thrown back as he rocked his cock into my ass.

He smacked my ass hard, leaving a sting on the cheek. "You need to be punished," he growled, smacking my ass cheek again.

"You think YOU can punish me?! HA!" I roared back. "You'll have to do better than that. I need a REAL man to punish me for all the shit I've done."

He spanked my ass again and again, but it wasn't having the effect he had anticipated. He had no idea how much I was getting off on it, and it was completely undoing him.

I know he could feel the humming of the vibrator through my body, tingling his cock as he fucked me. I was groaning and bucking as he nailed my ass and pussy both. I felt him getting closer again, just as I was peaking.

"That's right, Red. You come for my cock. Take it, Red, Take it all! Come for me! Come NOW!" he screamed, and I did. Our bodies locked together. I had nothing left in me, but the sensations gripped and wrung my body as I held on for dear life.

Finally, he pulled out and collapsed onto the bed, boneless, my mind was a haze of orgasm hormones.

I rolled and swung off of the bed, moving out of the room with speed. Yes, the sex was amazing, but I hadn't lost sight of the fact that he came over here to punish me for caring about him. He didn't seem a bit upset that he had lost me, only that it would reflect badly on his career.

He was slower, pulling himself together to get up, finding his pants, and pulling them on as he walked to follow me; if my body was any indication, all of the muscles in his legs, ass, hips, and abs were sore.

I stood by the door and swung it open while he quickly stuffed himself back into his pants and zipped them up.

"There, you got what you came for. Now get out," I said, my eyes narrowed in anger.

He glared at me, too shocked to move for a moment, before recovering his sanity and making his way to the door. As soon as he was out, he turned and opened his mouth to make a nasty reply, but I cut him off with a wave of my hand.

"Save it. Congratulations, Agent Murphy; you've become your father." And with that, I slammed the door in his flabbergasted face.

I paced my living room, furious. What a fucking idiot I had been to have ever cared about a heartless prick like Bax. He was cut out of the same cloth as his father. It had all been about sex for him, hadn't it? He hadn't ever really cared for me, only for making sure no one else had me. Hell, when he found out I hated his dad, his first thoughts were not that his father might have hurt me, but that I might have fucked him!

I was his dirty little secret, his side piece that no one could know about. How convenient that I just happened to be involved in a case he was working on. And when the world found out about me, he just disavowed all knowledge. Once he knew who I was and what I had done he had ghosted me like I was a piece of shit. No call, no note, nothing. And then, after he found out what had happened at Rocky's, I got the death glare, before he invited himself over to fuck me again? Was he serious?!

Did he think he could just use me, and I'd have nothing to say about it?

Well, I'd had the last laugh. Sure, he got his blowjob, but I made sure I threw him down and taken what I'd wanted. He had no idea that I was an accomplished fighter. And it had felt SO good to punch him in his smug face. I knew he wouldn't be able to resist once I was getting off with the vibrator. The spanking was a bonus. But the best part had been when I told him not to take my ass. If he ever had any idea how much I LOVE anal, he would be so pissed. In the end, I got what I wanted; the only thing he could ever give me. Not that it mattered now.

I just had one loose end to tie up with regards to Bax, and for that I had to call my girlfriend Amber. But I think my little act might have just finally convinced him to fuck off and leave me alone for good.

I am nobody's plaything.

Baxter

I sat in the chair in my hotel room, drinking my scotch. What the fuck had just happened? I hadn't meant to have sex with her... I hadn't meant to push her. I don't even know why the fuck I had gone over. I hadn't really planned out what to say, and it just... got away from me. It was, by far, the most erotic experience I had ever had in my life. I have never had orgasms like that before, and my dick was still hard just remembering them. But the rest of it...

Shame consumed me.

I had done it. I had crossed the line. How was I any better than Rocky? Or my father? She was right; I had become him. I had withheld evidence, slept with a fucking witness, and then I hid that, and then...

I had crossed a line.

In all of my life, I had never, NEVER, fucked a woman in anger before. I had never pushed a woman that far, tried to humiliate them the way I did to her. I had hurt her. Because I had feelings for her that I couldn't face, I had hurt her. And now she would never talk to me again. There was no chance I could ever face her, after what I had done. I dropped my head into my hand, feeling like a monster.

I drank the rest of my scotch down in one gulp and then got up to pour another.

I was supposed to be the good guy. I was the one who put the bad guys away and protected the weak. Who the fuck was I now? I was such a hypocrite. I had become one of the bad guys.

I flopped back down into the chair, some of the scotch sloshing over the rim of the glass, before I brought it to my lips and drank it down in one shot.

One thing was clear: I was going to need more scotch.

It had been two weeks since I had been down to Richmond to see Red give her statement, since I had...

Don't go there.

Back in Boston life went on. Thanksgiving had been just a few days ago, and having time off as well as a holiday, and no family, had sucked big time. I blew out a frustrated breath as a knock sounded at my office door. Before I could even answer, the door opened and Fiske stuck his head in, a big smile on his face.

"I'm heading to O'Malley's tonight, you in?" he asked.

O'Malley's was the local watering hole where Fiske found most of his nightly conquests. We had been there almost every night for the last two weeks, and I had buried myself in pussy, hoping to drown out the guilt that was eating me alive. It wasn't working.

"I don't know...," I started to say, before he cut me off.

"Don't back out on me now, Murphy! Rosa said there's a bridal shower there tonight, and I just know I can get a two- or three-way going. C'mon, help a brother out!" He gave me his rockstar grin.

I sighed. "Yeah... okay," I conceded. My heart wasn't in it, but what the fuck.

Something around my cock felt good... it woke me from my dreams. I had gone out to the bar with Fiske, and I had far too much to drink. My head was foggy and pounding, and my stomach was surging. I wasn't even sure where the fuck I was. Had I fallen asleep? It was dark. I looked around the room, a hotel room... before I felt the warm lips sucking on my cock and I groaned.

Red!

I ripped the covers off of the bed to find a messy blond bobbing her mouth up and down on my cock. Her hair was all over the place, and her makeup was smudged.

NOT Red. *Had I fucked her?*

She seemed to be enjoying herself, but she really didn't know what she was doing. It would start to feel good... really good... and then she would shift, or change what she was doing, dropping the sensation. I blew out a frustrated groan, which she took as a sign that I was enjoying myself, because I heard her groan over my cock and her lips smiling around it.

After the third or fourth time I'd finally had enough. I pushed up to sitting and pushed her back. She smiled broadly and spread her legs eagerly.

"You really need to learn how to give a blowjob," I stated flatly, getting off of the bed and heading for the bathroom. I needed to get out of there.

"What about ME?!" she whined in a high-pitched voice. "You're just going to leave me like this?!" She pointed to her crotch, obviously not satisfied.

"Go see Fiske next door, he doesn't care who he sticks his dick in," I said over my shoulder, before closing the bathroom door.

As I used the toilet, I could hear the door opening and slamming shut. *Good. She was gone.*

I immediately felt bad for being a dick to that unknown woman. Despair rose in my chest again, and no amount of alcohol or orgasms could seem to keep it away for very long. I was devolving into a self-absorbed monster, needing the next drink or the next orgasm to hide my own shame and guilt. Unfortunately, they never did, and I was back to needing more.

I sat at my desk the next day with my forehead in my hand. My temple was still throbbing from all of the alcohol I'd had the night before, and why the fuck did I have so many windows in my office? The sun was streaming in brightly, and making me nauseous.

Reaching over, I pulled a large manilla envelope off of my mail stack and tore it open. Inside I found the case file for Rocky's murder, with the added evidence found from the local clinic. It laid out just what Red had told us about "Jenna Gambelli," her alias. The doctors noted forced trauma, assault, rape... and the recent loss of a two-month old fetus due to excessive drug exposure and trauma.

I stared at the photos and documents in disbelief. It was clearly her. She hadn't been lying. Shame flared in me, threatening to bring me to my knees. I had treated her badly too. I would never be able to forgive myself.

I pushed the paperwork away from me, as if I was pushing back the truth, refusing to see it. As my hand came back a small detail caught my eye.

Jenna Gambelli. Gambelli was Victor's last name, but Jenna... The name of Max's girlfriend. Was it a coincidence? How many Jenna's are there out there? It's not a rare name, but it's also not that common.

I pulled Max's card out of my wallet. It was time to set up that get together.

Chapter 14

Red

I knew I had to call Amber, she was my best shot at getting answers and giving me closure on Bax. So why was it so hard to push the dial icon? My heart squeezed as I stared at the screen of my cell phone. Amber brought up so many mixed feelings from my past.

We had been best friends during high school. You never found Amber or me without Jenna and Andrew, and Andrew was gay, so it was like we were all girlfriends. We were a foursome, always there for each other, until we weren't.

I knew Amber had a crush on Victor, but Victor and I had been dating in secret for years. He even got me pregnant, not that I could tell anyone. If my family ever found out, they would have hurt him, bad. So he pretended to date Amber, my best friend, while he and I were together.

I had to listen to Amber talk about her boyfriend, and how much they loved each other, when he was loving me in secret. It was the perfect cover, but it made me physically sick, and I hated every minute of it. I couldn't tell her; if she told my family out of betrayal, they would have hurt Vic. I was stuck in the middle, knowing the truth. The guilt consumed me, and yet I loved him. I begged him to break it off with her, but he seemed to think it was a convenient relationship to pull everyone's attention away from us. I had worked up the courage to break it off with Vic, right before I found out I was pregnant. I never even got the chance to tell him he was going to be a father before Rocky grabbed me, and my world changed forever.

After I left they continued to date for a while, but it never worked out. She never found out about Vic and I, and the secret felt like a chasm between us. Maybe that's why I hadn't stayed in touch with her as well as I should have. I could never break her heart and tell her the truth, and I could never look her in the eye knowing it.

I clenched my eyes shut and pushed the button, as I let out a slow breath.

"Nat!" She squealed as she answered.

"Hey, Amber!" I tried to sound happy, but it sounded flat to my ears.

"I haven't heard from you in ages! How have you been?" she chirped.

"Well..." My stomach heaved. "I've been better. I'm sorry to do this, but I'm actually calling for your professional services," I said.

"You need a private investigator? I'm your girl! What can I do for you?" She was always so cheerful, and it made me hate myself a little bit more.

"Well, there was this cop in Boston; he was a detective who eventually made Chief. His name was Bill Murphy. Well, his wife Sophia disappeared about fifteen years ago," I recounted.

"Wait... Do you think your family had her..." She hesitated. My friends all knew who my family was, I was still a Giovanni then.

"No... actually, I think she left. Not because she wanted to, but because she might have had to. Anyway, I need her found. She has a son about our age, Baxter Murphy, and I was hoping you could find her for him." I let out another deep breath, having finally gotten it out.

"Well, I can't promise anything, but you know I'll do my best," she said cheerfully.

"I appreciate it, Amber. Just send me the invoice, it's an open budget, so spare no expense. I can send you her son's contact info, in case you find anything," I said.

"Oh, I love open budget jobs!" she said with a laugh. "I get to pull out all of the fun resources!"

I tried to chuckle along with her, but I was dying inside, and just wanted to get off of the call.

"Hey...," she said suddenly, "Did you get the invite to Jenna's wedding? It's on New Year's Eve, in Boston! Are you going?!" In my mind's eye, I could see her bouncing up and down on the balls of her feet.

"Yeah, I got the invitation," I said sadly. "I'm going to try. I may not be able to get away." My thoughts circled around Rocky's case; for all I knew, I might be in prison by then.

"Oh, you HAVE to come!" she whined. "Andrew will be there too! He has a new boyfriend, you know; it seems serious."

"I will do my best," I said, forcing cheer into my voice. "Oh, hey, I have to run! But send me an invoice, okay! Hopefully I'll see you at the wedding!" The lie fell off of my tongue like lead.

I fell onto the couch heavily. I was flooded with guilt, just like every time I talked with Amber, but now I was also seething with bitterness and jealousy. I loved Jenna, and I was glad she had found her "Mr. Right," but I was still too raw from my own betrayal not to feel feral at thinking about the "happily ever after" I so desperately wanted, and could never have.

Baxter

I stepped into the busy restaurant. It was a Saturday night, and most restaurants in the area were booked solid with holiday parties and family get-togethers. The noise level was high, more of what I was used to at a bar, rather than a five-star restaurant. I worked my way through the crowd, and finally spotted Max standing near the bar with a few friends; it still took me several minutes to get to him through the sea of people coming and going between tables.

"Bax!" Max grinned at me. "You remember my brother Ed? And this is Andrew."

I remembered Max's brother, and shook his hand. I turned to Andrew, having never met him, and instantly he reminded me of Fiske. The man was well-muscled, but not bulky. He had a feline-quality about him, like a large predator cat. He had waves of golden hair that must drive the women crazy, and a million-watt smile. I had a feeling he was gay; not that I cared, it's just one of those details my mind categorized. I shook his hand, and noticed he gave me a quick once over before smiling again. *Did he just check me out?*

Before I could say anything Max brought the attention back to him.

"So the ladies are all in the private room in the back, having their bridal shower, I thought we could head back to my place for a little poker tonight." He smiled slyly.

"Can Daniel meet us there?" Andrew asked.

Max laughed. "Andrew, it's supposed to be a night without the girlfriends."

Andrew laughed along with him, "Well, technically, he's not my GIRLfriend."

"Stop right there," Max said, holding his hands up. "I don't need any details. Yes, of course he's invited."

"I'm just going to use the men's room; I'll meet you at your place," I said, making my way towards the back of the restaurant, leaving them to pay their bar tab.

I was trying to think of a way to spin it so that I could either stay here at the restaurant, or leave Max's early to return. I needed to speak to Jenna, to see if she had a connection to Red. I didn't even understand why I needed to know, but I did. I felt like Jenna might hold the key to that first phone call I witnessed. Maybe she would tell me it was all a big misunderstanding... but I already knew better.

As luck would have it, as I rounded the corner where the bathrooms were located I saw Jenna walking toward me, and shot a prayer of thanks to heaven. She was gorgeous, and I watched her body move as she approached.

"Jenna!" I greeted her.

She eyed me warily; she clearly knew that she had met me before, but I could see her working it out in her head, trying to figure out where.

"I met you at the Holiday Gala," I said to put her out of her misery. "I'm Baxter Murphy, a friend of Max's."

Her eyes lit up. "Oh yes!" She smiled wide. "I remember you. They aren't still here, are they?" She asked, her brows pulling down.

I laughed. "They're just leaving."

She seemed to relax at that.

"Hey, I wanted to ask you a question; this may sound kind of strange, but I have a friend, Natalie Brooks. I'm wondering if you know her. She grew up around here, and I know she had a friend named Jenna." I tried to look curious; 'just another dumb guy.'

I saw the wall come up behind her eyes, and knew I had not succeeded in coming off casual at all. Her demeanor shifted instantly, and her body stiffened.

"I'm sorry," she said flatly. "I can't help you. If you'll excuse me." She stepped around me gracefully and quickly, rushing back to her party without a backwards glance.

That was a "yes."

I watched her go back to their private room, and another woman met her at the door; another hot body and nice face. *Did hot women all travel in packs?* The other woman was shorter than Jenna, and curvier, with amazing thick hair that seemed dark until it caught the light; there were golden red highlights that glowed around her like a halo.

The mystery woman reached for the door and caught my eye, smiling a very flirty smile as she looked me up and down, before she closed the door, ending my pursuit of Jenna.

I made my way over to Max's house. A part of me was in no mood to be social, but another part of me knew that I didn't want to be alone either. By the time I got there the guys had set the table up with pizza on the breakfast bar, and scotch all around. As I sat down Max handed me a cigar and then lit it.

Overall, it was an enjoyable evening. We played poker for hours, and laughed. Ed always seemed like he had a stick up his ass, but even he managed to loosen up a little bit. Daniel, Andrew's boyfriend, finally showed up and the fun really began. He was a pitcher for the Boston Red Sox, and I have to admit that I was very excited to get to meet him, never mind play poker with him. He ended up getting most of my money, and I didn't even care.

I had forgotten all about Jenna and her connection with Red, enjoying the company of other guys, when Jenna came up in conversation conveniently. It turned out that Andrew was her best friend, and had been since high school. I continued playing my losing hand while I fished for information nonchalantly.

"You went to school with Jenna, huh? Did you have any other hot friends from high school I should know about, since Jenna's about to be taken off the market?" I smirked.

"A few, actually." He smirked back. "But I don't know if you could handle them." He laughed.

"Who was the most untamed? SHE'S the one I want. Give me a name," I challenged him.

"Nat," he said without hesitation. "But I always called her 'Brat' because she was one. But I would never set you up with her," he said with mock sincerity.

"And why not?" I asked with mock indignation.

"Because she would hand you your ass, that's why." Andrew chuckled. "I watched her take down five black belts one time... together, mind you, not one at a time. And she was blindfolded. She didn't understand the meaning of the word quit," he said. "The woman is lethal, in more ways than one." He focused on his hand suddenly, before dropping his cards. "I'm out."

I felt the shift in the mood, even though no one said anything, and realized that the conversation was closed. I moved on to another topic casually.

I had my answer. It had been Red.

We played on, which resulted in me losing a lot of money, and then everyone said their goodbyes. I was exhausted, and wanted nothing more than to go home and get some rest, but I couldn't resist going back to the restaurant, where I knew their bar would still be open. I didn't know what I thought I would gain by doing it, Lord knew I needed the sleep. But I wondered if the girls would be tying up their party, and I might have another opportunity to get more information. It was a long-shot, and I wasn't optimistic, but I still made my way back there.

The restaurant was no longer serving dinner, but the bar was still open, with a fair number of people enjoying holiday cheer. I took a seat at the bar where I could see the door to the private room out of the corner of my eye. As I waited I ordered a scotch, and pretended to read something on my phone, but before my drink could even arrive I watched as a waitress came out of the room with a tray filled with empty glasses. The room was empty behind her. They were already gone, and I sighed.

The bartender put my scotch down, and I reached for my wallet to pay so that I could make a hasty retreat for some much needed sleep, but a hand perched gently on my arm.

"Is this seat taken?" a warm feminine voice asked, and I turned.

Standing next to me was the auburn haired beauty I had seen with Jenna in the private room, the one who had eyed me like a snack before shutting the door.

"It is now," I said, going into full flirt mode. She was no Red, but I couldn't have Red, so she was a nice consolation.

"I saw you earlier," she said, before ordering her own drink, and then turned to me coyly. "Have you been here this whole time?" Her hand touched mine on the bar 'accidentally.' I could see that her nipples were hard through her dress, which meant if I played my cards right I'd be getting some action tonight.

"No...," I said honestly. She knew Jenna, and Jenna and Max were an item. If I lied, it would get back to her, and I didn't need drama. "But I did return," I said, raising both an eyebrow and my glass as hers arrived.

"I see that," she purred, her finger tracing up the back of my hand.

"I'm Murphy," I said, extending my hand.

"Amber," she said, taking it in a quick shake, and then dropping her hand right next to mine on the bar again.

"Did you and the girls have fun tonight?" I asked, trying to be vague enough that it wouldn't look like I was fishing for information.

She lit up. "We did!" She smiled broadly. "Jenna is so happy! We were friends in high school you know! We were the 'Four Amigos!'" She laughed, letting me know she had already had quite a bit of alcohol before sitting at the bar.

"'Four Amigos?' Just the two of you?" I asked, smirking. "What kind of math did they teach you in that high school?"

She batted my arm playfully with her hand. "NO... (giggle) Jenna and I were two of the four, Nat and Drew were the other two! That makes FOUR," she pronounced triumphantly.

Bingo.

"Indeed it does!" I agreed with her, still chuckling.

She threw her drink back in a very unladylike fashion, and then shook her head and shivered as the heat of the drink worked its way down her throat.

"Hey, Murph..." She placed her glass on the bar emphatically, as she looked at me with hunger in her eyes. "You wanna get out of here and fuck?" The ends of her lips quirked up as she looked at me in challenge, daring me.

"Don't have to ask me twice," I said casually, swallowing my own drink. I dropped some bills on the bar to cover our drinks, and we made our way out... to her place, not mine.

She wasted no time getting us into her apartment, and we never made it past the living room. Amber was like a starving woman, and she was all over me. She knew what she wanted, and wasn't waiting either... she reminded me of Red. I shoved that thought out of my head as she shoved my pants down and face-planted on my cock. I groaned with satisfaction... she knew what she was doing! Again, my mind flashed to Red, and I had to push the thought back and focus.

Before long I was on top of her, pounding her hard. For such a small woman, she liked it extremely rough, and kept pushing me to go harder and faster. She placed my hands on her throat, wanting pressure, and begged for spankings. Then she was riding me, raking her nails down my abs and biting my shoulders like an animal. But when I went to take her doggie-style I got the biggest surprise of all...

Her eyes turned to look over her shoulder demurely, her ass cheeks on display in front of me, and her pussy dripping.

"Fuck my ass, Murphy," she purred.

I froze. Instantly all I could see was Red in front of me, telling me not to do it. Uncontrollable guilt surged through me, and I lost my hard-on immediately.

"Hmmm... not an ass guy, huh? I'm kinda surprised," she said matter of factly.

It was cold as I made my way back to my car in the early hours of that December morning. I had lived in Massachusetts my whole life and I still hated the fucking cold. Thinking of what we had just done kept my blood pumping; Amber was a lot like Red, and had I not met Red first, Amber would have been my dream girl. But I had met Red first, and she had ruined me.

I did get her number, but I didn't know if I would see her again. What was the point? I'd just compare her to Red, until I lost my desire. I had gotten the information I needed from her, she was no longer of any use to me, unless she could give me more insight into Red.

Four days later I was cursing at the snow for falling. I was really done with the cold, and I hated having to drive with people who couldn't drive in snow. I was fine... it was them who made the road a hazard. I shook my head as another idiot tried to drive too fast, and wound up spinning out and off of the road.

I had just put the car in park in the employee parking lot when my cell phone rang; I was surprised to see Amber calling me. I hadn't contacted her at all, and expected she would do likewise. Out of curiosity, I answered.

"Murphy." I kept my tone professional.

"Hey Murph!" she chirped.

"Hi Amber." I put a little bit of warmth into it, but just a little.

If she made this a habit, I would have to be blunt with her and tell her I wasn't looking for a relationship. Still, she was now a friend of Max's, and I didn't want to burn that bridge by being a douche.

"Murph, I have a weird favor to ask..." She hesitated, and I internally groaned.

Thus it begins...

She continued, "So you know Max and Jenna? Well, They're getting married on New Year's Eve, and I'm one of her brides-maids, and I don't have a date. I know you don't know me hardly at all, but I was wondering if you would go with me? I mean, you are friends with Max and Jenna... so it wouldn't be like going to a stranger's wedding..." She was babbling rapidfire, trying to talk me into it.

"I'd love to go," I said more warmly, a smile spreading across my face; not because I wanted to go with her, but because I might have an opportunity to get more information on Jenna and Red.

There was silence.

"You would?" she asked incredulously, and then her tone shifted suddenly. "I mean... that's great!" she squealed. "This way I have a date, you get to see your friends get married, and if all goes well, you're guaranteed to get some! I'd say that's a win-win-win!"

I laughed, but really found it a little presumptuous to assume I'd want to tap her again, but she was hot, so... maybe I would.

"Can you text me the details?" I asked.

"Yeah, of course! Thank you, Murph! I will *totally* make it worth your while," she teased suggestively.

My stomach felt queasy. "I'm just happy to help," I said with much more enthusiasm than I felt.

Maybe I wouldn't be tapping her again.

Fuck. Red HAD ruined me.

Chapter 15

Red

The days were long and dull when you really couldn't go out and get a job, and only left the house for absolute necessities. I felt like I was in prison already. So when Agent Pierce called me in the middle of December, I was ready to be done with the whole Rocky situation. It felt like an overdue pregnancy, sitting on my bladder and pushing at my spine; I wanted it behind me.

I was hauled down to the FBI headquarters again, and followed the same procedure as the last time: blue visitor's badge, hornery old fuck escorting me upstairs, and "Mr. Personality Pierce" meeting me in the elevator lobby. Except this time I wasn't brought into an interrogation room. I sat at what looked like a conference room table. Agent Pierce sat across from me, and next to him was a smaller woman whom he never introduced. She eyed me appraisingly, but never said a word.

I sat waiting in awkward silence for something to happen, but everyone seemed to be waiting on something I wasn't privy to. When five minutes turned into fifteen, I was about to open my mouth to complain, when the door suddenly opened, and a middle-aged man in an expensive suit sauntered in.

He stood out. His suit was designer, and tailored. Even though he was not handsome, he obviously took care of himself; I noticed his nails were manicured, and his shoes were expensive and polished. He made the FBI agents look like they were Walmart quality, next to his smooth composure and sharp appearance.

"Sorry I'm late,..." he said in a voice that told me he wasn't sorry in the least. "My name is Matteo Bianchi, I'm here to represent Miss Brooks."

My head whipped around so fast I hurt myself. Matteo was extending his beefy hand to the two other agents, who both shook it, but stared daggers at him the whole time. I could feel the anger radiating off of them in waves. I had to assume this was a new development for them, one they didn't like at all. Hope welled in my chest.

"If we can get started,..." Pierce said through clenched teeth, taking his seat.

I shook Matteo's hand, and the rest of us all took our seats as well.

Pierce cleared his throat, and stared straight at me, his jaw still tight. "The Bureau is prepared to offer you a plea deal for Involuntary Manslaughter in exchange for a guilty plea. This would mean you would serve less than eight years in a federal prison, instead of life. I think it's the best offer you are going to get." His look was calculating and condescending, it was clear he thought he was doing me a favor. And maybe he was.

"No deal," Matteo said without hesitation.

"Wha–" Both Pierce and I spun to him in stereo.

Matteo smiled a slick smile at Pierce. "Agent Pierce, aren't you going to tell my client the rest of the revelations about this case, before you offer her a plea deal that is not in her best interest?" he asked smoothly.

Pierce was grinding his jaw so hard I could hear it. A vein throbbed on his neck as he glared at Matteo. I watched as his hands clenched and unclenched on the table in front of him.

"I don't see how it's relevant–" He started to bite out.

Matteo laughed out loud, a braying mocking laugh. "You don't see how it's *relevant*?" he hooted. "You have received a signed confession, and two affidavits putting the confessor at the scene of the crime that day and at the time of the crime, as well as providing motive to commit the murder! How can that be irrelevant to my client?"

"She confessed as well," Pierce spat. "Perhaps they worked together?"

Matteo chuckled as if Pierce was clearly a fool. "So, you think *my client*, who had been chained to a bed for two weeks, suffered blood loss from losing a child and getting no medical care, as well as being malnourished and suffering the effects of long-term sedatives and abuse... you think SHE clearly killed a two hundred and sixty pound male, instead of the prostitute who was relatively healthy, and can be proven to be there at the time, and who also confessed and has witnesses?

"Where is your murder weapon, if you're going to pin this on my client? Where are your witnesses? You have two confessions; are you willing to gamble everything and lose this case for good? I'd suggest you think long and hard about that, Agent." He sat back, placing one hand over the other on the table. "No deal," he repeated calmly, with a smirk.

An hour later I walked out of the federal building and turned my face up to the sun, with a huge smile. I was a free woman at last. Rocky couldn't haunt me any longer. I didn't have to run anymore.

"You did good in there, kid." Matteo shook my hand with a smile. "Go enjoy the rest of your life."

"Thank you, Matteo." I couldn't help it, I threw my arms around him as the tears started to fall. He just smiled as he patted my back. "The... the person who confessed... what's going to happen to them?" I had to ask. I couldn't live with myself if someone else got the punishment that was intended for me.

He smiled at me in a very paternal way, "You don't have to worry about that, Renatta. She died five years ago. No one is going to prison today."

I smiled back with relief. "Oh, Matteo?... Tell Tony I said thank you too, please," I whispered, before pulling away.

As he walked away, I turned and walked in the other direction down the street: a free woman.

Baxter

"Are you FUCKING KIDDING ME?!" I screamed into the phone, before I hung it up. My hand curled around it, and I pulled my arm back instinctively, but stopped myself from hurling it into a wall. Somehow some hooker had confessed, and provided enough evidence to make it almost impossible to prosecute Red.

She was free. She was no longer a suspect.

I should have been enraged at the circumvention of justice. I knew, I just KNEW, that she had killed Rocky. She was the real murderer. But somehow, someway, someone else blocked the path to true justice. A murderer was still free, on the streets tonight.

I was mad that my case got derailed, yes. So why was I secretly ready to weep with joy? Why did the knowledge that Red was finally free lift a weight off of my chest I hadn't even realized I carried? Why did I want to celebrate her victory?

It wasn't my victory.

She wasn't mine.

Suddenly I ached with the loss of her, realizing the full depth of what I had lost. Now that she wasn't mine to have, she was free to be had. It was so fucked up. I wanted so badly to reach out and pull her to me, to hold her close, to smell the scent of her skin. I wanted to be there for her, to be the one she trusted again. But I had not only burned that bridge, I had fucking blown it up behind me.

I could raise a toast to her victory, but I would still be drinking it alone.

Red

I wasted no time booking flights to go back to Boston. It seemed like a miracle; in just a few short weeks my entire life of running had come to an end. I could go home and visit, without fear of being recognized or shot on the street. I could attend my best friend's wedding like a normal person. I also didn't have to worry about going to prison for Rocky's murder. It was more than I deserved, but I have to be honest when I say that I was never more grateful.

I couldn't keep the tears from forming in my eyes when I stepped out of the terminal at Logan Airport, a place I hadn't been since I was a kid. I saw Vic waiting behind the security barriers and made my way over quickly, the tears flowing openly. As I reached him he grabbed me into a bear hug and lifted me off of the ground. When he brought me back down his mouth was on mine instantly, tongue pressing into my mouth.

I pulled back in shock, my hands on his chest.

His cheeks flamed. "I've missed you, Nat. Don't make this weird." His eyes were tight with annoyance.

I honestly didn't know how to react to that. I didn't still have feelings for him, not after fifteen years of just trying to survive, and having not seen him in person. He had greeted me with an open-mouthed kiss, and a tongue down my throat. I didn't think *I* was the one "making it weird."

He tugged my hand quickly and pulled me behind him. "C'mon, let's get you out of here."

I let him pull me, as my brain struggled to catch up. Thankfully, Victor took me straight to Jenna's new place, a brownstone where she was living with Max. It was a shock to see her living in such an expensive place, after her humble beginnings, but I'd never seen her happier. She introduced me to her fiance, Max, and it was clear they were both smitten; the looks they gave each other were seeped in love, and they couldn't stop touching each other. I was so happy for my best friend, but the sight of their happiness was almost too much to bear after I had tasted it myself, and lost it.

Victor dropped my bag in the hallway. "I have a few errands to run, but I'll be back, Nat."

He leaned in and kissed me on the forehead quickly before rushing back out the door. Jenna shot me a confused look, but said nothing as I gently shook my head. Max said his goodbye as well, pulling Jenna in for a full lip-locked devouring kiss, and it was a moment before he finally pulled himself back, obviously aroused, and managed to get himself out the door too, while Jenna and I both stood with flushed faces.

Once he was gone Jenna grabbed my bag and headed for the stairs. "Let's get you settled in, and then I want to hear everything!" She shot me a pointed look over her shoulder.

Once in her guest room, it was like we were seventeen again; like we had never been apart. Jenna was always my best friend and closest confidant, and I hadn't realized how much I missed that, missed her, being away. I had done it to protect myself, but I still missed her.

First she filled me in on her relationship with Max, and honestly I had a hard time seeing how they ever managed to overcome all of their ups and downs. She also filled me in on the job she had given Victor, and why she had needed it. I just nodded without judgment. That was the world I came from, where you did what you had to do. And I was relieved that she called me, and her problems were over.

Jenna was a fierce woman, we trained in martial arts to-gether for years, so I knew it would take a very special and very strong man to be the one for her. Max seemed to fit the bill, and in the end their love had overcome everything.

Then it was my turn. Again, my heart ached.

I fumbled with my hands in my lap as I relayed the story of how I had met Bax, and our whirlwind sex life. Jenna already knew about my gift, so I could tell her all of the details. Only she and Victor knew that part of me... well, and now Bax. I brought her up to the day I kicked him out, and then told her about getting acquitted of the murder charges. When I looked at her face, her eyes were wide. I had never discussed the murder with her; she had been shocked when I disappeared, but I had explained later I needed to escape my family, and she had been a good friend and never questioned me.

For a minute she said nothing, and my insecurity rose. She had always been my best friend; was this the one place she would draw the line? Would she no longer be my best friend once she knew I was a murderer? Fear gripped my heart with icy fingers as I waited.

And a moment later she grabbed me into a deep hug, squeezing me tight. She said nothing, but I understood. A sob of relief burst out of my chest, and tears began to fall, as I finally found a sense of home again with my bestie.

Jenna pulled back quickly. "Nat. There's something I have to tell you! I met–"

But before she could continue there was a high-pitched squeal from the hallway.

"NAAAAAAAAAAAAAAAATTTT!!!" Amber bounded into the room like a kangaroo on crack, and leapt onto the bed with us.

I swiped at my tears quickly, but I knew my face was swollen and red. She noticed it too.

"Hey, what happened?!" Her smile fell, and concern filled her eyes.

"We–" Jenna started but I spoke over her.

"I'm just getting over a head injury. I have spells sometimes, and headaches. Nothing to worry about, I took some pain-killers." I smiled at her reassuringly.

I didn't know why I lied to her; I didn't know what it was in me that didn't want to share my story with her like I had Jenna. But there was something in my gut that warned me. I chanced a look at Jenna, and while her head was cocked with curiosity, she only nodded her head in understanding.

"Yeah..." Jenna picked up. "She just needs some rest. Come on, we can go to my room for a while. We'll catch up later."

Jenna climbed off of the bed, shooing a reluctant Amber with her, but as they got to the door Amber turned and looked at me.

"Oh, Nat, good news! I found that woman you were looking for! I've sent you my invoice... but I knocked a few hundred off." She laughed. "I took some payment from the client."

I froze. She had found Bax's mother... and *taken payment from Bax?!* My blood started to run cold, and a sweat broke out on my forehead and lower back.

"What do you mean?" I asked quietly and slowly, as if her answer would somehow be as clear and concise.

"Well, I met him! Of course, he didn't know who I was, but I had looked him up, so I recognized him. You didn't tell me he was man-candy! I took him home and had my way with him!" She laughed. "You'd have loved him, Nat; he's a little tentative, but trainable! Except he doesn't do anal. I asked him to, and he completely wilted! What the fuck? What guy turns down anal?" She laughed again, oblivious to my distress.

Oh God! It really was like we were all seventeen again. My stomach heaved, and I launched off the bed and into the bathroom just as all of the contents in my stomach came back up.

"...head injury," I heard Jenna saying in the bedroom, before she was beside me while I retched up nothing but bile.

"It's going to be okay," Jenna cooed beside me, smoothing circles on my back, but I knew it was NOT going to be okay. Nothing was going to be okay. My stomach kept trying to unload, while there was nothing left to purge.

I knew he had used me. I knew he didn't care. But the thought of him with AMBER. Of all of the people in the world WHY HER? All those years ago I had to share Victor with her, when he was my world, and now here she is telling me all about her exploits with Bax.

I must be a horrible human being to deserve this, twice.

Jenna helped me get cleaned up, once the heaving stopped. I couldn't stop the tears, but at least I wasn't bent over the toilet any longer. Just as she got me settled on the bed there was a knock at the door, and it creaked open to reveal Victor peeking in. I tried to stifle the groan in my throat. I didn't want to have to deal with his drama right then either.

Without asking, he made his way to my side silently. Jenna gave me a questioning look, and I nodded to her, giving her permission to leave us alone together. I really didn't want to deal with the elephant between us, but it was probably better to just get it over with, since I was already an emotional mess anyway.

The door snicked closed, quietly.

"Are you okay?" Vic asked quietly, studying my puffy eyes. He reached a hand out to push a red curl off of my face.

"I will be," I said flatly, without energy.

"I've missed you." His words were urgent and full of... passion? Hope?

"Vic, I..." I didn't want to break his heart again, but I couldn't lead him on either.

I wasn't seventeen anymore. I had lived a whole life without him, and I had grown out of the childish crush I felt when we were younger. There would always be a tender place in my heart for him, my first love, but I was no longer in love with him.

"Vic, we were kids..." I started.

"I know that," he snapped quickly, his brows drawn with annoyance. "But you're here now. I was hoping we could start over. I was hoping we could..."

I shook my head sadly, letting my eyes close.

"Victor, I loved you with everything in me when we were kids. But I've grown up. I've had a life without you. I will always care about you Vic, but I'm not that girl in love with you anymore." I looked up at his eyes, begging him to understand.

His face became a mask of guarded features, something I recognized from dealing with my family, but there was no hiding the hurt in his eyes.

"Is this because of that fuck-head Bax?" he spit out.

"No." I shook my head. "Vic, even before Bax I was living my life, moving on. I knew we were never going to be together, and I had to go on living. You need to go on living." I turned back to him again. "You deserve someone who gives you her whole heart. I can't give you that anymore," I said sadly.

I could see his eyes gloss with unshed tears, tears he would never allow to fall in front of me. He leaned down and kissed me on the forehead, chastely.

"I will always be here for you," he whispered, and then turned to let himself out of the room, closing the door quietly behind him.

My breath whooshed out of my body with all of the tension I had been holding in, and in the privacy of the bedroom the tears started flowing.

Baxter

I arrived at Max's to find a note on the door. He had run out for a few things, and asked me to wait for him, so I let myself in. The brownstone was impressive, not that I'd tell him that, with wood finishes and expensive touches. My bachelor pad apartment couldn't even compare; which is why I'd never tell him. We still had a competitive streak between us, even after all of these years. I allowed myself to look around as I stood between the living room and the kitchen.

I turned as I heard steps coming down the staircase, and was surprised to see Victor, in Max's house of all places. His eyes met mine, and there was murder in them. I had no idea what the fuck had set him off, but he was clearly furious.

"She doesn't want to see YOU," he hissed as he stomped over to me.

I had no clue what he was talking about.

"Who?" I asked, keeping my face neutral, but allowing my own heat to meet his.

"Nat. I think you've fucked her over enough. Leave her alone." He was in my face, inches away, and although he was shorter and smaller than I was, he was making the implied threat clear.

Nat was here?! My heart flew into my throat, and I had all I could do to try to remain unaffected by this news. I wanted to push him out of the way and run up the stairs.

"Is that what she told you?" I asked casually, knowing it would piss him off, but hoping he'd spill and tell me what I was up against. If there was *any* chance I could get Red back, I was going to grab it with both hands.

"She didn't need to," he gritted. "It's written all over her face. She told me you ghosted her, so stay GONE," he seethed. His jaw was tight, and his eyes were narrowed with malice.

Before I could retort a high-pitched squeal filled the room, followed by the pounding of steps.

"MUUUUUUUUUUUUURPH!!!"

I looked up in time to see Amber throwing herself at me, launching her arms around me with such force I had to take a step back, and then she had her mouth on mine possessively. I pulled away, untangling her arms and lips, and I caught the sneer on Victor's face as he shook his head with disgust.

"Oh yeah," he scoffed. "You care about her SOOO much."

"Victor? What are *you* doing here?" Amber suddenly noticed him, and pulled away from me like I was diseased. Her cheeks were flushed as she stared at him, and something like guilt passed through her eyes.

"I was just checking in on Nat," he said casually, suddenly very cool. I noticed that Amber suddenly seemed to stiffen up; her back straight and her jaw clenched, but she said nothing as she glared at Victor.

"I need to go," Victor said suddenly as he turned for the door. "Just remember what I said, Loverboy."

"Wait... what's going on?" Amber suddenly became aware of the tension still sizzling between Vic and I.

"Nothing," I stated flatly, watching Vic leave. "Nothing is going on. I was just leaving too," I added, needing to get away from this place. Max could wait.

"I'll come with you," she said, pulling back toward me again as Victor was no longer with us.

"That's not necessary," I stated as I turned, but her arm snaked through mine as she grabbed her purse.

"I insist," she said, as she dragged me toward the door.

Could this day get any more fucked up?

Chapter 16

Baxter

I left Max's place with my emotions all over the place. I had no idea what Vic's involvement with Red was, or Amber's with him, and I honestly couldn't give a fuck about any of that drama. I had enough to think about just dealing with Red.

It didn't help that I had Amber attached to my arm like a damn leech. She was uncharacteristically quiet as we drove; not at all her usual cheery self. I can't say that I was too upset by it, as she was usually annoying. I had never planned on anything other than a night of fun with her, so what the fuck was she still doing in my car?

I realized I really didn't have anywhere to go, and I didn't want to bring Amber to my place. There wasn't a chance in hell she'd set foot into my private sanctuary. So instead I took us to a small restaurant nearby, hoping I could buy her a meal and then get rid of her. Maybe I could even get a little insight into what had happened at Max's place.

I parked, and opened her door, walking her to the restaurant; she remained quiet and didn't argue. The small Italian place was dark and private, and importantly, quiet. Quaint tables with red and white checkered tablecloths gave the place an "old world" feel. We both ordered drinks and a light meal. I waited until we had both taken a few sips before I was ready to start peppering her for information, but she beat me to the punch.

"How do you know Victor?" she asked. It wasn't what she asked, but *how* she asked it. There was an emotion behind it but I couldn't pin it down, maybe irritation?

"I met him through a case," I said.

Her eyes narrowed, and she took another sip of her drink before asking, "Sooo, you work with him?" Her voice was dripping with accusation. She knew I worked for the Bureau, so I could see where this was going.

"No. I don't," I stated emphatically, letting her know I was not a dirty cop... well, not the dirtiest at least. "But my father did. Vic helped get me evidence against him," I added.

She seemed to relax at that. "What happened to your father? Is he in prison?"

I sighed. "No. He's dead." I stated it as a fact, but I couldn't help the tiny bit of hurt that I still felt at losing him; even if he was an asshole, he was still my father.

"Oh...," she said quietly. But she couldn't have felt too bad because she followed that with, "So did you kill him?"

"What kind of a question is *that*?" I spit, annoyed at her tactlessness. "No. I did not kill my father. My partner did when he shot... a witness," I concluded, not willing to give her anymore.

She stared into her glass, considering, and fortunately, she didn't push any further.

"So how do *you* know Victor?" I finally asked. I had a pretty good idea already.

"Oh... uh..." Her cheeks flushed, and she suddenly found her drink very interesting.

My suspicions were confirmed, she had slept with him.

"We, uh... we used to date. A long time ago," she finally supplied, never looking up.

"How long ago?" I asked, not even caring that I was prying.

"My senior year in high school, and the next," she said, but instead of looking nostalgic, she looked pretty angry.

"Did he break your heart?" I guessed.

"No... and yes," she answered vaguely. "It's complicated."

"I'm nothing, if not a good listener," I said more softly, hoping she'd volunteer more.

She sighed deeply, placing her glass on the table and washing her eyes over the room as if she wished she could avoid the topic.

"Victor always had a thing for Nat," she said with a little heat in her voice. It was obviously a sore spot for her, as she rubbed her fingers over her glass unconsciously. "I think he was cheating on me with her, but I could never prove it."

"What makes you think he cheated?" I asked gently, like a good friend would. It was probably a shit thing to do, to try to get her to trust me, but my gut said there was something important here I wasn't seeing.

Her eyes met mine for a moment, and I could see the pain in them before she looked away again.

"Well, a girl just knows... the way he looked at her, the way he'd drop everything if she called," she said.

"That doesn't mean anything necessarily," I said, trying to be gentle but supportive.

"No, no it doesn't. But I had been friends with Jenna for a few years, and Victor had known her most of her life." She paused, hesitated, before she started speaking again. "You have to understand that I wasn't very experienced... sexually, I mean... when I met Victor." Her cheeks turned crimson. "Jenna had shared her sexual experiences with me, it's what girls do; we talk. So I knew Jenna's 'tastes.' She liked rough sex, and she absolutely loved anal; like better than regular sex," she confided.

I tried to keep the look of shock off of my face. *Red loved anal?... so when we were together...* My cock hardened instantly, sending a jolt through my body.

Amber continued without noticing my discomfort. "So when I started having sex with Vic I found out he really liked rough sex too. I thought nothing of it. He taught me what he liked, and I grew to love it myself. Then he wanted anal, like all the time. He was obsessed with it." She paused for another drink. "It took me several months to realize that all of the things we did together were the same things Nat used to tell me she did with her lovers... It got me thinking."

Our food arrived, and we both picked at it. I tried to keep my body casual, but I was hanging on her every word.

"It could have been a coincidence," I said, unhelpfully.

"It *could* have been," she agreed. "But I was with Vic when we got her from Rocky's house one day. Rocky was supposed to be her boyfriend," she explained, not knowing I knew all about it. "Vic and I had been together when he got the call that she was in trouble, so of course he dropped everything, and I came along. He made me wait in the car while he went inside; I thought that was suspicious.

"When he brought her out she was a bloody mess. We both took her to the clinic and waited in the waiting room to find out how she was. He was having an absolute meltdown as we waited. I had never seen him that devastated before. She was my friend too, and I was upset, but he... he was just out of control. Something was just off. That was when we found out she lost a baby; a two-month old fetus." She looked me in the eye.

"She had been at Rocky's for two weeks, according to Vic, so someone else was the father," she supplied, her eyes as cold as ice. "Vic was devastated by that. He never really got over it. I couldn't understand why it bothered him so much unless it was HIS baby she lost." There was bitterness in her voice, and her lip curled slightly.

"Did you ever confront him?" I asked.

"What was the point? If they had lied all that time, why would he come clean?" She laughed mirthlessly. "Besides, Nat disappeared soon after that. I thought my problems were solved. I thought I finally had him to myself," she said.

"But?..." I pushed.

"But... I could never trust him again." She breathed out. "I would never know if Nat would just show up one day and he'd be gone. Or if he'd just cheat with someone else; I couldn't trust him not to lie. So I broke it off with him, and moved away to lick my wounds elsewhere," she finished and downed her drink.

"And now Nat is back, and Vic just showed up... I imagine that stirred up all sorts of feelings for you," I said.

"Look, it was a long time ago," she stated. "But even still, she hadn't even been back twenty four hours, and he came running like a lap dog. You don't find that a little odd?" She looked at me, the hurt still burning in her eyes. I could see she wanted me to validate her, to tell her how awful they were to hurt her that way.

"C'mon," I said, "Let's get you home." I paid the bill, and she let me walk her back to the car without comment, which was convenient, as I had nothing I could think to say to her about the whole situation.

I had some answers, but I also had a whole new stack of questions. *Were Red and Vic still involved, after all of this time? He had seemed so possessive at the house. Was there really no chance I'd ever get Red back? My stomach lurched.*

Red

A good night's sleep helped put things back into perspective. Bax was done and over; nevertheless, I was going to have to see him at the wedding, it turned out, and with Amber. But it wasn't about me, it was about Jenna and her big day. I was just going to have to put on my big-girl panties and deal with it. If Amber wanted Bax's level of fucked up, that was on her.

But I still couldn't help remembering what she said... *"Except he doesn't do anal. I asked him to, and he completely wilted!"* A small smile grew on my lips. *God, I hope that was because of ME. Petty, I know...*

Jenna was downstairs drinking coffee with Andrew when I finally descended, and I rushed to him for a big hug.

"There you are!" He smiled broadly as he hugged me and shook me back and forth like a rag doll.

"Drew, how is it possible that you've gotten even bigger?!" I laughed. The man was ridiculous with his muscles.

"And you haven't even seen my dick!" He smirked.

"Ewww... gross!" I squealed, scrunching my face and smacking his arm. He was like a brother to me, and the thought of seeing his junk was repulsive.

"Again, you haven't seen it. Don't judge." He chuckled.

I rushed around the table to sit next to Jenna, to demonstrate my disinterest. I knew he was kidding; this was our way. It always had been. The three of us together felt like family. I was realizing over and over again how much I had missed my friends.

"We're going to the dojo today to work out, you want to come?" She smiled at me.

"Of course I do!" I said enthusiastically. "But are you sure you want to do this so close to your wedding? You don't need a split lip in your wedding photos." I chuckled.

We had always trained HARD.

"No face shots," Andrew said, establishing the rules. "Can't mark up that pretty face of hers now can we, Brat?" He winked at me.

The doorbell rang before I could shoot off a response, and Jenna jumped from her chair to answer the door, while Andrew and I verbally sparred for a few moments, which turned into a wrestling match. By the time Jenna walked back into the room I was on Andrew's back, with his head in a headlock. I looked up to make a snarky comment and saw Bax standing behind her, a look of shock on his face. My heart sank.

That moment of distraction cost me, as Andrew flipped me over his shoulder easily, and flat onto my back on the carpet. He did it gently, though, the bastard.

Jenna scrambled over and helped me to my feet. Leaning in she whispered, "Bax is coming with us... will that be okay?" She nibbled her bottom lip with worry as she looked at me like I was fragile; which I was, but I would never admit. I got back on my feet quickly.

"Totally fine," I said flatly, while in my chest my heart beat a wild rhythm of rebellion. I could feel Bax watching me, but I refused to turn to him or give him my attention. I made sure I kept myself turned away from him at all times. I would get through this. *I could just ignore him, right?*

I couldn't just ignore him.

At the dojo Andrew was training Bax, who came in thinking that the Bureau had trained him to be the ultimate fighting machine. While Andrew never argued with him, he certainly did put a smackdown on him, repeatedly. I wish I had popcorn for that show. My pride for Andrew swelled a little each time he dropped Bax to the mat, or landed a good punch on his body, and I am not ashamed to admit I was jealous that it wasn't me. Bax finally had to concede he couldn't win against Andrew's level of proficiency, and to his credit, he asked Andrew to show him what to do. I almost felt proud of him...

Until I remembered what a lying sack of shit he was.

Meanwhile, Jenna and I picked up our bos, a type of staff, and began to work. It had been a long time since I had been in the dojo, or against someone as talented as Jenna, but it all came back to me as soon as the wood was swinging. We stepped, swung, grunted, thrusted, blocked, and repeated for the next hour. We were both dripping with sweat, and both sporting some nasty bruises on our arms and shins by the time we finally took a break. I know I definitely felt it in my body; I was out of shape, and breathing a lot harder than I should have been. I noticed Jenna was breathing a little heavier too, as she pulled out some bottles of water, so I felt slightly comforted.

After we drank some water, Andrew suggested a partner changeout, and asked Jenna if she would work with Baxter; but Bax immediately asked to work with me instead. I looked at him incredulously; *did he not remember our last encounter?*

"Oh..." Andrew interrupted. "I don't... think that's a good idea, buddy," he said slowly, his eyes shifting between us. Jenna jumped in, saying she'd be happy to work with Bax, but I wasn't going to play the victim. I told her I would work with Bax.

She and Andrew both eyed me warily. Jenna's eyes searched mine for the hurt, but a small smirk pulled at the corner of her lip when she didn't find it. She knew what I had in mind, and she turned to work with Andrew instead, pulling him to the other side of the mat. Andrew was still hesitant, but eventually gave in and went to work with Jenna.

"Open hand, no weapons," I said to Bax, all business, as he approached.

"Okay," he agreed easily, and then leaned in and said quietly, "Don't worry Red, I won't hurt you."

I burst out laughing, causing Jenna and Andrew to stop and stare at me for a moment before they went back to what they were doing.

"No..." I chuckled. "You won't."

The game was on.

We circled each other for a few moments, I was savoring this opportunity. I could pummel him within an inch of his life, legally, and he had literally asked for it. I was going to relish every moment.

He lunged, and I avoided easily. I took a shot at him and tagged him hard. *That would bruise.* I smiled to myself as we continued to circle.

"Red, I really want to talk to you," he said quietly, as we each evaluated our openings.

"People in hell want ice water," I replied casually, before kicking a shot at his quad and bringing him to his knee. *I know that fucking hurt.* I punched him in the jaw, snapping his head back. Then I stepped back, giving him an opportunity to get up and face me again.

"Red, please...," he said quietly, still circling, "Please let me talk to you."

"If you win this round, I'll talk to you," I said. Because there was no way in hell I was going to let him win.

He groaned. I feigned an uppercut, and then snuck another attack with my other hand; he was too slow to block the second, and my fist connected with his mouth, splitting his lip.

"No face shots!" Andrew scolded, having caught me.

We circled again, and I attacked again, landing shots. I noticed that Baxter wasn't attacking back, and was barely blocking me.

"Why aren't you attacking?" I asked, pissed.

"I don't want to fight you, Red. I want a chance to talk with you." There was sadness in his eyes, but I wasn't buying it.

"Well, you're not going to win it THAT way," I replied, as I swung again. He stepped out of the way, and I took advantage of his position to sweep his foot out from under him. He toppled over heavily, and I was on him like a monkey before he could blink. I had gotten six or seven good shots on his body, and another few on his face, before he could even get his hands in a defensive posture. I got him into a wrestling hold, and with my mouth beside his ear I said, "Thank you so much for not hurting me... THIS time."

Before I could move he answered quietly, "I thought you liked the way my cock felt sliding in and out of your tight little ass."

I stiffened, and in the heartbeat I hesitated, he flipped me, and had me crushed in an impossible hold beneath him. I could feel his erection jabbing into me, and it only made me more furious. I pushed and struggled, but it was no use. I was stuck.

"I think this means I win," he whispered into my ear with a slight chuckle, but I was too dumbfounded, and then pissed with myself, to say anything back to him. Bax released me and offered me a hand up, which I refused. I turned to see Andrew and Jenna staring at me with their jaws hanging open.

"What?" I asked, irritated. I could feel my cheeks getting redder by the moment.

"I think you're done for the day," Andrew said.

Jenna and I took off for the locker room, but not before I saw Bax shoot me a smug smile, his sweat pants still tenting in the front.

Bastard.

Chapter 17

Baxter

There wasn't a part of my body that didn't hurt, including my blue balls. While I had technically won the match, and would have my chance to talk to Red, I had paid for it. I was covered in bruises and welts, and she had split my lip and bruised my jaw. I moved really slowly to climb into the shower, hoping the hot water would help to get rid of some of the aches and pains.

Jenna had invited us all back for dinner at her place with Max, and while my body begged me to just lay down and die until I felt better, I was not going to miss an opportunity to be with Red. I don't know exactly when I had forgiven her for not telling me the truth... or maybe I hadn't. Maybe I just realized that I was too far gone for her to care about my pride. Either way, I wanted her back, and the thought that Victor might be trying to rekindle something with her lit a fire under me to claim her.

The shower did help, but only a little. I still walked with a slight limp as I made my way to the door and rang the bell. My breath left my mouth in foggy puffs in the cold December air while I waited.

"Come on in!" The door swung open, and Jenna smiled at me.

She took my coat and hung it in the closet, and I gave her a bottle of wine and a bottle of scotch I had brought with me.

She took them with thanks, and led me back into the dining room full of people.

Andrew, his boyfriend Daniel, and Max were standing in a corner, deep in animated discussion, while Amber and Red were at the table with Vic, obviously trying to make small talk, each of them looking uncomfortable.

"What happened to YOU?" The high pitched squeal pulled my attention to Amber, who was already racing over to me.

I froze, not sure what she was talking about until she brought her hand up to touch my lip, which instantly stung with pain.

"This?... Oh, it's nothing," I said dismissively, swatting her hand away.

Victor laughed loudly from the table, drawing everyone's attention. "Nothing, huh?" he said loudly, "Nat beat the ever loving crap out of you, Dude. You got your ass handed to you by a woman!" He threw his head back and laughed again.

I noticed no one else in the room thought it was that funny, especially Amber, who was suddenly livid.

"Of course she did," Amber spit under her breath, before dashing out of the room in a huff.

"What the fuck, Vic?" Red demanded, giving him an icy glare.

Victor jumped from his seat and ran after Amber, and we all heard the front door opening and closing with a loud thud. An awkward tension filled the room until Max cleared his throat and asked who wanted a drink; not surprisingly, we all did.

The rest of the evening went smoothly, partly due to the fact that Amber and Victor never returned, in my opinion. I watched Red across the room talking with Andrew, and I wondered if I could be lucky enough to have Amber and Victor reconnect, solely so that I would have Red to myself again while they were otherwise occupied. I wasn't going to hold my breath, but one could hope.

Red laughed at something Andrew was saying, and then she slowly turned so that our eyes met. For just a moment her laughing eyes made my heart squeeze with joy; until she remembered she didn't like me anymore, and her eyes went cold again. I thought she would turn her back on me, like she had all morning, but instead she turned and walked toward me.

My hands were sweating as she slowly made her way across the room to me. I had no idea what I was going to say to her. I suddenly felt pressure; the need to say the right thing. I needed for her to be mine again.

And then she was standing in front of me, drink in hand, eyeing me appraisingly.

"So, you and Amber?" She cut right to the chase.

I hadn't been expecting that, and my eyes closed on a groan.

"We're not a couple," I said. "She picked me up at a bar, it was just a one-time thing," I added, suddenly feeling the need to defend myself.

"Oh, I know," Red replied casually, and sipped her wine. "She told me about how disappointed you left her when you couldn't keep it up." A small smirk pulled at her kissable lips.

I nearly sprayed my drink as I choked on it.

"Excuse me?" I asked, incredulous.

"You forget, we've been friends for years. Girls talk," she said curtly. "She's under the impression that you have an aversion to anal sex," she added, a smile curling her mouth.

I could feel my cheeks reddening; not because of the accusation, she knew that wasn't true, but because of all of the things left unsaid between us. The fact that I stuck my dick in Amber was clearly an added challenge to overcome.

"Red, can I talk with you in private... please?" I asked, trying to keep myself from outwardly begging.

"Well, you did win the match, so I guess I have no choice, right?" She turned, and I followed her through room after room, looking for a private spot. We finally wound up in a guest bedroom, and she closed the door behind us.

"You wanted to talk. Talk," she said, her arms crossed over her chest, and her hip popped out to the side.

I looked down while my mind scrambled to find the right words… but nothing seemed to come to me. I decided to keep it simple.

"Red, I'm truly sorry." I reached to take her hands, but she backed up a step away from me.

"Exactly what are you sorry for, Bax?" Her look was searing.

I couldn't look her in the eye. I stared at the floor as my chest filled with shame. I knew she wouldn't make it easy on me, and I knew I had to spell it out if I ever hoped to have her back.

"Red…" I struggled to get the words out. "I crossed a line, and I am so deeply sorry about it. I have never had sex with a woman before in anger, and the guilt over the things I said and did to you… it's killing me. I can't live with myself. Please forgive me. I don't want to be my father." My voice cracked as I finished, still afraid to look up and see what she was thinking. If she looked at me with disgust, I would lose my mind.

She laughed.

My head snapped up, and I watched as she dissolved into laughter in front of me. I couldn't understand what she had found so humorous in what I had just said; I had laid out my soul for her.

Through her snickers she forced out, "THAT?!… *That's* what you are apologizing for?!" Her face was red, and she was almost doubled over laughing.

I froze on the spot in confusion. *Was she having a trauma reaction? She couldn't really think THAT was funny?!*

"That was not the response I had expected," I said calmly, watching her warily.

She finally got herself under control. "Bax, for someone who is so intelligent you are really dumb sometimes, you know that?"

I frowned at her, but waited.

"You didn't do anything I didn't push you to do." She held her hand up before I could get my argument out. "Let me finish. Yeah, you were a dick, and trying to get a rise out of me by implying I was a worthless whore only worthy of a blowjob..."

My heart sank in my chest.

"But I realized then that it had all been about sex for you from the beginning, that I was your secret side piece, even if I hadn't realized it, so I took the only thing you could still give me that mattered to me. Yeah, I GAVE you the blowjob. It's not like you forced me."

That didn't make me feel any better, and she was wrong about it being all about sex... but I'd correct her when she finished.

"When I saw that you were just going to leave me unsatisfied after that, I decided to take what I wanted. I do know your body after all, and it wasn't hard to get you inside of me. But after that, I needed a way to motivate you to stay if I wanted more, and I did. I knew you'd never be able to resist if you heard me getting off without you."

Realization started to dawn on my caveman mind. "So you locked me out and pulled out the vibrator," I stated.

She nodded with a pleased smirk on her face. "And then the cherry on top!" She grinned, maliciously. "I knew you were going to be too careful with me to give it to me the way I wanted–"

"So you used reverse psychology and ordered me not to fuck your ass," I finished flatly, my hand pulling down my face.

She stood grinning like the cat who ate the canary.

"So all this time I have been beating myself up mercilessly, thinking I had just about raped you, and I gave you exactly what you wanted?" I asked, already seeing it for what it was.

Her smile just got bigger.

I felt like an idiot. I turned and put my hand on the knob of the door, getting ready to just walk away with any dignity I might still have, but I stopped and turned my head one last time.

"It wasn't all about sex for me. It never was, Red. I was ready to give it all up, to walk away to have a chance with you. Just so you know. If you had told me, we'd still be in this together."

I pulled the door open quickly and walked out, even as she called my name behind me. I left the house quietly, not wanting to see anyone else. I needed some alone time.

I walked into my apartment thirty minutes later. My hands were full of mail: bills, Christmas cards, and a large manilla envelope. I dropped it all onto the side table by the door with my keys, and kicked my shoes off. I pulled my coat off lazily and threw it over the back of the sofa, not caring about being tidy.

I walked right over to my liquor cabinet and poured an unhealthy dose of scotch. I let the burn down my throat soothe my frazzled nerves and my broken heart. Maybe I should be glad that she had encouraged the rage fucking; maybe I should be relieved she didn't see me like a monster. But I couldn't be, because instead she saw me as the piece of shit my father was; someone who used women for sex without giving a damn about them... and was she wrong?

Hadn't I just proved that with Amber, and countless like her?

It didn't matter that losing her was the turning point that made me go back to those behaviors... They were always there, and like a junkie I just jumped right back in the first time I got my heart broken.

Now what?

I made my way back through the living room, chastising myself for leaving my coat and shoes lying around, even though I lived alone. I just needed the distraction for a moment, because I had no answers. The envelope caught my eye, and I reached and picked it up.

The return address was a company I had never heard of, and I ripped the envelope open to pull out its contents. A letter addressed to me sat on the top.

"Dear Mr. Murphy,

I have been hired to locate a missing person by the name of Sophia Murphy on your behalf, and I am just writing to make you aware that she has been found. Enclosed, please find photos, and some documentation including her address.

I hope that this information brings you peace. If you have any questions, please do not hesitate to contact me.

Sincerely,

Amber Borsari"

I nearly dropped the entire package. My mother! Amber had found my mother!

I flipped through the pages attached, a rental agreement, and some photographs that looked recent. She was older, but it was definitely my mother. I noted that the address was in Groton, Connecticut; close enough for a drive. Her phone number was also included. I flipped through the rest of the documents, random bits of her life on paper for me to see.

My heart swelled, and I felt tears prick at my eyes. I could have my mother back; after all of these years of believing she could potentially be dead, I could have her back again.

If she wanted to be back, that is.

I shut down that thought immediately. Knowing what I did about my father, I couldn't imagine my mother walking away voluntarily.

A new thought bubbled up to the back of my mind; Amber had found her. So Amber had known who I was when she approached me in the bar, more than likely. None of this had been a coincidence.

And who had hired her to do this? I suddenly had questions for Amber; but not before I called my mother.

It took me an hour of pacing, and two more glasses of scotch before I could bring myself to dial the number on the page. Anxiety ate at my gut. I had already been rejected once that day, and I didn't know if I could handle it again so soon.

What if she wanted nothing to do with me? What if she thought I was like my father?

Shame instantly washed through me. I was not a man a mother could be proud of. But I was also a man who wanted his mother back. Closing my eyes, I hit 'send,' and held my breath as I heard the ringing through my earpiece.

"Hello?" A sharp feminine voice spoke into my ear; my mother's voice.

"Hello, Mom. It's Bax." I held my breath again as I heard her gasp.

"Bax! My baby! You've found me!..." Relief flooded through me. "But... your Dad?!" Her voice was panicked.

"Dead mom. Dad is dead," I reassured her. "I know about his dealings, but you're safe now. Can I come see you, Mom?" I asked as tears started to build in my eyes.

"Oh, Bax, I'd love nothing more!" she whispered happily, and I choked on a relieved sob.

Red

"This is Agent Murphy, leave a message at the tone. (BEEP)"

"Bax... it's Red. I... I was hoping we could talk. Please call me." I hung up the phone with a heavy heart.

It had been three days since I shattered Bax's illusion. I thought it would feel empowering. I thought I would be happy to finally see him taken down a peg. But instead I ached with guilt. He said it hadn't been all about sex… but could I believe that? The look on his face after I had given my statement to the feds had been pretty damning. But the look of utter devastation and sadness as he walked out the bedroom door…

I had done that to him.

Maybe it was time for me to stop being so proud and just admit that I had feelings for him, and that I did want him back. Maybe it was time to stop fighting for dominance, the way my father had always taught me to. Sometimes it was more important to be happy, than to be right.

But would he even talk to me again? I knew that if it was me, I would never open that door again. Was he a better person than I was? I could only hope. I returned to the girls in the living room.

Amber growled in frustration and dropped her phone onto the coffee table for the fifth time. I raised an eyebrow but said nothing. She had been nothing but passive aggressive the whole time I had been back in Boston, and she seemed determined to take out her frustrations on me for some reason.

Jenna turned to her from her seat on the sofa next to me. "Something wrong, Am?"

Amber sighed deeply and flopped back in her chair. "Nothing… I was just expecting a call." She picked up her phone again, the phone she had been checking all day, and grunted at it before turning it over.

Jenna and I shared a look, but said nothing. We both knew that, of the three of us, Amber was the drama queen; it was better not to open that can of worms.

"Why don't we go clubbing tonight?" Jenna suggested suddenly, looking to change the mood.

"I don't know…" Amber started to whine.

"It would be fun! We could get dressed up and have a night on the town, like old times! I could invite Andrew as well." She smiled.

"Sounds great!" I chimed in, although I wasn't really feeling it.

"Fine," Amber huffed.

I looked at Jenna again. We both knew that her "fine" meant anything but. She was going to be a royal pain in the ass all night. I sighed, and we all got up to get dressed to go out.

Several hours later we were showered, dressed, and had hair and make-up done. We were even mature enough to make sure we ate before we went so that none of us wound up sick from drinking too much on an empty stomach... like we used to.

We walked up to the swanky club in downtown Boston and took in the line around the corner.

"Nevermind, we can go somewhere else," Amber whined.

I was really starting to get annoyed with having to babysit her, and her attitude, all night. I wasn't budging. The family ran this place, and I knew I could get us in. I walked to the bouncer and let him know who I was. His eyebrows climbed into his hairline, and he rushed to pull back the red velvet rope holding back the crowds to let us in.

As we walked past the crowds of people making nasty comments about us being allowed in, while they had to stay outside, Amber brushed past me.

"Of course they let YOU in," she grumbled snidely just loud enough for me to hear.

She stormed off ahead of Jenna and I toward the bar, and we shot each other confused looks in her wake.

What the fuck was up her ass?!

Amber was pounding drinks, where Jenna and I sipped ours and enjoyed people watching. I indicated that we should monitor Amber, as I didn't want to have to be responsible for carrying her home, and after her little outbursts I was more inclined to leave her on the floor of the bar if she got too hammered.

"There are my girls!" Andrew's hand came down around my shoulder for a hug, Jenna in his other one. Daniel stood behind him with his god-like smile. I watched as every woman in viewing distance stopped to ogle them, and laughed to myself, knowing none of them were taking these two guys home. It was cruel bringing them, really.

Amber popped off of her bar stool, right in front of Andrew. "Wanna dance?" she asked, taking his hand in hers and not waiting for an answer as she dragged him to the packed dance floor.

The rest of us looked back and forth at each other, wondering what was going on.

A few minutes later Victor showed up, and I felt my shoulders tighten. *I should have known that if I used my identity to get in, they would have made a call. Fuck.*

"Hey!" Victor beamed, and then he leaned in to kiss my cheek. He waved the bartender over for a drink, and I knew he wasn't going to be leaving any time soon.

So much for a girls' night.

Jenna and Daniel chose that moment to go and dance, snaking their way through the thick crowd, leaving Vic and I alone at the bar. My drink suddenly tasted sour to me.

"What are you doing here, Vic?" I asked.

"What? Can't a friend come to keep an eye on you?" He smirked.

He got his drink and swallowed it in a few gulps before turning to me and taking my hand. "C'mon, let's dance."

"I don't want to." I shook my head.

"Everyone else is on the floor already, don't be a party pooper," he said, tugging my hand a little more firmly, until I complied and followed him into the thick mass of moving sweating people.

The music was deafening, and the bass made the building around us pulse. It moved through our bodies like an external heartbeat. The floor was already full of hot sweating people, and the humidity from sweat and breath made the air cling around me.

I started to move to the beat, as the bodies around me gyrated with abandon, the alcohol loosening inhibitions. I tried not to look too closely, as plenty of couples were engaging in more than just dancing on the floor, if one looked closely enough.

I saw that Daniel had attracted a circle of females around him and Jenna, all of them trying to get close and rub up against him. I also noticed that Amber was grinding on Andrew, even though she knew he was gay and probably wasn't enjoying it as much as she was.

I nearly jumped when an arm latched around my waist, and I turned as Victor hauled me up against his body, my back to his front, so he could grind his hips into my ass while he danced. I pulled his arm off of me, but he just used his other to turn me and pull me back again; it was like dancing with an octopus. When he finally buried his head in my hair, his hands around my neck like he was about to kiss me, I pulled away from him violently, and stormed off of the floor.

Luckily, he didn't follow me, because I was absolutely furious about him treating me like a fucktoy on the dance floor. He didn't have a right to put his hands on me, and I didn't appreciate his hard-on stabbing me in the ass. I watched him pouring himself all over some other bimbo on the floor, and wondered what the hell had gotten into him.

I watched as Jenna laughed at all of the women trying to get Daniel's attention, and then my eyes caught Amber and my mouth fell open. Amber was wiggling her body down into a squat, as if she was about to give Andrew a blowjob right in the middle of the floor, and Andrew looked downright uncomfortable about it. It wasn't long before Andrew ditched her, and she was looking for a new target.

Andrew perched on the stool next to me, both of us facing the dancefloor and watching in confusion.

"What the fuck was that all about with Amber?" Andrew demanded harshly, as he used a napkin to wipe the sweat off of his forehead.

"I don't know! I was– ... oh... look at Victor." I said, pointing him out.

Victor had some girl's thigh up around his waist, her skirt barely scrunched above that... and I'm fairly certain his pants were undone in the front.

My eyes shot between Amber's antic's and Victor's lewdness before it suddenly made sense; they were each trying to make the other jealous. With each new move, they would up the ante, until one of them was just fucking on the dancefloor... if Victor wasn't already. I relayed this theory to Andrew, and his eyes opened wide with realization. He nodded his agreement, and we both sat in stunned silence watching the impending train wreck.

But why? They weren't dating... were they?

Just as I was about to suggest to Andrew that we intervene I was met with a beautiful pair of sparkling eyes above a mouth-watering chest that begged to be touched, barely contained in a tight black t-shirt.

"Bax?" I asked, surprised to see him. "How did you–"

Max stepped out from behind him, he had been completely hidden behind the wall of muscle that was Baxter Murphy.

"We couldn't let you ladies have all the fun." Max smiled, raising his hand to the bartender.

I felt Bax's nose by my ear, his warm hand on my shoulder. "You want to dance?" he asked in his warm sultry voice that gave me other ideas. Ideas I didn't deserve to have after what I had done and said to him.

I really didn't want to dance, but I found myself nodding mutely, and following him to the floor.

I had only had a few drinks, so I wasn't drunk, but I was definitely loosened up. Bax and I fell into an easy rhythm, and I felt myself getting warmer watching him. Damn, the man could move. He pulled me close, and we were gyrating and grinding on each other to the beat, our bodies pressed together, offering sinful friction that was making me crazy.

He dropped his head down, kissing my neck, his arms strong around me, and my head fell back onto his shoulder with the exquisite feeling of his touches all over me. As the dizzying heat between my legs started to become unbearable, I lifted my head to tell him we should leave, when something hard connected with my jaw, throwing my body back onto Bax and nearly knocking us over.

The crowd cleared, and Amber stood in front of me shaking out her hand and screaming at me. I couldn't even make out what she was saying over the music. And then Victor was scooping her up and dragging her off of the floor, literally kicking and screaming. I had never seen her so enraged.

Bax pulled me off of the floor and closer to the lights of the bar so that he could get a better look at my jaw. I had been hit plenty of times over my years of martial arts, and she hadn't even hit me particularly hard, but it had caught me off guard. I could taste the coppery tang of blood where a tooth had cut the inside of my lip.

Jenna, Max, Andrew, and Daniel were surrounding Bax and I, like a safety perimeter, while Bax assessed the damage. Other than the cut, I was fine, but I knew I may need to resort to makeup on the day of Jenna's wedding to hide any discoloration.

There was no discussion, we all just turned and left the club together. None of us saw where Amber or Vic had gone, and in that moment, none of us really cared.

Chapter 18

Baxter

We all left the club together, minus Amber and Vic. As we headed to the cars, Red pulled on my elbow, holding me back.

"Bax, can we go somewhere and talk?" She looked up at me with doe eyes, and my heart did a little dance in my chest.

I knew I should say no. I knew I shouldn't let her get back into my heart after she had just crushed it so completely, but I'm a fool, and I'd be lying if I said there wasn't still a part of me that hoped against all hopes that she would be mine again.

"Only if you promise not to use me for sex," I said teasingly, trying to lighten the mood.

"I can't make any guarantees..." she answered shyly.

I wrapped my arm around her shoulder and pulled her in so I could kiss her on the forehead. If she wanted to tell me we were done, I wanted to cherish every last moment with her I could. I was a masochist, and I knew it.

"Of course," I whispered into her ear.

Red skipped up to tell the others to go back to Jenna's without her, and met me at my car. I had it started, and the heater going, as the night air made the car feel like a freezer. I opened her door for her, and watched her slide in, before making my way to my own side. The heater was still only blowing lukewarm air on us, but it was better than the frigid air of December in New England outside the car. We drove in silence, and

I noticed her hands fidgeting in her lap, so I reached over and took one of them in mine. It felt natural and it made my heart tug. She smiled at me, but I noticed it didn't quite touch her eyes, and that only added to my anxiety.

I parked in the underground lot for my apartment and Red looked at me. "Where are we?" she asked, nervously.

"We're at my place..." I hesitated. "Is that okay?"

She nodded, and I walked around to let her out of the car, holding my hand out to help her up. We made our way to the elevator in silence, but I never let go of her hand. If she objected, she never said anything. Having her close to me in the enclosed elevator made me want to press her up against the wall and claim her mouth. Even with all of our winter clothing on, I could feel the heat of her body, and my own responded immediately.

Fuck, if this was the end, I was never going to be able to let her go. My hand grasped hers a little more tightly at my side.

The ride was thankfully quick, and I had her in my apartment and seated on my couch in moments. I was hanging her coat when I heard her say, "What's this?"

I turned to see her picking up the package of paperwork and photos I had taken out of the manilla envelope. I rushed over with excitement.

"My mother!" I exclaimed happily. "Amber found my mother!"

"Oh, she did? That's great!" Red smiled up at me, but I could tell it wasn't her usual bright smile. Her eyes still held some lingering tension. It doused the joy that had been swelling up at the revelation.

I poured us each a drink and then sat down next to her, pulling her close to me so that I could smell her scent. She wore a musky perfume with slight floral notes, but not too much, the scent always went straight to my groin. I savored it like a starving man smelling his last meal.

"What's on your mind, Red?" I asked, trying to hide the anxiety I was feeling rolling in my gut.

She swallowed some scotch and then put the glass down. "Us," she said simply.

"What about us?" I asked, not doing a very good job of hiding the anxiety after all.

"I... I need to apologize," she said at last. "I just... the look you gave me the day I made my statement, that look of disgust, after you hadn't called me again since the warehouse... It hurt." Her eyes were downcast, and her voice broke.

"Disgust? When did I ever look at you with disgust?" I asked her, confused.

"You were in the viewing room, off of the interrogation room; the one with the two-way mirror," she said sadly.

"That... No. NO, Red! I wasn't disgusted with you at all!" I placed my hand under her chin and tipped her face up to see mine. "I was horrified at hearing what you had been through, at what you were still going through."

"And then you ghosted me," she said quietly.

I sighed. "Red, I thought you were the main suspect in a murder case, and that you had used me for protection. I thought you had purposefully sought me out and engaged in the relationship and withheld that information on purpose. I was hurt and confused. But even when I had convinced myself that you were just using me as a pawn, even then, I knew I cared about you. That look wasn't aimed at you, it was aimed at my own weakness."

"But you knew enough, and you never broke it off either," she said. "Don't you think it's a little hypocritical to judge me based on what I withheld, when you withheld too?"

"Red, I couldn't tell you. It's my job. I'm not allowed to share case information," I explained.

"And I'm supposed to share information that can get me killed? I should have trusted you after how you acted when I didn't want to be around your dad?" she pushed. "If I had told you, I WOULD have been using you for protection."

"So that call you got that day in the gym... that was just a coincidence?" I asked, suddenly unsure.

"What call?" She faced me full on.

"Jenna called you about a family matter... you said you had a contact..."

Her eyes went wide. "You heard that?" she whispered.

"The whole thing. That was one of the first reasons I started investigating you," I said honestly.

"Well, it's not entirely my story to share, but I want to put all of my cards on the table with you. If I share what that call was about, Bax, it has to stay between us. You can't report it." She eyed me seriously, and I nodded.

"Jenna called me out of the blue because someone had put a hit on her to get back at Max," she said quietly. "She's my best friend, Bax, I couldn't let someone kill her. I called Victor, and he handled it. It is the one and *only* time I have EVER gone to my family to solve a problem. You can't tell the Bureau, Bax. This has to stay between us. You can't even mention it to Jenna. Swear to me." Her hand grasped at my knee.

"This stays between us, Red," I assured her. She nodded at me, but stayed silent for a few moments, processing her thoughts.

"So where does this leave us?" Red finally asked. "I spent all of the time we were together trying to convince myself we could never be together. Can we?"

I cupped my hand under her cheek and looked into her big sad eyes. Honestly, I had fought the same fight she had, knowing if she was attached to a case it could never work. But now she was cleared, she was just another citizen.

"I want to," I answered, as I leaned in and placed my mouth gently over hers.

Her arms worked around my shoulders and I pulled her onto my lap as I deepened the kiss, until she winced and jerked under my mouth.

"Oww... jaw," she said, rubbing the swelling that had risen where Amber had hit her.

"Oh fuck, I forgot!" I swore under my breath, as I jumped up, putting her back onto the sofa, and rushing to the freezer to get an ice pack.

When I returned she was chuckling as she took the pack and pressed it against her swollen jaw. I watched her, and was suddenly struck with a panic attack; *what next?* We were communicating, we were happy. I didn't want it to end. I didn't want to burst the moment. I couldn't let her walk out my door, only to wonder if things would stay okay between us. I had never felt so insecure in all of my life.

"Stay with me here?" I blurted out, and I could feel my cheeks burning.

She looked up at me, startled. "Tonight?" she clarified.

"While you're in Boston... will you stay here with me?" I didn't know why it felt so important to me all of a sudden. I needed her to stay, I needed to keep this going. She was the only woman I had even let into my apartment, but now that she was here, I wasn't about to let her go.

A huge grin split her face. "You want me to?" she asked.

"Well of course I do," I said. "How else am I going to use you for sex if you're not here?"

She picked up a pillow from the sofa with a feigned huff and threw it at me, and with a chuckle I let it hit me.

I was over the moon that she had agreed to stay with me. I had spent some time taking care of her injury, and getting her a drink and some snacks, but every time I walked back into the room she took my breath away all over again. I couldn't believe that she was really in my apartment, with me, that we were to-gether... even if it didn't last. I had her for a time, and I wanted to memorize every breath, every look, every laugh. I wanted to hoard them all selfishly, and try to make them last a lifetime. I still felt an impending sense of doom in my heart, and I refused to look at it while I still had her within arm's reach.

I pushed off from the doorway, where I had been staring at her for the millionth time in only the last hour, and brought her out the t-shirt I had gotten for her to sleep in. She looked up at me with confusion as she took it from my hand.

"To sleep in," I said with a small smile.

"But I sleep in the nude," she countered, looking at the t-shirt.

"Not if you don't want me fucking your ass all night you don't," I said back with a chuckle.

"Duly noted."

I had already set up a spare toothbrush in the bathroom, and laid out some towels for her. I brought her into the ensuite, so that she could shower and get ready for bed. As I turned to give her privacy her fingers reached out and touched my arm gently.

"I've had another head injury tonight... do you think it's safe for me to shower... alone?" She batted her eyelashes at me, as she started peeling her dress off in front of me.

My cock leaped in my pants.

"The real question is, are you safer showering alone or with company?" I answered her with a smirk.

"Oh, I definitely think I'd be safer with company." This time she smiled up at me seductively.

I watched as her dress fell off of her body. She stepped out of it, and used her foot to push it out of the way. She was standing in front of me in only her bra, panties, and high heels. I had everything I could do to control myself, as my cock just wanted to bend her over and bury itself inside of her until I exploded. There was a part of me that was still unsure about us together sexually, after our last encounter, but she was testing my willpower.

"That can be arranged... if that's what you want," I answered casually. While my outward appearance was calm and playful, my cock was fighting to get out of my pants like a rabid badger.

"Well, I wouldn't want to impose on you further,..." she said shyly, and began rubbing her hands up her body. "I guess I could take my chances..." Her hands reached behind her and unclasped her bra. She slid it off of her arms, and then crossed her arms in front of her, under her amazing breasts, as if showcasing them on a platter for me.

"It's no imposition... I assure you," I said, my voice starting to crack with my need.

She smirked knowingly, and then turned and bent at the waist, latching her thumbs into the material of her panties and slowly began to peel them down her long straight legs.

"Only if you're suuuuuuure," she said, her bare ass in the air in front of me.

I couldn't take it any longer. I rushed up so that my erection was pressed into the cleavage of her ass snuggly, only my pants between us, and my hands on her hips to steady her.

"Careful, Red, I wouldn't want you to fall over now," I whispered as I ground my hardness into her soft ass.

She brought her torso up partway, but didn't stand all the way back up.

"Thank you for that," she said breathlessly, grinding her ass back to meet my thrusts, "It's good to know you've got my back." A low moan escaped her mouth.

I leaned forward and grabbed her hair into my hand pulling her head back, and whispered into her ear, "Back, front, top, bottom, sideways... I've got you, Red. Don't worry about that."

"God I've missed your cock!" she exclaimed suddenly on a groan.

"God I've missed that filthy mouth of yours," I groaned myself.

"I need you to fuck me, Bax," she moaned, her breath coming out in short pants as she rocked her ass against me.

"But you promised not to use me for sex," I whispered in her ear, before sucking her earlobe into my mouth.

"How about just for today?" she asked.

"Alright," I conceded. "But it's getting late, so we'd better get at it before it's midnight and we run out of time."

I pulled away from her lush cheeks, begrudgingly, to turn off the shower, and scooped her into my arms as she yelped and laughed with surprise. My arms were still sore from our workout the day before, but nothing was going to stop me from burying myself in her as soon as I could.

"So no shower, huh?" She chuckled into my chest.

"No time," I said as I shuffled her quickly into the bedroom and launched her onto the bed. She bounced with a laugh, before spreading herself out before me, raw desire burning in her eyes.

I made quick work of my clothing, ripping them off and tossing them onto the floor. I'd deal with them later, at that moment my sense of urgency had everything to do with the soft wet opening I craved displayed in front of me for the taking.

As I made my way to the bed naked I watched as her eyes roamed down my body, stopping on my erect cock. The tip of her tongue snaked out to wet her lips and my cock jerked.

"Like what you see, Red?" I asked casually, stroking myself before her as I slowed my approach.

"I love what I see," she purred, her eyes locked on my hand as I pleasured myself. "I wish my mouth was in better shape so I could suck the pleasure right out of you."

My cock jerked again in my hand, and I groaned. Her filthy mouth was my greatest fantasy.

"I don't think either of our mouths are going to be doing too much of that tonight," I groaned with regret, my own split lip still stinging, "But there are plenty of other things I can do to your body." I promised.

"Oh yeah?" She quirked an eyebrow and spread her legs for me. "Like what, Loverboy?" she teased.

I didn't answer her with words. Instead I was on top of her in a few quick strides, taking her mouth with mine, more gently than I would have liked, but acknowledging that we were both still healing. One of my hands worked its way between us, and my fingers swiped up through her wetness.

"So wet, Red," I growled into her mouth. She only moaned into my mouth in response.

My fingers got busy, my thumb working her pearl of nerves while two fingers slid effortlessly into her warmth, lubricated by her own desire for me. Her body writhed and bucked under me, pushing her harder onto my fingers, as one of her hands reached between us, taking over my pleasure with a strong sure grip.

I felt her start to stiffen beneath me, her back arching into me, and a loud groan leaving her throat, just before the orgasm tore through her, clamping her down hard on my fingers and greedily milking them.

I couldn't take it any longer. I pulled myself out of her hand and positioned the head of my cock at her entrance, just as another wave of her orgasm rolled through her. With one solid push I was inside her, her walls clamping down hard on me, and her wetness surrounding me.

I had to stop. I had to hold still to avoid blowing right there and then, and even without moving, her muscular walls working my cock still made it damn near impossible to hold back. As her breathing started to calm, and her muscles slowly released their death grip on my cock, I started rocking into her slowly, savoring the feel of her hot juices and muscular walls taking me deep.

She groaned loudly as I pumped in and out of her, just relishing the feel of her velvet wetness surrounding me. My head fell as I groaned in bliss. I was still too close to do much more than tease myself with her body.

"More!" she gasped. "Bax, I need you to fuck me hard!" Her breathing was already ramped up, groaning. I looked up to see her flush face, her eyes half lidded with need, her perfect fuckable mouth open, and as crazy as it sounds I wished I had another cock, just so I could watch that perfect little strawberry mouth suck it off while I fucked her.

My cock reacted to her immediately, and I knew there was no more holding back. I was all-in. I pulled her thighs up around my waist, and she hooked her heels behind me as I thrust into her hard and fast, my balls slapping against her wet ass where her fluids had leaked down her beautiful crevice. I fucked her hard, furiously, letting all of the anxiety and anger wash through me, pushing my hips at a demanding pace. I was punishing her pussy with my cock for every moment of despair I had felt at being apart from her.

And she fucking loved it.

Red cried out and writhed under me like a porn star, her body hyper-responsive to the frantic beating my cock was giving her.

"Yes, Bax!" she cried. "FUCK ME!"

I didn't last long. Watching her falling apart under my cock was enough to tip me with her. I felt her start to clamp down, and my balls drew up tight, aching for release. The spasms overtook my body as I shoved into her hard one last time, and unloaded deep inside of her spasming core. I felt each wet spasm as my cock drained inside of her, and continued to pump her heavily until I was completely drained, my own orgasm rocking my body in a bliss-induced haze. Our mixed fluids leaked from her body to run down her ass cheeks and down my balls and thighs, evidence of our shared climax.

My body gave out, and I fell on top of her, trying to catch most of my own weight on my elbows, as my lungs heaved for breath. *Fuck, she was amazing.* There had been no other woman that had been able to own me so completely as Red did. Anyone else had just been a placeholder, a means to a very frustrating end, as they could never give me the satisfaction that seeing the sated smile on her rosy face gave me. It was like her body came alive under my touch, purred with contact, and I know mine responded to her the same. We were made to be wrapped around each other like this.

Chapter 19

Red

It was just a few days before Christmas, and I was like a kid again. For the last fifteen years I hadn't really celebrated the holidays, there had been no point. I had no family, and my friends were all far away, for their own safety. Christmas had always stood out as a sad reminder of just how much I had lost in the world.

But this year was different. I had family again, and I was surrounded by friends. Today I was going to visit Tony and the family, as a sort of homecoming. All of my friends had plans to spend Christmas Eve at Jenna and Max's place to exchange gifts; Bax was bringing his mother up for Christmas Day, and had invited me to join them and meet her.

It was heartwarming, and a little overwhelming all at once. I had lived so many years alone, depending on no one but myself, that the thought of being surrounded by so many people was a little scary. But at the same time, I had watched happy families shopping, or going out to parties, and my heart had been lonely, wanting to be a part of that. I realized that I missed being a part of something; I missed being loved.

Bax was driving to Connecticut to visit with his mother again; apparently he had gone down the day after he called her, and it had gone really well. There were lots of tears, and lots of catching up. I couldn't wait to meet her myself, and that was a little nerve wracking too.

I had spent the better part of the morning shopping for Christmas gifts while Bax was gone, and I was ready to just call it quits and get everyone alcohol. Knowing that I had to get gifts for people didn't make the crazy crowds or rude sale nazis any more relatable. For about the hundredth time I had to resist the urge to throat punch some crazed shopper who seemed to think that she was the only person of importance on the planet.

Tis the Season... Fa La La La Fucking La.

Having gathered all of my purchases, I made my way back to Bax's place to set about wrapping everything. I was nervous that people wouldn't like my gifts, but hey, I had two week's notice that I was coming up, sooo... Truthfully, the only one that had really made me nervous was Bax's gift, but I'm pretty sure he'd smile and say he loved it even if he absolutely hated it.

It took another hour of cutting paper, getting tape stuck to my fingers, trying to figure out how to wrap soft items, getting tape stuck to my fingers again, trying to figure out how to wrap bottles, and finally just going back out and paying someone to wrap all of my gifts for me, before I was finished. Between crazy shopping crowds and gift wrap, suddenly a solitary holiday wasn't seeming so bad any longer.

With my shopping done, I grabbed Tony's gift, and got a cab to his house. Waves of nostalgia washed through me as the cab drove through the old neighborhood, and I watched memories pass us by. I saw the corner where I had met Jenna for the first time, and the small corner store, which was now a bakery, where Victor had started flirting with me when we were kids. Each old house brought a tear to my eye, and each building, which had been replaced and taken my memories with it, brought even more. It was like the current day had been smashed together with the past, so that some parts were disjointed, while others were exactly the same.

I got out of the cab and walked by old man Bailey's house, noticing that it had a fresh coat of paint and looked well-loved; something it had never looked like when I lived nearby. The small wooded area we used to hide in and smoke cigarettes was now a laundromat. I was only a few steps away from the gate going into Tony's yard, but a part of me wanted to wander the neighborhood and see how many of my memories had been demolished since I had been gone.

But it was just like me, wasn't it? I had picked up and left. Yes, I was the same girl that walked these streets, and snuck down them after dark, but I was also a whole new person, with a whole new name, and a whole new life. Wasn't it just a reflection on me as well? Same bones, with a few new looks?

"Renny!"

I turned to see Louie standing in the doorway, wearing the same white t-shirts he always wore. Well, he hadn't changed a bit.

"Louie!" I called, smiling, and made my way through the gate and up the walk.

Louie was all smiles. He had been a sweet old guy when I was here last, and I was surprised to see that he was still around. He was older, and a little more weathered, but his smile was just as genuine.

"Come in, Bella! I know Tony will be happy to see you!" He ushered me in quickly, and shooed me into the kitchen like a mother hen. Tony was sitting at the kitchen table with a few of his guys as I peeked around the corner. When he saw me he jumped from his chair, nearly knocking it over, and rushed to me with his arms wide.

"Renny!" He grabbed me in a bear hug and squeezed so tight I couldn't breathe. Pulling back he grabbed my face to examine me. "Renny, you haven't hardly changed, 'cept for the hair. I'm so glad you came!"

He turned to the guys still sitting at the table, and yelled loud enough for the guys who were probably in the back as well. "Hey, fellas! Renny's here!" Soon there were footsteps descending the stairs, and coming out of the back rooms, as everyone came out to welcome me back.

My first thought was that it was all a set up, and Tony was going to have them all beat the crap out of me. I froze as they all surrounded me with hugs and kisses on the cheeks, until I finally began to believe that they were all just happy to see me. Tony finally sent them all back where they came from, so he could monopolize my time, and I had to laugh. He really hadn't changed much... his eyes had more wrinkles, and were a little softer, but he was still the same guy.

I handed him his gift: the bottle of single-malt scotch that was supposed to be excellent, if the price was any indication. Tony looked at it and whistled, and I smiled knowing I had picked well. Tony liked *the best*. We settled at the table, with a cup of coffee each and Tony with his cigar, and caught up on each other's lives. Not much had changed for Tony, except that now he was in charge, but my father's health had been deteriorating for years, so even this wasn't new for him. I told him about my life in Richmond, that took me all of a minute, as I didn't really have anything in my life. I filled him in on what had happened with Rocky's case, and the looks of fury on the feds' faces when Matteo had strolled in and dropped his bomb on them.

I also told him a little about Bax, testing the waters. Tony had known Bax's father, Bill, and never liked him. From what he told me, Tony had tolerated Bill because my father had insisted on it, but Tony had seen that Bill wasn't loyal, and had predicted he would disrespect the family sooner or later.

Bill had been telling the truth when he said he was dismissed from the family; Tony had found out how much he had been skimming off of the family's funds, and how many liberties he took in the family's name, and they were not amused. They had enough cops, judges, and prosecutors on the payroll that cutting the Chief of Police out of the network wouldn't hurt too much. He was a loose cannon, and was starting to draw fire from people on the outside.

So he wasn't thrilled with me dating Bill's son, Bax, whether he was dirty or not. I reassured him that Bax wasn't a dirty cop, and that I wasn't in the know anymore, so I couldn't really give away any family business to him. But the fact remained that it was still Bax's job to investigate my family, and that fact hung heavy in the air like Tony's cigar smoke. Sooner or later, they might wind up on opposite ends of a barrel.

"I've got something for you," Tony said as he slowly climbed out of his chair, his years showing in his calculated movements. I followed him into a back room where he moved into the closet and opened a safe. He pulled out a box about the size of a shoe box and handed it to me.

"These were your father's. He wanted you to have them." He pointed his cigar at the box.

I stared at the box dumbfounded. Until a month ago, I had thought my father had hated me, and suddenly I was inheriting his possessions.

"You can open it later, if you want to," Tony said softly. "There's also the house. He left it to you to decide what you wanted to do with it. If you decide to sell it, I have some folks who would pay top dollar for it. Just something to think about."

I didn't think I could go back to living in that house again, not with all of my memories. I knew Tony wasn't trying to push me to sell. Even though the houses around here were old, they were in town, and that made them valuable... and expensive to buy. The family always tried to move close together, safety in numbers, after all. They would put another member of the family in the house if I didn't want to keep it.

"Yeah, Tony. I'll probably just sell it. I'm sure you know a good family who would like this neighborhood, right?" I played along.

"In fact, I do." He smiled at me. "And they can afford what it's worth." He winked.

We made our way back into the kitchen and resumed our chat, the box sitting like a ticking time bomb on the floor next to my purse. I managed to put it out of my mind as Tony and I reminisced about the crazy things that had happened when I was still a kid growing up. It was like having my Dad back… not the father I had when I left, but the Dad I had when I was still little; the one who made me feel cherished and safe. For the first time in a long time, Tony really felt like 'Uncle Tony.'

I got a little teary-eyed when it was time to go, wondering if I'd see Tony again; or if I'd wind up stuck in Richmond for the rest of my life. This little vacation had opened my heart to all of the people I had closed out so long ago, and with each new reconnection, I was finding I didn't want to close the door on them again. I didn't want to run back to Richmond, and gloom, and loneliness.

Tony gave me another hug before I pushed out the door and made my way down the porch steps. I had just shut the gate to his yard when I saw Victor leaning up against his car on the street ahead of me. His hair was disheveled, and a cigarette hung out of his mouth as he scowled in my direction.

"Vic? What's up?" I tried to sound upbeat, but he really didn't look good. His hair fell over his eyes, making them look darker. His hands were stuffed into his pockets.

"What's up?" His voice and body left no doubt that he was upset about something. His tone was gruff, his eyes were narrowed as if I had insulted him instead of having greeted him. The way he pulled his cigarette away from his mouth, before jamming it back between his taught lips painted a picture I remembered well. He smelled of liquor. Victor had a bad temper on the best of days, but get a drink into him and you'd better run.

"What's the matter Vic?" I tried not to roll my eyes. He could be a stubborn drama queen.

"Amber's FINE, by the way... in case you were wondering," he spit, taking the conversation in a completely different direction.

I stared at him in confusion. "Was she NOT fine at some point I didn't know about?" I spit back.

"Well, you're her fucking friend, so you tell ME," he shouted back, arms exploding at his side.

"Well, she seemed fine, right up to the point where she sucker punched me in the face for no reason, Vic!" I shouted back. I shouldn't let him bait me, but it was like my mind stepped back in time, and we were seventeen again. We loved deep, and we fought hard.

"Maybe she had a reason, did you ever consider THAT, Nat?! She was your friend first, Nat! Before your fucking fed fucktoy, she was your friend! Maybe you should be checking on your FRIEND instead of running back to suck some fed's dick!"

My hand flew out and connected with his cheek hard, knocking his head to the side with a CRACK.

"You're out of line, and you need to sober up, Vic," I seethed as I turned on my heel and walked away from him. He was drunk, and there would be no reasoning with him.

"That's right, Nat!" he bellowed after me, "just keep running away!"

I almost jerked to a stop, but forced myself to keep putting one foot in front of the other, as tears rolled down my cheeks. Victor was one of the things about this neighborhood that had clearly never changed.

Baxter

I walked into my apartment to find the lights off, and my heart started to race. My visit with my mom had gone great, and I was excited to share my news, but the apartment seemed empty and dark. Red was supposed to be here! I snapped the lights on quickly, and heard a groan in the corner as Red lifted a hand to shield her eyes from the light of the hallway.

"Red? Why are you sitting in the dark?" I made my way to her without even taking off my coat.

"Diddd'n nnneeed light," she slurred. I looked at the mostly empty glass in her hand, and the largely empty bottle of scotch on the table beside her.

I squatted down beside her. "Do you want to talk about it?" I took the glass out of her hand carefully, and put it where she wouldn't be able to reach it.

"Nooooo..." She moaned. "Ssssallll buuusssshhhit anyway." She made a sour face. "Fuck'n Vic annn hisss fuck'n priooor-rrtiies."

"What about Vic, now?" I asked, suddenly concerned.

"Hhhheeee'sss aaalll 'poooooor Ammmberrrr.' Like ssshee's th'victum. SHE hit ME." Red yelled.

I wasn't sure what to make of any of it, but it was clear that Red was too far gone to get the whole story tonight.

"You're right!" I said to her adamantly, causing her to open her blurry eyes wide. "And I know just what you need! You deserve to be taken care of tonight." I smiled at her.

"FFFucckkk yaaaaaahhh, I dooo," she insisted, waving her finger drunkenly. "Where'ssss my drink?" She began searching her skirt and the chair.

"I'm going to get you something even better," I said, as I backed away, hiding her glass behind me and taking the bottle while she searched for her missing glass.

I took the alcohol into the kitchen and got her a tall glass of water and some ibuprofen. It was clear she was going to need it for the hangover she was undoubtedly going to have. I made my way back into the living room, only to find her passed out asleep on the chair, curled into a ball like a little fiery kitten. Even though she was a drunken mess, the cute factor had me over a barrel.

I brought the glass and pills into the bedroom and put them on the nightstand, and then I went and collected Red. I got her into the room, laid her out on the bed, and began to undress her, when she suddenly decided to come to. Apparently, in her mind, my undressing her signaled that it was sexy-time, so she started trying to undress me as well. This went on for a few minutes, with me trying to respectfully remove her clothing and swatting her drunken hands out of the way, or taking my cock away from her so that I could get her into bed. All the while she was slurring up a storm of filthy suggestions. She kept trying to sit up so she could pull me down, but she was far too drunk, and just kept falling on her back in the end and begging me to join her.

I finally had to tell her in my sternest voice that she was being naughty, and if she didn't keep her hands to herself, and let me undress her, I wasn't going to fuck her ass for her.

That did the trick.

She whimpered and moaned a little bit, but by the time I had her undressed, she had thankfully fallen back asleep. It was still early, but I didn't want to leave her alone in that condition, so I went back out and took off my coat, hid my Christmas gifts, and undressed to climb into bed behind her, spooning into her warm ass.

I couldn't even imagine what would cause a firecracker like Red to want to drink that much. It sounded like the drama with Vic and Amber was far from over, though.

Red groaned loudly as the sunlight streamed through the curtains and into the room. Without opening her eyes, she pulled her hands up to her head and squeezed, as if trying to keep it from breaking apart.

"I have water and ibuprofen for you, Sweetheart," I said softly. "You should take it."

She cracked an eye open, and the look on her face begged for mercy. There were dark circles under her eyes, and her skin had a yellowish-green hue that really clashed with the orange-red of her hair.

She stretched a hand out carefully, and I placed the tablets in them, and then I helped her to sit up slowly while she groaned. Once seated, I handed her the water, and watched as she took the tablets. Once I had the glass back from her, she fell back onto the headboard, as if the task of holding her body upright was just too much to ask.

"You going to make it there, Tiger?" I asked, trying not to chuckle at her obvious distress.

"I don't know yet," she croaked. "Ask me in an hour."

Her eyes started to close, and I gently settled her back into bed to sleep it off a while longer. Even with her hair going in every direction, clearly hung over, she was still the most adorable woman I had ever known.

I made my way into the living room and quietly began to work. I had bought a fake Christmas tree, and a ton of decorations while visiting my mother. I wanted to transform the house for both her and Red, and make it a Christmas to remember. My original plan was to send Red out shopping, but she probably wasn't going to be getting up any time soon, so I had the opportunity to decorate.

I snuck around gleefully taping up garland, and hanging decorative bulbs... in fact, I may have gone overboard. I looked around my living room, and decided that it looked like Christmas had thrown up all over it. Every square inch was decorated.

Every surface was lit up. The apartment was so bright, I'm pretty sure they could see it from space. Perhaps the "Santa's Village and Railroad" that I had set up around the perimeter of the room had been a bit too much as well… And the fake snow on all of the flat surfaces… the gift-wrapped pictures hanging on the walls… But I couldn't bring myself to take any of it down.

"What the hell happened here?"

Her voice startled me, and I jumped and spun like a cat.

"You're up." I smiled.

"Are you trying to land the space shuttle in here?" she asked with a smirk.

"No, just a certain sleigh," I answered haughtily. "And if you expect to get anything you had better make sure you are on the NICE list."

She just chuckled, and shook her head slowly, taking in all of the details… and there were a LOT.

"How are you feeling?" I moved to her side, and noticed her color had returned.

"Better thanks. I still need a shower." She scratched her head absently with one hand like a bear, crumpling her already messy red hair in all directions.

"Tell you what, you go hop in the shower, and I will make you pancakes," I offered.

"Only if there's coffee too," she said hopefully.

"As much as your precious heart desires," I answered, as I swatted her ass out of the room.

This was going to be the best Christmas EVER.

Chapter 20

Red

Everyone howled with laughter as Jenna tried to shove the monogrammed butt plug back into its gift box before anyone else could see it. Her face was crimson.

"It matches the one you got me." Max laughed, setting the group into peels of laughter again.

"I will get you for this," she promised him in a hiss, but her lips pulled into a small smile.

"I'm counting on it," Max answered, his eyes glued to hers, as they shared a heated moment.

Bax leaned in until I could feel his warm breath on my ear. "Would you like another drink?" he asked quietly. I turned to him and nodded, sharing our own moment, until he smiled and pulled away.

Someone handed Max his gift and I held my breath; I had drawn his name in the Secret Santa, so I had bought it. Max unwrapped the box, and then pulled out the piece of paper I had enclosed, describing what he was receiving. It was a year-long subscription for a new bottle of whiskey every month, all of it sourced from international indie distilleries. I know that it went against conventional "Scotch whisky is the best" sentiment, but some of them were really good.

Max's eyes opened wide, and a huge smile spread across his face as he looked up to me like a child receiving the toy he had requested.

"Nat, thank you! I can't wait to try them!" He beamed, as Jenna read over his shoulder to see what he had gotten. She too beamed as she looked up at me.

Bax was suddenly beside me again, handing me my glass of wine, before sitting next to me and kissing me on the temple. My hand rested on his thigh as we turned to watch the others opening their gifts. I heard the door open, and footsteps in the hall, and everyone turned to watch as Amber and Vic made their way into the room, presents in hand.

Amber walked in, to place the gifts on the pile, smiling her hello's, but I noticed that as she saw me sitting next to Bax her eyes narrowed and her nostrils flared for just a fraction of a second, before her face became blank and expressionless and she rushed back over to where Victor was sitting, never looking in my direction again.

I looked at Bax, and noticed he was watching her too, before he turned to me with the same puzzled expression I must have been wearing. He shrugged a shoulder as if to say, "I don't know either."

The group went back to opening gifts, most of which were gag gifts, filling the room with laughter. We were a raunchy and ruthless group. I noticed Amber never laughed, she sat and sulked next to Victor. While Victor wasn't sulking, I could see something going on behind his eyes, and it made me uncomfortable.

After our last encounter, I realized that something was going on with Amber, and it somehow involved me, but for the life of me I couldn't remember having said or done anything to piss her off, nor any reason Victor should be involved. Until one of them was a grown up and willing to actually confront me with it, I chose to just ignore it and enjoy my time with my other friends.

Andrew opened his gift next, and didn't even take it out of the box.

"Really?" he deadpanned, one eyebrow raised.

"What is it?!" Jenna squealed, but Andrew pulled the box out of her reach, and unfortunately into Max's reach, because he grabbed the bottle out and showed it to everyone.

"Midol," Max read, "For temporary relief of menstrual symptoms, such as cramps, fatigue, and bloating.... Doesn't say anything about mood swings, though." He laughed.

"You're an ass." Andrew laughed at him.

"And apparently you're a moody bitch." Max laughed right back, the rest of us joining in.

All of the gifts had been opened, and I adored the wireless headphones Jenna had gotten me. We all sat back with our drinks, eyeing the coffee table filled with an array of cheeses, crackers, and fruits. We were all stuffed and sated with alcohol, but we couldn't help but graze from the buffet of goodies laid out before us either. It felt so easy being with my friends, and with the exception of the cold front coming from Amber's side of the room, I felt more relaxed than I had been for a long time.

The hour was getting late, and Andrew and Daniel got up to say their goodbyes. I nudged Baxter to let him know we should head out as well. As we stood up I heard Amber's voice behind me.

"So Bax, what time are you picking me up for the wedding?" Her voice was laced with faux saccharine. She had a smug smile tugging at her lips.

I looked at Bax, and he turned to look at Amber. I could feel my irritation rising. *What was Amber's game?! Why was she suddenly so angry with me, and why was she taking it out on Bax?*

"I'm sorry, I didn't realize you still needed a date for that," he replied, his cheeks flushing slightly. "Wouldn't you prefer if Victor–"

"YOU said you would go with me, or are you backing out?" she demanded flatly.

All conversation in the room stopped, all heads turned toward Amber. Behind her, Victor was trying to calm her down, but she wasn't having it.

"N-no... of course not," Bax fumbled, turning to me for help. I could see the concern in his eyes; not for hurting Amber's feelings, but worry that I might get offended and leave him.

"It's fine, Bax," I said gently, wrapping my fingers around his arm in support. "You told her you'd go with her. I'll be there too, it's not like it's a date."

"No, it's definitely NOT a date," Amber said, and I had to wonder what the hidden meaning in THAT was. "I mean, after all, we had an arrangement. And I DID find your mom for you..." She threw that piece of information out to try to guilt Bax into going; pissing me off because it was ME who hired her to do that.

I said nothing, my lips drawn into a thin line to keep from saying something I would regret. Thank God for Jenna.

"Yeah, you found his mom, but it was Nat who hired you to do it. I mean, you didn't even know who Bax was when you took the job," Jenna interjected, having had enough of Amber's pity party.

Bax's eyes swung to me in surprise. I hadn't wanted to make it about me, and I was furious that Amber was forcing all of our personal information out into the open so that she could make it all about her... yet again.

"Come to think of it,..." Jenna continued, staring daggers at Amber, "you knew who he was based on the case Nat gave you when you hooked up with him. You told us so. So why are you being such a bitch to Nat now?"

"I'm leaving," Amber announced with a huff, ignoring Jenna's question. She stomped quickly out of the room. Victor shot me one glare, his upper lip pulling up to reveal teeth, before he spun on his heel and followed like her lap dog. The door slammed a moment later.

"What the fuck was that all about?" Andrew asked, looking from person to person. But none of us had any answers. Whatever was brewing with Amber was clearly festering, and just like always, Amber wasn't going to talk about it except to fling accusations. She hadn't changed at all, either.

Baxter

Nat and I drove back to my place in silence. When Amber had confronted me about being her date for the wedding, I had a moment of panic. I had completely forgotten about it. I had looked to Red, to try to gauge her reaction, and Red was the mature rational voice. She hadn't seemed upset with my still taking Amber, but I wanted to discuss it openly with her. If she objected, even *a little*, I would tell Amber no. I wasn't risking it.

Then there was the little tidbit about her hiring Amber to find my mother. That surprise had blindsided me; I knew that *someone* had hired Amber... I had just never guessed it would have been Red.

"That was crazy,..." I started, keeping it in neutral territory.

"You can escort her to the wedding, Bax. I'm really fine with that. You had arranged it before we were together; although I'm fairly certain that was her plan all along. Like I said, I will still be there, it's not like it's a date. It's not like you're going to fuck her, right?" She seemed far too calm and casual for the words leaving her mouth, especially when I knew how passionate she was.

"I know I told her I would, but I honestly don't want to. Not after her hitting you, and treating you like shit. I want nothing to do with her; not date or fuck her," I said. "Red, what was it that Vic told you about Amber last night that got you so upset?"

She went silent suddenly, pausing for a moment, before she slowly replied.

"He didn't say much. In fact, it's not just what he said, but the way he said it that bothered me," she began. "He said that she was my friend before you and I were going out, and that maybe she had a reason for punching me. He implied that I'm a bad friend because I chose you over her, and because I'm not running back to her to find out what I supposedly did to hurt her, and falling over myself to apologize."

"That's what this is all about?" I asked, incredulously.

"No," she said. "And that's what concerns me. If Amber is bent out of shape with me, why isn't she calling me? Why isn't she confronting me, instead of sending Victor to be her middle-man? She's not exactly a shrinking violet herself. What does she expect to gain by forcing your hand to take her to the wedding? Does she think she's going to seduce you away from me? And if so, why is she playing Victor as well? I can see he has a dog in this fight somewhere, even if I don't know where." Her jaw was clenched tight, as she stared out of the windshield.

"When did you hire her to find my mom?" I asked quietly, the curiosity getting the best of me.

She looked down at her lap. "You weren't supposed to find out it was me," she said. "I called her after our last encounter at my apartment."

I had no words.

"You... after I... I don't understand." I finally managed to force out something coherent. "Why would you do that for me, after... what happened?" I could feel the guilt lapping at me again, even though we had already been over what had happened.

"I'm not sure," she said, looking up through her lashes at me. "Part of it was because I felt responsible in some bizarre way, because of your father's association with my family. And part of it was because I miss my mom, and wish that I could believe she was still out there alive somewhere, waiting to be found. You deserve to have your mom, Bax. Regardless of anything that ever happened between us, it was the right thing to do. So, I did it."

I sat in stunned silence as the car crunched through the snow, moving through the largely deserted streets. Snowflakes fell heavily in the headlights, making it look like we were traveling through space at warp speed. It wasn't until I had parked, and helped Red out of the car, that it hit me. I pulled her into a tight hug, burying my nose in her hair.

"Thank you," I whispered. "That was the greatest gift anyone has ever given me."

Then I kissed her... and kissed her... and kissed her... until I could feel her shivering with the cold. I pulled her in close to me, not wanting to let go of her for even a moment, as we made our way inside.

And I knew I would never willingly let her go again.

Red

I lay with my head resting on Bax's chest, feeling his heart beating under my ear. It was like a soothing cadence that calmed me. We had explored each other's body ever since we made it back to his apartment, in our usual crazed and hungry fashion. I could never seem to get enough of him. And now we lay in exhausted silence, waiting for sleep to take us, but I couldn't quiet my mind.

I had been so happy reconnecting to my friends and family, and Amber's dramatics had twisted a knife in my heart, the bitterness of her words still echoed in my mind, until I couldn't push them away any longer. Perhaps it was because she pushed against the raw nerves in my gut which always held the fear that in the end I would lose Bax; that I would lose everyone, all over again.

"You don't have any feelings for her, do you?" I asked quietly, my voice sounding small in the dark room. The fear I felt was like a toxin seeping into my bloodstream, threatening to take me under. I hated that I was so insecure.

His head turned to me instantly, and I could hear his heart rate speed up.

"Amber? No. None," he said emphatically, pulling my chin up. In the dimness of the room, I could just make out the shape of his eyes, staring down at me. "It was a mistake hooking up with her, but I didn't know who she was. Still, it was a mistake. I was on a downward spiral after I thought you betrayed me, and I lost you, and... I made some pretty shitty decisions. I did things I'm not proud of. Unfortunately, she was one of them," he said sadly.

"If I lose you because of what I did with her... Red–" His words were urgent and laced with pain. His fingers tangled in my hair as if he could hold me, keep me from flying away.

"We all make mistakes," I said gently. "As I said before, I think this was all a part of her plan. I just wish I understood why."

"She told me she dated Vic, both before you left, and afterwards," he said. "She said she broke it off with him because she believed he cheated with you, and she could never trust him again. She thought he was the father of the baby you lost."

I closed my eyes against the truth. It was a truth I had never wanted to share.

"Did you cheat with him?" Bax asked me gently.

"It's not like that," I said too quickly. I was never a cheater and I didn't want him to even consider it.

"Vic and I had already been dating for years." I felt the tears rolling down my cheeks. "I was Vinnie's daughter, and Vic was one of his boys, so we could never be together publicly; my father would have made an example of him. But I thought I loved him, so we saw each other in secret.

"When Amber came into our circle of friends, and she saw Vic coming around every now and then, she let me know she had a crush on him. I tried to talk her out of it, but she was bound and determined to have him. Part of me thinks she only wanted him because he paid so much attention to me, even though we were supposed to be hiding our relationship. She was always jealous of me for some reason. It absolutely killed me that she pursued him, but I couldn't tell anyone; not even Jenna and Andrew knew.

"I found out later that Vic had agreed to date her, 'for appearances,' he told me. I was furious with him, and we fought over it all the time. He said no one would suspect us if he had a girlfriend, and Rocky was making moves to claim me, but I always saw it as the ultimate betrayal. He didn't just date her, and he didn't just fuck her. He had a full-fledged public relationship with her. The one I could never have with him.

"You have no idea how many nights I had to listen to her gloating, on and on, about 'her and Vic this... and her and Vic that...' She gave me a play-by-play of everything they did, sexually and otherwise. And I had to pretend to be happy for them. I couldn't say anything about how he was also fucking me, and that I was his real girlfriend. I grew to hate her, and him.

"When I found out I was pregnant, I didn't tell anyone, not even Vic. I was angry, and scared, and a thousand other emotions. My dad couldn't know it was Vic's or he'd kill him. I didn't know what I was going to do. I was ready to give Vic the ultimatum: me and the baby, or Amber, but then Rocky decided to make his move and it became a moot point.

"He grabbed me after school one day and took me back to his place and tied me up. He was deranged, unhinged. He said he planned on getting me pregnant, and then my father would have no choice but to let him marry me, since we'd be having his grandchild. That baby was his ticket to run the family someday, and I was just the womb to provide that. I was nothing more than livestock to him.

"After two weeks of him drugging me, and then raping my unconscious body, big surprise, he gave me a pregnancy test and it showed up positive. He never even guessed I was already pregnant when he took me. Thank god he wasn't the sharpest knife in the drawer.

"I was desperate to get out of there, I knew that once he had that baby he would make me disappear. But Rocky was super paranoid, and made it really hard for me to find a way to escape. He did lots of drugs, drank a lot, and I found out skimmed quite a bit of my father's protection money. He had reasons to be paranoid.

"Once he knew I was knocked up, he started getting sloppy. One night he opened the safe in the room I was in, and because he was so high he didn't bother to make sure I couldn't see the combination. The next day when he gave me my drugged drink I took advantage of a distracted moment and dumped it on my bed, and then covered the puddle up with a blanket. He left soon after to go out whoring, and I worked at getting the ropes off of my wrists. It was a lot easier when I wasn't unconscious. You know how the rest of the night went," I said quietly.

"After I... After Rocky was dead, I panicked. I found my cell phone and called Vic; he was the only person I thought I could trust. Vic raced down to get me, and I cleaned out Rocky's safe so that I'd have some money to get me started. I knew I had no choice but to run, at that time I thought my father would have killed me for taking out his second in command. I didn't even consider that he'd listen to my side of the story.

"Vic insisted I needed to see a doctor first, and it wasn't until I was in the car that I saw that Amber was with him. She didn't say anything to me, just stared at me with pity. They brought me to the local clinic because there was less chance that my dad had people watching there, and I got the treatment I needed. I was an absolute mess. I was convinced my father was going to walk in and catch me any minute. I was really hysterical.

"After the doctor released me, Vic told Amber he was taking her home. She seemed really pissed that she couldn't come along, and they argued; like full-blown screaming-raging-argued. But in the end Vic got what he wanted. He always did. We dropped Amber off, and she stormed into her house, never looking back.

"We sat in a parking lot and came up with a really quick plan, and he put me on a bus out of town. I begged Vic to go with me. He was my world, and I had just lost our baby. I begged him not to send me away alone, but he insisted he had to stay, that his absence would draw too much attention to me, and it was safer this way.

"That was the last time I saw either of them in person, although Vic kept in touch with me via a burner phone. At first he called me every week... but as the years went on, he called less and less often, until it was down to once or twice a year.

"I knew he continued dating her," I said finally, the bitterness coating my tongue like poison. "I guess I know now why he really stayed behind."

Bax kissed my forehead gently, and stroked his hand down my hair; my nerves calmed at his touch, and my breathing relaxed. He didn't try to give me uplifting words, or try to say something to make me feel better. Instead, he just cared for me with his touch.

I don't know how he had this control over me, when I couldn't even find this control in myself. He was my candle in the darkness, my ray of hope against an otherwise murky future. If he was by my side, I just knew everything would turn out alright. I laid still on his chest, having nothing left unsaid, until I fell asleep to the lullaby of his heart beat.

Baxter

Despite the tension we had felt on Christmas Eve, Christmas Day was like a miracle for me. My mother drove up from Connecticut to join Red and me, and I couldn't wait to introduce them. My mother had been the first woman I had loved, in the way young boys idolize the woman who birthed them and loves them unconditionally. And Red was the woman who I currently loved, clearly in a different way, but just as unconditionally as my mother had loved me.

I loved her.

I stilled in my chair, staring at Red as she hung a few more ornaments on the tree, humming Christmas carols. The realization shocked me, although it shouldn't have. She was a part of me, she was the best part of me. As if sensing me watching her, she turned her head to me and smiled at me. That smile turned me inside out, my heart started to spasm in my chest.

"What?" she finally laughed, as I choked on my emotions.

"Red... I–" The doorbell interrupted me, and frustration at our moment being stolen temporarily flummoxed me.

I climbed out of my chair and made my way to the door, washing my irritation away, and reminding myself that it was a gift to have my mother back in my life. There would be time later to confess my emotions to Red. But right now...

I swung the door open.

"Bax!" My mother grinned up at me, her arms stretched wide. I pulled her into a tight hug and lifted her small frame off of the ground.

"MOM!" I said loudly, with the enthusiasm of a six year old at Christmas. I put her back down and pulled her into my apartment, taking her coat like the gentleman she had taught me to be.

"And who is this angel?" she asked, turning her twinkling eyes on me, before returning to look at Red, who had joined us.

"Mom, I'd like you to meet my girlfriend, Natalie." I held my hand toward Red. "Nat, this is my mom."

"It's nice to finally me—oof!" Red never even got to finish. My mother launched herself at Red and pulled her into a tight hug. Red's face was washed with surprise as she looked at me over my mother's shoulder, until my mother finally released her.

Mom held Red's face in her hands, as if Red was just a little girl. "I am so very happy to meet you, Natalie. I have heard so much about you! Thank you for making my boy happy," she said in a broken voice. I could see tears forming in her eyes, and in Red's.

"The pleasure is mine Mrs. Murphy," Red said, her own tears threatening to overflow. "But I think you're confused. It's your son who has made me happy." She chuckled.

"Nonsense." My mother chuckled, releasing Red's cheeks. "And don't call me Mrs. Murphy, that was my mother-in-law. Call me Sophie, or... Mom... if you'd like."

She smiled one of the smiles I used to pray for as a child. My mother knew very little happiness in her life, but when she smiled like she did right then, I was a little boy again, and I was eternally grateful that my saint of a mother was truly happy. I lived for those smiles.

"Okay... Mom." The tears were flowing freely now, as Red tried it on for size. I knew she had lost her own mother when she was young, and I couldn't imagine what she was feeling at that moment, but I was happy to share my mom with her. And I was glad that my mom had accepted her so easily; they were both easy women to love, and impossible to forget.

Several hours later I sat with Red on the couch, each enjoying a drink and just watching the lights on the Christmas tree. Red and I had cooked dinner together, which had been a real joy. I knew my way around a kitchen, and Red was a pretty good cook as well, so it made our playful banter easy, and the meal delicious. Mom supervised, and told Red all of my embarrassing stories from childhood. We had eaten, cleared the table, and then opened gifts. I knew my mom didn't have much money, although I was already working to fix that, but her gifts were thoughtful and touched our hearts.

As the night wore on, and Mom started getting tired I brought her back to the guest room to settle in. She shut the door behind me, and I raised an eyebrow in question.

"I just wanted a moment alone with you, Bax," she said, looking worried.

"Is everything okay, Mom?"

"Yes, yes, Sweetie. I just... well, I wanted you to have this." She pulled a small box out of her suitcase and handed it to me. "I didn't want to give it to you in front of Natalie," she added.

I opened the box to find a beautiful solitaire diamond ring inside.

"Your father gave it to me, but he didn't buy it," she explained. "My father passed it to him when he asked for my hand in marriage. It has been passed down in the Sullivan family for generations, but I was an only child. There were no sons to pass it on to."

She looked up into my eyes. "I want you to have it, if you want it. It would mean a lot to me if my future daughter-in-law would wear it."

I didn't know what to say, as I again choked on my emotions. My mother seemed to mistake my distress.

"Oh, of course, if you don't want to... I don't expect you to have to Bax. I'd be happy to see any ring on your wife's hand–"

I shut her up by pulling her in for a hug and I squeezed. I could feel the tears leaking out of my own eyes.

"Mom, I would be proud to give this ring to my fiance," I said quietly, for fear that I would start bawling.

"Well then, you'd better get on that," my mother laughed. "My grandchildren aren't going to make themselves, you know. I'm not getting any younger."

Chapter 21

Baxter

New Year's Eve, the day of the wedding, had finally arrived. I had tried calling Amber to work out a plan for the wedding, but she wouldn't take my calls. Finally I left her a message saying that it just wasn't going to work out, and so I was planning on going to the wedding with Red. In fairness, it's not like Amber *needed* a date; the people attending were all friends of hers, so she wouldn't be alone. And the fact that she wouldn't even talk about it made me less willing to try to work it out.

Red spent most of the morning with Jenna, and her sister-in-law-to-be, Joelle. She texted me to let me know that tensions were high because Amber, who was also a bridesmaid with Joelle, hadn't shown up. They had a contingency plan to have Red stand in, if Amber pulled a no-show, and my heart tugged a little at the thought of not getting to sit next to her. I was jealous of all of her moments, and even a day without her burned in my heart.

I offered to call Jenna and apologize, feeling that it was my fault for having backed out on Amber, which caused her to then back out herself, but Jenna texted me herself to tell me to "knock it the fuck off," and that "Amber is a big girl, responsible for her own fuck-ups." So at least I knew where I stood. It seemed that everyone was done with Amber's nonsense.

I was invited to hang out with the boys for the day. Nothing is more intimidating than hanging out with Andrew and Daniel, who both look like a love child of Mr. Universe and a rock star. At least Max was slightly smaller than I was, but only slightly. We spent the day doing manly things like smoking cigars and drinking ridiculously good scotch in the cigar bar attached to the hotel, and then we got massages and manicures, at Andrew's insistence. I wanted to say I hated it, but truthfully, I will probably be booking those once a month from now on. Of course, I didn't tell Andrew that.

We didn't do any of the usual tacky bachelor stuff, like looking for strippers or hookers; having two gay guys with us helped to balance the crazy. I know I had zero interest in watching anyone but Red, and I have a sneaky suspicion that even if Max *did* want that, Jenna would have castrated him. She was scary-lethal, just as much as Red.

So we spent the last afternoon of Max's bachelorhood being pampered and enjoying ourselves in a more laid back way than is traditional. The hours slipped by easily, and Andrew made it a point to ensure that Max didn't have too many drinks before the time came to tie the knot. Our only job, according to the girls, was to get him there in one piece, un-laid, and sober enough to get through the ceremony. And none of us was willing to endure their wrath.

As shadows fell outside our windows we got our tuxes on, and were putting on finishing touches. I got the text from Red to say that Amber had finally shown up; so it wasn't surprising when a few minutes later there was a knock on the door, and Victor came in. He was frosty, and kept to himself, which was fine with me. Red and I had already agreed that if they were here, we would stay away from them, for the sake of Max and Jenna's big day.

Afterward, however, all bets were off.

The wedding planner was the next to knock, coming to collect all of us men-folk to get us staged in the ceremony space. I watched Max straightening his bow tie for the millionth time, before Andrew reached over and smacked his hands away and set it back to straight. Max twitched nervously. His eyes were large, and his breathing was rapid and shallow.

"Thurston, you okay, Buddy?" I asked him quietly. The other guys were following the wedding planner out the door.

He looked at me, his eyes a little wild, like he might start hyperventilating or take off running.

"I... I just..." He swallowed loudly, and I noticed a tremor in his hands as he tried to fidget with his tux.

I put my hands on his shoulders, pressing firmly as I stared into his eyes.

"You are just so excited to watch that amazing woman of yours glide down that aisle and choose you in front of all of your friends and family. Isn't that right?" I suggested.

He looked at me, and I watched as his panic attack slowly slipped away as thoughts of Jenna filled his mind. His breathing became deeper, and his eyes seemed to return from their dilated state to normal.

"Yeah,..." he said, slowly pulling himself together. "Yes."

"Good man," I said as I pulled him in for a hug, patting him roughly on the back, before I whispered, "And the sooner you do, the sooner you'll be buried in her, my friend."

I walked away before he could hit me. The one thing I knew about Max Thurston was that a horny Max trumped any other kind of Max, any day of the week. I chuckled. He'd be fine.

I exited the room with Max right behind me, and we made our way to the ceremony space behind the hotel, in their atrium. The room had glass walls facing the snowy exterior, but inside was humid and warm, offering tropical flowers and palm trees. A quaint canopy had been set up on the dais at the far end of the room, and chairs lined either side of the hall draped in rose satin. There were flowers everywhere in all of the colors of the sunset: rose, peach, yellows... It was a stark contrast to the white of the snowbound exterior just beyond the glass walls, devoid of color in the dying light.

The wedding planner got Max into place, and pulled his brother Ed and Andrew to get them into place down the aisle as his groomsmen. I stayed nearby until things seemed to be rolling along smoothly and the chairs were beginning to fill with family and friends. Red found me, and we took some chairs on the bride's side so we could sit together. *Sorry, Max.* I watched as everything fell into play with rehearsed precision until it was time.

It was just like every movie I have ever seen, or any other wedding I have been to; the music started, the guests stood and turned to the doors expectantly, and pair by pair the groomsmen ushered the bridesmaids up the aisle, until, finally Jenna came into view. She was absolutely stunning; still nothing on my Red, but I can admit that she was an amazing woman. She walked down the aisle slowly, as they are taught to do, to prolong their future husband's torture, and I found myself reacting.

I wasn't sure what was going on inside me, but I felt like I was watching Red walk down to me, instead of Jenna to Max. I suddenly wanted to be the one waiting at the end of the aisle, looking down to see my blushing bride as she made her way past everyone else, stopping next to me. Committing herself to me. Choosing me. I wanted it. I wanted it more than anything. I wanted Mrs. Natalie Murphy. I wanted "his and hers" towels. I wanted to have to stock feminine products in my bathroom, I wanted two toothbrushes in the holder...

I felt a hand on my arm, and I swung my head to Red who was staring at me with concern. I realized I had tears on my cheeks, and I wiped them away with an embarrassed chuckle. Let them think I was emotional about the wedding... I was...

just not *this* wedding. I kissed her cheek and then turned back to take in the rest of the ceremony. I held her hand tightly in mine, and promised myself I would have this with her.

"I now pronounce you man and wife! You may kiss your bride!"

The crowd erupted in applause as Max took Jenna into his arms and dipped her low for a kiss that would never have been appropriate in a church. They straightened, with huge grins on their faces, as they made their way back down the aisle, and toward the reception area. There was happiness and a buzz of conversation as the room emptied behind them, with Red and I near the end of the pack.

I waited until even the officiant had left the room before I pulled Red up onto the dais with me. She looked at me with her brows drawn in confusion, like I had lost my mind, and I chuckled.

Not my mind, Darling, my heart.

I pulled her in for a hug, and she let me. I knew she didn't understand what was going on in my head, but being who she was she allowed me time to process.

"Red," I spoke into her ear, my head snuggled close to hers, holding both of her hands by our sides, my fingers intertwined with hers. "I love you. I have always loved you. I will always love you." I whispered. "It terrifies me, and it sustains me. I need you, and I can't live without you. You are the heart I never knew I lost. Stay with me."

I didn't know what I was asking for; I just knew I never wanted us to end. I kept my mouth by her ear, so that I couldn't see her reaction. If she looked unsure, or if she rejected me, I couldn't bear to see it.

She gasped and my heart stopped. *What did that mean?*

I froze where I was, afraid that my heart was going to burst out of my chest. And then she threw her arms around me and started bawling.

Not the reaction I had anticipated.

"I (hiccough) I love you too!" she managed through ragged sobs.

"Then why are you crying, Red?" I asked, pulling back slightly to look into her eyes.

"I'm just so RELIEVED," she sniffled. "I... I wasn't sure if you... I didn't know..."

I chuckled and pulled her back into me, and she clung to my shoulders as she released the last of her tears.

I would do my best to make sure she only cried happy tears from now on.

Red

Why the hell did he have to choose a very public WEDDING, with all of my friends, to confess his undying love for me?!

It took me the better part of twenty minutes to wipe off most of my makeup and re-apply it, and even then my eyes were still red and puffy. Thank God I wasn't in the wedding party; those would be photos to burn. When I couldn't make myself look any better, I finally just gave up and headed back down to the reception.

People were mingling and drinking, waiting for the wedding party to return from their photo shoot. I found Bax with the other guys in the back of the room.

"Another sentimental one?" Andrew teased me, seeing my telltale eyes. "I saw your man spouting waterworks when Jenna came down the aisle. I never knew you were both such softies!"

"I noticed a certain someone with tears in HIS eyes, as well," his boyfriend Daniel said behind him with a wicked grin. "So you can include yourself in that group of softies, where your BabyGirl is concerned."

I laughed with him as Andrew blushed deeply and Daniel threw an arm around his shoulder. I loved that Daniel called

Andrew on his bullshit; they had the most genuine relationship, and adored each other. They were good for each other.

"There's my Tiger." Bax's voice was warm and vibrated
against my neck as his arms enveloped me from behind and I
couldn't help but notice the firm ridge in his pants against my
ass cheeks as the satin of the dress helped me to slide across
his groin. He breathed a groan that I felt more than heard at
the sensation.

I purposefully shifted so that my ass slid over his hardness
again as I tipped my head back to whisper quietly into his ear,
"I'm not wearing any panties."

The ridge in his pants instantly transformed into a club,
jutting in between my cheeks.

"You're going to need to stand here for about thirty minutes
now," he growled into my ear. "Because I can't move."

Again I whispered, "What, you don't want to show off your
massive cock to everyone in attendance?"

His nose burrowed further into my hair, as his cock pressed
harder into my ass. For a moment it felt like he was going to go
ahead and take me right there, right through our clothing.

"There is only one person I want to show this massive cock
to, and it's pointing at her." He chuckled, and I could feel it
rumble through my back.

Unfortunately for Bax, the wedding party chose that moment to rejoin the party. I laughed as I walked in front of him
awkwardly, his arms still wrapped tightly around me, until we
got to our seats, and then I sat on his lap until he could get
himself under control. Of course, I had to wiggle and press
myself against him, just to make it that much harder.

"Keep it up," he groaned. "Payback's a bitch."

"I think I am."

I felt his finger smooth its way down the slippery fabric of
my dress until it rested just inside of my ass cheeks and over
my tight hole. My face flushed.

"Try me," he whispered.

I stopped moving immediately, suddenly very hot and clammy.

"Is it cold in here, Darling?" he whispered with amusement, and I noticed in horror that my nipples had pebbled into hard nubs pressing through my dress. I might as well have been naked.

I immediately removed myself from his lap and took my own seat. Bax took off his tuxedo jacket and placed it over my shoulders, ... and breasts. I shot him a grateful look, but he still had his gleeful smirk on his face.

Damn him and his hot body!

The bride and groom were announced as they danced onto the dance floor together, the wedding party fanning out around them, and I brought my attention back to the room. It turned into the best wedding I had ever attended. There were all of the usual wedding traditions: the first dance, the cutting of the cake, and of course the bouquet toss.

Apparently Jenna had her own ideas about the bouquet toss, because she first threw a very real looking training sword over her head and behind her, so everyone ducked except me; I simply stepped out of the way. THEN she threw the bouquet, so that I was the only woman left standing behind her. I tried not to catch it, on purpose, but I was too shocked to move so it bounced off of my head, and into my hands. Defeated, I trudged back to my table with the offending flowers, where Bax was howling with laughter.

Jenna and Max made their way over to us with huge grins on their faces and I cringed. Max walked up behind Bax, placing his hands on his shoulders firmly.

"Murphy, my friend, she's caught the bouquet. You need to up your game before someone else asks her first." And with that he chuckled and pulled Jenna off behind him.

"Thanks for the pep talk!" Bax called after him, but he wasn't laughing anymore.

We sat through another hour of frivolity, we danced, and we drank. I noticed everyone having a good time... except... I couldn't find Amber. Nor Vic. Both were conspicuously absent.

Not my problem, really.

I was on the dance floor with Bax, dancing to a slow sultry song, his arms around me tight, and my nose filled with his scent. My body thrummed with need to feel more of him. My dress was thin, and it was working against me; giving me slide but no friction. I could feel his warmth ghost over my skin, but never stop, never quite give me satisfaction. I groaned in frustration.

"What's the matter, Tiger?" He kissed my forehead as we swayed, and I felt his bulge slide across my abdomen.

"I want your cock inside me," I answered so that only he could hear me. Instantly he was jabbing me in the gut.

"Clarify," he stated quietly in command. "Do you want my cock inside of you as in 'find a broom closet and bend you over?' Or do you want my cock inside of you as in 'take me upstairs and ride all of my holes as hard as you can all night long?'"

"The second one." I panted. "DEFINITELY the second one!"

I felt his chuckle through his chest, but his cock didn't diminish at all.

"But you'll miss the ball dropping," he teased.

"The only balls I want dropping are yours while you fuck me," I retorted.

"It's New Year's Eve. Don't you want to ring in the New Year?" he taunted me.

"I can think of no better way to ring in the New Year than by making you blow inside of me so hard you scream," I whispered into his ear, and then took his earlobe between my teeth for good measure.

"You make a good argument," he replied, as he slowly steered me off of the floor and toward the doorway.

I giggled as I turned and pulled him by the hand behind me, his pants obscenely tented in front of him. I was about to say that we were lucky that most of the room was facing the dance floor, and we had gotten away unnoticed, but just as we rounded the corner into the hallway we came face to face with a very pissed off Amber, with a sulky Victor behind her. She stopped and glared at me, noticing me pulling Bax with me.

"Leaving so soon?" she snapped at me, and then took in Bax... and his erection. Her eyes got big, and she couldn't seem to tear them away from his crotch, much to Victor's displeasure.

"Yes," I replied, head up, pulling her attention back to me. "Bax wants to fuck my ass, hard. Who am I to say no? Come on, Bax!" I pulled him along with me as I jogged down the hallway toward the elevator, leaving Amber standing with her mouth open, and Victor sputtering.

Baxter

We couldn't keep our hands off of each other the whole ride up the elevator. It was all I could do not to rip the thin satin fabric of her dress off of her. Our hands were buried in each other's hair as our mouths grappled for dominance. I surged forward, pressing her body into the back of the elevator, feeling her hard nipples as they pressed into my shirt through the flimsy satin. I was sure she could feel the length of my cock straining against my pants to get into her.

When the doors slid open with a DING, I grabbed at her, pulling her behind me as we ran to our room. As I pushed the key card into the slot, I noticed her face was flushed, and her breathing was coming in heaves, but her eyes were glued to mine with need. I pushed the door open roughly and yanked her inside with me, letting the door slam closed behind us.

She turned to kiss me again, but I used my body to press her back, corralling her toward the bed. When her knees hit the mattress, she fell back onto it, sitting before me.

I towered over her. "This is how it's going to go, Tiger," I said thickly, reaching out to move a lock of her red hair from her forehead. "You were a naughty girl tonight, teasing me. So tonight I'm in charge. You will do what I tell you when I tell you, and if you don't, you won't get your reward. Do you understand me?" I wrapped my fingers in her hair tightly, so that it would give her just a little sting.

I saw the heat flame in her eyes, and she nodded up at me with big doe eyes.

"Words, Tiger. I need to hear you," I commanded, still gripping her hair.

"Yes!" she whispered breathlessly.

I tugged her head firmly. "Yes, what?" I demanded.

"Yes, Sir," she said, and a small smile edged her plush lips.

"I'm glad you find this entertaining, Tiger," I said harshly. "I need you to take that dress off right now before I shred it. I need you naked, except for the heels. Do it."

I released her hair, and she stood and began to slowly slide the spaghetti straps of her dress off her shoulders coyly.

"I said strip, not tease me." I moved behind her and spanked her ass hard through the satin material. She yelped and immediately slid the dress off of her body. Her thin bra followed, but she hadn't been lying when she said she had no panties on. My cock jerked.

She stood before me naked, like a buffet I wanted to gorge myself on, but I held myself back. She went to sit back down, and I cleared my throat.

"Forgetting something, aren't you?" I demanded.

"What?" She looked at me, confused.

My hand snaked out to grasp her hair again. "That's 'What, *SIR*,'" I reminded her, giving her hair a slight tug. She moaned softly under my hand, but I pressed on. "You need to pick up that sinful dress and hang it properly. We're in no hurry, there's no need to be sloppy," I commanded, knowing it would tick her off.

She shot me a glare, but pulled out of my hold to get her dress and bra and put them away as I instructed before coming to stand in front of me again. This time, she waited for instructions, like a good girl. I smiled at her obedience.

"Undress me, Tiger," I commanded.

She didn't hesitate to reach out and start unbuttoning. She took my jacket and hung it up, before pulling my shirt off and hanging that too. I fought the smile that wanted to rise to my mouth. Next she undid my pants, forcing me to hold back the groan as her fingers swept over my fully hard cock. Once the pants were hung, and my underwear and socks were in the dirty laundry bag, we were again standing face to face; this time both of us naked.

"How may I please you, Sir?" she asked with a small smirk, as she looked up through her lashes at me. My cock jerked as the words spilled from her lips, and I ached with desire watching her play the game along with me.

"Get on your knees, Tiger," I said, my voice gravelly and low, almost a growl.

She complied immediately, kneeling before me, her big eyes looking up my body.

"I want those talented little hands of yours out of the way, Tiger. You're going to keep them under that plush little ass of yours. And you're not going to pleasure yourself with them, either. Do you understand?" It was hard to keep the act up, when looking down I saw my own cock just inches from her sweet fuckable mouth.

She slowly slid her hands between her ass and her calves, but I noticed an irritated bow in her brows as she did it, although she said nothing.

"I asked you a question, Tiger. Don't make me repeat myself. Do.You.Understand?" I growled.

"Yes. SIR," she answered heatedly.

I suppressed a chuckle. God, I loved the fight in her.

"Open your mouth and stick out your tongue," I instructed. She looked surprised, then confused, but she did as I requested. I tangled my hands into the hair at the back of her head, gripping tightly for a little sting at her roots.

"You've been naughty, and disrespectful, so I am going to take my pleasure with that filthy little mouth of yours. You are not allowed to help. You are not allowed to enjoy it. Nod if you understand," I commanded harshly.

Her eyes widened, and she nodded, her tongue still out.

"I'm going to fuck that perfect little mouth of yours. I'm going to fuck my cock down your throat so deep, and then I am going to come deep down that throat. I am going to fuck myself with your filthy mouth, and for once, you will remain quiet." With that I shoved my cock past her open lips and into her mouth.

"Close!" I instructed, and she did. With both hands I grabbed her head roughly and pulled her mouth back and forth over my throbbing cock, which had been begging for attention.

I threw my head back and groaned at the sensation of her warm wet tissue around me, and I pumped her face in and out, chasing my release. Her small moan vibrated around me, sending shivers through my body. I looked down to see her watching my face as I fucked her mouth, I didn't see any sign of anger left in her, only desire as her eyes blazed into mine.

I might have been in charge, but we both know she owned my cock at that moment.

"I'm close, Tiger. You've done a good job of following orders, so you may suck my cock now to suck me off good. No hands, though," I ordered with a groan, fisting her hair again as I dragged her up my hard length.

Instantly her tongue was laving my cock inside her mouth, as her cheeks hollowed, sucking me in deep. I groaned loudly, pumping my cock between her lips faster. I fucked her face hard, and I watched as the girth of it slid into her lips to the hilt, and then back out, over and over. I could feel my balls smacking against her chin, and feel her saliva dripping from the corners of her mouth and down her chin onto my balls. She was so fucking amazing. She made my cock feel incredible, my entire body was lit up like a live wire that she tripped with her mouth alone.

My balls started to tighten. "I'm going to shoot down your throat, Tiger," I huffed out. "Take it! Take my cock! Suck me dry!" I cried, shoving my cock hard into her mouth as I felt the spasms overtake me. I felt the spurts of warmth rising and shooting out of my cock, into her waiting throat, and I realized I held her head in a death grip over my cock, forcing it deep into her. I pulled back, and pumped her mouth a few more times, letting my fluids coat her mouth and tongue, and letting her get air again. I groaned as the waves of pleasure took over my body.

"That's a good Tiger," I cooed, pumping her lips, letting the last of my fluids drain from my cock as it started to slowly soften. "You suck my cock so well. Your mouth was made for me."

I was working really hard to give her what she wanted sexually, a man who was arrogant, dominant, and as filthy as she was. It was a little out of my comfort zone, especially after I had done it before out of spite, but I knew it turned her on. Now that I understood how she liked it, I was determined to be that man for her.

When the last of my orgasm had passed I looked down at her. "Lick it all clean, Tiger. Don't waste a drop." I smiled condescendingly at her. A part of me expected her to quirk an angry brow at me, but instead, she devoured me with her tongue, cleaning my entire shaft, and even licking my balls until I thought I couldn't take it anymore.

"That's good, Tiger. I don't want you to enjoy it too much." I chuckled. We both knew the truth, that it was ME enjoying it too much.

"On the bed, Tiger," I commanded, as I turned and made my way to my suitcase. When I turned around she was on her back, spread before me, and my mouth watered. My cock instantly went firm.

"Tiger," I said gently, and her eyes turned to meet mine. Then she noticed my hands. I held up the handcuffs. "I want to restrain you, Tiger. I need to be sure you will do what I want. Give me a safe word, so I know I won't hurt you, and I will agree to be as rough as you need it." I watched her process my words.

"Orange.... Sir," she amended quickly.

"Your safe word is orange," I repeated, making sure we were clear. "And what will you do if you are uncomfortable or I cross a line, Tiger?" I asked arrogantly.

"I will say orange, Sir," she said, her voice breathy and her eyes half-lidded.

I was suddenly glad I had planned this, seeing how it was getting her off. I hadn't even touched her yet, but I could see her pussy glistening and wet for me. But I had plans to drag this out for a long while.

I walked up to the bed, noticing she was already rubbing her thighs together with need, and I chuckled. I took her wrists and handcuffed them, firmly but not too tightly. I then went back to my suitcase, and to the smaller bag I had hidden behind it. I unzipped it and pulled out a bowling ball. I walked toward her, with the ball in my hands. Her eyes flew open wide, and I laughed openly.

"Hands above your head, Tiger," I ordered. She raised her arms above her head, watching me warily. Once her arms were extended, I placed the bowling ball on her hands to weight them in place. "This way you can't lose your mind and disobey me," I said. "You hold that right there, and don't let it move, Tiger; otherwise I will stop and prolong your suffering."

I walked to the end of the bed, admiring her body laid out before me. Her hands were extended over her head, the weight of the ball keeping them occupied. I washed my gaze down her beautiful face, her swollen lips, down her long graceful neck, her full breasts heaving, her dainty rib cage fluttering, her waist, her full lush hips, and of course her wet pussy lips. Strong legs reached out, open and begging me to fill them with my body heat, but I wasn't giving in that easily.

I had a plan. I was going to bring her to the brink of nirvana, but I was only going to let her have it if she would promise to give me what I wanted as well. I couldn't risk it any other way.

Tonight was the night.

Chapter 22

Red

I had never been so turned on in all of my life. He had handcuffed me, something I was completely unwilling to do with anyone else, and the restraint made me feel vulnerable... and excited! I watched him look over my entire body with approval, and I noticed that his cock was growing harder again with every second that passed.

My core ached to have him inside of me. The need for release pressed hard in my abdomen, making me moan and rub my thighs in anticipation. Bax paid me no attention at all as he went back to his things, searching for something. I wanted to groan or scream for him to get on with it, but we were playing his game tonight. My turn would come. Letting out a frustrated breath, I rubbed my thighs together again, clamping them tight for the friction.

Bax walked back to the bed with a large box in his hands. First the handcuffs and bowling ball, now a box; I had to wonder how long he had been planning this, and I had to admit my curiosity peaked. He placed the box at the head of the bed before he straddled himself over my chest, his cock between my breasts.

"I got something for you," he said with heat in his voice. "But really, it's something for me. You will wear it."

He reached into the box and pulled out a leather collar with a leash attached. It was wide and made of soft black leather. In the center, it was decorated with a large gem, surrounded by smaller gems in dark reds, which got progressively lighter as they fanned out from the center, giving it the appearance of a small sparkly explosion of fire. There were smaller starbursts made of stones decorating the rest of the collar, as well.

No fucking way.

I must have made a face because he stopped, with the collar hovering over my body.

"This is not a request, Tiger. You WILL wear it. You are MINE. You will do whatever the fuck I tell you to do. Is that understood?" he asked fiercely, leaving no room for argument.

I must have taken too long to answer him, because he shot off of my body faster than I thought he could, and swept my legs up with an arm, leaving my ass exposed in the air, before swinging his other hand to smack hard with a crisp CRACK. I yelped with the pain, and tears formed in the corners of my eyes, before he dropped my legs unceremoniously back onto the mattress.

"I don't like to repeat myself," he hissed. Then he reached down and worked the soft collar around the column of my throat, before tightening it in place. It was snug, but didn't stop me from breathing, and it fit from just above my collarbone to just below my jaw. He wrapped the leather leash attached to it around his hand and gave it a good jerk, pulling at my neck like a dog on a lead.

"There's my good little bitch," he said, eyeing me with approval. I wasn't thrilled with the collar, but I also wasn't willing to use my safeword and stop it. I wanted to see where he was going with this. I liked this new side of Bax, so I had to trust he wasn't going to do anything I didn't want.

"Seeing as I'm here, already..." He had moved back onto my chest to put the collar on, and I watched him pull a few of the pillows and stuff them under my head so that my chin was tipped down toward my chest, his cock laid out in front of me between my breasts, already starting to seep from the end.

"I'm going to use your body, Tiger, for my pleasure for as long as I desire. Right now, I'm going to fuck these gorgeous breasts of yours. How does that sound?" he hummed.

Frustrating... that's how it sounds.

"Please, Sir!" was what came out of my mouth.

But he didn't start fucking my breasts, instead he moved off of me, palming one breast roughly and pinching and pulling the nipple, while he brought his warm mouth over my other nipple and nipped it hard. I screamed, and then groaned, as the pain morphed into pleasure under his flickering tongue. My hips writhed as the pleasure sent jolts right into my pussy.

"Such a responsive little Tiger," he murmured over my nipple, sucking it in hard, before releasing it with a pop. "Your body responds to me, and only me, from now on Tiger. I own you. I will be the only man who gets to enjoy your tits like this." He moved his mouth to the other nipple and kneaded my wet breast with his other hand. "Say it, Tiger. Tell me," he commanded, nipping my nipple between his teeth roughly.

I yelped again before blurting out "Yes... Sir! Only you!" I groaned, rubbing my thighs, trying to bring the release I desperately needed.

"All of it Tiger," he growled into my nipple. "I want to hear all of it."

"You... No one else will get to enjoy my body... Only you... you... own me," I whispered on a mewl, my clit begging for relief.

"That's a good Tiger," he hummed, flicking my tender nipple with his tongue. "You get a reward for that."

He slid down my body, bringing his face over my mound, and I moaned in anticipation. My core was begging for release, and it almost hurt as I waited for him to bury his face in me.

Of course, he took his time, gliding his fingers through my folds and making me jerk and buck. He kissed and nipped at my thighs, stroking and licking around my sensitive areas, but never where I needed it, until I was going crazy with need.

And then finally his mouth was on me, the warmth of his tongue licking me up the center and delving deep, before coming back up to service my clit with rough attention. I screamed and bucked my hips up into him, trying to ride his mouth and chase my release, but his hands clamped down roughly on my hips to hold me in place, his fingers digging into my skin.

I thrashed and screamed as he plunged two fingers inside of me, stroking through my wetness with a sucking sound that echoed in the small room. My back arched, as I sucked in breaths around my groans and screams of pleasure. He curled his fingers to hit the spot I so desperately needed, and I felt myself tightening as I got closer to release.

"Such a good little Tiger. You've been such a good girl I'm going to let you come on my mouth. You're lucky I am so generous, Tiger; I could have made you wait all night. Thank me for my generosity, Tiger," he commanded, looking up at me.

"Th-Thank you, SIR!" I screamed, as another wave of pleasure tore through me, my body flexing.

"Just remember who owns your pleasure, Tiger. I give this to you. No other man will ever put his hands on you. His mouth on you. His cock on you. You come for me, and me only. TELL ME," he commanded, his voice booming, as his fingers fucked into me harder, sending my mind into a hazy fog of bliss. I was so close…

His hand stopped.

"TELL ME." he commanded, his fingers poised and unmoving.

"I'M YOURS!" I screamed with frustration. "NO ONE ELSE CAN DO THIS TO ME! PLEASE, SIR… PLEEEAAASSEE!" I was begging, screaming, pleading. I was so close to falling off of the cliff, my body twisted with need and pain...

His fingers slammed back into me, mercilessly, punching into my core, and pulling my release out of me with force. I screamed his name as my body convulsed on itself, every muscle seizing with an orgasm that completely overrode my body and mind. The edges of my vision grew black, and I fought to get air into my lungs as I released long keening screams of pleasure. His hands continued to pummel my sore swollen pussy, while he fawned over my orgasm.

As the last of the shock waves tore through my body, Bax ran his tongue through my folds, licking up all of my wetness, groaning and humming his pleasure at having brought me to such ruin under him.

As much as it irked me to admit it, this "game" of his was my reality. He did own me. He did own my pleasure. He did control my body. Outside of the bedroom, I would never give anyone that kind of power, but here, I was his plaything. I was his to do with as he wanted. As much as my independent side hated it, I WANTED it. I needed it. Nothing made me come faster or harder than a demanding alpha.

Bax finally finished playing with my pussy, enjoying his feast. He wore a smug smile on his face as he dragged his body up mine, his mouth wet with my arousal, again straddling my chest as he looked down at me arrogantly.

"I love making your pussy come for me," he said. "I love the way you break apart under me, and the way I give you permission to release."

I couldn't even argue. I was still floating in post-orgasmic bliss.

"But now it's my turn," he said, reaching a hand back into the box, and coming out with a small clear bottle of lube. My core tightened as I saw it, anticipation making me salivate, and my insides clench with need.

"This isn't for you, Tiger," he laughed cruelly. He poured some of the liquid into his hand and then stroked himself over my chest, the head of his cock just inches from my mouth. My need only intensified as I watched his hand firmly stroking his glistening hardness with a 'thucking' sound that filled the space around my ears.

"You want this cock inside of you, don't you Tiger?" he teased. "You want this cock in all of your holes, don't you? You want me to fuck your mouth, and come down your throat. You want me to beat your pussy with this cock until you're bruised, and I feel you come all over it, don't you?" He stroked himself a little faster, his breathing becoming more uneven.

"But what you REALLY want,..." he pressed the head of his cock to my waiting lips, but didn't let me take him in, "is to feel this fat cock fucking your tight little asshole and making you scream, isn't it, Tiger?" With one hand he pulled the collar tighter around my throat as he taunted, rubbing the wetted head over my lips, his hand still stroking base to tip.

"Tell me, Tiger, or I'm the only one who will get all that pleasure tonight... and I'll make you watch." He smirked.

"Yes!" I yelped. "Yes... I ... I want you to fuck me everywhere! I want you to punish me! I want you to make me sore! I want to come all over your cock!"

Watching him getting himself off, right in front of my face, I would have said anything he wanted. I needed him. The orgasm he had just given me had been earth-shattering... but it wasn't enough. I needed more.

"That's a good little Tiger!" he praised, spreading the lube over my breasts, kneading it into my skin roughly.

He leaned in, placing his cock between my breasts, and then reached over me. I realized he was removing the bowling ball from my hands, and lowering my arms. I rubbed my hands together to get the circulation back in them, as he brought my arms down and around my torso. Lifting up, he brought my arms over my chest, pulling my breasts to stand between my upper arms, before he brought himself down over me again, sandwiching his cock between my constrained breasts, his hips keeping my arms in place over my belly.

"I'm going to fuck your gorgeous tits now, Tiger," he growled, pumping his cock slowly between my slick breasts with a groan. "I'm going to shoot my load all over that beautiful face of yours." He rocked his hips, back and forth, pleasuring his cock with my chest. Leaning forward he braced himself on the headboard behind me.

"FUCK, you feel so good, Tiger. You fucking undo me," he rasped. "I just want to come all over you. I want to fucking bathe you in my fluids. I want you dripping in my come." His pace became more rapid and his breathing became heavier, groaning.

"I wish I could walk you down the street in that collar, Tiger. I'd parade you around in nothing but that collar and my come, dripping off of your beautiful chin, all over your tits, leaking out of your pussy, dripping off of your ass..." He was huffing hard, pounding his cock against my sternum at a punishing pace and pushing me into the mattress under his force.

"Fuck.. I'm going to come!" he hissed, throwing his head back with a loud groan he reached down to grab his length in his hand. I saw the spasms rolling up his muscular cock before the hot milky fluid was spurting onto my mouth and chin, dripping down my neck. He backed up, letting the next few spurts splash onto my chest and collarbone. Groaning, he stroked himself hard, trying to squeeze every last drop out and onto my body.

"Fuck, Tiger, you look good in my come." He smiled, as he reached out to smear his juices over my lips, down my neck, and lastly to spread them out over the globes of my breasts with his hands like he was fingerpainting my body in his essence.

"This body is mine," he said firmly, meeting my eyes, while his hands continued to coat my tits in his fluids. "No other man will ever come on you or in you. Do you understand, Tiger?"

"Yes, Sir," I answered. He was adorably possessive, marking me as his own.

"No man will ever have his fingers in you, or his cock in you. You exist for my pleasure and mine alone. Do you understand?" His eyes never left mine, his command clear.

"What about my OBGYN, Sir?" I asked smartly, a small smirk on my mouth.

"Get a female doctor," he growled. "And for that, you get punished!" The smirk was on his face then.

Fuck.

Baxter

I rolled her over onto her hands and knees, with her ass in the air. I loved the way she leaked her arousal down her thighs. I loved knowing I did that to her. She craved my cock, as much as I craved giving it to her.

"Count them out, Tiger," I ordered as I smacked the soft flesh of her ass hard. The CRACK echoed in the room, sounding loud to my ears.

She screamed and then whimpered. "One."

I immediately cracked her again. "One, WHAT?!" I demanded harshly.

"One, SIR!" she yelped.

"That's a good Tiger. Pick up at three," I stated rubbing my palm over the angry red mark forming on her porcelain ass cheek. I dipped a finger between her legs, sliding it over her clit and causing her to jerk with pleasure before I brought the flat of my hand back to her other ass cheek with force.

"THREE... SIR," she groaned, shifting her ass under my hand.

Again, I gently rubbed over the redness that bloomed where my hand had landed. This time I ran the fingers of my other hand through her wetness, just outside of her opening. I could feel her muscles trying to lure me inside, wanting to fill the needy void.

I brought my hand down hard at the base of her ass so that the force would hit her clit, and she groaned loudly, bucking her hips to follow my hand.

"FOUR, SIR!" Her breathing was in pants, her chest heaving for breaths, and I could see more of her arousal slowly sliding from her opening.

"Am I making you wet, Tiger?" I asked, running my fingers through her silky fluid.

"Yes, Sir," she answered breathily, turning to look at me over her shoulder. Her eyes were heavy with desire, her eyes dilated and glassy.

"What do you want me to give you, Tiger?" I asked magnanimously.

"Please fuck my ass, Sir?" she all but begged.

"Hmmm... I don't know..." I teased, still running my fingers through her pussy, occasionally tweaking her clit and sending her reeling. "You were very naughty today. I have to be sure I have tamed you, Tiger, before I can give you the ultimate prize."

She whimpered, her head falling, and her ass grinding back against my fingers, searching for relief.

"Maybe I should just make you suck me off again, Tiger," I said casually.

"Whatever you want, Sir," she answered immediately.

"*Whatever* I want?" I questioned.

"Yes, Sir," she answered without hesitation.

"Good little Tiger," I praised, slipping two fingers inside of her wetness and pumping her. She responded immediately, groaning and grinding.

I moved up onto my knees behind her, pulling her hips toward me, as I fucked her with my fingers, feeling her squeezing them inside her tight body.

"I think you deserve more, Tiger. I think you deserve to make me come inside of you."

"YES, Sir!" she agreed enthusiastically, still wiggling and groaning.

I placed the head of my cock against her opening, holding her with an arm around her waist to stop her from moving.

"I'm going to fuck you now, Tiger. This is for my enjoyment, not yours. You are not allowed to come. If you do, I will not touch your ass tonight, do you understand?" I asked harshly.

"WHA– Yes, Sir."

I knew she was close, it was going to be hard for her to hold back, but I wanted to try to save her final orgasm for the grand finale. I brought one knee up beside her hips and I thrust inside her hard, filling her to my base. I groaned with pleasure as her warm wet walls enveloped me like a gloved hand, pulling and sucking on my cock deep inside of her.

"FUCK," I growled, before I pulled out roughly, and slammed back into her. I held nothing back. I fucked my cock into her as if I hated her, being as hard and as ruthless as I could. Faster, harder, HARDER; I beat her ass with my hips, trying to lodge myself so deep inside of her that she would taste me. I pounded a punishing pace, feeling her struggling underneath me; not to escape me, but to punish me back. She met me blow for blow, screaming her pleasure, swearing, and cursing. She was a wild animal, my Tiger, and the only way to tame her was to give her the orgasm that calmed her into submission.

I felt her body starting to climb, I felt the beginnings of her release, and I pulled back out of her suddenly. Her hips shot backward, trying to impale herself on my cock.

"NO! NO!" she screamed, but I smothered her arguments.

I pressed my cock into the seam of her ass, and let my body drape heavily down over her back, my face in the crook of her neck. She stilled immediately. I bit into the fleshy part of her shoulder muscle, and she screamed out a moan.

"Listen to me, Red," I stated clearly into her ear, one hand jerking her collar to get her attention. She quieted, her breathing still ragged. "You are MINE. You are all mine. Now and forever. Do you know why, Red? I'll tell you why... because you own ME. My cock is yours. I can't even imagine being with another woman. My heart is yours, I will never love anyone the way that I love you. I don't even want to try. My soul belongs to you, and I am an empty shell without you.

"So I HAVE to own you, Red. I HAVE to claim you. I have to dominate you in the way you dominate me, because if I don't then I am NOTHING.

"Make no mistake, Red, I am claiming you tonight, here, now. I OWN you. You are MINE. I will fucking kill any man who lays a hand on you or hurts you ever again, Red. I am claiming you. You WILL wear my collar. You ARE MINE."

"Bax,..." she whimpered.

I lined the head of my cock up with her asshole and felt her flutter against me.

"There is no argument, Red. The only answer is YES, SIR. You give me what I need, and I will give you what you need." I pressed my cock against her opening more firmly, and reached under her to tease her clit. She groaned and pushed back against me, but I stopped her.

"SAY IT," I demanded gruffly, holding her in a hold I knew would leave bruises on her hips.

"I... I'm yours." She breathed out, conceding. "You own me." The words came out very small, almost defeated, and it broke something in me.

"No, Tiger," I said, pulling her hair to make her look into my eyes. "We own each other now. Don't you dare lose your fight now. I will tame you, but I will never break you."

"Then fuck my ass, Sir!" she insisted with a snarl. "And I'll show you fight."

"That's my Tiger." I smiled, right before I reamed her ass with my cock.

She went feral, screaming and growling, throwing her hips back and arching her ass up to meet my violent thrusts. My hand with the leash wrapped into her hair as well, tugging at her, pulling her head back, and putting pressure on her throat. She roared with pleasure beneath me, her body demanding I take her harder.

"You love that, don't you Tiger?" I ground out between heaving breaths, as I pistoned my hips against her ass mercilessly. "You want me to come in that tight little ass don't you, you filthy Tiger? Take it all, Tiger, make me fill you," I commanded, cracking her ass cheek hard again with my other palm.

She could only scream incoherently, she was beyond language. Her movements were primal, grinding and fucking her ass on my cock as I slammed in deep to meet her. I reached my hand down to find her clit as I felt her building again. I grabbed it and pinched hard while I continued to pound inside of her, and then she was coming.

Her ass clamped down on my cock tight, and I felt my own orgasm rising while she screamed long and low, her face buried in the pillows, unable to move, a quivering mass of sensation. I plunged in hard, throwing my head back and arching my cock to push as deep inside her tightness as I could, and I roared my own release over her. I felt her wetness dripping down over my hand, as my own wetness shot deep in her ass, coating my cock in my own sticky fluid. I continued to massage her clit as I pumped in and out of her, milking the last of myself inside of her warm body, losing myself to the sensation of her muscles contracting around me. When there was nothing left I fell on top of her, spent.

We both lay there, our sweaty hot skin sticking together, heaving in deep breaths of air, our muscles tired and sore.

"I love you, Red," I breathed in a huff, and leaned in to kiss her temple, hidden under her tangled hair. She turned her head to face me, unable to pick it up as she continued to huff breaths.

"I love you too, Bax." A smile split her face, even in her post-orgasmic haze as she looked at me, and it made my stomach flip inside of me.

"I meant what I said, Tiger. You're wearing my collar," I said, suddenly serious.

Her eyes widened. "Bax... you're joking?"

"Of course..." I cut her off. "I realize it's not socially accept-able. So I have prepared a compromise." I turned to reach into the box, now behind me, while she eyed me suspiciously.

I brought my hand between us, my fingers curled to hide the content. "I'm not taking no for an answer. You're accepting my claim, and you're wearing it," I said with more confidence than I felt. I held my breath as I uncurled my fingers to reveal her surprise.

Her eyes shot open wide, and she gasped, as she took in the solitaire diamond ring my mother had given me sitting in my palm.

"This is more publicly appropriate, I think," I said calmly, trying not to squeak.

"Bax," she whispered. Then her eyes narrowed as she looked into my eyes, "Is THIS your proposal?" she hissed.

"I knew if I fucked your ass hard enough you wouldn't be able to say no," I smirked. "Put it on."

"Wait." She drew in a breath, and I froze. If she refused me, she would crush me. I felt my heart crack with that one word. "I will agree on one condition," she said, giving me a hard stare.

I swallowed. "Go ahead."

"I'll wear it, and agree to be yours and only yours..." She paused for dramatic effect, "But next time *I* get to be in charge."

I laughed with relief, all of the air whooshing out of my lungs. "Alright, Tiger. Anything you say."

I slid the ring on her finger and watched her stare at it, turning her hand to catch the light until she finally looked up at me with a goofy smile on her face.

And I was complete.

Chapter 23

Red

We laid there, hot and sticky, for a long while, until Bax finally lifted up onto his elbow and suggested we shower. We made our way into the hotel bathroom together, and when I went to take the ring off he grabbed my hand.

"NEVER take this off," he whispered. "This has been passed down through my mother's family for generations, but she had no brothers. You are her kin now too," he said softly into my ear, rubbing his thumb over the ring at my knuckle.

I didn't know what to say. It felt like it was too important to be given to someone like me. I wanted to give it back to him, tell him it was too special, but he placed his mouth over mine in a kiss, his hand still rubbing the ring into my finger as if to brand it into my skin.

"I can't wait to tell her she'll have a daughter soon," he whispered over my mouth. "She loves you, you know." He pulled back, his eyes sparkling with joy.

I swooned. I wanted to be the woman who made him so happy, but I couldn't help the feeling in my gut that said I wasn't worthy of all of this attention. I didn't deserve a diamond ring. But I also couldn't be the villain and steal that look off of his face, either, so I stuffed down my inadequacies and kissed him with all of my heart.

We made it back to bed in time to count down the end of the year. We kissed as it turned midnight, and the year turned over. The first moments of our new year were spent naked and sated in each other's arms.

"How is this going to work?" I asked suddenly, and he looked down at me. "I live in Virginia, you live here. How is this going to work... us getting married?"

"We'll think of something," he said calmly, his hand caressing my hair the way he does when he wants to comfort me. "I mean, you don't really have a lot down there, do you? You don't have that job anymore, and the apartment wasn't in the best neighborhood. Your family and your friends are all up here already. You could just move up here with me," he offered simply.

"I don't know if I'm ready to move," I said quietly.

"You don't want to be with me, Red?" he asked, and his hand stilled on my hair.

"I didn't say that," I answered. "I just need some time to process all of this change. It's all happening very quickly."

He didn't answer me, but his hand continued its slow strokes down my hair. I didn't want to upset him, but I also didn't want to get railroaded into making decisions I wasn't ready to make.

"Can we talk about it again, later?" I asked hopefully.

"Of course, Red," he said, and leaned down to kiss me on the top of my head. "We don't have to make any decisions right now. We should get some sleep."

He pulled his body down into the covers, and I wrapped my leg and arm around him as I snuggled into his chest. When I felt him look down, I looked up, and he took my mouth in a reverent kiss, pulling me closer to his chest.

"Goodnight, Tiger," he whispered, as he reached to shut off the bedside lamp.

"Goodnight, Bax."

When I woke up the sky was only just starting to brighten with the sun. I hated the winter schedule where both mornings and evenings were dark, with a tiny window of sunlight in between. I stretched and startled when I didn't come into contact with Bax. Sitting up quickly, I found his side of the bed empty.

Scratching my head in confusion, I got out of bed to check the bathroom, but it was empty as well. I pulled on a robe and headed for the coffee maker when I heard the key card swipe in the door, and it pulled open.

Bax strolled in with his gym bag, his sweats on underneath his winter coat. He made his way over to me with a huge grin, pulling me into a hug before handing me a large steaming cup of coffee.

"The in-room coffee is terrible. I couldn't make you suffer through it," he stated, as he smothered my face in kisses. His lips were freezing from having been outside. I squealed and pulled away from him and his cold face and fingers.

"Are you naked under that robe?" he asked me suddenly, a mischievous smile spreading on his lips.

"Bax! No. I'm- NO! BAX!" I shrieked as he chased me around the room, shucking off his coat as he went, and pulling his sweatshirt off. The room was only so big, there wasn't anywhere for me to really hide, so he had me cornered in seconds, and was snaking his hands into the warmth of my robe to torment me with his icicle fingers against my warm flesh.

We ended up rolling on the floor together, laughing and screeching like children, until Bax pulled me up to join him in the shower, which ended up taking far longer than it should have, as neither of us is great at resisting temptation.

We had breakfast with all of our friends; except Amber and Vic who were, again, conspicuously absent. No one mentioned it, as I was sure no one was really missing either of them. After check out, Bax and I went back to his place, and I started some laundry. I marveled at the 'normality' I seemed to be fitting right into.

Could I see myself living in this apartment with him? Making dinner and doing laundry? He was right when he said I didn't have much in Richmond, I really didn't. There was nothing holding me there, and everything luring me here. So why was I hesitant?

Bax breezed through the hall and kissed me on the head.

"I have to run a few errands. Will you be okay here while I'm gone?" His hand lingered on my hip.

"I'm fine, Bax. Go do you." I smiled back at him.

He gave me one more assessing look, before he nodded to himself, and then started for the front door. "I shouldn't be too long," he called over his shoulder as he put his winter coat on, and in moments I heard the door click shut softly behind him.

Finishing my laundry, I headed into the bedroom to prepare for MY night with Bax. I pulled out one of his silk ties, and then another one; one to tie, and one to blindfold. I put the lube with them and searched for the buttplug I had ordered. Payback was indeed a bitch.

I turned, and the small box Tony had given me caught my eye. I stopped and stared at it for a moment, my stomach churning. I hadn't opened it yet, too afraid of what I would find inside. It was just a harmless cardboard box, but it represented all of the emotions I associated with my father; many I had not even identified yet.

Stop being such a wuss. Just get it over with.

I took small halting steps as I inched closer to it as if it would reach out and bite me. Picking it up gingerly, I brought it to the bed and sat down with it in my lap. *It was just a cardboard box.* There was nothing extraordinary about it, but it gave me a visceral reaction.

I gently eased the top off and placed it on the bed. Inside I could see photos, small trinkets, and an envelope that had yellowed with age. I pulled out the pictures and looked through them one by one. Each were scenes from my childhood.

One showed my mother, father, and me at the beach; I was very young then, and we were all smiling like a happy family. My heart squeezed in my chest. The next few were of my mother and father together, doing ordinary things; sitting at the table, dancing, and playing cards. I shuffled through them, taking in every memory, every smile. If someone had only seen these pictures, and didn't know us, they would have thought we were an average loving family and not a family involved in organized crime.

The last photo was of my father holding my shoulders as I looked at the camera with a huge smile on my face. I was missing my two front teeth. His head was above mine, and he wore the same adoring smile on his face. Tears threatened to leak from my eyes. I remembered thinking the sun and moon set with him when I was younger; I remembered him adoring me back then.

Putting the photos back, I pulled out the envelope and slid it open. Inside there was a handwritten letter, and I recognized my father's messy scrawl.

"Renny,

You've been gone many years now, and I have asked myself every day what I did wrong that I failed you so badly. You reminded me so much of your mother that when you left it was like I lost you and her, again, that day. I had always promised her I would protect you. How did I mess it up so badly?

I found out what Rocky did to you, and it killed something in me, Renny. I don't understand why you didn't feel you could tell me, but clearly, I gave you enough reason to think you couldn't trust me with that. I will forever regret that. I had made it clear to all of the people who came to work for me that no one was ever allowed to put a hand on you; obviously, I didn't do a good enough job of protecting you from the dangers of my world. I take full responsibility for that.

I know I can never undo what was done. I know I can never have your trust again, the way I used to when you were just my little girl. That, more than anything, is the thing I regret most in this life. Everything else I have done pales in comparison.

You were always my bright star, my Princess. I'm sorry that I lost sight of that.

I could never be mad at you, or hold a grudge with you for anything. You are my blood. You are the part of your mother that I loved the most. I wish I could tell you this myself, but the doctors say my health is failing. I may never get to see you again.

If I could have one wish, it would be to see you again, to hold you again. I know it's selfish, but I am an old man now. What was all of this worth, if I had to lose you in the process?

I know it won't make up for the ways that I have failed you, but I have left a substantial investment behind for you, to make sure you never have to worry about anything again. I hope that you find love, get married, and have a family of your own. I know your mother would have wanted that for you too. This money is all that I have to give you, and while it's no substitute for the years of love that I have not been able to give you, I hope that you will take it in the spirit in which I intend it.

If you know nothing else about me, please know that I love you. I never stopped loving you. You will always be my Princess.

Love,

Dad"

Tears streamed down my face as I held the delicate paper in my hands. I didn't have the energy to ponder the "what if's" of my life decisions; what was done was done, and there was no going back. Still, it warmed my heart to see the photos of the man I had adored as a child, while I still felt he adored me back and it was even nicer hearing that he did value me, at least in his own way. I was loved.

I started to put everything back into the box before I could have a full emotional meltdown, and I heard my cell phone ringing from the other room. I put the lid on the box hastily and rushed to answer the call before it went to voicemail. Scooting through the room I snatched the phone up, surprised to see Vic's name on the caller ID; I hesitated, wondering if I should just let it go, but decided to just face the issue head-on. I'd rather get our drama out of the way sooner than later.

"Vic," I answered.

"Nat. I need your help." His voice was urgent, laced with panic. "It's... something has happened, and I need to talk to you in person. PLEASE."

"What is it? What's happened?" I asked. His fear was compelling, but my gut told me something was off.

"I don't have time, Nat! Please! Just meet me at this address, I promise, I'll explain everything!" He rattled off an address to me, and I had to stop him so I could find a pen and a piece of scrap paper.

"Let me call Bax–"

"NO! Nat! This is personal, just you and me. I don't need everyone knowing about this. Promise me! Just meet me." His voice was nearly hysterical, and then the line went dead in my hand. I chewed my lip, debating. I didn't trust him, it didn't feel right. There was NO reason he needed to see me alone, and I knew it.

But my guilt crept into my belly; he had saved my life once. He had gotten me to safety. He had watched over me from afar all of those years. This was VIC. He would never do anything to hurt me.

I quickly dialed Bax's number, needing to hear his voice, his opinion; suddenly not trusting my own. The line rang and rang and finally dumped me into voicemail. It was unlike Bax not to have his phone on, and my stomach turned. I shot him a text next, telling him what Vic had said, and that I was going to meet him; as well as the address where the meeting would take place. I knew he wasn't far away; if he saw the text, he could just meet me there. This way I would be arriving alone as requested, but I wouldn't be without backup. Satisfied that I had taken sufficient precaution, I grabbed my purse and coat and ordered an Uber to get me there.

The streets of Boston were still snowy and congested. Every delay set my nerves on edge, as I watched the driver edge through traffic aggressively. My hands were rolling nervously in my lap, and my knee was tapping an impatient cadence as I checked the time on my phone again. I was nervous to get there, and I was also wishing I wasn't going there at all.

When the driver finally pulled up in front of a laundromat I stared in confusion.

"Is this the address I gave you?" I asked. He just grunted in the affirmative, pointing to the faded numbers over the peeling paint on the door. The building was old and neglected, and there was no sign that anyone had used it anytime recently. Warning alarms were blazing in my head as I stepped out of the car. With one last look at the building, I was turning to tell the driver to just take me home when I heard Victor.

"Nat! Thank god you're here!" He rushed up the snowy sidewalk, and taking my elbow he steered me toward the building.

"What are we doing here, Vic? Why can't we talk at your place?" I asked, suddenly very uncomfortable with stepping inside the building.

"Because Amber's there," he hissed. "There's a lot I need to tell you, and I don't want her to hear it." His eyes softened as he looked at me. "I need you to trust me."

I nodded at him slowly, and he moved back toward the door again, pulling me along with him and I let him. He made his way into the back, past rows of ancient washing machines and dryers. He had been there before and knew the layout. He stopped in a large cinder block room in the back which was cluttered with dusty tables and some chairs, but otherwise empty. Vic reached the switch by the door and flicked the overhead lights on, but they did little to disperse the gloom leaking out of the shadows.

"What's going on Vic?" I demanded, keeping myself close to the door in case I needed to run for it.

Vic stood stock still, his forehead bowed in his hand. "She has my child, Nat. She was pregnant when she left, and she's holding my kid over my head," he gritted out.

His eyes rose to meet mine, and there was a tortured quality to them.

"I lost a baby with you. I can't lose another kid," he said urgently.

The shock left me reeling. "Wha–... Vic, do you think she's telling the truth?"

We both knew Amber was a drama queen, and more than capable of lying or spinning the truth to meet her goals.

"You think I didn't already check?" he demanded. "Yes, she's telling the truth! I've seen the birth certificate, the timing matches exactly. Of course I'll demand a paternity test, but I've seen pictures; Nat, she looks JUST LIKE ME."

He started pacing in a small circle, his hands clenching and unclenching, as if he didn't know what to do with himself.

"So why did you need to see me, Vic?" I asked calmly, sensing the storm approaching.

"I'm so sorry, Nat," he said, his voice cracking.

Baxter

I cursed as a car tried to cut me off, but ended up sliding in the slushy snow and nearly careening into me. As he pulled away my phone rang with a number I didn't recognize, and I answered it through my car sound system.

"Agent Murphy"

"Agent Murphy, this is Tony Giovanni. I have a proposition for you." His voice was calm, denoting a man who was clearly used to getting respect.

"You must have me mistaken for my father," I bit out. "I am not interested in any proposition from you."

"Oh, I think you will be, Baxter, if you want to see Nat alive again," he stated flatly.

My blood turned cold with fear. "Go ahead, I'm listening," I answered through gritted teeth.

Red

"So, what? You had me come here to kill me? For HER?" I demanded, the anger from fifteen years ago rising and demanding to be heard. "You put me on a bus, beaten, and having lost a baby, ALONE, so that you could stay and continue to fuck her... and NOW you're willing to kill me? FOR HER?!" I was shrieking.

"It's not like that—"

"DON'T YOU FUCKING LIE TO ME!" I bellowed. "For over a year you CHEATED on me, with HER... IN PUBLIC. You gave her all of the things I could never have. You could hold her hand, you could kiss her on the street, while I had to be your dirty little whore in the background. And I DID THAT to protect YOU! And how did you thank me?! By letting me have to listen to her giving me the play-by-play of every dirty thing you two ever did together! Do you have ANY IDEA what that did to me?!"

A loud noise rang in the other room, and Vic and I both spun to face the door as Amber walked in like she owned the place. Her head was held high, and her walk confident, but her eyes burned with rage.

"So let me get this straight," she snapped, her eyes shooting between Vic and me, "You two were already dating when Vic agreed to go out with me?!"

Vic opened his mouth to say something but she just shot him a look and he shut it.

"It makes so much sense now," she seethed. "All those times Vic came around, the way he was always sniffing after you... I thought he just hadn't gotten over you. But he'd been fucking you that whole time. And when I told you I wanted to go out with him, you never fucking said a WORD!" Her eyes and her rage were turned onto me like a spotlight.

"I couldn't tell you, Amber. My father would have killed him. It was supposed to be a secret," I shot back heatedly.

"And YOU!" Her finger shot up, pointing to Vic. "You took me out, you FUCKED ME. And the whole time you were out fucking her too!" she screamed.

Vic stared at his feet dejectedly and said nothing.

"You BOTH knew! You both knew I was being used, and neither of you... my *FRIENDS*... ever said a word," she sneered at us. "Did you laugh behind my back too? Was it all a big joke to you both?!"

"I wasn't happy about it either!" I screamed. "I never WANTED to share my boyfriend. But if I told anyone, he'd be in danger. My dad would have beaten him half to death AT LEAST. I had no choice but to keep his secret." I turned to Vic. "What's YOUR excuse?!"

Vic looked gutted. His shoulders sagged and his eyes were wide and pleading as he took in our combined rage aimed in his direction.

"I loved you, Nat. At first, I loved you more than anything," he said softly, before turning to Amber. "But I fell in love with Amber when we started going out, and I didn't know how to end it with you. You kept telling me that you loved me, and I didn't want to hurt you by breaking up, and I didn't want to risk you telling the family to get back at me. I thought that if you started going out with Rocky, it would kind of solve the problem for me." His voice cracked, his eyes glossing.

"So you continued to selfishly use us both?!" I demanded. "You fucking COWARD!"

"You are so full of shit!" Amber screamed. "After she left that's all you ever did was fucking moon over her. You think I didn't know about all of your late-night calls with her? I saw the fucking phone bills, Asshole. You think I didn't put it together?! You think I'm going to believe that I was the one that you wanted after you had a fucking baby with her?!" she roared, her control breaking.

"I didn't even know about the baby until that night!" he screamed back, finally finding his fight.

"She used YOUR fucking last name at the clinic!" Amber screamed. "Don't fucking tell me you didn't know! If she had that baby, were you just going to dump me? Was that the plan? Use me and then just leave me behind to have your perfect little family with the Mafia Princess? Did you think that would move you up the ladder faster, Vic?!" She was screaming, her arms flailing, and her face red. Any semblance of control or reason was gone.

Victor said nothing, he only stared at me with apologizing eyes, begging for something, but I had no idea what.

"Red!"

The three of us turned to the door just as Bax ran into the room to stand beside me.

"It's about fucking time," Amber hissed, pulling herself together. "Vic."

She turned to him with a nod. He pulled a pistol out of the back of his pants and aimed it at me.

"I know you have one too," Vic said to Bax. "Drop it on the floor and kick it away."

"You wouldn't shoot Nat," Bax said calmly, but his eyes were a little too wide.

Amber chuckled. "You'd be surprised what he'd do, *Bax*. I'd suggest you listen to him. He knows what's at stake if he doesn't play along."

"Bax, don't!" I urged, but he was already pulling out his pistol and placing it on the floor. He kicked it, sending it skittering away from him across the concrete floor. Then he moved to me and pulled me further behind him and into the room, away from Vic and Amber.

"It's going to be alright," he whispered to me soothingly, but there was no hiding the concern on his face.

"I knew you'd never come alone," Amber gloated. "You never could take orders, could you, *Princess*?" she hissed. "And now it's time for payback! The way I see it, you took something I wanted, and ruined my life; so now it's time for me to take something YOU want. How's it going to feel knowing you are responsible for Bax's death, huh?"

"What is your fucking problem, Amber?! Vic cheated on ME with you, NOT the other way around. If you've got a beef, it's with him," I hissed back at her.

"Oh, I do have a beef with him, but we're settling that, aren't we Vic?" She sneered in his direction.

"It was fifteen fucking years ago, Amber. What do you hope to gain by any of this NOW?!" I was regretting not having punched her in the throat at the wedding when I had the chance.

"Well, I was willing to put it behind us, let bygones be by-gones, but you're such a fucking whore that as soon as I find a guy, you've just got to go and fuck him away for yourself!" Her lip curled up with disgust.

I shook my head in disbelief. "Again, Vic was MINE first... I didn't steal him. Secondly, I didn't steal Bax, he wanted me, and he wasn't in a relationship with you. And again, I dated him before you even met him! You need to get over yourself."

"Oh, is that what they teach you in the mafia, Nat?" she threw out condescendingly. "You can just take whatever you want, and to hell with anyone else? Because you are 'Renatta Fucking Giovanni!' Because you want it, it's yours for the taking, and to hell with anyone else's feelings?!"

"Amber, you and I were never a couple. We fucked. That's it," Bax spoke up suddenly, stepping forward to draw her attention.

"So because you don't care, that makes it okay? Is that more mafia ethics? Well.. if that's the case, maybe I should just kill Nat, since I don't care. How does that sound?" She shot him a glare filled with poison.

"Stay out of this, Loverboy, this is between Nat and us!" Vic spit.

"Yes, it is," The voice was calm and clear as it rang into the room. All heads turned to watch as Tony slowly made his way into the space as if he had all of the time in the world. He stood between a frozen Amber and Vic, two of his men at his back watching the door.

Baxter and I were completely cut off from the only escape by all of them.

"Agent Murphy, I assume," Tony said, staring at Bax.

"Tony," Bax said back, with a slight nod.

"That's 'Mr. Giovanni,' to you, boy. You are not on a first-name basis with me. And I assume you understand how I deal with people who interfere in my family business?" His eyes were narrowed on Bax.

"Uncle Tony, he came here for me! He's not interfering!" I tried to explain, but Tony just turned to Vic, and my gut dropped. I knew right then Vic was going to throw Bax under the bus. He was going to save his own ass.

"Victor... tell me... is this federal agent interfering in my business?" Tony asked calmly, like he was discussing the weather, or what to have for lunch.

"He's... yes, Tony." Vic's jaw tightened.

"And your little girlfriend here..." Tony indicated Amber, where she stood stock still and made no sound. "Has Agent Murphy interfered in her business as well?" he asked shrewdly.

Victor shot a look at Amber, and then back to Tony, before nodding mutely.

"I'm a busy man," Tony sighed heavily. "I don't have all day to deal with petty problems." He pulled a gun out of a holster and I screamed.

"UNCLE TONY, NO!"

Beside me, Bax went completely still. "Mr. Giovanni... Please,..." he begged.

"Renny, I'm sorry, Honey," Tony said quietly. "Trust me, you'll thank me one day."

Before I could even breathe the BOOM of the pistol filled the small space, almost deafening me. I jumped and screamed as I watched Bax take a couple of staggering steps back, his hands clutching his chest before he went down hard on the concrete floor on his back. A cloud of dust rose up around him, and I flew to him, still screaming.

"Victor, bring your girlfriend, we can discuss business in my office," I heard Tony's voice, and the sound of retreating steps on the concrete, but they were irrelevant. My chest heaved with sobs as I screamed and screamed, tearing at Bax's coat, trying to get it off of him so I could find the wound and stop the bleeding.

But my fingers were numb, I couldn't get them to work right. I threw myself at his coat, trying to tear it off or pull it away, but I couldn't manage anything at all. I was beyond hysterical, and finally just collapsed on his chest wailing.

Chapter 24

Red

I felt his hand on the back of my head before I heard his voice rumbling, muffled by his coat.

"I'm okay Red. It's okay."

My head shot up to see his head was tilted up to see me, worry lining his eyes.

"H-HOW?!"

I started to hyperventilate, not able to catch my breath. My hands clawed at my chest.

Bax groaned as he sat up quickly, pulling me into him, and pushing my head down toward my knees. "Easy, Red. Slow down. Deeeep breaths… there you go." He ran his hand down my hair, speaking soothing words, and occasionally wincing in a breath.

I heaved and hacked, overwhelmed with emotion, but when I finally got my breath back, I turned to him. I knew I must look like a nightmare, but I felt like I was seeing a ghost. He had been shot! I had LOST him! I wanted to grab him and hold onto him to prove I wasn't imagining this.

"How?" I asked again, my lip trembling, my eyes and nose running from grief.

"I'm wearing a vest," he said simply. When I stared at him blankly, he filled in the blanks. "A bullet-proof vest, Red."

I let out the breath I had been holding and then erupted into sobs all over again. He pulled me in close and just held me, letting me cry, telling me that he was okay, that we were okay, but I was not okay. I had lost him. I lost the most important person in my life that day. I was far from okay.

When I started calming down Bax finally slowly pulled himself up to standing with a groan and a wince, grabbing his ribs.

"I thought you said you were okay!" I shouted in fear, my terror rising again.

"Honey, they stop the bullet from penetrating, but they don't stop the impact," he groaned. "It's like getting kicked by a horse. I need to see a doctor and make sure I don't have any broken ribs," he said patiently.

That spurred me into moving. I threw his arm around my shoulder and steered him back through the door. The others were long gone. Bax told me how to get to his car, and although I was in no condition to drive, I wasn't going to make him do it. I cursed the snow as we snaked through the slick streets.

"What the hell just happened?" I asked, overwhelmed by everything I had just seen and heard.

"After I left the apartment today, I got a call from Tony," he said.

I turned to him in shock, my mouth hanging open.

"Yeah, that's the way I felt too." Bax chuckled, and then groaned, clutching his ribs again.

"Amber got pregnant all those years ago, and then left without telling Victor; now she's using the girl as leverage to force Victor to get her revenge for her. But Vic knew better than to kill you, he couldn't go against Tony and the family. But if he did nothing, he'd lose his only chance to find his child. So Vic finally did the adult thing and called Tony for help. He told him the whole situation, and where and when he was bringing you to her.

"Then Tony called me. He didn't want there to be any chance that you would get hurt, so he wanted me to be there to draw fire. We came up with a plan of our own. We couldn't take the chance that Vic or Amber would shoot you, nor that they would shoot me anywhere that the vest didn't cover. So Tony would shoot me, where he knew I would survive it.

"Amber would think that her revenge had been served, so she wouldn't come after you again, and Tony could use that to his advantage and say that she owed the family now, so he could force her to give Vic access to his daughter.

"For a criminal, he is pretty brilliant." Bax wheezed a laugh.

"I am going to fucking kill him the next time I see him," I seethed. "HE SHOT YOU!"

"Because I told him to," Bax said gently. "Neither of us was willing to let you die, Red. I'd do this a thousand times if it kept you safe."

"You could have said something," I grumbled, trying to be grateful.

"There was no time, Red. We wanted this to be believable."

"So when you were begging him?..." My jaw went slack.

"It was to shoot me so that they would leave you alone," he confirmed.

Tears formed in my eyes again, and before I could say anything else we were at the Emergency Room and getting Bax inside.

I sat by his bedside as they taped his ribs and wrapped him. He was lucky to have only one fracture, but the enormous black bruise on his chest made it look much worse. When the staff had all left the room I moved to his side.

"I guess I don't get my turn tonight, huh?" I teased, trying to make him smile.

"I'll move to Virginia," he said suddenly.

My smile fell.

"Why would you do that?" I asked.

"If you're not ready to come to Boston, I can request a transfer to Richmond. I don't want you to feel you have to make all of the sacrifices for this to work. I want to be with you; I don't care where we are, as long as we're together." He reached a hand up to tangle in my hair, while his eyes searched mine.

"Bax, don't be an idiot." I laughed. "Your job is up here. My family and friends are up here. Hell, I own a house up here."

"You own a house?" he asked in confusion.

"The point is,..." I continued. "I never said I wasn't ready to move up here. But I had just gotten engaged only moments before, and suddenly we were discussing moving. I need time to process the change, Bax. I've had fifteen years of controlling every aspect of my own life, you're going to have to be patient with me while I navigate this whole 'partnership' thing." I smiled at him warmly.

"Take all the time you need, Tiger." He pulled me close for a kiss.

"If you're really good,..." I teased over his lips, "I'll let you live in my house with me."

Bax was assigned bed rest for a few days, and while I can confirm that he spent most of it in bed, I cannot honestly say that he was resting. I will say that I got to take a lot of control during those days, to keep him from "over-exerting." I can also confirm that he was extremely satisfied with his level of care over those days, as he told me so, and demonstrated by painting my body in his milky essence, his new favorite pastime.

I told him about the box my father had left for me, and showed him the contents. I didn't break down and cry, but the 'feels' were definitely there. Bax went through all of the small items in the box, and then he handed me a small key with a tag attached.

"What does it go to?" I asked, eyeing the key.

"It looks like a safety deposit box key," he said, picking it out of my hand. "Look, the tag has the name of a bank and the box number. Are you up for an adventure?" He smiled his brilliant smile that made me fall for him all over again.

We were at the bank in no time, and once we had the box in front of us and the room to ourselves, I opened it. "Substantial Investment" was an understatement. There were deeds to several properties, both in the US and internationally. There were several loose gems and other precious jewelry. There were stock and bond certificates. And lastly, there was a card for a financial planner, with a note simply saying "call him." I had no way to evaluate the worth of what I was looking at, but even I could tell it was a LOT of money.

I bit my lip as I looked through the paperwork once more. I snuck a side glance at Bax and noticed that he had his "work face" on. When he concentrated, his brows would dip, as if he was contemplating a puzzle he needed to solve. That was the face he wore, as he took in the massive amount of wealth my gangster father had left behind for me.

We emptied the box, choosing to take everything home so we could thoroughly investigate just how much money we were looking at. As I pulled the strap for the briefcase over my shoulder I turned to Bax.

"What's wrong?" I asked.

"Nothing," he stated flatly.

"That 'nothing' means 'something.'" I looked up at him. "I need words, Bax. What's going on in your head?"

He stopped. His eyes flitted from spot to spot, still in "puzzle-solving mode" before he finally settled on me.

"I think I need to transfer to a different position within the Bureau," he said finally.

"Why?" I asked, wanting to understand his reasoning. He had spent years training for his current position. I wanted to be sure I understood why he would choose to leave it.

"Because," he started, then paused. "It's a conflict of interest for me to hold a position where I am expected to investigate my wife's family. Your interactions with your family should be private, and I can't be a part of your family but not associate with them. I no longer have the passion to pursue them that I used to; now I'm only interested in pursuing one member of that family." He smirked at me slyly.

"Besides, there are lots of other positions which I am equally qualified for, and would require less travel and less time away from my family." His million-dollar smile dazzled me again.

"And you won't grow to resent me someday for giving up this position?" I asked.

"Tiger, there is only one position I am not willing to give up for you. I'd gladly demonstrate when we get home if you'd like." He waggled his eyebrows at me suggestively, as he grinned.

"I have created a monster!" I groaned.

"I'll play Godzilla if you'll be Tokyo!" He laughed. I groaned and slapped his arm, and we made our way out of the bank.

The next day I contacted the financial advisor from the business card we had found in the safety deposit box. Apparently, my father had been working with him for quite a while and had amassed quite a retirement portfolio; including the deeds and other items from the box.

"Four hundred and twenty-two," he said as I heard his adding machine clicking away in the background.

"That's it?" I asked incredulously. "The properties alone seemed to be worth quite a bit more," I added.

He cleared his throat. "*Million,*" he clarified. "Four hundred and twenty-two million dollars; that is the current value of all of your father's assets, including his Boston home of course."

My jaw fell open, and my mind stuttered. It was incomprehensible. *Millions?! What the hell was I supposed to do with millions?!*

"Miss Brooks? Are you still there?" he asked.

"Y-yes,..." I stuttered. "I'm going to need some time to process this, thank you."

"Of course. Call me if you'd like to transfer any of this, or liquidate any of the properties. I am glad to be of service, Vinnie was a close personal friend."

Baxter

I was sweating bullets as I shut the car off. Taking a deep breath, I unbuckled my seat belt and got out of the car. The neighborhood was eerily quiet, and I saw many faces that turned to watch me silently, like a warning. My palms were sweaty when I held my hand out to Red.

She bounced out of the car with a smile, seemingly oblivious to the danger surrounding us; although, to be fair, it wasn't really a danger to her... only to *me*. She led me to the small metal gate in the fence surrounding a small neighborhood yard and house. It was quaint, and surprisingly... normal.

"Are you sure you want to do this Bax? You don't need to." She studied my face with concern, her fingertip tracing my cheek.

"I'm sure," I groaned. "I've already fucked this up, so I need to do this now before I make it any worse."

"Bax,..." She soothed. "I'm sure you're worrying about nothing. It won't be that bad." She smiled at me reassuringly.

"Yeah... considering he shot me the last time I saw him, things can only look up," I said under my breath, just as I heard the front door creak open.

"Renny, Agent Murphy, won't you come in?" Tony stood in his expensive suit, with a cigar propped in his mouth, at the top of the stairs watching us.

"Uncle Tony!" Red chirped happily, running up to grab him in a hug. He happily hugged her back with an adoring smile on his face, but as I approached his smile fell, and his business mask met me.

"Mr. Giovanni," I said politely, extending my hand.

His eyes flicked to my hand and back to my eyes. He paused, taking a deep puff of his cigar, and then breathing out a billow of smoke before he spoke.

"Call me Uncle Tony," he said, taking my hand in his and squeezing it. A smile pulled at the corner of his lips.

He ushered us inside and pulled out an expensive bottle of scotch. Pouring two fingers into three glasses, and then passing them around, he finally turned to me.

"So, Baxter, what did you need to talk to me about today? My niece tells me I may be getting some good news?" Tony stood tall, every bit the boss.

"Well, Mr. Giovanni—"

"Uncle Tony," he corrected me in warning.

"Uncle Tony... I... I wanted to ask for your blessing, I wish to marry Natalie." I could feel the sweat beading on my forehead, and I was suddenly blazing hot.

It didn't help that Tony was staring at me in a way that could either mean "I am going to have you skinned alive" or "I need to think about this." He took another long drag on his cigar. Finally, ever the king of the dramatic pause, he spoke.

"You've already given her a ring and asked, you're a little late, aren't you?" He didn't sound insulted.

"Well... no offense, Uncle Tony, but I'm not asking for your permission. I'm marrying her. I can't live without her. If I'm going to die anyway, I'd rather die married to her. I'd like your blessing so that I can actually get to live with my wife," I clarified.

Tony's eyes opened wide. I saw a couple of his guys stand up a little straighter and move a little closer. Then Tony threw his head back and laughed loudly, his hands wrapping around his belly. His goons made their way back to whatever they had been doing, and I blew out a breath in relief.

"I can see why she likes you!" He chuckled, before turning to Red. "Renny, does he make you happy? Does he treat you right? Does he treat you with respect and make you his equal?"

Her smile lit up the room. "He does, Uncle Tony," she said and sent me an adoring look.

Tony harrumphed and then turned back to me. "You have my blessing, kid. Partly because I know she can kick your ass, even without me. Good luck. You'll need it." Then he laughed again, before pulling me in for a hug and slapping me hard on the back.

A few minutes later I walked Red back to the car under my own power, with all of my limbs, and without needing to stop at the Emergency Room afterward. When dealing with Tony Giovanni, I call that a win.

Red

Time seemed to pass quickly. I was settling into Bax's apartment, and enjoying playing house with him, but there was a shadow lingering to the light of my happiness. I sipped my drink as I stared out the window at the setting sun over the Boston skylight as I pondered. I now had a small fortune, but I had no direction.

"What's on your mind, Tiger?" His voice purred beside my ear, and I looked up to find Bax behind me, his fingers already tangling in my hair, stirring the heat between my legs.

"How would you feel about getting a house together?" I asked, pulling my lip between my teeth nervously.

"I think it's a great idea," he said happily. "What brought this on?"

"I inherited my father's house," I said quietly.

"You want to move in there?" he asked, curiously.

"Oh God no," I breathed out. "I love my family, but I don't think it's a good idea for us to live so close to them."

I heard him breathe a sigh of relief as if he hadn't been looking forward to that either, and I smirked.

"No, I just thought…" I looked up at him uncertainly, and then pulled my eyes down again. "If we ever… you know… if we wanted a family… It would be nice to have a yard and a nice neighborhood." I shuffled my hands in my lap, too nervous to look up.

We hadn't discussed kids. We hadn't really discussed anything about the future.

"Well, if we're going to do that, we'd better make sure it has a lot of bedrooms," he said in a serious tone. I looked up at him then, unsure where he was going with it, and he couldn't keep a straight face. "Because we're going to need them for all of the babies I'm going to put into you."

I felt the blush creep up my cheeks, but I couldn't stop the goofy grin that came to my lips.

"You're putting the cart before the horse, aren't you?" I asked. "We haven't practiced nearly enough."

He rushed around the chair and snatched me up into his arms while I squealed with delight.

"I'm on it!" he shouted as he carried me quickly through the apartment and into the bedroom, launching me onto the bed.

We were walking down the street a few days later when I happened to notice a tattoo parlor on the corner. I stopped, taking in the pictures in the windows.

"You want a tattoo?" Bax chuckled in my ear, clearly seeing my interest.

"I don't know," I answered honestly. "I've always been interested, but it seems painful."

Bax seemed to contemplate this, and I turned to him. "How about you? Would you ever get a tattoo?" I asked with a smirk.

"Absolutely," he said without hesitation.

"Really?" I was taken aback. He had always seemed so straight-laced. "What would you get?" I asked.

"I'd get 'Red's' tattooed on my cock, so everyone would know who owns it," he said, completely seriously.

A laugh burst from my lips. "Why would you damage such a beautiful cock with a tattoo?!" I asked, still laughing.

"First, it wouldn't be damaged, just engraved. Second, you think my cock is beautiful?" He smirked at me, and I couldn't believe I had walked right into that one.

"It is beautiful," I breathed. "Why do you think I can't keep it out of my mouth?"

I watched as his eyes widened slightly and his body stiffened as if a tremor had run down his spine. He leaned in to whisper in my ear.

"I am so fucking that tight little ass tonight... right after you suck my beautiful cock."

Chapter 25

Red

I looked over the brochures and blew out a frustrated breath. There were hundreds, literally hundreds, of wedding venues, hotels, or reception halls to choose from, and that was just in New England. It had been five months since Bax had asked me to marry him, and I had been so busy that we never sat down and actually picked a date until last night. I now had a year to plan our wedding, and based on what I was seeing, it was never going to be enough time.

To be fair, we were both dealing with a LOT.

I told Bax about my new financial status soon after I spoke with the advisor, and he had nearly passed out. Neither of us needed to work ever again, we didn't need the money, but that's not who we are. Bax was reassigned within the Bureau doing something involving behavioral analysis, and some other psychological terminology, but not in the Organized Crime Division.

I had floated for a few weeks, lost without purpose, until Jenna and I chatted over lunch one day. Jenna also had a lot of money that she had inherited but never wanted. We talked about putting it to better use, and that was how we went into business together. We started a charitable organization that provided shelter, counseling, and support for people who are battered, recovering from addiction, homeless, or otherwise marginalized. I even pulled Tony and the family in to help me. I wanted to change the streets I grew up on, and help the families that lived there.

The family was a lot more reliable with getting the truth of a situation than the government ever was, and a lot of the people we served were the people from our own neighborhoods. We were helping the people who needed it most, and not the people who gamed the system. I felt good about giving the boys legitimate jobs, and in turn, the number of homeless and sheltered around Boston dropped dramatically.

We had enough money to do what was almost impossible; we offered child care so that people could get job training, and Tony ensured that a lot of local businesses would give our new trainees a chance. We built housing and provided for the most vulnerable or needy of our community members and their families. We provided drug and alcohol counseling, as well as mental health counseling. We had food and clothing programs. Almost immediately Jenna and I had been forced to hire an army of staff to manage the day-to-day needs of the steady flow of new people. Our business had mushroomed overnight, becoming an all-consuming machine.

And Jenna and I finally had a purpose. Neither of us was happy about the way we had come into money, knowing where it had come from, but we were sure that we were doing the best things possible with it going forward. I know we both felt a little lighter, and smiled a little easier, with each new person that we helped to forge their new life.

Bax and I sold my father's house, and despite not wanting to keep it, I bawled like a kid when I signed it away. Uncle Tony promised me that the young family moving in truly appreciated it and that their little "Princess" would love my old room. But as I walked through the empty rooms for the last time, I could almost see my father, sitting in his favorite chair with his cigar, smiling at me. I was saying goodbye to another piece of my childhood.

And then we found this house in a quiet suburban neighborhood, on the perfect tree-lined street. I had fallen in love with it instantly, and it grew on Bax. We had only moved in a month ago, and we still had boxes left to unpack in the back of the garage, and in a spare bedroom. I tried to get at least one box a day done, but it seemed never-ending.

It wasn't until last night that Jenna and Max had asked us just *when* we were going to get married, as we had dinner together to discuss more business details. We had included our men on the board, and Andrew and Daniel as well. It was truly a "family" business; my chosen family of lifelong friends.

Thus, this afternoon I was pouring through all of the brochures I had been collecting, and all of the web information I had been printing out, and I was ready to just cry and pour myself a drink to forget about it all.

Maybe we should just elope.

"Honey, I'm hooooooome!" Bax's voice called through the house, and I heard the front door close.

He did this every day, and I loved it each time. I rushed to the front foyer and threw myself into his arms for a panty-melting kiss. My man was home!

"How was your day?" I managed to squeeze out between smothering kisses dominating my mouth and jaw.

"It was good," he said briskly, his hands tangling roughly in my hair, and his mouth moving hungrily down my neck. "But I think you should suck my cock."

"Well hello to you too," I laughed.

I felt his erection stabbing into me insistently, and his mouth and hands never stopped moving. I didn't know what had gotten him so hot and bothered, but my mouth started salivating, and I was on board.

"Now," he growled into my neck. "Suck my cock now."

I didn't need to be told again.

I dropped to my knees in front of him, quickly undoing his pants and fishing his cock out, and my mouth was on him in seconds. His head fell back with a groan as his hands snaked into my hair, tugging the roots to pull my mouth over his length. I loved the way he dominated me. His musky scent filled my nostrils, while his thick cock filled my mouth.

My eyes swung up to meet his when a flash of color caught my attention. Just below his shirt still hanging over his abdomen, I saw a flash of orange. I pulled off of his cock immediately, and my hands flew to his shirt, pulling it up off of his abdomen.

There before me sat a female tiger, sitting face-on in a sphinx pose, her front legs dropping lower into his pubic line to showcase the base of his cock. Between her paws was the word "RED'S."

"Like what you see, Tiger?" He smirked down at me.

I looked up at him incredulously as a laugh erupted from my chest. "You got a TATTOO? You got my name tattooed on your body?!"

He pretended to act offended. "Red, I'm not sure it's polite to laugh while your face is examining my cock." A huge smile slowly grew on his face. "You only told me not to damage my beautiful cock, you never said not to get it; I think this pretty much says what I needed it to say. No woman is ever going to get that cock again, you own it."

I looked back at his groin, my fingers itching to trace the lines and color over the clear plastic bandage they had put on it to protect it. The tiger was fierce, but regal, clearly claiming ownership of the thick cock protruding below her.

"Did it hurt?" I asked, not able to tear my eyes away.

"Not as much as losing you did," he answered sincerely.

I tore my eyes away from the incredible artwork to see the adoring look in his eyes bathing me in emotion. If I hadn't believed I was his everything before, I certainly did now. We sat there for a heartbeat, just looking at each other, lost in the feelings, until he finally broke the spell.

"So are you going to stare at it all day, or suck my cock, Woman?"

His cock jerked under my hand, and I smiled as I brought my mouth back down onto him and worshiped him, watching the tiger watching me. I took him deep, stroking him roughly, massaging his balls, and it wasn't long before he was groaning and shooting down my throat. But I didn't stop. I worked his softening cock in my mouth and lips and pressed my finger against his asshole until I felt him starting to harden again, and then I did it all over again until he was ready to come into my mouth a second time.

I was on my knees for about a half hour, sucking and working him in the foyer, getting him off, and then working him back up again. He had dropped his jacket onto the floor behind him, and his pants and underwear were pooled around his ankles. I didn't even care if the neighbors could see us through the side windows that framed the door, I lavished his cock like a starving woman until he was finally so sensitive that he couldn't take it any longer.

"Enough, you animal! I can't,..." he hissed, pulling his cock away from me as I tried to start again. "I'm only human!" he laughed. "I need a break!"

He pulled his underwear and pants up and hissed as he put himself away, the skin stinging from every sensation over his raw nerves. I noticed he didn't do up his pants, and just let them hang open as he finally made his way inside the house.

I smirked with pride as I wiped my mouth, and he pulled me in for a deep kiss. He hissed again as his cock bumped me, and jerked his hips away.

"I think you broke me," he said with a laugh and ushered me back into the dining room where I had been working.

I flopped into my chair, knocking over a small tower of pamphlets with a flutter of paper as they fanned out over the other pamphlets, already spread out.

"Make any progress?" he asked, looking over all of the brochures. "Have you decided?"

"I have," I said grimly, pulling a face as I took in the mountain of information on the table. "We need to elope."

He laughed gently, putting his hand on my shoulder and patting me conciliatorily. "Tiger, we can get married right now in the bedroom with a JP if that makes you happy. Arrange whatever you'd like. I'll be there for it." He leaned over and kissed the top of my head, and my thoughts swirled around what he said.

Baxter

It was Red's night to play, and I looked up at the handcuffs she was placing on my wrists as my arms extended over my head.

"Where did you get the handcuffs?" she asked absently, as she threaded the cuff through the headboard before cuffing my other hand tightly; tighter than I had secured hers.

I looked up and arched an eyebrow at her in response. Her mouth opened in an "oh." expression.

"You forgot I'm law enforcement?" I laughed. "I don't know whether to be insulted or delighted. Although to be fair..." I added, "it ceased to matter to me that you were born into a crime family a long time ago, so I guess we're even."

She chuckled and slapped my arm.

"Now, Agent Murphy," she said seriously, "You are my prisoner. You will do whatever I tell you to without question, or suffer the consequences."

"Are you going to torture me?" I asked casually, "because I will never break."

"Oh, you will break, Agent Murphy," she asserted. "It's only a question of when."

I could feel myself getting harder, just listening to her talk. *Damn. This was going to be tougher than I thought.*

Red left the bed to get her own box and placed it beside us on the bed where I couldn't see into it. Apparently, I had set the bar, bringing props to use during our domination sessions. I watched as she slowly made her way toward me, like the prowling tigress she was, working her way up between my legs, and I couldn't help but spread my legs wide to give her access to my waiting cock, which was twitching for her attention.

"Maybe we should have a repeat of this afternoon," she said, her lips ghosting over the head of my cock so I could feel her warm breath on my skin. Her fingers traced over my clear bandage, protecting my new homage to my mistress. "Only this time, I won't stop."

She smiled at me wickedly, and I groaned. My cock, however, leaped at her words, wanting to feel her warm mouth sucking it down. She trailed her tongue up the underside of it, before swirling it around the head, and I fell back onto the pillow with a groan of desire.

"Suck it... please..." I begged, needy to feel her.

"Oh no, Agent Murphy," she teased, her tongue flitting out to flutter just under the sensitive base of my cock head. "My goal is to make you talk. You're going to tell me everything. You're going to keep talking; because if you don't..." She pulled her mouth away and looked up at me. "I stop."

I met her eyes. "Yes, Mistress," I smirked. "What do you want me to talk about?"

Her wicked smile was back, as her hand slowly took my length and began to stroke me, but only gently, not enough to slake my need.

"Tell me how it feels. Tell me how I make your cock ache for me. Tell me what you want me to do to your cock," she said, her voice low and husky, as her grip tightened around me.

"Fuck," I groaned, the sensation in my groin lighting me up.

"Tell me," she said, and her hand stilled.

"Red... I... I want you to stroke my cock until it is rock hard, and then I want you to take it all into that perfect fuckable mouth of yours," I started, meeting her eyes. I saw my own desire reflected there. Her hand began to stroke me harder and faster; she knew just how I liked it.

"Just like that, Tiger," I growled, and it rumbled out of my chest. "Get me hard. I want to feel your mouth around me. I want to hit the back of your throat while you suck me off like I was your last meal." My breathing was becoming labored.

She brought her mouth down over me, sucking me in deep, and I groaned loudly, my body jerking off of the bed. I pulled on my arms, wanting to feel her hair in my fingers, but the handcuffs held me in place, at her mercy. She moaned over me, vibrating through my length and I groaned again.

"That's it, Red. Suck my cock. Take it all in, Tiger. Work it with your tongue," I hissed out in shallow breaths. My eyes closed involuntarily at the incredible sensations of her warm wet mouth milking me in, and I had to fight to keep them open so I could watch her beautiful face as she bobbed up and down on my shaft, fucking me with her perfect lips. It was the most erotic sight I had ever seen. There was nothing as perfect as Red sucking me off.

"Deeper,..." I begged. "Take it all, Red. Uuuuuunnnnnngggg... Fuck my cock with your mouth. It's all yours, Baby. Aaaaaaaaar- rrggg... My cock is yours to take, however, and whenever you want. I want to shoot my load right down that pretty little throat, Tiger. Take it all," I was groaning and panting, barely able to get the words out.

I watched as she slurped me in deep, moaning on me, her eyes flicking up to take in my desire as I started to come undone inside her mouth. Suddenly, she pulled off with a pop.

"Wha–?! No!" I groaned loudly.

"Agent Murphy, you didn't think it was going to be that easy, did you?" She laughed, still teasing my rock-hard shaft with her hands. I was a panting mess, my cock straining for release.

"Please... Mistress..." I begged, before groaning under her hands again.

"I think it's time for me to use this cock, Agent Murphy, for MY pleasure. How does that sound?" She gave me her evil smirk as she pulled herself upright. "Agent Murphy, you are MINE. Your cock is MINE. And I will use it however I want. I am going to use your body today. I am going to get myself off all over you," she said, her own voice gravelly with need.

The thought of her fluids leaking all over my cock and balls sent another spasm of need through my already straining cock, and I could only groan. I don't know if there is such a thing as a "come fetish," but the thought of smearing our fluids on each other gets me off every time, and she knew it. When I wasn't actually coming all over her naked body, I was jacking off imagining it.

She perched herself over my waiting cock, her back to me, and she spread her ass cheeks wide. I watched as she reached into the box for the bottle of lube and poured it down the crack of her ass, and then worked it into her own hole with her finger, moaning. I groaned, my hips trying to reach up and bury myself in her waiting wetness. Then she ran her slick hands all over my cock and balls, coating me in the slippery liquid. I could only groan and writhe under her touch, needing more. She stopped suddenly, turning to face me.

"You're awfully quiet, Murphy," she said wickedly.

I groaned. "Do it! Take me, Mistress! Please, put me out of my misery! Let me come all over you!" My hips jerked upwards, trying desperately to feel her, but she kept herself above me and out of reach until she was ready to take what she wanted.

Slowly she lowered her ass down over my cock, and I practically screamed at the amazing sensation of her tight ring of muscle slowly working its way down my shaft. I was ready to explode. Instantly I started babbling, anything to get her to ride me and release me from my misery.

"That's it, Mistress! Ride my cock! Impale your ass on me! AAAARRRRGGGG! Ride me! Ride me hard! AAAAAAAAAR-RRRGGG! FUCK! You feel so fucking good on my cock!" I said anything and everything that came to my mind, desperate to make her fuck me into coming.

She took her time with long slow strokes, rising up my body until just the head was sheathed, and then slamming her ass back down onto my hips with a wet slap. I pulled at the cuffs, wanting to pull her into submission, wanting to fuck the living daylights out of her ass, but she only groaned and repeated her slow torture until my balls ached with need.

"PLEEEEAAASSSEEE!" I begged with a ragged breath.

"Agent Murphy, are you willing to surrender?" she asked me wickedly over her shoulder. I stiffened instantly. Although my cock was screaming "YES!" my pride held out.

She smirked at me as she pulled herself slowly up my length again, spreading her ass cheeks so I could watch as she pushed back down violently, and my cock disappeared deep inside of her tight hold.

"I can see you need a little more motivation," she said with a gleam in her eye. She reached into the box and pulled something out, something I couldn't see. My hips twitched as I tried to fuck up into her for the friction I needed, but her body weight made it impossible. Suddenly there was a hard wetness pressing into my asshole.

"What are you doing, Tiger?!" I asked warily.

"Motivating you, Lover. Now surrender," she commanded.

"Never!" I gritted out, still panting.

"You will, Agent Murphy," she said as I felt the hardness slowly push past my outer ring of muscle and deeper into my ass. I groaned and jerked, trying to pull away, but there was nowhere to go.

"You are MINE," she said, as she pulled the toy out slightly, only to slide it back into my ass while I clenched. "Take it!" she insisted, "Take it all, Agent Murphy. I want to fuck your tight ass, while you are fucking mine."

She pushed the toy into me even deeper, and the strangeness of the sensation of being full overwhelmed me. My cock got uncomfortably harder, and she groaned as she felt it stretching her ass around it.

"TELL ME," she ordered. "Tell me you are my fuck toy. Tell me I can use you however I want. Tell me you are MINE to play with!" she barked, as she fucked the toy in and out of my ass with smooth strokes.

"I'm yours!" I screamed. "I'm your fuck toy. Use me! Use me any way you want! Just PLEASE!..." I screamed her name again, my body convulsing with need. And then I felt the vibration turn on in my ass.

Instantly she was impaling herself on my cock, and I could feel the vibration hitting the walls of my ass and moving straight through my balls, and up the base of my cock into her tight asshole. Everything in me clamped tight. I screamed as a wave of pleasure overtook me hard. My heels dug into the mattress, lifting my hips, with her impaled on me, right off of the bed. We fell hard, her sliding even deeper over my cock as the orgasm rocked my body and shattered me beneath her. I was shooting into her, my body completely out of my control.

My vision blacked out as pleasure more intense than I had ever felt gripped my groin and shook my body like a ragdoll.

I could hear Red screaming out her orgasms over me, and as I came back to awareness, sucking in breaths, I could feel her wetness running down my balls and groin, working down my thighs.

I could only lay there, boneless, gasping for air. I felt like I had short-circuited. Red slowly pulled herself off of my deflating cock, and came to rest by my side, my hands still cuffed over my head, and the vibrator still buzzing in my ass.

"You have an anal fetish, don't you?" I asked her with a smirk.

"Tell me you didn't enjoy it, Agent Murphy," she smirked back confidently.

"Oh, I absolutely did!" I conceded. "Especially since you are the ONLY one who has ever had me there."

"Really? You've never had anyone finger or fuck you there before?" she asked, surprise in her voice.

"Not a chance, Tiger," I answered. "But I guess I'm your fuck toy now, so I might as well get used to you sticking things in my ass." I laughed.

I knew I previously had prejudices against ass play for men; too many insecurities about being perceived as "gay"... but I'd let her do that to me anytime she wanted. She gave me earth-shattering orgasms, and she did let me fuck her ass... So fair is fair. And it really got her off too, so there was that.

"Shower time, Agent Murphy," she announced.

She reached up to undo the handcuffs, and I rubbed my sore wrists as I brought my arms down. I went to reach for the vibrator, still buzzing away happily in my ass and sending all kinds of sensations into my cock, but she stopped me.

"It stays," she said, with no room for argument.

I wasn't really sure how that was going to work. I climbed off of the bed gingerly and practically waddled into the bathroom with my ass feeling stuffed full. While the sensation in my ass was great, the size and girth filling me unnaturally was weird. I had the urge to push it out but forced myself to hold it in.

Red got the shower started, and brought the water to temperature, before ushering me in with a giggle. She was enjoying my discomfort at having to move around the large vibrator shoved deep into my ass. I gave her a side-eye but moved under the water.

"Wash yourself thoroughly, but leave the vibrator in place, Agent Murphy," she instructed, and then sat on the shower bench to watch me.

I lathered the soap and proceeded to wash as she had instructed, noting that every time I twisted or turned, it still felt like I was being fucked from behind. It wasn't *bad*... it was just *different*. The vibration worked itself through my entire groin.

Then I watched as she soaped up, and cleaned herself as well, paying special attention to her own ass for my benefit. I was already hard again.

She sat back on the bench and then leaned her upper body against the back shower wall, spreading her legs wide in front of me.

"Agent Murphy, I have a new mission for you," she cooed. "I want you to come over here. Stand over me. You're going to watch me pleasure myself in front of you, and you are not to move a muscle, do you understand me?" She looked into my eyes intently.

My cock was rock-hard as I stood before her, inches away from touching her, my hands uselessly at my side, and the vibrator in my ass humming through my balls and cock.

"Words, Murphy," she singsonged.

"Yes, Mistress." I gulped loudly.

Her hands moved down her body, stopping to massage her breasts and tweak her nipples. She moaned as she pulled the little pink button harshly. My fingers twitched, wanting to join her, but I stood still.

Then her hands were moving down to her pussy. She pulled her lips open, revealing the soft pink cavern inside for me. Her delicate fingers drew up inside of herself, fucking herself lazily, as her other hand worked her clit in tiny circles. Her eyes watched me as she gasped and moaned, bucking under her own hand.

My cock was starting to burn with need. She leaned forward and took me into her mouth for just a minute, and I cursed at the amazing feeling of her mouth collapsing around me. Without thinking I pulled a hand forward to secure her head over my cock, to finish the job.

She pulled back out of my hands and sent me a dirty look.

"I didn't say you could come yet, Murphy." She continued to pleasure herself, moaning and writhing and really putting on a show. I groaned with need, my cock standing at full attention before her.

"Agent Murphy," she said, her voice low, guttural, "I want you to jerk yourself off all over me. I want you to coat me from head to toe in your come. I want to be a wet, sticky, dripping mess with your come all over me. NOW! Do it NOW!" she commanded.

Red

He moved in a flash. Falling forward, he caught himself on one arm, leaning over me and supporting his weight on the wall behind me. His other hand stroked his cock at a rapid-fire pace, the 'thucking' noise even louder than the water hitting his back from the shower head. He was groaning and roaring, his eyes clenched tight as he chased his release.

I knew he got off coming on me, and that he had some sort of fantasy about 'marking me' as his with his ejaculate. I loved playing into his fantasy, even if it wasn't a fantasy of mine. He had done so much to be the lover I needed him to be, I was happy to be able to give that back to him.

I bucked on my hand and pulled it up to smear my wetness all over his chest.

"I want you to wear me too," I moaned, before returning my hand to stroke in and out of myself for his viewing pleasure. I was a little over the top, but I wanted him to enjoy it.

"Fuck!" he swore. His hand flew over his cock with a death grip, trying to force himself to unload on me. His face was red from exertion. "FUCK! NO! NO! I need to cover you!" He was desperate, his face taking on a panicked expression. It was then that I realized that he wasn't losing himself to his arousal, he was having a panic attack.

"I need to cover you! I need to mark you! I need every man to know they can't fucking have you!" he roared. My hands stilled as I watched him start to fall apart. "THEY CAN'T HAVE YOU!" He screamed. "THEY CAN'T TAKE YOU! You can't leave! YOU CAN'T LEAVE ME!" he roared, his eyes wide on his cock, as he tried to force the orgasm to claim me.

"Hey! Hey! Hey!" I jumped up, pressing myself against his body; still, he tried to pump his cock, trying to empty the evidence of his ownership onto me.

"Bax, Bax look at me!" I pulled his face up to look into my eyes. He crumpled, dissolving into tears as sobs tore at his chest.

"You can't leave me!" he croaked with a sob.

I threw my arms around him, pressing him against me as I pulled his head onto my shoulder. His fingers dug into my skin as he held onto me for dear life, his body heaving with anguish.

"Bax, I'm never leaving you. Do you hear me? NEVER," I soothed, as I stroked my hand down his wet hair. "You are mine, and I am yours. I can't leave you, Bax. You have my heart, you have my body, you have my soul. I could never leave you, I wouldn't survive it. No man could ever tempt me away from you; you are exactly what I want, what I need, and what I crave.

So you get that thought out of your head right now, Baxter Murphy, because you are my today and all of my tomorrows. You are going to be the father to all of my children, and we are going to grow old together. I will never leave you, and no one could make me."

We stood there for endless moments with the water running down his back as I spoke gentle words of reassurance in his ear, while he cried out every last bit of his fear. And when he finally calmed I pulled his face to mine.

"MINE," I said possessively and kissed him deeply. His kiss was wounded and tentative at first, but I thrust my tongue into his mouth, deepening it. I kissed him long and hard. I kissed him with all of the intentions in my heart. I kissed him, wishing him to see the picture of him I held; my protector, my lover, my joy. I kissed him until he finally pulled away from me gently, wonder in his eyes as he searched mine, looking for the lie, until he found none.

Finally, he spoke.

"Can we take this thing out of my ass now?"

I laughed as tears rolled down my cheeks, and I reached around him to gently slide the vibrator out. He jerked and hissed, but I felt his cock hard against my belly.

I looked up at him again to see his face flushed and sheepish with vulnerability.

"I think..." I said quietly, "that someone needs a reminder about who owns my body," I said. "I think I need you to claim me again, Baxter Murphy. I think you need to do it right fucking now."

I stepped out of the shower quickly, but he grabbed me by the waist and threw me over his shoulder, caveman-style, as he launched us into the bedroom.

And then he did claim me. All night long.

Chapter 26

Red

"Calm down!" Jenna said again, chuckling.

I wrung my hands in my lap, wishing for patience. I was nervous. I had only two weeks to pull my plan together, and I wanted it to go smoothly. I wanted to surprise Bax. I needed for him to understand how much I loved him, and to know I would never leave him. I felt like so much was riding on this night.

"Does it hurt?" Jenna asked, gently touching the clear plastic bandage wrapped around my throat, protecting the collar I had just had tattooed there, matching the one Bax liked to use on me.

"It stung at the time," I said, fingering it gingerly. "But it's just a dull burn now."

She looked at me unsure but intrigued at the same time. She and Max both knew that Bax had gotten a tattoo for me, but neither of us would tell them what, or where. Max had been relentless, trying to get the secret out of Bax, but he remained staunchly close-lipped.

Tonight our company was being honored by the Mayor at an enormous event, for all of the work that we had done in the city. We were getting a plaque of some sort, and a huge financial donation. Since we would have all of our friends there, it wasn't a stretch to invite our families and loved ones, and it wasn't much more of a stretch to take advantage of that gathering to surprise Bax with our wedding.

He had said to arrange it, and he'd be there, so I was taking him at his word. I didn't want a huge cathedral and white gown. I wanted vows, a party, and an all-night fuck-fest with my husband. So that's what I had arranged.

However, after Bax's meltdown in the shower two weeks prior, I knew I had to add one last piece. He still had insecurities about me, no doubt some lingering abandonment issues from when his mother had been forced to leave him when he was young. So I decided to do what he had asked me the night we got engaged. I was going to wear his collar.

The tattoo was an outline, so it didn't stand out as garish. There was a thin line under my jaw which ran around my neck, and another above my collarbone. In between those was a huge starburst of circles of red tattooed jewels, radiating out in flame colors. There were other, smaller, starburst decorating the rest of my neck as well. It was tastefully done, and I was pleased. I just hoped Bax liked it, as there was no going back now.

But that created another problem in itself. My dress had been strapless; a lovely creation in maroon lace, with an under-the-bust black satin corset over it. I had been forced to have the seamstress create a lace overlay that climbed all the way to my jaw, like a victorian gown, to hide the bandage until I was ready to unveil the tattoo. It had taken her the better part of the week, but she had been able to do it in such a way that the overlay looked like it was a part of the dress.

We left the tattoo parlor and headed for the seamstress, to pick up my dress. As we walked my phone rang again: Bax. We had put Max on duty to keep him occupied all day so that we could pull the wedding together, but Bax must have been suspicious; he kept calling and texting me.

"Hi, Honey," I answered, while Jenna snickered beside me.

"Hey, Tiger! Where are you? Are you coming back to get ready?"

"Ugh, I'm sorry, Bax. The printer had an issue, and it took longer than expected," I lied. "Look, why don't you and Max just meet us there?" I offered, crossing my fingers that he would just go along.

"Are you at the printer now? We can just pick you up there if you'd like," he offered hopefully.

I smiled at the thought of my sweet guy.

"No, Honey. We just left. We still have to get my dress from alterations, and..." My mind stuttered, trying to find an excuse to keep him away.

"Makeup!" Jenna hissed quietly beside me.

"And get our makeup done," I finished quickly.

"Oh," he pouted. "Alright then. Well, I guess we can just meet you there." I could hear the disappointment in his voice, and my heart tugged a little.

"It's just a few hours, Lover. I'll be yours all night. I promise."

He had no idea.

"Alright then," he said. "Call us if you need anything."

"You know I will, Bax. I love you!"

"I love you too, Tiger." He let the call end, and Jenna and I scurried to get my dress and get to the event.

It was showtime!

The lace of the dress itched over the plastic protecting my throat, and it took everything I had not to scratch at it. Bax looked over at me curiously. He kept eyeing my neck, and I had all I could do to distract him. His eyes had lit up when he saw the corset over my gown, but the high neckline really threw him for a loop; I had never worn anything this conservative, normally choosing to show as much flesh as possible. I knew he had to be suspicious. I chewed my lower lip as he looked at me out of the corner of his eye again.

"Is everything okay, Tiger?"

"Yes." I said quickly. "Just nervous."

"You don't need to be nervous." He chuckled. "We're all here with you. You've gotten awards before. Don't let politicians intimidate you."

I let him think it was the Mayor I was nervous about. I wasn't going to say anything to the contrary.

His mother made her way over to where we were standing, and I saw tears forming in her eyes. I shot her a death glare in warning. I had told her, thinking she could keep the secret.

"Bax, I'm so proud of you!" she said, as a tear rolled down her cheek. She pulled him into a hug, and he patted her back gently.

"Thanks, Mom," he said, looking at me over her shoulder with a bewildered expression on his face.

"Mom, let me show you where you'll be sitting!" I interjected quickly, but she pulled me into a tight hug too.

"I love you, Nat. You know that, right?" she asked me.

Bax shot me another confused look, and I just played along. *If she tipped him off, I was absolutely going to kill her, mother or not.*

We had all sat through dinner, and my nerves were getting worse and worse the longer I had to wait and pretend. Jenna finally pulled me away and snuck me outside to smoke a joint, just so I could calm down. Back at the table, we finished our desserts, and Bax leaned in to sniff me, giving me an accusatory stare. I just smiled back at him and shrugged my shoulder. He didn't say anything. *Yes, I smoked a joint. So shoot me.*

Finally, the MC announced the Mayor. We sat quietly through his twenty-minute speech about community and giving back, blah, blah, blah... the words went in one ear and out the other.

FINALLY. Our names were called to represent our company 'A Family of Neighbors,' and we all made our way up to the small stage. The Mayor read our plaque out so that everyone would know all of the amazing work we had done for the citizens of the city, and then we took endless pictures. We held the plaque, we took turns shaking his hand, and we stood in front of the giant fake check; all the while huge smiles were plastered to our faces while photographers clicked away. And at last, the Mayor thanked us one last time, before handing me the microphone.

Bax turned to walk with the Mayor, but I spoke up, addressing the room.

"If I could have your attention please, for just another moment," I began.

Bax turned around to look at me in confusion but came back up to stand with Max, Jenna, Andrew, Daniel and me.

"We have one more surprise in store for you folks tonight, and I hope that you'll indulge us."

Max steered Baxter to stand next to me, with Max and Daniel behind him, while Jenna and Andrew stood behind me.

"Bax, I have someone I want you to meet," I said to him, still speaking into the microphone so the room could hear. He stared at me in confusion, as a small older man approached us from the back of the room.

"This is Tony Balfore," I introduced, and Bax took his hand, still looking at me.

"He's going to marry us."

Baxter

"NOW?" I asked, stunned.

"Right fucking now," she said with a smile, and then brought her hand up to cover her mouth as the room filled with laughter. The microphone had broadcast it.

I stared at her in shock, and then I felt joy filling my heart. We were getting married. Right here. Right now. She was going to be my wife.

Max leaned in and whispered quietly in my ear for only me to hear, "And the sooner you get through it, the sooner you'll be buried in her." He chuckled as he pulled away.

"Is this okay?" she mouthed at me, worried.

I just smiled at her with what must have been the goofiest grin ever. And then the panic hit me.

The RINGS!

I turned to Max in terror, but he just chuckled and held his hand up.

He had known! The bastard was in on it!

I narrowed my eyes at him, mentally promising him retribution, but he just laughed harder.

The officiant got us started, walking us through the ceremony, but I hardly heard him. My eyes were glued to my beautiful bride. I recited my vows as he had said them, placing the ring onto her delicate finger, and something inside of me clicked seeing her wearing it. Memories of our engagement and the collar I had given her, surfaced, causing me to blush. The ring had been my smaller version of the collar, of the sign that she was mine and only mine and now she wore it on her hand for all to see. Every man would know that she was taken: by me.

Before the officiant could recite Red's vows for her she asked for a moment. Uneasiness settled in my gut, as I wondered what she was up to. I didn't think she would put all of this together just to get cold feet, but the way she fidgeted with her dress worried me. Finally, Jenna stepped up behind her and adjusted her collar for her, and she pulled it down over her chest to reveal her throat.

My jaw dropped. Her beautiful neck was adorned with the pattern I had put on her collar. I could see the lines of it under her jaw, and delicately flowing over her collarbone. The starburst in the center was the fire that was the fight in her, it was my north star. I stared in disbelief, while she stood back in place, resuming her position, ready to speak her vows to me.

She didn't have to bother. The tattoo said it all.

She was mine. One hundred percent mine, and only mine. Willing to give herself to me fully and wholly, just as I had dedicated myself to her.

I watched her mouth move, as she said the vows to me, and let her take my hand to slide my ring onto it. My own tiny collar on my finger, for her.

"...You may now kiss the bride!"

Max smacked me, and I jumped into action, pulling Red into me for a kiss that was far too long and deep to be publicly appropriate, but not caring one bit.

The crowd swarmed around us to congratulate us, and the DJ put some music on for dancing. A cake was wheeled out from the kitchen, and placed at the front of the room

"How did you manage this?!" I asked her, still floored.

"You said arrange it, and you'd show up... so I did," she answered, with a shrug of her shoulder.

My fingers reached out to trace her delicate throat. "I love this, Red. You have no idea. This is the best wedding gift ever. I can't imagine what I can get you that will ever live up to this." I stared at the intricate design, brushing my fingertips over her collarbone, and feeling her shiver beneath me.

"Well... you could always give me a pearl necklace to go with it." She smirked up at me.

We danced, we drank, we had cake. My mother was a crying mess, overjoyed with finally having a daughter-in-law. Tony and some of the boys were there too, and Tony was uncharacteristically warm to me. We had come to a mutual understanding that we were family, and we had enough respect to leave our work lives out of our family business, and vice versa. Fiske made his way over to congratulate me, and I noticed he sidled up to one of the women by the bar afterwards.

It was a wonderful night full of laughter and fun but as the hour wore on I was ready to take my new bride back to our hotel room and consummate this marriage.

She must have had the same idea, because I caught her eye across the room. She smirked, and nodded, and then turned and made her way to the side door. I turned, finding the nearest exit, and rushed out to find her.

We rushed into the Bridal Suite like teenagers. I tore the strings out of the back of her corset, frustrated that it was taking so long to get my hands onto her bare body. I was ready to just flip her dress up and fuck her with it still on, but the corset finally fell away. I unzipped the back of her dress, and she shucked it off quickly, letting it pool on the floor. She reached back to undo her strapless bra as she launched herself onto the bed.

I tore my clothing off, tearing buttons off in the process. I didn't give a shit. I needed to be inside of her, immediately. I grabbed her lace panties in one hand and twisted, tearing them off of her. She spread her legs wide for me, groaning, and I launched my body over hers, sinking myself deep into her pussy, already wet and waiting for me.

I rutted her like an animal, with only the need to make her come all over my cock driving me frantically. I fucked her hard, pushing her into the matress with my hips, groaning as I devoured her mouth. One of my hands was clamped into her hip bone, and I wanted so badly to clamp my other hand around her throat, to dominate her, but I didn't want to hurt the delicate skin that was still healing from the tattoo. MY TATTOO. My brand on her skin. Instead I pulled her arms over her head and held them there while I pounded into her, urging her to give me everything.

And she did. I felt her body coiling beneath me, her pussy clamping down on me, and my own release rose to meet her. As she pressed her walls down around my cock, it only grew harder, pressing back into her, until we were both arching, convulsing. Our wetness seeped out of her and down our legs as I continued to pump her for every last bit of her wetness.

Our chests were still heaving, and a thin sheen of sweat coated our skins, as I released her arms and she threw them around me.

"You are mine!" I growled possessively into her ear, biting the muscle on the top of her shoulder, being careful to avoid the inked lines.

"And you are MINE," she groaned, before biting me back.

I let my weight fall on her gently, my cock still deep inside of her as her fluttering walls calmed around me. A deep sense of happiness filled me as I stared into her glowing eyes. *My Tiger.*

"I have one more gift for you," she whispered breathlessly.

"What could you possibly have for me, after you have given me everything, my Love?"

She reached back with one hand, and pulled a large sheet of paper out from under the pillow. I stared at it in confusion, sitting up to take it from her. She sat up with me and just held it for my inspection.

It was a drawing from her sketch book. It was a scene of her and me sitting together in a field of flowers. Beside her was a small girl who looked just like me, and her belly was swollen with another baby, soon to be born.

"WHEN?!" I asked in shock. 'When did you see this?!"

"That night, in the shower," she answered shyly. "Afterwards, when you fell asleep."

She was searching my eyes, as if scared about what my response would be. I couldn't help the shit-eating grin that spread across my face as I took in the scene of our future family. Our family! I watched as a smile slowly spread across her face as well.

"On your knees, Tiger!" I commanded, flipping her over. "I have work to do!"

THE END

Fay Smith is an avid reader, as well as an author. She's lived a very diverse life, having moved every few years. She's worked as a soldier, a carnie, a translator, a business owner, a minister, and a medium, among other jobs. Her interests are as diverse as her background, including spirituality, travel, meditation, and of course writing. She currently writes romance, erotica, and Science Fiction, but has plans to branch out into other genres as well. You can find her on Instagram, TikTok, or Facebook as FaySmithAuthor.

www.ingramcontent.com/pod-product-compliance
Lightning Source LLC
Chambersburg PA
CBHW070610300726
48975CB00006B/1769